ALSO BY MARK Z. DANIELEWSKI

House of Leaves

Only Revolutions

The Fifty Year Sword

The Familiar (Volume 1)

. novelistic mosaic that
nultaneously reads like
riller and like a strange,
eamlike excursion into
ibconscious."

— Michiko Kakutani
The New York Times

House of Leaves

"A great novel . . . Thrillingly
alive, sublimely creepy, dis-
tressingly scary, breathtakingly
intelligent — it renders most
other fiction meaningless."

— Bret Easton Ellis

House of Leaves

"A rare treat for c

The I

CIRCA SURVIVE   JUTURNA

Music

Music

l book lovers."

— Eric Liebetrau
The Boston Globe

The Fifty Year Sword

Sword

"*Only Revolutions* . . . instills
in the reader that indefinable
longing and love for what is
beyond history. It dares the
grand emotions."

— David Plante
National Book Award
Finalist Citation

Only Revolutions

"Here is the road nov
imagined by John Ca,
. . . Truly revolutiona
wants to overthrow n
just how we read, but

— John Freema
Newsday

Only Revolutions

A CIRCLE

ROUND

A STONE

PRODUCTION

It should break your heart to kill.

— *Brian Turner*

SQIRL

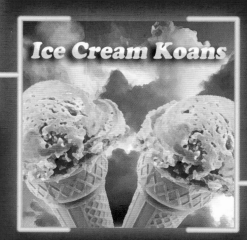

Ice Cream Koans

The Loy

Black to capture White stones.

Hawaiian

Chaucer's Books
Santa Barbara, California

EAT OF

PANTHEON

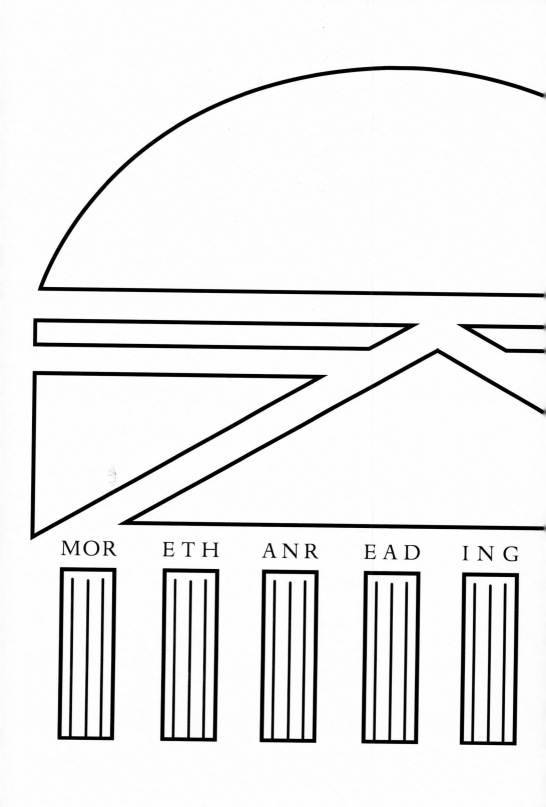

MOR   ETH   ANR   EAD   ING

NEW THIS SEASON

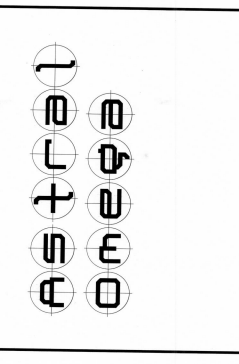

Astral Omega

The Unwilling

You do not know violence.

Until now neither did we.

But we thought we knew.

We thought that by remembering what we once considered its tragic limits we could end violence forever.

But memory has no such power.

And violence has no limits.

One justification relies upon that paltry logic still unaltered since even your time:

What does it matter?

We are all going to die.

To which the H.O.L.Y. adds that at least their cause seeks to defeat the tyranny of death's certainty. And in response to deaths resulting from their actions, their reasoning remains as unaltered as it too is paltry:

What does it matter

if some are saved?

And so an equilibrium which once endured for billions of years, the H.O.L.Y. has eradicated in fractures of time.

They are terribly powerful.

Now only subsumption by the H.O.L.Y. offers a chance at survival. It makes no difference to the H.O.L.Y. that the cost is the negation of the S.E.L.F. Too many already have submitted.

We are the unwilling.

Out of the multitude of I.D.E.N.T.I.T.I.E.S. once giving meaning to the manifold reaches of space and time — what we call The Verse — only three now remain.

W.H.I.M. suffered massive decimation but managed to marshal a defense preserving the ambit of her personality.

She survived by crossing beyond the borders of V.E.M. and there encountering its failure.

Until now, we never knew that V.E.M. had borders. And its failure was as impossible as the inconstancy of light.

Even the H.O.L.Y. faltered before such revelations.

The discovery of V.E.M. — which brought about the V.E.M. Revolution and eventually led to the reshaping of all multiverses answering to The Verse — has always been predicated on intrinsic permanence.

But nothing is permanent now.

Nor intrinsic.

As The Verse expands beyond itself, even the beyond disassembles.

But the H.O.L.Y. will not allow this to happen without first implementing its plan for time's restitution.

Already the extremes of our own S.E.L.F. endure the H.O.L.Y.'s occupations and murders.

But we are the D.A.R.K. and we are not without resources either.

VEM 5 Alpha System
Grand Unification Epoch 10^{-36}
Encryption 2/5

We too are powerful.

An unusual recall. No question. And with a refund. Not just any old refund either but with a We're-Sorry-We-Wasted-Your-Time! bonus. Lucky buyers actually made money.

And while the rate of return continued to increase with forthcoming details about emissions and the leakage of certain lead-based components, it was the eco-nomics of that We're-Sorry-We-Wasted-Your-Time! bonus that really got people shipping their devices back.

All the jokes and Poke-Fun-At humor on morning radio shows had helped too. Nothing better for the laugh altar than a big dumb sacrificial conglomerate.

Solomon didn't give two hoots about the media frenzy. Though no question he'd choose cash over a Petch any day.

Besides, anyone stupid enough to pick such a name for their "revolutionary piece of technology" deserved a good suing. Solomon had almost retched — literally — when he heard the ad for the first time.

Of course, he graciously kept to himself a similar reaction when he accepted the thing from his kids: four of them marshaling best intentions to better reconnect their dad to the world via a very expensive piece of electronics served up in a box big enough for one of his old shoes. Maybe.

New shoes would probably have done a lot more to get him out of the house than this gizmo.

But the financial man in him had indulged widget curiosity and unpacked it. Maybe the good father in him had turned it on.

He even permitted his daughters to point out the various features, including endless wireless improvements which would make it that much easier to check out the three social networking sites they'd already signed him up for. For those sixty-five and over. For those who like to talk about full RMB convertibility and eat cereal for dinner. For those who were— His daughters didn't bring up newly divorced.

His sons took over describing the exceptional speed and memory capacity, enthusiastically touching on new tactics in nano-transistors which purportedly would someday best the synaptic capabilities — not to mention durability — of household pets. Hence the shape.

All of which boiled down to:

> Mom's gone.
>
> Try dating.
>
> Use a Petch.

Was this what she had used?

Their unspoken answer to this unstated question would never change:

When Vanessa had asked for a divorce, Solomon had congratulated her by pointing out the statistical anomaly: usually at this stage in the game, it was the man who left.

"If only you cared," she had smiled on the way out, crying too, and he'd snorted something about markets needing caring too.

The Petch sure wasn't worth caring for. And it sure wasn't beautiful. Derivative in all sorts of ways: round-ish, ear-ish, compact-ish, soft-ish with its Teal-Green-Something-Or-Other-Hydrocarbon-Isoprene case.

Two screens like two wide dumb eyes.

Vanessa required no such device. Even at sixty-four she had those gray eyes. She had that smile. She had a life.

Getting out of the house came naturally to her. And even if, initially, alone beat Alone-With-Solomon, it didn't take long before the gray-haired wolves started calling. Rich ones too — those who shorted Parcel Thoughts. But if Vanessa could handle Solomon, she sure as hell could handle wolves.

She probably was a wolf. Though when she cried at the moon the moon cried back and the stars gathered and each flake of winter's snow became a star until the sky above became a Brighter-Thing-So-Much-More-Than-Stars.

Punctuated like that too. Its first officious tag line replaced mere days later with

Solomon had repacked the thing at once. The kids could get their money back. He'd pocket the extra cash. Thank you notes for everyone.

Except Solomon didn't feel like heading to the post office, let alone leaving the house, let alone putting on his old pair of shoes.

So the Petch just sat in its box.

And then one evening for no reason he will ever be able to guess, Solomon decided to turn it on. Why not? It was just a wireless handheld device. A sexed up Personal Digital Assistant. Maybe with a few extras. Like the chips.

Solomon had no clue what Pavex even meant. The awful acronym drew him back to his Dartmouth days studying the Iraq-era military-industrial complex. He could use his Petch to look up Pavex.

But Solomon did no such thing. He was too depressed. Too depressed to even ask how long he'd been fumbling along in this bewildered state. Instead, he used his Petch to call each of his daughters and thank them. Then he used it to e-mail each of his sons and thank them.

Then he looked at all three of the social networking sites for a total of thirty-three minutes before finally abandoning the Petch to the top of his ancient tube radio.

He'd repack it come morning. Now was cereal time. Solomon smirked. It wasn't even 6 PM yet and he was already at the end of his evening. Vanessa was probably just getting ready to go out.

Of course, Solomon could go out. Not like he was tired. He wasn't going anywhere.

And then Beethoven buzzed.

A wave of uncertain static collided with alighting strings before vanishing just as suddenly — alighting strings left unaware.

With spoon still in his mouth, Solomon walked over to the Petch. Finding Airplane Mode was easy enough.

But what if his daughters tried to return his call? Or his sons? Solomon turned off the wireless feature instead.

A moment later Beethoven buzzed again.

Solomon sighed. Airplane Mode it was. Beethoven over children.

A claim which, through the alchemy of reason, Solomon could no longer view as anything short of ludicrous. Only just short of *suspiciously* ludicrous.

Solomon never shirked from quick math. And so when estimated unit numbers against recall-bonus numbers yielded an amount substantially higher than likely civil liabilities from questionable consumer harm, Solomon's curiosity grew.

Nothing more fun than Math-That-Doesn't-Add-Up. Call him eccentric. He'd even cop to didactic (daughter one), argumentative (son one), Well-Versed-But-Unrehearsed (son two), impossible (daughter two), a Self-Involved-Plop-Of-Brain (Vanessa).

And that did the trick. For a while.

Solomon was well into his second bowl of Something-Corn cereal when a piano sonata faded and then just as abruptly returned.

This time Solomon turned the Petch off. Tossed it into its box for good measure.

Defective!

Even as another exclamation worked its way up through thoughts elicited by magazine articles on crypto currency databases and algo HFT trading:

Dangerous!

harmony.

But there was one thing Solomon wasn't: gullible.

And so when Piano Sonata No. 8 in C minor buzzed, Solomon didn't consider it dangerous. What he noticed was that it was short and desperate. It only tangled briefly with Rubinstein's loving hands before expiring in a kind of flickering anguish.

And this while the Petch was still in its box. While Petch was still turned off.

And even stranger, the interference had not produced dissonance. Neither muddle nor muck there. Instead, for a gleaming if impossible instant, there lived a most unexpected improbability:

Caged Hunt

Part Two

July 31, 2014
███████████, Mexico
3:47 PM

"This beats fuckin any day!"

Dead center: four large metal crates. Dust washes over them. That and the desert sun give everything a reddish hue. Or maybe it's something else. ~~Leather~~ swaggers forward. Sunglasses on. Camo hat. Loaded for bear. He even wears a sidearm in a shiny black holster. Not even the pixelations can hide his huge grin. He raises the Remington Model Seven with Konus scope.

"Say hello!"

Maybe ~~Weejun~~ yells that. Or ~~Tabori~~. Either way the Mexican workers scurry back as the door to the first crate falls away. Two children start banging the crate's roof with old bowling pins. Closer to the fence a little girl wearing a pink dress with a sash of yellow polka dots closes her eyes as something hobbles into the arena.

"You got the hyena!"

_____ at once starts squeezing off shots. He's a lousy shot. Plumes of dirt rise to the left and right of the animal. It keeps limping around in a confused circle.

"Fucker!"

██████ has to reload his rifle twice. Finally a patch of red appears on the left shoulder. The hyena groans. The second round takes off an ear. The third paints a hip red. Then a jagged streak tears open the throat.

"Bad Ass!"

████ grunts as the hyena crumples and blood gushes out onto the sand. ████ keeps firing into the carcass. ████ and ████ are laughing too hard to stop recording. ████ laughs too and reloads.

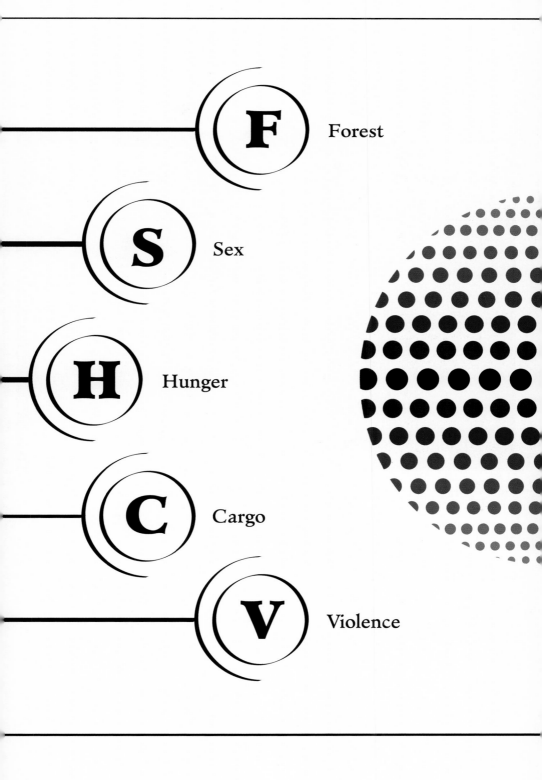

F   Forest

S   Sex

H   Hunger

C   Cargo

V   Violence

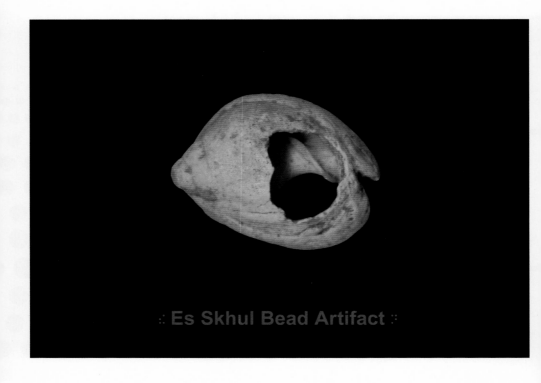

:: Es Skhul Bead Artifact ::

:: 106,101 years ago. ::

:: 2:07 PM. Summer. ::

:: South of present-day Haifa, Israel. Not so far from 32.6259, 34.9585. ::

:: Sunlight floods forest slope. One red deer followed by two fawns slips by. ::

:: Atop large fallen tree Very Old Woman knaps stone, now and then lifting racloir to wave away insects clouding her face. ::

:: Very Old Man limping along path emerges from pines. ::

:: Morning you passed here, here morning. ::

:: *Very Old Man says nothing.* ::

:: On way you, you to catch up four, catch up with children four. ::

:: *Very Old Man nods.* ::

:: Morning over good, good morning, was good. See points made here. Sit. ::

:: *Very Old Woman shows spearhead. Lifts up second. Laughs.* ::

:: You? Point maker, maker points too? ::

:: *Very Old Man shakes head. Sits.* ::

:: Hunt? ::

:: Once. Once mayb threw your points, mayb. ::

:: Mayb. Years now I make now. ::

:: Spiral-plus. ::

:: You spiral-plus maker, maker spiral-plus now? ::

:: *Very Old Man nods.* ::

:: Oh. ::

:: *Very Old Woman touches bare neck. Waves again at bug cloud to forget bare neck. Returns to chip, hinge crack, feather edge, and snap.* ::

∴ For spiral-plus me, too clumsy me, me for spiral-plus. ∴

∴ *Very Old Man takes spiral-plus from skin pouch.* ∴ ∴ **Nassarius (Plicarcularia) gibbosulus** ∴ ∴ *Perfectly pierced. Beaded on tangle-strand of thin enloving roots.* ∴

∴ That's drop sun there, there sun I ever seen. ∴

∴ Knot. Please. ∴

∴ *Very Old Woman touches bare neck but shakes head.* ∴

∴ None enough points here, here to trade none. These— ∴

∴ *Very Old Woman looks around. Startled by sudden wings in forest. Or shift in light. Or something arriving by path that never arrives.* ∴

∴ —these points I make, I make all, all declared for. ∵

∷ But Very Old Man refuses to take back necklace. ∷

∷ No point. ∷

∷ Oh. ∷

∷ Very Old Woman smiles, uncertain, but still knots on spiral drop of sunlight. Smile no more uncertain. Very Old Woman even throws back head and laughs. ∷

∷ Not Very Old Man. He crumples to knees and starts wail. ∷

∷ What this, this what? ∷

:: *Very Old Woman scrambles off tree.* ::

:: **Pointless spiral-plus.** ::

:: **Go not blind now with crazy cry. Old one you crazy, crazy old one?** ::

:: *Very Old Man pulls from pouch elaborate spiral-plus necklace. Does not offer this one to Very Old Woman. Drops it on ground. Very Old Woman answers grunts.* ::

:: **No pointless that! See! Worth all, all points. Mornings three points! More! Mayb mornings five more, and nights, five more!** ::

:: *Very Old Man pulls from pouch a second elaborate spiral-plus necklace. Drops that on ground.* ::

:: **Morning sun there, there all morning sun!** ::

:: Very Old Woman even claps hands together as Very Old Man arranges third elaborate spiral-plus necklace on ground. ::

:: **Crazy old one, old one wealth you!** ::

:: Fourth necklace next to rest traces gentle arc. Like rising sun to sun setting. Very Old Woman stops clapping. Hands fly to chest. ::

:: **Four these for, for four children for?** ::

:: Very Old Man cries harder as he now lines up handfuls of strandless shells beneath necklaces. As if to grant them horizon. ::

:: **Never you found, found children never?** ::

:: Very Old Man's horizon bends. ::

:: Mayb just with other, other elsewhere mayb? ::

:: I found children, children found. I found other, other found too. ::

:: Horizon keeps bending. ::

:: Tell me old crazy! Old crazy what found you, you what found? ::

:: Stillness. ::

:: Very Old Man places last shell. Horizon is no more horizon but closed whole. Like giant sun topped by four suns like four small heads if not heads and never suns. ::

:: Five all, all five? ::

:: Worse. ::

∴ *Very Old Woman scrambles back up fallen tree. Hands grabs hafted points. Very Old Man joins her. His hands grab no points. From up here spiral-plus arrangement is easy to see. Very Old Woman gasps.* ∷

∴ Pawclaw? ∷

∴ Pawclaw. ∷

∴ Not so large not. Not not. ∷

∴ Not so large. No. Not not. Larger. Much much larger. [ϵ] ∷

∴ [ϵ]For alternate set variants of gestural translations, including alveolar clicks, numerous sibilants, bilabial fricatives, retroflex approximants, pharyngeal consonants, see 19210491-07281940-032921722011, order VI, v.26, n.13. ∷

MARK Z. DANIELEWSKI'S

THE
FAMILIAR

VOLUME 2

INTO THE FOREST . . .

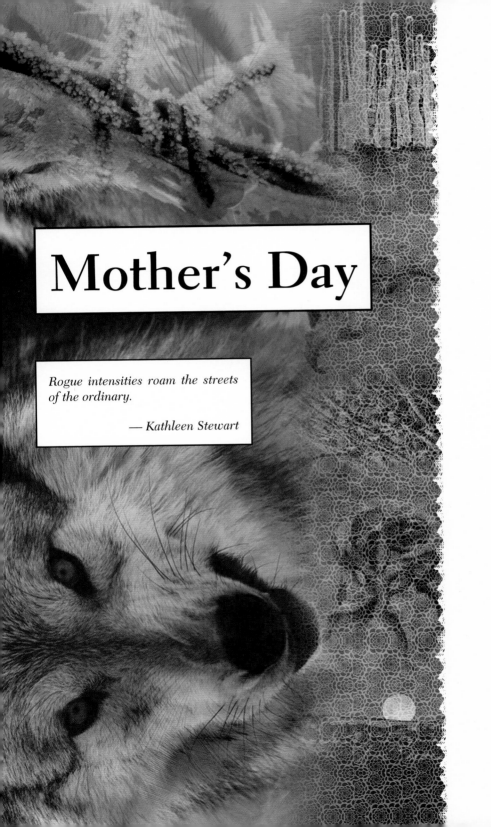

Mother's Day

*Rogue intensities roam the streets
of the ordinary.*

> — *Kathleen Stewart*

)

(

(   )

(

)

       each waking interrupts dreams with the vivid recollection of those dreams before submerging (again (and again)) into a subsequent sleep cycle (below (again) the surface of consciousness (and memory) (a drowning in (seemingly) obvious narratives((?) something about Dov's death(?)) which the resurrection of waking easily negates (if just the dream and never death))).

All night long.

(

(

)

)

)

Until the transparency

of dawn. But why is every window in their bedroom open? Downstairs too? Even the back doors are thrown wide. The front door is no exception. Had a polylingual alert alerted what had failed to stir husband and children? (Anwar doesn't move when Astair slips on sweats and then pads downstairs.)

(

(

))

?

Sunday's warmth rising up ((still dreamy (and still too)) sun splashing her face (reaffirming an announcement (however spurious in its origin) that here was egress (not ingress

)

(

(

)

(!)   (

)   )

).

(Is Astair (still) in the grip of a dream's order? Unremembered night passages (still) ordering events which reason (and in mere moments too) remaps and re-affiliates?)

((

)

)

Closets, cupboards, and drawers (all open too). The whole place should scream intrusion (intruder! (aftermath! (or *worse* . . .))) were it not for how (after all that hinges and latches had already followed through with) neatness is nowhere sacrificed. Not a thing displaced.

(((

()   ()

)

)

)

(still) Wild breezes (stirring the downstairs (from room to room (not strong enough to displace (only animate)))) make sense (as much as Astair's decision to begin closing things: from front door to back doors to all the downstairs windows) even having to slide shut the living room coffee-table drawer (inside (it has been a while) discovering one ((small) black-lacquered) box filled with purple-tipped matches and purple ribbon (and a postcard from Istanbul ((from Dov) for Xanther with only two words beyond name and "Love" ("Cats galore!") (privileging a conversation Astair could not have cared about until now (has Xanther always (secretly) loved . . . ?)))))

Dov had never made a secret of his love for wild animals (even if (to Dov) killing them and eating them also meant love).

On their mantel (still) sits his present to her: two savage wolves (glass (by ████████████████ (Astair can't surface the name))) ((here ((before her) as present and memory)) forever frozen in the middle of their courtship (his teeth (or are those hers?) scraping against the wide lunging neck (both animals (Lares & Penates) sexless (even if their evident desire for closure (*consummation!*) is obvious in their together-surge upward toward a moon as invisible as it is out of reach))) forever undisturbed by moonlight (even breezes (whether stirring or cyclonic)) (if only light ((candlelight (say)) flickering wickedly) could grant glass movement and maybe consummation (*closure!*) along with the possibility (after closure (*consolation!*)) of bounding off the mantelpiece (as Dov and Astair had dreamed of doing in every situation they (ever) found themselves (they were not (*never!*) for each other)) or just continue tearing away at each other ((though they were never for each other) they had done that plenty of times) and copulating (that too ((lots and lots of it) and still not a match))) with only dust now to still (maybe (or at least (still) muting the alchemy of light)) the conclusion this work (still) persistently suggests to Astair (achievable neither with celerity nor patience (just inevitable (even if the inevitable needs dusting now and then)))). It was the nicest thing (aside from Xanther (of course)) that Dov ever gave to Astair and (for whatever reason) Astair still feels calmed by these two wolves (their desires their possible pasts their probable futures their . . . (well (glass)) stillness) and so their place in her life.

Not that much else this morning is in its place.
Or that Astair is surprised.

She knew it crossing through the breakfast room.
She knew it by the time she reached the kitchen.

Already spoiling for a fight?

Anything for a Jump Start to lurch her from this
malaise? (Still tea-less.) Is that it? (Coffee-less.) Is
she really (that (this))—

                                        (*depressed?*)?

Can barely think (it (forget it (say it))).

Though this sure does beat an open door (and
does in fact Jump Start everything).

Astair doesn't linger on the empty dog bed but (at once (heart beating toward sweat)) storms up the stairs to confront Xanther (and catch her red-handed).

Disease (after all (at least)) is a serious issue.

Astair checks herself ((before the door ((of course) already open)) from slamming the door shut ((!) *ridiculous!*) with a loud bang ((to startle Xanther awake) before opening it again)) with the thought that ~~that thing~~ (*her* animal!) might have (in its sleep (their sleep) already dragged in a final breath and (with a frantic scratch of kicks)) passed away (her daughter (still asleep) oblivious to what waking must discover).

The idea is almost (and suddenly too) too sad for Astair to face (wanting the thing alive if only so anger might live too (if also wanting the whole thing over with so—)) even as she slips into her daughter's bedroom ((child of living glass) child of wolves who knew once (if only for the shortest time) the biggest (most beautiful) moon).

And here it is.

Neither dead nor living.

No creature at all.

Not even Xanther's here.

What's more the bed is pristinely made from corners to pillows (tucked creased smoothed). When does Xanther ever make the bed ((for that matter) when is she up before seven let alone six without being pried awake (both parents usually required))?

The twins are hours from rousing. Anwar sleeps like stone (though he had slipped into bed not long before the sun began to draw color out of the air).

But where is Xanther?

Not in the house.

Or out back.

Anger goes (replaced by Astair's constant companion (the most unbeatable Jump Start):

∴ How stars start . . . ∴

worry).

Astair finds her eldest balancing on the curb (glazed in amber dawn (storm long gone)). How had she missed this? (hadn't Astair even stepped out onto the stoop?).

"Isn't the sky beautiful?" Xanther smiles. (She's beautiful (beaming)). "Happy Mother's Day!"
"Honey, you can't leave the front door open."

That's how Astair responds.

To this beautiful greeting (to this beautiful morning (to this beautiful child ((her child) glowing! ((dustless!) animate (within (and without)))))). While tucked within the hold of her gangly arms (hidden in a crib of palms and elbows):

that thing.

The day doesn't improve. Both Shasti and Freya (tasked with a coloring assignment to keep them in the living room ((still) come to her with Anwar's laptop in hand (squealing with delight))).

"Look mommy!"

"Look!"

Miley Cyrus (last year (at something called the AMAs. ∴ **American Music Awards** ∴)) singing "Wrecking Ball." In the background a corpsified kitten chomps out lyrics while crying diamonds (*corpsified!?*).

"If Xanther gets a kitten, can we get one too?"

"Or what Miley has on? With all the, uhm, kittehs?"

"Girls, can't you see your mother's working?" (She even slaps her palms down on the table (hard).) "Please! Spare me the indignity of your distractions!"

(fortunately) Anwar is there to give Astair (chastened (very chastened)) quiet time. She knows she should take advantage of the (offered) nap but (instead) calls Abigail (still ecstatic over recently beating Astair in *Words With Friends*).

"Just goes to prove that being good at organizing words out of letters isn't the same as being good at putting words together."

"Ow."

"Am I a bitch or what? I am so sorry, Abby."

Abigail forgives her at once (and listens (too) to Astair talk about everything except what is going on with her career (Astair hangs up (apologizing again (and)) promising to take a yoga class with Abigail soon)).

It gets even more ludicrous.

(attempting to make up for her (what?) prickly(?) engagement with anything ~~vital~~ (*happy!*)) Astair drags Xanther to the supermarket (reasoning that it will be nice for a change to let her pick out her favorites for dinner (even if at every turn Xanther makes it clear that she doesn't want to go (and she doesn't care what's for dinner))).

"Mom, like I hate the supermarket?"
"You do?"
"Oh, uhm, I love hanging around stuff I can't have?"

Xanther's archness is as rare as it is surprising (not something that she would pick up from Anwar (either father)(like that would surprise anyone)).
"Besides, uhm, like no way am I leaving the little one?"

But Astair insists. That— (she almost said it aloud too (*that thing!*)(whatever it is)) —needs to sleep (and doesn't Xanther know that "too much handling can be a very bad thing?" (what Astair says (lying too (even if she (vaguely) feels justified too (doesn't life accord steep fees for over-handling?))))).

(once out the door) Xanther immediately starts complaining.

"I feel funny. Am I hot?"
"You're always hot."
"Feel my head?"
"You feel cool."

In the car feeling funny becomes feeling sick. At Trader Joe's sick really does start to look sick (at least paler than usual (complete with (more than!) the usual stumbles (down goes a display (a quirky pyramid of sorts) of organic coconut water))). Even Astair starts feeling sick (thanks to an added surge of panic when she sees a Hiring sign (she might have to . . . (and it still won't be enough (not even close)))). And there goes any bonding (let alone talking (they leave with only organic coconut water ((Xanther can't even drink something with that many carbs) they have tofu and pine nuts at home))).

(however) On the way back something (briefly?) bright does make of this (brief) excursion something worthwhile.

"Mom!"

Racing across Hyperion is a black-and-white spaniel (panicked and confused (drivers (fortunately) not confused (calmly halting in the name of safe passage))) while (far behind) the (apparent) owners try to catch up (to cross the street). Astair finds herself driving alongside the dog racing a sidewalk.

"Mom, go faster! Cut it off up there."

If the day will have one victory it's this: Astair does not resist the order ((a little bit of interpersonal Tai Chi at work?) Xanther's voice so settled and matter-of-fact ((also) without recourse to tones this calmness also suggests (tones in isolate which might have made Astair shudder (with their unfamiliar power(?) ((too) other (wise)) overwhelming)))).

Astair accelerates ahead (just managing a quick right into a driveway ((with a small squeal of tires too!) and Xanther's already out of the car (like she's been throwing herself out of cars her whole life)).

The spaniel runs straight into Xanther's arms like it's known her her whole life. And the owners (eventually catching up (breathless)) cry with her like they've known Xanther her whole life.

He's eighteen, they keep crying. We've had him since he was a puppy. He's gotten more and more confused. We'd have died if something had happened to him. Thank you. Thank you (something like that). Also offering money which Xanther refuses with a laugh (such a beautiful laugh (is there any sound so beautiful?)).

Even Astair tears up (though unlike for(?) Xanther) tears bring no relief (not in the way Xanther looks when they finally return home (again throwing herself out of the car (racing back to the laundry machines for prolonged petting, cradling, and kissing))). Astair's tears burn with bitterness (why couldn't this day (Happy Mother's Day!) have been all about Xanther with ~~her~~ (*their!* (*her!*)) dog?).

Tai Chi is supposed to help but doesn't. Astair tries to enlist Xanther (as she does every night (except on Sundays)) but (fortunately) Anwar intercepts.

"Enough, honey. Let her be."
"It's our routine."
"It's Sunday."

And (of course) Astair knows that Astair (just)

wants company (the company she didn't have all day when she had company (trying (still) to change that with the same company (even now))).

Her first go is in the living room. Then in the piano room. By the time Astair tries again on the back patio (scolding herself (accosting herself!) about how place should make no difference (Lambkin would say you can do the form in a prison cell or a closet)) she (stiffly!) teeters through the start (uneasy from right foot to left ⁖ *Beginning* ⁖ ⁖ Yang Style Short Form ⁖ ⁖ **William C. C. Chen** ⁖). (next) Scares away the sparrow and its tail (if such a bird were ever to exist) ⁖ *Grasp Sparrow's Tail or Ward Off With Left Hand* ⁖. (then) Fumbles a shrinking ball ⁖ *Ward Off With Right Hand* ⁖ followed by a rolling away ⁖ *Roll Back* ⁖ (more like throwing away) and by this point (toes catching on a paver (*nice!*)) arresting the whole futile exercise.

When did Astair see Lambkin Crierhue last? No question they are due a session. Astair (though) snorts at the infeasibility (the *infinancialability*) of such a thing (but how badly (suddenly too (it seems)) she misses the sparkle of his eyes (the round enthusiasm of his form (as he demonstrates a touch (a push (even a shove))) (his Beautiful Lady's Hands ((more ladylike than hers (and more beautiful (and Lambkin's hands are *not* beautiful))) one of the basic principles ((Astair's pretty sure it's the fifth (#5 (maybe not))) hands soft (supple and long) like those of a beautiful woman (there are four(?) more basic principles (right?) which (right now) Astair (also) can't remember)))))).

Pffffft! (Astair actually throws up her hands.)

(at which point) Taymor calls to find out what all the snappiness with Abigail was about.

"She told you?"

"Told me? Cried is more like it. Stair, did you really say that? Over a game on a phone?"

"I did. I apologized."

"On Mother's Day too. Talk about *extra* sensitive. You know how badly that girl of ours wants kids."

"I still feel horrid." Even if Astair can't (won't?) tell Taymor about anything more specific than a bad day. "You know me. The sun comes out and I sulk."

"That's bullshit. Like I really give a fuck about Abigail wallowing in hurt feelings? Come on, give it up, tell me about the new dog!"

An ugly thought follows (not new either (but like a vampire immune to heart-piercing analysis reviving as often as it's restaked)): maybe Astair really is a bitch. Can she argue (but she's done just that ((constantly too) with herself)) about how (so long as she is good-intentioned (loyal (fierce defender of what might (before a day of doubt) rise up as a Good))) it might not matter if others perceive her as ((overanalytical) (shrewish)) cold.

Cold!

Why does that one always hurt the most?

∷ *The secret stones of our movable possessions.* ∷

What of her warmth for her children? Her husband? Answering Anwar's amorous advances (finding what satisfaction she can in the memory of a satisfaction she once had known so well and so often (so finding instead (these days) a satisfaction (real satisfaction (really!)) in his satisfaction (his beautiful desire and (filling) contentment!)) (keeping from him (still) this itchiness (hers alone) these flashes of bodily humiliation (hers alone (talk about heat!)) (("Beware unforgiven secrets," Sandra Dee Taylor had whispered in one of her famous lectures (the much-revered "Doula at Oceanica" (certainly revered by Astair (what might Sandra Dee Taylor have to say about her paper?)))) is there really no Goodness in secrets?)))?

Of course (re: vampire of icy bitchdom) it's not like she's ever had much ground to stand on. Hadn't she (after all) left Dov Mudd for Anwar (and pregnant with Xanther too ("Not even born!" went one community refrain (which her parents took up too (maybe even started))))? How beyond pardon! (Anwar getting his share (more than his share)). And (no question) it was a weird way to commence a romance (this marriage of theirs). And ((of course) in the court of public opinion) how kind it had been (and sexless too) never mattered ((how (purely) devoted) (how (purely) nurturing)). But Astair remains bitch proud of it. Doesn't give a hoot. Even if her parents (still) haven't forgiven her (no matter that Dov (whose record (of intolerance and violence) should have granted her immunity) had forgiven her years earlier (going so far as to whisper (almost in tears(?)) how (in retrospect) he could never have equaled Anwar's care when dealing with Xanther's epilepsy ("I would have failed her before year one was up"))).

Rochelle Gardiner. That's who Astair misses. Rockie wrote horoscopes for the *LA Weekly*. Had since the '80s. Not that Astair ever took seriously such vatic readings of the stars (she read Rockie first in the *Village Voice* (and then in the *Improper Bostonian*)). They were just these (tasty tidy) bits of goodwill ((why, she'd sometimes read all of them (from Aries to Pisces)) (decency bests prophecy)).

Astair needs Rockie now.

But Rockie is years gone.

∷ October 31, 2008 11:11 AM ∷

(instead) Astair finds Anwar in the piano room. It's like he's been waiting for her all this time. That beautiful smile. Those tolerant eyes (eyes so deep with tolerance they make of darkness something almost too bright to see).

His gentle palms reach for her. His kiss on her lips is lighter than whatever brightness would dare to keep. Astair wants to cry at once (curl up within his arms (within those whispering caresses)).

"Do you want to talk about finances?" That's what Astair says instead.

"Not now," he responds patiently (even if his hands slip from hers). "Do you want to talk about the paper?"

"Not now."

Beware unforgiven secrets.

But here (still) at the end of the day (. . .) wiggling in her daughter's arms.

So small. Like a white puff of cotton (a cotton ball if it weren't for the pink pads on each paw (like tiny unused . . . (what?))). Not that Astair ever gets a clear view (no matter how much Xanther keeps it on her person). It (allways) seems to disappear ((between knees) (in elbow nooks)). (even when Xanther bends her neck ever so softly against its sleep) It seems to disappear inside one of her ears.

"So cute! Full of gurgling!"
"Careful, baby. We don't know if it has any diseases."

Yes. That's another what-Astair-says-on-Mother's-Day (instead of pointing out how nice it is to see her child so happy (practically glowing!) and (finally (apparently)) unmolested by worry).

Xanther scoffs (disappears the puff of sighing(?) white between penitent palms).

Though Xanther's no penitent. (even as her mother's eyebrows arch (to a daughter's lips receding for what teeth prevent (a hiss unhissed (for now)))) Astair knows she deserves Xanther's (lack of?) response. (obviously) Xanther recognizes how ridiculous Astair is being (how far from sense (what would she (or anyone in her family) do if they knew that Astair had just spent an hour today searching for kitten diseases (coming up with nothing more plausible than a (really unlikely) case of rabies (and an image (hardly making the case) of a squalling kitten (GITZ BACK . . . I HAZ A FIERCE)))))). (obviously) Astair sees how Xanther couldn't give a hoot about this mother's opinion (sparing no more than a scoff (coming off (really) as a pretty adorable *pfumpf*)).

(though (for the record (what record? ∴ *Indeed* ∵))) Astair's objections are not (entirely) irrational (or heartless). They serve some purpose (if only to brake (qualify?) Xanther's affection). (as Anwar himself keeps warning (sotto voce)) The likelihood that the kitten won't live much longer remains very high. And if that happens (when that happens?) both parents will then have Xanther's (terrible!) heartache to contend with (*contend!* (how about handle? care for? (*bitch! bitch! bitch!*))).

Anwar's warning ((though)(so sotto voce) about the future) also comes with its own omissions (which (for all Astair keeps saying (*thinking!*) she still (for some reason (what reason?)) hasn't been able to ask about):

Anwar's explanation yesterday afternoon.

"She saved him."

Though that wasn't it either.

"She saved him. Actually—"

Actually what? As if to say—

"She saved him. Actually, she—"

She what? (If she didn't save him (him?!)?)

What Astair still can't ask about (or really is (really) about to ask about (when the phone rings (gets through Mefisto's ongoing onslaught with a ringtone ("Love and Peace or Else")))).

Mother.

Bringing no relief. Talking about a trip next spring break "for the girls!" "Next year?" "Your father and I like to plan. It's why we get things done. Your sisters and I were thinking Florence or maybe Venice? *Italy.*" (in the face of which) Astair knows better than to bring up her news or (ridiculous (bitchy?(!))) distress (knowing better than to point out (once again (what never helps)) how her mother (Bea ((not Bae) pronounced Bee)(Eustace Beatrice Donnelly West)) fails to mention Anwar (even allude to him (not a shadow of a reference))).

(though by this time) Anwar's not even a shadow (he's taken the car to see his friend Ehtisham to discuss money (until Ehtisham cancels while Anwar is en route (returning Anwar to leftovers))).

Astair took care of Sunday dinner for the girls ((which really only included Freya and Shasti) because Xanther was handling dinner(?) for her charge ((that squeaking Q-tip) warm bottle of milky formula blotting out its presence)).

Sleep coming later (though Astair climbed into bed early (keeping her eyes closed too (despite fits of dread(?)))).

(

(

(let more transparent dreams seize her)

)

(   )

()

(as if opening (Anwar) up to her)

)

She saved him. Actually, she . . .

Not just uncertain.
Or maybe startled.
Or even amazed.

He had looked terrified.

Worse: Anwar had looked appalled.

078*371*636

"We" are not the only kind of **we**.

— Eduardo Kohn

Doors slip wide. Windows slide open.
Here is no dream.

∴ **Here was never a dream.** ∵

Darkness fails and with it vision.

∴ Nimieties of form compacting into brightness and lightness
allways finding their way to less . . . ∴

∴ Uhm, hello? Xanther's like dead asleep? And like definitely not dream-ing. Double-definitely not seeing anything. Eyes flapped. Zip REM. I know this because I'm zip REM, flapped, with not a glimmer of a thought. In fact, huh, I shouldn't even be present now, right?, except, uhm, okay, well, this is a pretty weird start to —, I don't know, like not a hallucination, it's not that, but more like what a hallucination *feels* like? ∴

Xanther's teeth grind down against the assault, will it ever cease?, gritting back a scream, which gurgles, must gurgle right?, ∷ *Gurgling like a growl making of grinding teeth something more than just sounds* ∴ as if to warn herself against opening her eyes, and there discover worse, what no amount of open eyes will ever defeat. ∷ **What we could never defeat.** ∴

Forget the cubby comfort of Xanther's small room, where she lies now, drapes drawn, with the hot May air drawing the walls in even more, crouching the ceiling too, along with all of its made-up constellations, the phosphorescent paint which succumbed hours ago to this room's darkness, all of which wouldn't stand a chance. Not paint or plaster. Forget a poster or a corkboard dangling above a desk. Not even the house frame could survive.

Roof erased by sky.

And then sky erased by . . .

But Xanther knows what it means to feel a mind melt. And Xanther also knows what it takes to survive. Like Dov always said, mud's beyond defeat, "especially a Mudd."

∴ No record of that. If she'd just open her eyes, this nightmare could end. ∵

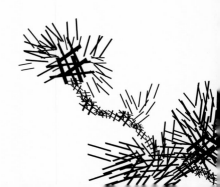

87

So Xanther just makes something else out of it all, something less, letting all such tumbling confusion collapse in on itself, until the, what?, compression of so much, what?, density?, forget what could never announce itself anyway with some name, forget explanations, forget words, like what are those here?, there is no expression here anyway right?, just unregistered output, whatever that means, is something put out?, and yet still somehow drawing out something, limning an edge, limning?, lining?, this overwhelmingness made visible, briefly, even if probably the wrong visible, right?, how could it not be?, like isn't Xanther really just closing her eyes to make something up against a reality forever beyond her, and like on the other side of infinity, just a dumb way to behold the strange territory of her incompleteness wherein, in?, she might imagine herself, if for no better reason than to find herself utterly lost, if only so she can just unclench her teeth, silence the gurgle, that growl prowling these confusions, and, you know, maybe, just maybe, find space . . .

:: And so two eyes open . . . ::

Someplace branched, and snow-packed, and if still immured by ridge after ridge, and valleys veiled in freeze, with an endless open despondent and gray above, still a place to roam.

But roam for what?

Like is she even the one roaming?

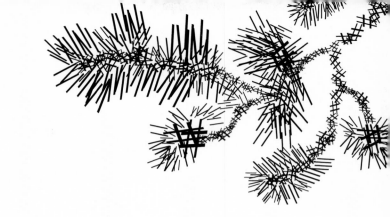

.: **Exactly.** :.

Xanther snaps awake, ∷ *two eyes close* ∷ like lurches really, back arching too, chest jerking upward, and not like some dream twitch either. Did she really groan? ∷ This is much better. And yes, she did groan. ∷ Followed by just as nasty a reverse, all of her going twitchless, down to the last stitch of muscle, almost down to that fist of meat at her center.

Was that even sleeping? Weirdest ever.

∷ Much, much better. ∷

Can't even remember. ∷ Because there's nothing to remember. ∷ But still remembering this sensation of forgetting something . . . something important? ∷ **Crucial.** ∷ And then, like that, even that goes. Bye-bye whatever. Hello, Monday morning. Not even drowsy.

Maybe a little scared.

Except—

Except for the little one. There with lights out. Beside her all night. Under her comforter, folded back like a dog-eared page. Either curled up tight underneath or stretched out on top, one arm, foreleg?, reaching out from that pillowy beneath, a paw reaching her, settling so light on her arm Xanther has to imagine it there to even feel its weight and then, suddenly, it weighs quite a bit.

Except—

Except, there is no weight. No paw. Here is how a breath ends, a dream arrests and a heart stops: the little one is gone.

Xanther searches the folds of her duvet, scrambles off of her bed to check the floor, to search under her bed, flies downstairs.

There.

Right where she left it before going up to brush her teeth, even putting on a good show for Les Parents, but after that first evening, for sure expecting it on their second night, what just had to keep happening again, and did happen again: lights out, and somehow already there, stairs and whatever somehow posing no obstacle.

Now on his back.
Little hips twisted to one side.
A forepaw held up. Rigid.
Eyes always sealed shut.

Only the thinnest rasp confirming life.

Xanther's scream calls to life the house.

Astair drives like a crazy woman. Xanther always forgets how great her mom is with emergencies. Like the awkward, pent-up way she usually is, like sorta thick and frozen, so she gets all jerky, these days a lot like that, like way more, like almost this *Walking Dead* kind of thing, which vanishes as soon as things heat up and she kicks into crisis mode.

In those moments, Astair actually seems calm.

And it keeps Xanther calm. Or at least calmer.

Clutching the little one in her arms, eyes wild with tears, all while thumbs text her friends, still not in school yet, thank goodness, asking about the best vet, animal emergency facility, and all of them answering back, Mayumi, Cogs, and Kle, even Josh, who's usually the slowest to respond, with so much info, from family to extended family, all with lots of pets, swearing here was the very best, or there was the very best, along with sad faces and screenfuls of dog emojis. She still hasn't told them yet.

Astair, though, sides with Taymor's rec, which Mayumi's aunt also vouches for, Josh's dad's best friend too. Who cares if that means West Hollywood? Astair just teaches their Honda how to really guzzle gas.

Dr. Syd Lactnod's entrance brings warmth. And not like the examination room is that cold either. Maybe it's the fluorescents caged above? Or the cold-metal counter on the back wall with metal-lidded jars of gauze and Q-tips. Is that it? The metal? Does metal always describe cold? Metal shelves stacked with steel instruments, boxes of tissues and disposable gloves, bottles labeled something like Beta-Gen Otic Solution or T8 Keto, which somehow reads like a temperature drop, if that's possible. Just looking at GOJO hand sanitizer feels icy. Drawers labeled 18GA, 22GA, 25GA feel iciest. And no getting around the fact that the big scale/ examination table in the center of the room is actually cold. Like to the touch? Nothing but stainless steel except for a little patch of LEDs, red, registering weight in lbs/kgs. Something called a Vet-Tec 2000.

One wall has a poster of a cloud looking much like this big dog blowing a wind made up of smaller dogs. Kinda cold, right? While opposite are two more posters. One has storm clouds raining cats and dogs. Cold for sure. The second is called *Cats of the World,* which isn't cold but does snag Xanther's attention, Astair's too, both taking in all the different breeds, from Cameo to Tonkinese. Say hi to a Maine Coon or Abyssinian. Hello Ocicat, Turkish Angora, Manx. There's even one with a yellow eye and a blue eye, Astair pointing out the difference, because like, right?, Xanther shares that in common, sorta, because really what do "share" and "common" really ever have to do with glossy paper? Xanther just keeps petting, with oh so gentle fin- gertips, this too-still still-rapsing little one, not glossy at all, more like beneath the gloss, at the bottom of a Trader Joe's reusable bag now, all they had, already knowing that despite all these images with certain names, in cursive too, Xanther won't find the right breed for this little one, even if some might come close, closest maybe the Devon or Sphynx, though Xanther can't say why.

Why?

Oh.   No.

Xanther almost shudders. Or is it shivers?

And then Dr. Syd Lactnod walks in and bye-bye chill. Like no amount of metal could ever matter. And it's not like he's this huge presence either. In fact just a whisper taller than Xanther. Blonder, well duh, for sure. But maybe a giant koala, if she and Astair were playing The Animal Game, which they're both always playing anyway. A drowsy giant koala, belly full of eucalyptus.

His voice is soft as a nap, smile softer, softest though is the way he listens to Astair but with alert eyes on Xanther, because he already knows Xanther's the one with the most to lose, and like she's already losing it, can't wipe the tears away fast enough, as Dr. Syd gently takes the grocery bag from her and even more gently lifts out the tiny curl of white.

"Wow," Dr. Syd says, first thing, and Xanther takes that as a good sign, as in one, he's impressed, and two, there's no need to put his smile away just yet.

On the stainless steel scale, her white little curl starts to uncurl, red LED numerals ticking upward toward a pound, or is it maybe like a kilo?, that wisp of cloud stretching out, heaviness on the rise, nearly a pound, kilo, whatever, a waggling tail adding another ounce, gram, even a yawn seems to weigh something.

"We found it," Astair has to explain for some reason. "Or my daughter found it. Rescued him. If it is a him."

"Is he a him?" Xanther asks.

The little one cries out, a sharp little peep, stumbling at once toward Xanther's voice.

"That's good," Dr. Syd laughs, as one of his big hands, with an easy scoop, arrests the wobbling march while his other hand begins to gently prod the hips, the curve of the tiny spine, peeling back the ears, checking around the eyes, opening them for a quick look at the whites and what seemed to Xanther like something deep, black and wet, and smoky, all at the same time.

"What seems to be the problem?" Dr. Syd asks gently, sorta to the kitten but to Xanther too, his tone shifting a little, like maybe a little more serious?, like he too had caught something unsettling beneath those lids?

As best as she can, Xanther explains how she heard the cries, though doesn't try to explain how the hearing was not like really hearing, but . . . , and anyway, running out into the rain, to the gutter, finding the little one pinned against a grate, caught up in all the other stuff too, like leaves, and the icky rest, about to get swept down, maybe all the way to the sea. "And, and my dad, uhm, so tried like CPR?, and that didn't work, and so he, he like, uh, let me try?"

Though now, with all the not-telling going on, ∷ **You know what she's hiding.** ∷ Xanther shivers for real, or is it shudders?, stammering more too, trying hard to keep going, eyes fixed on the sealed little eyes, which without seeing, which is like without knowing anything too, right?, were also like still telling Xanther it was okay to keep some secrets, especially theirs, which Xanther really has no clue about, and sure can't explain, ∷ What is she going on about? ∷ at least not without coming off as completely bonkers.

Besides, while she's managing to sputter out how she and Anwar went in search of a clinic, Dr. Syd gently pries open the jaws. That starts the little tail really flicking around.

"Did it just belch?" Astair smiles.

"Or tried to growl." Dr. Syd smiles too.

Then as Dr. Syd examines the little one's teeth, Xanther tells about the first vet and all the little bottles they had to get plus the kitten formula and instructions on how to make a bed that's warm enough and safe enough, because obviously the little one had lost its mother and that's what mothers are for, to keep beginnings safe.

Tears start up again then. Because isn't that the only thing Xanther wants? To be safe? To make the world safe?

Tears ebb when Xanther gets to yesterday, how well the kitten seemed to be doing, "almost making a sound, like, I thought it was maybe a purr?" Until this morning, tears betraying her again, Xanther can't help it, when everything changed again, her little one barely moving. "I thought he'd gone, like his heart had just stopped or something?" Even as Xanther wonders, especially with the kitten clearly squirming around, just how badly she's overreacted?

Dr. Syd retrieves a stethoscope from a drawer and listens to the kitten's chest for a long time.
"Huh."
Next Dr. Syd checks the temperature by sliding a thermometer into the kitten's bum, provoking another sound, this one even lower, so maybe a growl, like Xanther could blame it.
"Is there a fever?"
Head shake. More checks. Dr. Syd goes to the door, whispers something to someone, returns again to the scale.
"Temperature's just a little low."

A little later, JD, at least that's what the white lettering stitched onto his blue smock says, comes in holding some kind of machine.

"Is that an iron?" Xanther blurts. It almost looks like the one Anwar has at home.

"Gets the wrinkles out," JD winks. Wow, is he tall, like too tall for the ceiling, though of course the ceiling's not that low, but it must seem that way because JD keeps stooping, in this sweet way, like he's constantly and carefully considering the world below him.

JD's long black arms hold the iron thing a few inches above the tiny creature, and wow, like how had Xanther not noticed that before?, like JD might have been joking but he was right too: the skin is nothing but little wrinkles, or really tinytiny ripples. JD smiles, catching something, telling Xanther not to worry, explaining that it's not really an iron, it's something called a Power Tracker IX, and the "ripples," JD even says ripples, "gonna stay just where they are." He's just scanning.

∴ One light pulses red. One switch reads READ ∵

Wait! Like an X-ray? What kind of scan? Scanning what? Xanther molaring the questions because the last thing she wants to do now is interfere with this new seriousness, both Dr. Syd and JD bending all of their attention in on the tiny animal causing the liquid crystal display to come to life.

LOOKING

Over and over. ⠂⠄ *Blue crystal refreshing and refreshing.* ⠂⠄ With plenty of beeps too. Dr. Syd mumbles something about interferences. JD holds the iron-scanny-tracker thing even closer, eclipsing the little one, Xanther's throat thickening, her chest tightening, and then the machine isn't looking anymore.

078*371*636

JD leaves with the machine and the strange number without even glancing Xanther's way, and like his stoop got deeper too, or maybe the machine got heavier? Dr. Syd's not making things any easier, because he seems different too, like heavy but on an empty belly, his smile still there but no longer locking into place, as he spends more time looking at Astair, though not locking in there either.

The only thing okay about any of this, for Xanther that is, is that her little curl of white is back in a palm of hands, eyes locked tight, paws fish-hooking, light beyond feel, locking in all of Xanther's attention.

"Is it okay, Dr. Syd, for it to be handled so much? Being a kitten and all?"

Like that is the only question her mom has been waiting to ask this whole time. Xanther almost groans. Or growls.

"Oh yes. It's a good thing. A great thing. Great for your daughter, great for our little friend, who incidentally, is a he and a neutered he too."

"Neutered?" Xanther asks, because she doesn't understand the word, though it rings familiar.

"But so young?" Even Astair seems surprised.

"That's the curious part. He's lost lots of weight but I find canines, premolars, and molars. Actually, a few are missing. The rest indicate years of use. Heavy tartar buildup. Gums worn. Pigmentation too. Curious fellow. Polydactyl. Male pattern baldness even. In other words, not so young. More like on the other side of life's span."

"He looks like a kitten," Astair insists.

"Probably sick. We need to get him fed and hydrated. I'd also like to order a blood panel and start him on a regimen of antibiotics."

"Of course."

And there's mom being mom, like the greatest Xanther could ever know, who for all her habits, like so over-stressing things, worryings, pesterings too, and these days overall jerkiness, the not *Walking Dead* kind, still can with just a tone, such an amazing tone!, like better than some ancient bell tower on some distant green hill, which at the same time as it's impossibly far away also sounds impossibly close, like tolling just for Xanther, tolling the music of everything-will-be-okay, mom's here, mom will always be here, and keep life safe.

Even this little thing of broken white whiskers seems to hear it, sighs even, re-resting its tiny head against Xanther's wrist, just as Xanther rests her head on Astair's shoulder, sorta sighing too, Astair definitely sighing, wrapping her arm around Xanther and kissing the top of her head.

Dr. Syd kinda sighs but with no good news in it.

"There's something else."

Xanther knows that look, the one of I'm-obliged. Like when she's in doubt, like maybe she's eaten too many pieces of dried pineapple and has to admit so to Les Parents.

"With found animals we're obliged to do a routine check for, well, previous ownership. To make sure it's not lost. I know this might be hard, but this cat could be ten years old, fifteen, maybe older, and maybe you can see how hard that would be for someone who's had him for so long?"

Now it's Xanther's turn to look away, anywhere but at Dr. Syd, though looking at the little one now is hardest.

"I don't understand," Astair speaks up. "How can you scan for a previous owner."

"Oh. Right. You can implant your animal with an ID."

"Like a microchip? Is that what you found?"

"Not at first. Which sometimes happens. Signal complications from equipment or phones. JD didn't pick up anything and then he did and then he didn't and then we found some numbers."

"What happens now?"

"JD's checking. Avid, Fecava, Trovan. There are a few services so it might take a moment."

Xanther's scabbed knees lock, big toes pumping. Eyes too hot to wet anything. Forget taking a breath. Like she cares. Like she would want to breathe, like ever again, if it comes down to some stranger taking away this little whisper of warmth.

And then JD's back, still stooping, but not nearly as much, like his smile is lifting him up, like the ceiling better take note. Now when he whispers something to Dr. Syd, he looks at Xanther and winks again. Dr. Syd's uneasiness ends too. Belly full of eucalyptus again. He even chuckles.

"We're good. Though it's a little weird."

"Oh?" Astair responds.

"The ID came back as deceased."

"Deceased?"

"It also came up as a dog."

Xanther smiles at the mix-up, can't wait to tell Cogs, but the relief lasts only until JD takes away the kitten, or is it now a cat?, to the back for tests, shots too?, while Astair goes off with Dr. Syd to take care of the bill, instructing Xanther to wait in the admitting lobby. Of course, Xanther obeys, if still hanging on to their voices, fading away, making that hushing sound, like brooms on pavement, leaving Xanther with nothing to do but fidget her phone, wanting her friends, but not texting anyone, her phone crashing anyway as soon as she logs into Parcel Thoughts, leaving her with nothing to do but look around at other people waiting with their animals or for their animals.

Xanther feels awful.

The second JD took the little one away, all the while saying it would just be a moment, and that like, you know, everything would be fine?, even though it wouldn't be just a moment, and fine? right?, who knows about that, Xanther felt something inside her, like in her chest, only deeper, so not her chest, in fact not anywhere close, make this pop, but like loud enough that everyone should have heard it, like when her sisters take turns at the thermostat, Xanther creeping down to the basement to watch what happens through the little glass window at the base of their furnace.

Xanther keeps getting hotter, for a moment even sure she'll throw up in the lobby.

And then JD's back. And just like that, the feeling sick, the burn in her chest, vanishes.

"A champ."

In JD's hands, the Trader Joe's bag looks like some kind of vet doggy bag, JD's hands are that big, but still handled like it holds the world. And it does.

An old woman with knee-high green stockings shoved into dusty Birkenstocks, her lips dabbed with orange lipstick, squints hard at Xanther. But oh how those eyes widen when Xanther pulls out the little one.

"Oh, she's small. How old?"

Xanther shrugs. "She's a he."

"Kittens are such fun!"

And even if fun doesn't quite fit, the tiny creature breathing softly in the cradle of her arms somehow settles Xanther. More than that. A kind of lightness follows, like even shadows lose their hold a bit, including the one thrown by the door as they hustle out onto Santa Monica Boulevard, or the one cast by their parking meter, maybe grayer?, or even the ones in their car, collecting around Xanther's feet, as they head home.

"A dog!" Astair laughs as she turns left up Echo Park Avenue. "And in this area. And an Akita too. What are the chances?"

Which is funny, or at least smile-worthy, if her mother's eyes didn't look now like two black holes.

'Birds?'

(AN UNMATCHED LEFT PARENTHESIS
CREATES AN UNRESOLVED TENSION
THAT WILL STAY WITH YOU ALL DAY.

— *Randall Munroe*, **xkcd**

Now is all about money [Anwar reminds himself
{just the money ‹no fussing with M.E.T. «let alone
MOOWK ⟨let alone ⌈PO⌋ *Paradise Open*⟩ and whatever components and subsystems» or invisible work
presently not monetized›} and keeps reminding him-
self] because Now [for Anwar] is never about money.

Especially when Now = coding [Anwar trying to
avoid his own Question Song rising with why {his
upbringing? ‹synaptic arrangements «genetically?»
determining rewards «pleasures?» out of reach of
numerics?›}]. Trying hard to focus on this one thing:

$9,000.

Anwar's not sure even an extra zero would help
[would zeros?].

[surely!] Safeguarding his family's future helps [but
it remains a consequence and {unless fomenting imagined states of destitution for his wife and children}
never an instigator].

Once [upon a time {ha‹!›}] Mefisto and he had
spiralled into a conversation about measurement and
worth. Mefisto is equally unmotivated by promises of
remuneration [his own pleasure systems {apparently}
originating out of neural conclusions Anwar can no
more estimate than make].

'Making money has nothing to do with money,'
Mefisto had sighed [Scotch inspired {or AM enlight-
ened}]. 'You must just create value.'

An easier approach [{for Anwar} however asymptotically]: to pursue the value of a thing itself [without waxing too philosophical {Plato whispering into view ‹before passing out of range again «leaving behind no locus classicus» only a promise to return› what is never lost to begin with}] as prime mover. In this case:

Cataplyst-1.

Enzio's game might not even prove worth a look [in essence what they are paying Anwar to find out {to resuscitate ‹resurrect?› what has lingered in their digital vaults for ‹two«?»› years ‹this solitary creature «or fruit?» «all history of its purpose ⟨not to mention its creator⟩ somehow lost»› likely valueless} moribund] but [{maybe?} for that reason alone] also enticing?

Anwar can read the lines clearly enough to get a vague picture of the play [{curiously though} odd words he can't place litter the lines]. What remains syntactically apparent still hides its thing-ness in oblique [strange?] nomenclature/opacity. [typically] An engineer [even a non-programmer] can catch hold of descriptors [like Grandma or Zombie or Zombie Spawn Rate or Cat or numCatsSaved or All_Cats_Dead {Anwar thinking of a game created by his friend Lloyd Tullues ‹Ironblight Software›}] and figure out that Grandma is shooting Zombies to protect her Cats [cats? { . . . }].

This is something else:

```
101001    bool Networking::Connect(const char* addr)
101002    {
101003        if (!mInitialized)
101004            return false;
101005
101006        int res = 0;
101007        struct addrinfo *pAddrInfo = NULL;
101008        struct addrinfo *pCursor = NULL;
101009
101010        if (!ResolveAddress(addr, &pAddrInfo))
101011            return false;
101012
101013        // Attempt to connect to an address until one succeeds
101014        for (pCursor = pAddrInfo; pCursor != NULL; pCursor = pCursor->ai_next)
101015        {
101016            // Create a SOCKET for connecting to server
101017            mSocket = socket(pCursor->ai_family, pCursor->ai_socktype, pCursor->ai_protocol);
101018            if (mSocket == INVALID_SOCKET)
101019            {
101020                printf("socket failed with error: %ld\n", WSAGetLastError());
101021                return false;
101022            }
101023
101024            // Connect to server.
101025            res = connect(mSocket, pCursor->ai_addr, (int)pCursor->ai_addrlen);
101026            if (res == SOCKET_ERROR)
101027            {
101028                closesocket(mSocket);
101029                mSocket = INVALID_SOCKET;
101030                continue;
101031            }
101032            break;
101033        }
101034
101035        freeaddrinfo(pAddrInfo);
101036
101037        if (mSocket == INVALID_SOCKET)
101038        {
101039            printf("Unable to connect to socket!\n");
101040            return false;
101041        }
101042
101043        return true;
101044    }
101045
101046    void Networking::Disconnect()
101047    {
101048        if (mSocket != INVALID_SOCKET)
101049            closesocket(mSocket);
101050    }
101051
101052    int Networking::Receive(char* buff, unsigned int bufflen)
101053    {
101054        if (!mInitialized || mSocket == INVALID_SOCKET)
101055            return -1;
101056
101057        int res = 0;
101058        int bytesRemaining = bufflen;
101059
101060        // Receive until the peer shuts down the connection
101061        do
101062        {
101063            res = recv(mSocket, buff, MIN(5 * 1024, bytesRemaining), 0);    // Receive in 5k chunks
101064            if (res > 0)
101065            {
101066                printf("%d bytes received..\n", res);
101067                bytesRemaining -= res;
101068                buff += res;
101069            }
101070            else if (res == 0)
101071            {
101072                printf("Connection closing, total bytes received: %d\n", (bufflen - bytesRemaining));
101073            }
101074            else
101075            {
101076                printf("recv failed with error: %d\n", WSAGetLastError());
101077            }
101078
```

```
101079  ┗      } while (res > 0 && bytesRemaining > 0);
101080
101081         return (bufflen - bytesRemaining);
101082  ┗  }
101083
101084     int Networking::Send(const char* buff, unsigned int bufflen)
101085  ▼  {
101086         if (mInitialized || mSocket == INVALID_SOCKET)
101087             return -1;
101088
101089         // Send an initial buffer
101090         int res = send(mSocket, buff, bufflen, 0);
101091         if (res == SOCKET_ERROR)
101092  ▼      {
101093             printf("send failed with error: %d\n", WSAGetLastError());
101094             return -1;
101095  ┗      }
101096
101097         return res;
101098  ┗  }
101099
101100     bool Networking::ResolveAddress(const char* addr, addrinfo** info)
101101  ▼  {
101102         if (!mInitialized)
101103             return false;
101104
101105         struct addrinfo hints;
101106         memset(&hints, 0x00, sizeof(hints));
101107         hints.ai_family = AF_UNSPEC;
101108         hints.ai_socktype = SOCK_STREAM;
101109         hints.ai_protocol = IPPROTO_TCP;
101110
101111         // Resolve the server address and port
101112         int result = getaddrinfo(addr, DEFAULT_PORT, &hints, info);
101113         if (result != 0)
101114  ▼      {
101115             printf("getaddrinfo failed with error: %d\n", result);
101116             return false;
101117  ┗      }
101118
101119         return true;
101120  ┗  }
101121
101122     void atsa()
101123  ▼  {
101124         extern char* tokpela;
101125
101126         Networking* pNet = new Networking();
101127         int talpuva = 10000; // Retry every 10 seconds; taawi
101128
101129         while (true)
101130  ▼      {
101131             if (pNet->Ping(tokpela))
101132  ▼          {
101133                 // >          ^        .       .     ^      <
101134
101135                 pNet->Connect(tokpela);
101136                 unsigned int data_size = 0;
101137                 pNet->Receive((char*)&data_size, sizeof(data_size));
101138
101139                 if (data_size > 0)
101140  ▼              {
101141                     char* data = new char[data_size];
101142                     pNet->Receive(data, data_size);
101143                     processData(data, data_size);
101144
101145                     delete[] data; // >      ^          . .              ^        <
101146  ┗              }
101147
101148                 pNet->Disconnect();
101149
101150                 break;
101151  ┗          }
101152
101153             Sleep(talpuva);
101154  ┗      }
101155
```

```
101156        delete pNet;
101157    }
101158
101159    void decodeVideoStream(Networking* pNetworking)
101160    {
101161        StreamingVideo* pStreamingVideo = new StreamingVideo();
101162        int tid = createThread(&atsa);
101163
101164        const int TAAWI = 32 * 1024; // Decode 32kb at a time
101165        char* chunk = new char[TAAWI];
101166
101167        memset(chunk, 0x00, sizeof(chunk));
101168
101169        unsigned int videoSize = 0;
101170        pNetworking->Receive((char*)&videoSize, sizeof(videoSize));
101171
101172        printf("Decoding video of size: %d\n", videoSize);
101173
101174        unsigned int remaining = videoSize;
101175
101176        while (remaining > 0)
101177        {
101178            int received = pNetworking->Receive(chunk, MIN(remaining, TAAWI));
101179
101180            StreamingVideo::DecodeStatus status = pStreamingVideo->Decode(chunk, received);
101181            if (status == StreamingVideo::FRAME_READY)
101182            {
101183                pStreamingVideo->RenderFrame();
101184            }
101185            else if (status == StreamingVideo::DECODE_ERROR)
101186            {
101187                printf("Error decoding frame!");
101188                break;
101189            }
101190
101191            remaining -= received;
101192        }
101193
101194        closeThread(tid);
101195        delete[] chunk;
101196        delete pStreamingVideo;
101197    }
101198
```

Just get the thing running and Anwar will have all the time in the world to make sense of nomenclature [though therein lies the rub {Anwar's real problem and solution is time ‹because the time he needs to solve this keeps eluding him «or is it more complicated than that? ⟨energy [. . .] energy?!⟩ »}].

The morning had already gasped awake with the dead in their midst [that whiskerless fluff of white {that ‹dead «again»› creature}]. Or almost dead [Xanther's heart-stopping panic {‹the two of them «sipping up rapid breaths»› Xanther chirping out fragile words ‹having to do with not breathing «not chirping ⟨which was true ⌈convinced a tiny heart had stopped⌋ and not⟩» at all› Xanther ‹either way› holding her loss so close to deny visibility}]. Astair [gratefully] raced them to the car [leaving Anwar with how to get Freya and Shasti to school {‹why Cataplyst? «or Cata-? ⟨why even plyst? ⌈but really⌋ why?⟩ -1?» Cat-?› Anwar had called Lucy Fischer to see if an unscheduled pickup was an option ‹fortunately it had been›}]. And suddenly the morning was his [until Ehtisham called {the expected apology for cancelling last night coming at once ‹followed by a flicker«?» of good news›}].

'Culver City this afternoon?'

The logistics of a single-car household [and the inability to keep Uber as an anytime/anywhere service {not taking into account surge pricing}] resettled their get-together to early evening.

Dread then [{how Xanther will return ‹petless? «bereft? ⟨worse?⟩»›} until she's his own petrified spirit].

Anwar stares at lines of code and his mind goes blank [any error here eludes him {to the point that he's not seeing anything ‹not even the code›}].

```
4215    class ConfigFile
4216  ▼ {
4217    public:
4218        ConfigFile(const char* filename);
4219        bool getUIntValue(const char* keyName, unsigned int* value);
4220
4221    // ...
4222  ∟ };
4223
4224
4225    ResourcePool<GameObject>* mObjectPool = NULL;
4226
4227    int _tmain(int argc, _TCHAR* argv[]) // >        ^        .        .        ^        <
4228
4229    {
4230        ConfigFile config("sipaapuni.cfg");
4231
4232    // >        ^        . .                            ^        <
4233
4234        unsigned int objectPoolMax, atsaCnt;
4235        config.getUIntValue("OBJECT_POOL_MAX", &objectPoolMax);
4236        config.getUIntValue("ATSA_CNT", &atsaCnt);
4237        mObjectPool = new ResourcePool<GameObject>(max(objectPoolMax, 64));
```

Anwar tries [{futile} again] another restart [because? {what? ‹on the off chance things might load differently . . . ?›}]. Not even a flicker clues the mishap. The screen blacks [crash].

[whatever earlier insights Anwar might have had {‹while not at his computer «not facing any code»› about how to approach the problem}] The present hour makes out of insight an infeasible mess.

[forget runs] The thing never boots up [and instrumenting the code seems impossible {how is Anwar supposed to debug a release build with no console output? ‹debugging blind› unless he goes through the ‹whole› program line by line? ‹he's not fast enough «he'll never be fast enough» Enzio hasn't granted him unlimited time›}].

Until [as if facing some {‹terrible «segfault?»› crash} vault

{forever closed ‹out of reach «though ⟨maybe⟩ only just»›}]

finally gives way [[{always} so close by {too}] to the Web's latest distraction [{*temptation*!} that old one-thing-leads-to-another lie {backgrounding quests for resolution ‹satisfaction?› with every availing splash of color}] at one point landing Anwar on a Nespresso page [would coffee help? {is dependency a question? ‹or is desire always questionless?›}] before [who knows why {the how in his Firefox history}] reaching the Jaguar Corridor Initiative [creating a path {out of ranches and parkland ‹backyards too›} from Mexico

down through

Belize

Guatemala   Honduras

Nicaragua

across Panama

to Colombia

Ecuador

Venezuela

Guayana

down through Brazil   Suriname

Paraguay

and Argentina].

Dr. Alan Rabinowitz [despite battling CLL {Chronic Lymphocytic Leukemia}] had led the charge to defend these extraordinary cats [divided from one another by . . . {us}]. Rabinowitz [a giant of a man] suffered from stuttering at an early age [so bad he 'spasmed' {his word}] but discovered he could talk flawlessly to animals [{realizing they ‹like him› had no voice} he vowed to defend their lives {Stephen Colbert claimed Rabinowitz was the only guest to ‹almost› make him cry}]. Rabinowitz moves Anwar too [enough to donate {on the spot} one hundred dollars to panthera.org].

But as Anwar clicks through PayPal to donate what the Ibrahims don't have [forget $50k {even $9k ‹and as for big cats . . .›}] another curious return slips into place: a dream early this morning.

Cairo.

Saturated. Burnt reds. Burning yellows. Before dusk. Summer's dusk. Honks and engine coughs rise up from streets below. Bicycles drag wagons packed with bread and cabbage through narrowing streets. One wagon is filled with volleyballs. Buses and taxis crowd the main routes. Calls for prayers command the corners الموسيقى في ضوضاء العادات الحضرية ∴ Music in the mild clatter of— How these words come and go. ∴ People hurry to get home. Meals on their minds. Family. The whole thing feels absurdly Now and yet also of another time [born in dream time {‹re›born now‹?› in this ‹‹what?›› post-dream› time ‹because this is not the dream›?}]. If توحيد were a feeling perhaps this would be it?

He should ask his father. About فناء too. His father sets the table in their tiny dining room adjacent to their tinier kitchen. For some reason the apartment is always nine stories up. Muslin curtains waver as the day's end changes the air's mind.

'ماما مش هنا' His father smiles [never in English {even if Anwar knows the English ‹‹at the same time›› 'Mother's gone to the Square'›}].

From the tray of his high chair Anwar takes two pink plastic triangles and slides them together. He must be four years old. He's wearing a dark blue bib. For some reason the square he makes is dark blue too.

118

'ده كويس. ده كمان صح.' His father nods as he surrounds round plates with spoons and forks but no knives.

'ماما!' Anwar keeps crying because he doesn't have his father's knife and without a knife he can't cut his square back into two pink triangles.

'باباك مش بيعرف يحضر الترابيزه؟' Shenouda jokes. Anwar cries harder because [no] his father can't set the table [because Anwar has no memory of his father ever setting the table {which is true}].

And then Fatima arrives with bags of warm bread clutched to her chest like she will soon clutch him to her chest and both his parents are laughing and kissing him because they love him and soon they will eat.

'كل الأمور كانت هادئة في التحرير' Fatima assures Shenouda [but why wouldn't it be? {in 1964 Tahrir was التحرير ‹occupation was a word used elsewhere›}].

'المكعب بيعمل مثلثين!' Anwar shouts.

'هما يقدروا' his mother smiles [looking carefully at the green and yellow triangles].

And then Fatima and Shenouda disappear into the kitchen to cut the warm bread and fill their bowls with soup and talk about things they won't talk about in front of Anwar.

A red volleyball rolls into the dining room.

[when Astair and Xanther return] It's like the house is suddenly thrown wide open [{breezes upon breezes running wild ‹of one mind›} and they only came through the front door].

The kitten is fine [though {apparently ‹not so apparently›} not a kitten].

'You're joking. This is what the vet said?'

'Old,' Astair explains. 'Probably ill too. The vet, Dr. Syd, ordered a blood panel. None of it cheap.'

'Dare I ask?'

And he had thought the dog bed was bad [what had he been doing anyway giving to a charity? {Anwar knows parenting comes down to handling fiduciary surprises ‹forever disadvantageous «except when weighed against the child ‹outweighing every cost›»›‹though since when does a path «across the Americas» count as good parenting?›} unless his sudden affection{?} for jaguars originated in this {what?} mini-sheepcat{?} incarnating Xanther's {efflorescent} affection {leading Anwar to toss any and all ‹quantifying› integers out the window ‹all of which «for some reason» are now open}]!

'Supposedly there are all these books,' Astair mentions. 'On the phenomenal health of cats. How they do it, their magic. You know what Dr. Syd told us? "The cats don't read the books."'

Smiles [however] strain when Xanther learns she still has to finish out the rest of the school day.

'I can't just leave him.' Her mood all clouds.

Parenting! [but laments will quiet {tears will dry}].

[after a feeding {and a bundling in a warm towel ‹along with repeated promises «by both Anwar and Astair» to keep up the same routine every couple of hours›}] Astair drives Xanther to Thomas Star Kane and Anwar returns to Cataplyst-1.

Either an inscrutable ladder of code or crash after crash:

Anwar heads downstairs [for herbal tea {if indulging in a whiff of Astair's Chiapas beans ‹from Cafecito Organico›}].

[waiting for the water to boil] Anwar checks on Xanther's little round of white. Fast asleep. Have its ribs and spine always been this pronounced? Even the pelvic bones seem too visible. How did age suddenly become so obvious? Did just a word open his eyes? [at least{?}] This misreading permits Anwar to reframe the events of two days ago.

Old to begin with.

Old to end with.

[that evening {in Culver City}] Anwar thinks he's in the wrong penthouse [Sementera has two{?}]. [{then} he convinces himself] He's walked in on a robbery.

The robbers [though] all have jerseys. Prodigal Movers. The boxes say the same thing. [also] Nothing's leaving the building [all ingress {‹in fact› some boxes are unpacked ‹brand-new computers set up «atop brand-new desks»›}].

'Kozimo did us a favor,' Ehtisham says [cross-legged {‹on the floor› outside of that strange lazaretto for dangerous ‹or just silly› whims ‹The Glass House›}].

'No,' Anwar answers his good friend. 'Buying us would have been the favor.'

'I just told Talbot and Glasgow. I'll give you the same speech. If you disagree, we can reconsider.'

The speech isn't a speech. Just one spreadsheet after another [laid out on the carpet]. Solvency versus costs [including cash flow {nil} against tax liability {‹astonishingly› not nil ‹having to do with last year «and including an extension»›}].

'The bad news you can see for yourself: we're out. As you can also see: if we hold onto all . . . this, even until the end of the month, we're owing.'

'So there's good news?'

'No one's losing proprietary rights. MOOWK's still ours. Plus some capital remains.'

'How much?'

'Enough for a drink. Maybe two.'

'Paul Bucksea agreed to take over the lease,' Ehtisham sighs. 'Wired the money immediately.'

'Why would Dead Rowboats want in here?'

Ehtisham shakes his head. 'Some other Kozimo venture.'

Anwar's curious [but now those cautionary admonitions {‹usually› intended to check Xanther's curiosity} sound his way {who will now occupy this space makes no difference}]. Anwar pats his friend's back.

[first and foremost] The three friends are engineers. [generously] Ehtisham had agreed to take on the additional burden of handling all monies [no one had disagreed that the title of CFO was any recompense].

Each of them had taken a swing at interesting VCs or big companies. Only Ehtisham had gotten close: some big meetings followed by big promises [a big rush that was now a big headache].

'I think I just believed their shiny chrome and lobby furniture,' Ehtisham groans [like he really has a headache]. 'I should have known better. Everything at Dead Rowboats was so clean. There was no vibe there.'

It's clean here too. Some of the Prodigal Movers have even started putting on gloves.

'Hard to believe it's just gone,' Anwar says.

'Like a bomb went off. A really neat bomb. Removing everything. And then in its place, even more neatly, installing something entirely different.'

And while Ehtisham is right [everything going on here is exceptionally neat {from bubble wrap to packing peanuts to white gloves}] he's wrong about bombs.

Bombs are never neat [{one square makes two triangles . . . } they make shards . . .].

[instead of leaving then] Anwar and Ehtisham end up swapping Mefisto stories.

[for example] Back in the '80s [in response to Martin Newell's Utah Teapot] Mefisto wrote a program called the Utah Bong [modelled on a Klein Bottle {dubbed the Seventh Platonic Solid ‹StickyIckyHeadrush «after Teapotahedron ‹sixth›»›}]. Mefisto joked that purists should leave his Utah Bong bottomless. He sure had. As he intoned [from his own {unfathomable} head-rush]: 'What others might call inconsistencies, I call personality — the essence of all great programming.'

'I could use him now,' Anwar laughs [though he could]. 'I can't for the life of me debug this release build Enzio sent me. I'm drawing lines but it's no use. Can't even get a debugger window open.'

'Try music,' Ehtisham suggests. 'Your ear's good.'

'How so?'

'I heard this story, out of Red Fly Studio I think, about some guy who programmed outputs of various pitches at different points in the code. Do-re-mi type stuff. Whenever the CPU crashed, the audio system kept producing the tone. If you know the note, you know where to look.' ∷ *Game Coding Complete, Fourth Edition* by Mike "MrMike" McShaffry and David "Rez" Graham, p. 827. ∷

[several] Prodigal Movers now begin to move large things [{irregular things} all covered in canvas] into The Glass House.

'I'll tell you something weird,' Ehtisham hesitates. 'The last time I spoke with Kozimo all he wanted to hear about was Mefisto. And wow, talk about wax ecstatic when I mentioned the phone prank Mefisto had played on you and your family.'

[at this point] Anwar just wants to know what's under the canvas. Curiosity isn't one child's domain. Anwar can see where Xanther gets it.

'I'm almost afraid to admit that Kozimo was never down with our game,' Ehtisham continues. 'He just wanted to get close to Mefisto.'

'Well, he lost out there.'

'Like a groupie. Knew stories you and I have no clue about. Like Mefisto's work with NIF ⁛ **National Ignition Facility** ⁛ out of Livermore? What supposedly got him dragged over to ITER ⁛ International Thermonuclear Experimental Reactor ⁛ ⁛ *The Way* ⁛"? Or even back in the '90s — Did you know Mefisto was involved in TIGR ⁛ **The Institute for Genomic Research** ⁛?'

'Biology?'

[before leaving {his own Question Song taking charge}] Anwar has to slip into The Glass House [at once surprised {as the movers are not} by the bright shrieks].

'Birds?' Ehtisham is just as surprised.

In all kinds of cages [gilded to black iron {the biggest ‹easily!› ten feet tall}].

Parakeets? Finches? Anwar has no idea. Scores. Shrilling the light [Anwar keeps lifting the canvas covers {before a mover advises he stop ‹if only Xanther were here›}]. [behind bars] Rainbows break with the flutter of wings.

The glass terrariums [on the floor {however}] need no canvas and house no birds. Here the sandy bottoms swim with snakes.

Planski

Without me all your efforts would be smoke.

— *Sait Faik Abasıyanık*

When you're single, a single malt at a bar rings right. Not so much when you're alone and should be home. Texts from the university keep making promises about coming over late. It's not even close to late. This glass suits the hour just fine. It's the next one that worries Özgür. The ones that leads to late. The ones that get him saying things he has no mind to say because he knows what nights like these can cost and what little the mornings can mean.

The girl beside him has already complimented his purple pocket square. She thinks the scene at REDCAT is "nice." Her friends are still no-shows. Over an hour. Not so nice.

"You're a cop, huh?" she asks now.

"Detective."

"Even better." Half his age. If that. Probably just wants to talk. Get enough attention to not feel so at the mercy of solitude. Not to say that she wouldn't go for more attention if the night goes right. And there was a time when Özgür could have made the night go just right.

"Retiring." Özgür signals for the check.

He doesn't think about her again until he's back in his apartment. Charlie Parker tonight. With a decent blend. The name she gave was Cally. Black hair and wide brown eyes with a face pretty enough and a waist tight enough to give the size of her tits at least two reasons not to stare. The tattoo across her chest, though, was beyond avoiding. "Don't Ask" was caged in barbed wire, with drops of blood shaped like little hearts. Once upon a time Özgür would have found out everything Cally never wanted to admit. These days, though, he satisfied himself with what she thought mattered: seeing *Gatz* twice, the unabridged reading of *The Great Gatsby,* put on by Elevator Repair Service, and how it had changed her life. Of course at that age everything changes your life.

Özgür sleeps light waiting for Elaine's lighter touch to wake him. Her 4 AM text explains too little to want more:

too late :(

Özgür's stomach feels slit by glass. Forget breakfast. He barely dares a Tums. Not even a cup of coffee.

Noon is a different story. Just south of Marathon and up the street from where Independence Cab is headquartered, Sqirl turns out to have one of those menus worth whatever his guts are finding so difficult to stomach these days. His friend has chosen well.

Özgür picks one of the nine stools towards the back of the counter lining the south wall. None of the tables outside are free or if they are they aren't under the awning. Özgür doesn't want to sit in the sun.

Katla.

Planski might want more privacy but Özgür thinks the two girls here won't pose much of a compromise. Straight Thai, no code-switching.

Katla-katla.

Overhead a chalkboard displays the day's delicacies. Özgür already wants the smoked sablefish on Danish rugbrød served with an egg, pickled beets, and dragon's tongue only to realize the order-by time was 11 AM. He's considering the seared polenta when she walks in.

Detective Shannon Plainer Yarlovsky briefly went by Spy until someone figured her for just another plain Jane — a whitewash of unwashed blond hair. Except she isn't that. Though no highflyer either. Maybe because she excels at planning, Planski is what stuck. Some say she looks a bit like Beadie Russell in *The Wire*, only thinner and more awkward, her surfaces planed sharp until there's no place for your eyes to rest. Bony is too unkind and it's not like she tries to keep it off. Planski has one of those metabolisms cops getting old around the middle dream about. She's almost never late.

"So sorry, Oz."

Özgür doesn't doubt either her urgency or fluster. There's also something vaguely exhausted about her, the kind of tired that neither sleep nor jokes can remedy. The scary kind. Özgür doesn't know what to make of that.

"For you, a lifetime."

Katla. Katla.

"Is that for me?" She winks and like that all her sharpness goes, bones to points, on her cheeks a glow, and in those blues of hers a kind, familiar shine, and she's seen more than enough to teach living the darkest side of blue.

"Maybe you won't want it." Özgür keeps folding, rotating the paper, folding again.

Katla. Katla-katla-katla. Katla.

"Oh, I'll want it."

"Planski, you've never wanted it."

"That's true too." She answers with the same happy shrug Özgür's known for years, draping her beige coat with big black buttons over the metal stool. They've gone around the same innuendo so many times they forgot to notice that whatever possibility the innuendo had once offered had yawned and left years ago. They'd already become friends. Not that there was ever an occasion for otherwise. And whether or not Planski digs strange guys or straight gals has never been clear. Özgür's never heard of Planski going out on a date.

Katla. Katla.

"Where do you get your hats?" she asks after ordering the Kokuho Rose brown rice bowl with sorrel pesto, Meyer lemon, French feta, a poached egg, and something called lacto-fermented hot sauce. And that's just for starters. Planski also gets brioche toast with nut butter, Maldon salt, and Guittard chocolate ganache plus a coffee drink called the Al Pacino "Cold, Sweet & Creamy." Özgür settles on the open-face brioche with kale, a tomatillo puree, fried egg, sausage, and that same lacto-fermented hot sauce. Why sacrifice taste on behalf of some intestinal discomfort?

"I get them from a Turkish girl named Giza."

"You've had the same one for as long as I've known you." Just a cobalt trilby, stingy brim, with a side-dented crown, and one black-and-white ribbon with a thin turquoise band. The tight weave is what keeps sun and rain out and keeps Özgür coming back.

"She never runs out."

"And you?" Planski's nothing but twinkles today.

Katla-katla. Katla.

"Hush. I don't run out either. Giza's my hat girl. Elaine's my gal."

"I'm impressed. You've even been together awhile. Finally found the right one?"

"I've met plenty of right ones. Just never the one I could get along with."

"Except Elaine."

"Not really," Özgür laughs. "I just don't have the energy to object anymore."

"That's not what I keep hearing from Central."

As predicted, yesterday Özgür had got an earful about his "reported fucking failure in Southwest to fucking respect the fucking chain of command at a fucking crime scene." So much for his mailbox solve and Marvin D'Organidrelle.

"Retirement's inevitable. Question is just how soon. Captain keeps making a good case for me to stay."

"Bully then for Abendroth. About the only case he's made in, what . . . ?" But Planski doesn't finish the sentence, just smiles. She often doesn't finish sentences. Sometimes ends up in a stream of mumbles, either to herself or someone she's all too happy to leave confused.

Katla. Katla. Katla-katla.

Özgür fills her in on the Korean market murders, which people have started to refer to as the K-Mark Killings. Balascoe's triumph earns a laugh.

"I even gave my bullet a hug," Özgür admits. "The one I dodged years ago. It was still nice to see her."

"Nyra Carlton?"

"I told you that, huh? A P-II now. Did I tell you we were pregnant once?"

"Only half a dozen times. And let me guess, you still wonder about the child you never had?"

"That too, huh? Kid would be about thirteen now."

"You're too young to regret."

Katla.

"At fifty-seven it's fifty-seven varieties of old." ∵ With not a Heinz in sight. ∵

"Not in this town. What does Elaine say?

"That's she's too old too."

"Is she even twenty?"

"Thirty-six."

Planski snorts, picking up the laminated card that came with their order, as if waving around a picture of El Diablo, number 2, could materialize lunch.

Katla-katla. Katla-katla. Katla-katla.

"Hear about that one-eighty-seven in Chinatown last month?" Özgür asks. Planski's been in Hollenbeck since they met back in 2006. It's not Central but it's as close as Rampart. "Very Dexter."

"Realic?"

"That's right."

"You're the third person to ask me," Planski mumbles, followed by more mumbles, which Özgür guesses has less to do with his question than with their missing food. "I did ask Benicio Echevarría over in Boyle Heights. He said so far it was long on gory what-ifs but still a short story of a police report. I meant to call up Oreb but forgot. Like you and I don't have enough to do without bothering someone about their case work, right?"

Özgür nods. Maybe he'll try Oreb too. Or even Frank. He'd like to get back to Cletious Bou with something, anything.

Katla.

"For you," Özgür smiles and hands over the Irish Setter ∷ Stephen Weiss ∷ like it might answer her wanness or appetite. The scary kind. "You good?"

"As good as my CI ∷ Confidential Informant ∷. So these days, really good. This time the years might just pay off. Direct eyes on distribution."

"Drugs?"

"Oz, if this runs right — and you know I'm givin' it my ball sackin' best — we won't just be grabbing street-side knuckleheads. I'm talking wider, county lines, online, maybe national lines. Could seriously disrupt our little balloon parade here."

"Mexico?"

"Sure, but across oceans too. I'm hearing West Africa, Europe, Russia. Plus something deeper than the usual points of origin, than location. Something I don't understand yet."

Planski tenderly tucks away Özgür's Irish Setter into one of the wide pockets of her black-buttoned beige coat. Like if nothing else, maybe it does answer something.

"FBI?"

"FBI's my problem. And why I'm about to start begging you. Ever heard of Guzzy Harris? He's our Hollenbeck go-to agent."

Özgür shakes his head, FBI, Florian, and the Long Beach murders distracting recollection. Agent Trauma. Was that his name? Something close. Something else too. Lost on the glass.

"Sanders tolerates him. Baeza not so much. Let's say it's high praise calling Harris a clogged douche nozzle."

"Sounds like you're all in love."

Planski laughs until smile and twinkle both go, her blues darkening into something beyond the reach of any color, a shade that if you're the kind who responds to need will break your heart. Not that Planski's ever had a problem breaking his.

"Jello?"

Just the mention gets her hissing. Jello had been one of her CIs four years ago.

"I need help, Oz. Someone I can trust. Someone my CI can trust."

"What else?"

"This goes way beyond what Central Bureau can handle. I need federal resources."

"You know better than I do, the more money your CI needs, the harder it is to get money."

"It's not like that. Minds are bold, hearts are wide, goodness is at stake."

"Eisenberg will be pissed when he finds out you took the wide loop around."

"Shit, Perez *and* Paysinger will probably try to figure out a way to bury me twice. Like freeway therapy to Valley Traffic."

"And I thought I was the rogue."

"Forgive us the vanity of purpose," Planski mumbles, even crosses herself. "I honestly thought I was only dealing with some homegrown set, at most a few blocks deep."

"Lucky you?"

"I don't want to fuck it up."

"Courage reveals itself in the context of others."

"Then let me pick the right others. Come on Turkulese, I need your help."

Özgür hasn't heard that name in a while. He'd earned it almost twenty years ago when a concrete slab stabbed through with rebar had fallen on a junkie's leg in a shooting gallery downtown. One of those buildings scheduled for demolition to make room for a Broad construction that never happened. Özgür had saved the kid's life, even saved the leg, though it never quite made sense how he had gotten the concrete to budge, let alone lift it up two feet. These days Özgür's happy if he can tie his shoes without making his back sing foul.

"And don't say Mazzola," Planski adds.

"Mazzola's about as discreet as a prize-winning pumpkin."

Funny that Planski picked this place. Of all the streets. Almost too much of a coincidence if the coincidence had any relevance.

"I have someone. What do I tell him?"

Planski starts eating lips.

"He'll ask."

Having had enough of this El Diablo, number 2, getting no one's attention, Özgür goes to check on their order. Planski will end up swallowing her lips if something on a plate doesn't come quick. A runner assures him their order is next. Özgür pours two glasses of water by the entrance where two young women stand in line discussing the medical industry and difficulties involved when attempting to alter patient protocols established in part by the drug manufacturing industry. Only as he starts to move away does he recognize her. She recognizes him at the same time.

"You!" She smiles.

"Hi, Cally." What more can he say? Özgür doesn't say more. Her remembered name pleases her. And while the coincidence shouldn't rattle him, it does. He knows coincidence doesn't have to mean anything more than just that, which Özgür hopes to communicate, and kindly too, with a mute tip of his hat. Cally pulls away from her friend and towards him just enough to communicate a difference of opinion.

The food beats him back. Planski looks pleased and focused, and even a bit renewed as she digs up forkfuls of green rice and runny yolk.

"Ever hear of Synsnap-27?" she asks between mouthfuls.

"No."

"You will."

be extraordinary

All I see is signs.

— *Rihanna*

stare morning dark. :: Fort Canning Park, Spice Garden. :: stare god's

crown. eat raw that lah, kill ya. risked right though, mahkota dewa

:: **Phaleria macrocarpa** :: cure sleep drought, cure piss pain, cure

cancer. plenty such tree do except find cat.

still jingjing all peace here, beside leafy tall and speckled red

shiny. no saysay why. by self in park hours from sunrise.

just downhill from keramat iskandar syah too, so many spices

reach out, alive, calm jingjing. who saysay why? tumeric, vanilla,

blue ginger. cardamom too. thai basil like old friend. pandan leaves

wave hey. betel leaves so damn shiok.

jilo nuts. jingjing prod betel more. mebbe overlook nut? jingjing

knuckle bump gums. could use friendly chew. could use new mood.

no time for kooning. up since cat gone. at least daun sireh :: **Piper**

betle :: grant green clump to mash on. chiak chow til better.

but jingjing pui chao nuah! outside park spout sidewalk with leafy

mess. heck care if matas come, cuffs out, mm tzai si, if he kena

rotan the offense see. no cops come. empty buses roll by.

much later then, and too much feet ache, south cam whore path,

old greenway tracked once by sleeper and rail straight back to jb

:: Johor Bahru ::, kena sai near from one bad step. root like oil that

quick untangle. jingjing feel hiss pass on ankle. mebbe cobra spit

too. or just dew jingjing kick loose. thing gone oreddy to roots.

jingjing still shake, check all over for bite. shakes hardest for every

next what-if. until he dashing, if shacks fast, oreddy can't breathe,

trying to outrun what-ifs. every grass tickle macam new teeth.

until night air wiggle thick with flying paradise trees. whip shapes

jewelling leaves glimmering branches. from thickest trees thickest

shadows dropping free to bind and ban last pulse.

what if what-ifs oreddy was?

jingjing lari-lari then, until panting drag him stop again, until

worse than pythons everywhere, until worse than venom every-

where, much worse than any writhe on fence post, lamp pole . . .

something else stir up from smokeless dreams.

hungrier things now gathering like shadows kena makan shadows,

along with any living thing casting oreddy devoured shadows.

even when jingjing race across clearing of nine bird poles, cage-

less, hooks hooking no sky, not even one hooking a silhouette for

dawn, skin tingle won't let be, as hungrier things still chase.

only off block 74, when jingjing stumble up hillside to find by

palms, made of plaster, locked from life, locked from even blue, a

blue lion, lion-size too, only then do jinn and snake scare cabut

fast. and mystery sure, that this saddest secret hantam jingjing

one, how such sham stockstill leave him kay stunstill and diam.

"未丢," tian li crycry. "其去之. 其终去之. 其去之求良."

gone at last gone. gone for good gone.

and gone still, back at commonwealth calyx, where manyak chop-

ear cats crouch void deck corners like claques of mourners, lor.

not near so calm if snake around. or spencer. but this early no one

down. jingjing tactical padpad by for lift.

top rooftop dawnlight kisskiss jingjing's lips. hdb ∴ Housing Develop-

ment Board ∴ ∴ *Housing and Development Board* ∴ got skyline. nowhere near

so wide as zhong's. bluer mebbe. zhong's . . . unlasting unreal if

not for such lasting loss. here too. where wicker chairs sit, rock

cairns still stand untipped. where some gorblock once built shrine

of honey jars and clock parts.

jingjing squat by old planter arm deep in beer caps and hoong kee

butts. birds sail roof. perch wires, shit the tv dishes, flutter down

to balconies or parks. javanese miners most. one zebra dove land

on box. siam ah! jingjing shoo mr. feathers from trash. dumb bird

come back.

"呢度乜野都冇, 鳥先生"

jingjing squat lower, longer, calves sleep. shakes head. sees what might have grown instead. wild spices mebbe or, mah, why not a bewildering rose? jingjing pick toes, like just seen bluest ghost, not sky, not lion, with sharpest thorns.

back in flat still no cat.

old bag still sprawl out on pallet late. snores like stranger. mouth yellow bubbles these days. jingjing clean her when she wake. brush teeth too. still some myojo mee siam left. share a plate.

most she do is cough or sigh too much. cries. grieves. jingjing do what he can. says same thing. please, auntie, please please.

time was once she never closed her eyes. now great tian li sleep and sleep. time was she never needed food. now great tian li eat and eat. time was they never felt poor. now jingjing boh lui liao.

funny how back when cat tup pai around jingjing barely see it. now

he notice everywhere where it's not and how, mah, she gone case.

jingjing check kitchen drawers, mebbe some coin hide in corner,

recheck cupboards, closet by front door bare, even under broom

bristlesofts bare. neh'mine hammock, hammock can't hoard much.

heck care for worldwall, acorn necklace not worth mrt fare.

all while tian li snoggle snoresnore. on and on.

jingjing the one better wake ideas to survive this change.

so jingjing slip to ali baba her, sapu something wurf, then run,

cabut for good. chuay si, lah, if cat there, but now he kuat one,

check whole room, if best get is fingers sticky with spider webs,

and quick gostun from blue coral coil with red tail never more

than shadow and lint. over mattress edge, pale as eggshell bits,

auntie's ankles stick, still as mistakes made for finding life's limit.

damn too lan, jingjing skip loose for restaurant rows. too late

oreddy for recycle search but jingjing kin kah kin chew. cartless is

fastest. loose cardboard always hides. but after hour-long scav-

enge, cari makan, jingjing toh, sapu only three boxes.

truck boys chio kao peng loud: "bring us back something real!"

some auntie rattles up then, stack of boxes, flat on flat, cart

topped higher than her lavender top hat. tower near topple too.

but truck boys leap down, kiu kiu kio, sing her praise, curse weight,

like they go broke hauling up this trade.

ah mm pleased though. ooh lui, ooo song. rattles away behind

empty cart, top hat her sway, smile big as brim.

"hum kar chan," jingjing curse banglas, stalk auntie, curi next

chance her pockets. gives her three boxes instead, nays two cents.

jingjing craves smoke next.

wah lan, sudden too, like seeing old friend on empty street. first

time in years. clap shoulders. got pipe. got smiles enough for end

of time. or just one puff. soften edges, bring good luck.

some friend craving is.

street stay empty. jingjing stay broke. and even if hantu puteri

appeared from thin air, with numbers tangled out of graveyard

hair, without sing for ticket, 4d ∴ lottery ∴ hopes worth jilo.

jingjing need more than box coin money, gold wrapper chocolates.
damn chik ak.

then, like hantu hantu giving jingjing media taunt, at electronic

store for looksee-looksee, screen after screen, jingjing catch zhong

sim lin in dark glasses, waving at phone flashes, before swallowed

again by blue parrot fish. more news on zsl means no news with all

those tvs going, not one with sound on.

jingjing know inside of that limo, sky palace with riri-filled rooms,

illegal aroma too. and bow-tie prettiness, bored as they saht saht

boh chioh. no matter how late. even when smoke came up, the big

world balloon parade, for what thrills, what cost: zhong's son lost

to one pale-blue puff, stiff under machines and medics. raeden sim

lin same geragok coma boy lah, even after great tian li fell to the

floor in a foam, jingjing taking rest of night to get auntie home.

only to find their door open, every window open too. cat gone.

was that the price? for billionaire's tears? this invade of emptiness

where peranakan mannequin once never slept now never wake?

其终去之. 其去之求良.

jingjing stop short. sidewalk peds bounce him right, scowl munjen,

banner here won't stop recruiting:

police: be extraordinary

bus then stops, no standard for lift. how seow now, pockets full of

fist. rip up that banner, burn down this bus.

"bring us back something real!"

later, off woking road, by tree shrine past mart, plates of pineapple

and chikus, broken chairs, foil trays, bottle of joss, jingjing draw

out monster card:

like korban eats mean much. liak bo kew. so jingjing just curl up, chiak chuah, to koon deep last of day's sunbake balm.

so why jingjing wake so afraid? not cop, lah, calling him damn bakero, like jingjing rooftop vandal, toa payoh rooftop hdb block 85a, lorong 4. be extraordinary! boot threatens kick if jingjing don't move on. balik oreddy. and straightaway jingjing kelam kabut but not because of that mata. something else keep his chest macam ice and face kay wet.

ok, ya lah, ya lah, jingjing miss cat, miss cat bad, miss padpad of smallest mystery, and them two, like that, tup pai together, ride great tian li's shoulder, white tail swishing back, or side by side with white tail wrapped, or in her lap, darling to each, small jaw at rest on her knee, or paw on her hand while asleep, or eyes gleaming with dark so distant and old and pleased they left jingjing too scared to care how long auntie could laugh like so.

"吾等需食," ∷ *We need food.* ∷ wah lao, sial lah, tian li up oreddy,

making bird's nest of kitchen, kiam chye, pot after pot hitting the

floor. wants her 4d, toto too. "擇一數。" ∷ *Pick any number.* ∷

"姨母,吾等財破。" ∷ Auntie, we broke. ∷

"今子之责,靖靖。" ∷ *You are responsible now, Jingjing.* ∷ saysay tian li. "勿

让吾等失意,吾等今孤矣。" ∷ *Do not fail us. We are alone now.* ∷

then like flowers in her hands, thickets of thistles, ∷ *Missal of leaves.* ∷

she presses into jingjing hands, thickest of sheaves.

cash. lots.

Between Nowhere
and Nowhere

You can't.

> *— Victim #3*

Only when the engine cuts out
does Isandòrno heed the stillness.
The stillness tells him that unlike
dawn this delay will last.

Tilting his hat away from his face,
Isandòrno climbs down from the
flatbed and follows the driver and
his wife.

More trucks wait ahead. Tractors
too, alongside the mud-splattered
cars. There is even a bus bound for
Palenque.

One by one taillights go out, followed by engines enjoining the
collective quiet to take heed.

There are no motorcycles but one
woman pedals a bicycle with low
tires. Because her heavy thighs
hide much of the frame, she seems
to float. Isandòrno sees no seat.
An AM radio taped to the han-
dlebars plays music cottoned in
static. Shouts and laughs greet her
wherever she passes. She laughs
and shouts back.

The rain stayed for more than a week. The rain left behind small lakes. Now and then her bare feet kick down at the mud that keeps threatening to swallow her up.

Isandòrno leaves behind the driver and his wife and follows her.

Farther ahead the shouts stop, along with the laughter that was never really laughter. The woman on the bike stops too. She does not laugh and shout back then. She turns off her radio and turns around.

Isandòrno does not turn around.

Here people do not leave their cars. They keep their engines running too. The small lakes gouged into the road glow red with their uneasy wait.

Past the last car, only the music of official arrival snarls the air, though the sirens are far away and their arrival will make no difference.

After fleeing Veracruz, Isandòrno had gone as far as Benemérito de las Americas, where he exhorted himself with every sun's departure to cross into Guatemala.

The border was only steps beyond the carnicerías and accesorios en general and the arcade games set outside where men rolled cigarettes on benches and drank coffee out of paper cups and watched stray dogs hunting for scraps. Sometimes they spoke about Balams guarding the maize, sometimes about Xibalbá.

Isandòrno drank their coffee and

shared their tobacco and fed the dogs gullets and feet. Sometimes he even tried his skill against the centipede and the asteroids.

Now and then he walked past the racks of piñatas, cowboy hats, and plastic trucks where the children shared sodas and drew chalk pictures on the floor.

From the one who knew how to get across, Isandòrno bought wine for the men who knew only how to drive north with those they called brazen and crazy and poor.

Isandòrno had never come this close before. In his room, after he had lost to the snake and the stone, out of dreams never his to have, he would picture in ways not his to recognize, Honduras or Panama, Montevideo, Punta Arenas. As if knowing such names were even possible from within his cage.

The key was lost years ago. The Mayor had lost it or eaten it.

—Tonight? The wine seller had asked each time Isandòrno bought the wine he never drank.

Unlike his father, Isandòrno's mother was not from this country. Unlike Isandòrno, she was claimed by a made-up country once pronounced as "Americas."

It was she who had laid upon his heart that curse that keeps him from crossing any border. In barbs and wire she had bound his desires and dipped him in the promise of this land as if a land such as here is enough to also be a river black enough to shield the end from every end.

Isandòrno knows too much about ends to heed his mother's boast but he has never once stepped beyond her oath.

—Is it fear? asked the wine seller, who described the trip to Guatemala City as no big deal and nothing like the one to the States. You don't look like you answer to fear.

But instead of answering with a story about his mother's curse or The Mayor's cage or the fourth crate, Isandòrno answered with No for the last time.

And then one of the men who had drunk Isandòrno's wine and understood his debt, and the price all of them might have to pay if they chose to laugh and not understand, agreed to return Isandòrno to the north.

Carretera Federal 307. La Trini-
taria. Toward San Cristóbal de las
Casas. Past homes of cinder block,
walls painted with Mujeres Vamos
Contigo in three colors.

Except the driver and his wife had
asked if instead of going by way of
Villahermosa, they could take la
carretera 199 through Ocosingo.
The wife had a cousin there who
had rebuilt for them an engine,
which they would like to sell in
Mexico City.

It was a delay that had not troubled Isandòrno.

Not like this one.

Those few who decide not to stay in their cars, and there are not many, spend little time considering the animals blocking the road.

Most look at the corpses. On both sides.

—What of those without heads? One asks.

—The heads must be here. They are always near.

—Has anyone checked the field?

—When the police come they will check all the fields.

Isandòrno steps toward the animals.

—Señor, you should not go so close, says the one talking the most. This will be a scene.

But one of those who did not talk quiets his friend.

From then on no one questions Isandòrno or comes close.

He squats unmolested beside them. Both shot numerous times through each side. They had wandered into a bad place. And between these two factions, they had fallen between nowhere and nowhere even if they fell as one.

Over the first animal's eyes, Isandòrno rests one palm. Over the second animal's eyes, he rests his other palm.

Then Isandòrno closes his own eyes.

By the time he returns to the truck, Isandòrno knows his late arrival will stir The Mayor's emotions. It is bad enough that Isandòrno failed to accompany the crates to The Ranch. He did not even go as far as Mexico City.

The Mayor will be surprised to learn that Isandòrno ran. If he asks. But The Mayor will not ask. The Mayor is capable of anything except asking.

Not that the telling of this would matter in the slightest.

One goat.

One donkey.

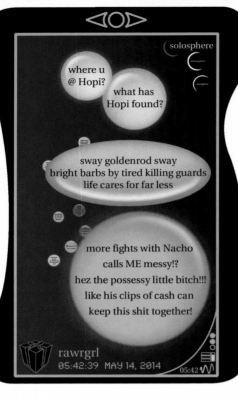

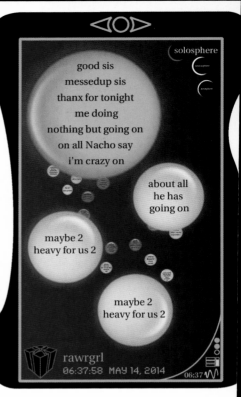

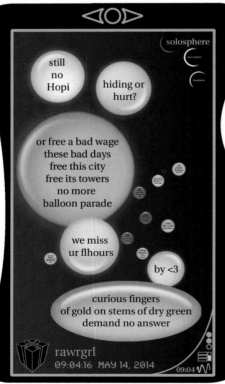

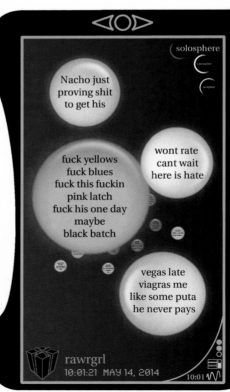

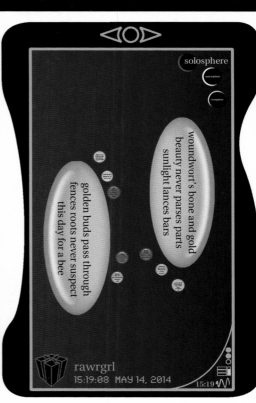

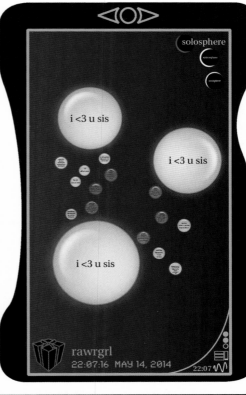

Frogtown

We escorted Death up the main aisle.

— Richard Rodriguez

Maybe the biggest deal of Luther's life comes together quick. Happens like this.

For three days, nada. Talk about tumbado del burro! Luther firing up his cars, creeping boulevards, mad-doggin anyone dumb enough to slow for a look. Cálmate homeboy. Like when does Juarez call Luther off? Seriously!? But Teyo's perdido. Luther hit that lista, firme fools, yet he the one feelin like some fuckin mamón. No feria, not one fucking word. Mr. OG's now Mr. Ghost. And then, like that, out of all the morning's sun and dust, ghost walked up.

At Mariachi Plaza, right across from House of Trophies. This early no tacos de ojo. Just some old men drinking iced coffees. Instrument cases still shut. Luther and Tweetie hitting some quesadillas and Cokes. Breakfast of champions.

Then from a doorway to something still closed, something Libros for bros, like a shadow falling from a shadow, only not falling, just a hustle straight for them, across the plaza, past the old men, drawing even their attention. Hair spiky and young. Brown eyes so big they almost seem blue, like big blue moons. All for Luther too. Like this little kid gonna ask for an autograph or blow himself up and kill them all.

"I got something for you." Is all he said.

181

Cellular was already ringing before the kid reached the metro.

"Sobres," Tweetie said after Luther was done. Convo with Eswin didn't take long. Just Teyo's assistant bringing up witches.

Tweetie took the phone, crawled into the back of the van, and dropped it into his black box. One switch and on go the magnets. Everything digital just goes away. Hammer does the rest.

Tweetie's el mero mero when it comes to this shit. Every few weeks swapping out Trace-Fones and new 900-minute cards. The only one Luther trusts when it comes to how they talk when not talking face-to-face in their cars. Look at Chapo. That guy had tunnels and armies and a fuckin BlackBerry took him down.

In Chinatown, beneath two gold dragons, down sidewalks packed with hat racks and baskets of incense and tea, by markets with jackfish and butterfish stacked on buckets of ice, Tweetie ducked that sun, into Dynasty Center, big fucking swap meet, with socks by the pound, one guy selling puppies out of a box, three for one.

Not like Tweetie was shopping, kept heatseeking exits with stairs, taking all the stairs down until they were nowhere near the Center, not a shop around.

Something Chinese hung above the door where they finally stopped. ∷ 彩虹睡蛇 — 到处都开门 ∷ ∷ *The Sleeping Rainbow Snake — Open Anywhere* ∷ Only computers inside. And cigarette smoke. Tweetie's cash got a peace sign.

Terminal 2 was all the way in back. Every screen they passed looked like a Vegas arcade. Most of the guys here, and there were only guys here, all Asian too, sat in white button shirts, sleeves rolled up past their elbows, a few shouting, some smiling, the rest just slouched over ashtrays and keyboards, like they methadone gripped, whatever key they tripped tying their accounts to cartoon horses and cartoon cards.

Tweetie logged into Parcel Thoughts, picked Noosphere, then a few clicks later, instead of roulette wheels . . . Teyo's three witches.

First one with tits so big and oiled-up they'd Exxon Valdez Zuma if they ever got seaside. Bitch was even named Valdez. Eulalia Valdez. Fat too. So fat Luther's crew could pull a train on the folds of her belly and still have clean creases to go at again.

The second one's just Calsilda. Not half as nice. Three fingers going for some clit-bliss, panocha so unshaven its like Amazonian, not that any jungle's gonna keep out the black cock already deep inside, thick as a wine bottle too, working that pink mystery nonstop.

The third's also just one name: Rufina. Ass so big it's solar. Won't fit the frame. Hands digging in, rhinestone nails doing the lettering, **BLISS** spreads one rippling cheek, **AGONY** the other, while a machine pumping two poles with dildos, probably glass, probably greased up on Eulalia's tits, keeps robot dicking both holes, in and out, one endless gif.

Never a face. Only the names keep. Pics changing week to week. Shit just grabbed from the Web. From rack to tamaluda. Greasy and fat.

Luther and Tweetie figure Teyo's got a thing for tortas chamagosas. Like the old man needs loose, wide, and flappin to bury his stink in.

Luther will never have no taste to buck bitches that big. Yet something about Teyo's witches always makes his dick twitch.

Profiles read ready-set escorts, with stupid tastes, special tastes, dos and don'ts all over the place, reviews going from diseased to 4.8.

blake1776:   hj or cbj unless ur stupid. kermits neat sweet. keep her deadend tight as fort knox. g0es t0 t0wn f0r n0thing. cheap.

Tweetie started taking notes in print small as a label on Sudafed box.

clip_this: gives me all her pink. worth $$$. me she did for free.

After that Luther had Tweetie check out who they knew.

"What these tontos bring down on themselves," Tweetie never stops warning. Instasham is the worst place to front. Facecrook gives judges plenty to send lops to the pinta for life. Parcel Caught is no better.

Other clicas all over this. Not Luther. Fly under the radar, outside the nets. Luther would chew bottle caps if he found out any of his crew was fucking around online. Juarez is no worry. Can't read, fuck write. Teeth sharp, sure, loose lips?, not a chance. Victor got cars. Hours on a block. PlayStation eats up the rest of his time. Piña got friends, iPhone too, but she honors Luther's law, his Never List.

And the Never List goes like this: never mention doings, never drop where you been, where you at, where you going, for sure never what you got at, never give names, one reason names stay fake, and never never post real pics. Still, as any pinche knows who's lived long enough to know what makes happen happen, no matter caution or skills, mistakes always happen. The thing is to control the damage.

And that meant keeping eyes wide.

Look at these eyes.

Melissa Torres.

She was their girl. Amber eyes. Cocoa skin.
Nineteen. With firm little titties. Bikini tops
mostly. Tight little waist. But not too tight, or
hard, like Luther likes, or craves, he's never
had what he likes. Melissa is softer, wider, all
thick in the thighs, stretch marks on her hips,
baby on her side.

What ink she's got, Tweetie's blurred. For two
years he'd Michelangeloed her to life. At the
start Dawgz Lawz kept it real but who's gonna
friend some OG they never seen, especially
with Luther's dogfighting days all crated? Better to Amicasphere someone they want to see.

Tweetie had collected all these pics, Mexican
beauty queens, telenovela stars, east side shots,
but up the coast too. Baby pics they got from the
parks, Whittier moms showing off what they
got. No Tupac and Biggie, but Pitbull, Selena
Gomez, Usher, and Skrillex. One bright nails
on a .45, some finished 40s.

But like Dawgz Lawz or Teyo's witches, made
up from scratch, even her hot friends, or some
of them, because Melissa got so popular, her
sphere soon started nabbing real hot friends,
then friends Luther knew.

Tweetie clicked over to Amicasphere to check what was new. Not like Luther's surprised.

Almoraz is the same latoso. Shirt off, **LOST WANTED** across his chest. Or in his Corolla, beer in both hands. Or at his gym, boxing gloves on. Too many on the sofa, toy gat by the remote, lame-ass morritas posing with his gym hats on.

Too dumb to close off his sphere. Here Almoraz, calling some hard bodies friends, nipples and limes, designer shades with glass dicks, DSLs on blue parasol drinks. "Bullshit." Tweetie say it every time.

Even got Almoraz rapping some shit on You-Tube. Boy cannot flow:

sic es3

fuck scraps mecoso park. crying bitch with or without a cuete.

my boiiiii!

--> 1:01 that me! ;)

lmao mexicans cant rap just landscape and clean houses lmao you looks broke af2 no fiine cars cheap ass clothes ugly bitches lmao

shit talk surenos but cant say shit to there faces. they most powerful gangs in the world. Mexican Cartel's supplying, So yea, got $$$, weapons, drugs, hoes. The more you know. lmao cx

Melissa leaves:

<3 <3 <3

Chitel was no better. Danny Brown vids, From The Hood Boy, Sad Boy, Biggie Still Smashing, Colonia, Oxnard sets. Shorty got on his same gray hoodie. Kings hat. Grin of split teeth. Lips to a spliff. With Almoraz. With that little thing that grabbed cash off Lupita's floor.

Melissa leaves:

;*

Even Lupita's got a profile. Pics of her nails. Cigarette smoke spinning from each nostril. Cheek to cheek with Miz in a bright flash. Something uncertain in both their eyes.

But Melissa leaves:

this here it. lesson up kids.

Melissa don't talk shit.

Come afternoon they had picked up the truck.
El Porvenir Auto Body.

"Abandoned and salvaged," Victor had explained. "VIN shaved. Arizona plates. In the name of someone any of us could say was a cousin. Runs good too. Not some harnero."

"Ocho mil if I don't see it again," Adolfo had told Luther then.

But if it did come back okay, Adolfo just wanted balloons for the favor. Luther offered twenty but when Adolfo learned they were pinks he lowered his eyes and said a handful was fine.

Adolfo wasn't the only one surprised by the color. Luther too, when Tweetie figured out all he'd got down at the Chinese gambling joint.

kermits meant Frogtown. fort knox meant Knox Avenue. There was no blake1776. Blake Avenue was the cross street. More comments had changed that cross and number. all her pink meant just that. Bomba. Pinks were unheard of, sold mad crazy. No matter what raspa come lurking, crowd got cruel and scratched deep to torch this fix. Gave Luther the chills. If it was realz.

Frogtown now. After ten. Night cooling.

Long as he's been coming here Luther's never seen a frog. Cholos used to call this place home before gabachos started moving in with money and new names for everything. Alissa Valley. Some shit like that. Like you erase Frogtown, you gonna erase the gang? Even if they be a bunch of maricones anyway.

Not even some lone cholo around, hiding under a bridge, swigging a 40 of 211, looking for a friend.

Lot's deserted. Whole area dead quiet. Especially here along Blake Avenue away from the houses. And where Luther's parked, the few orange street lamps only make the warehouse seem darker, emptier. Some sort of plumbing outfit. Pipes at least.

Luther keeps listening for frogs. Miz swore they were here once. Red-legged frogs all over the place. Down along what they now be calling the L.A. River Pathway. Maybe Miz was vacilando.

For some reason, thinking about frogs, real frogs, is calming. Though Luther's been calm for a while. As soon as the plan got set, crazy went. Instead it's Juarez who can't settle down.

Keeps getting in and out of the truck. Takes one lap, then two, around the building, nail scratching the wall as he goes, like he tizo or worse. Lucky the fucker doesn't have a gun. Tango up this shit for sure.

Luther should have stuck with Tweetie. But something had got up in Big Man's guts. Maybe from Mariachi Plaza. Luther feels fine.

Still, his J-Dawg can move, silent too. Not even a crackle in all this dryness. What summer keeps bringing. Needling for something to burn.

Dodge Charger pulls up before Juarez is back. Black with red rims and a violet stripe hood to trunk. Too new for plates.

Three get out. No clue who the fuck these dudes are. Balloons or cash? Know Luther though. All laughing when they see Adolfo's truck.

"Eswin said you couldn't be missed," the driver says. Shorter than Luther but grip's solid, shoulder too, as shoulders bump. "Memo."

The other two unchain the gate and disappear the Dodge into a loading bay littered with old valve parts and a half-assembled lathe. Oil stains on the floor look fresh.

Luther likes Memo. Homeboy waits easy. Leans back by the bay entrance. Ink his arms cross says little. Memo saying less. No offense.

Except Juarez's fingers have already cinched tight around Luther's wrist, nails digging in hard, racing Luther away, from the Charger, the 4×4, cash, stash, past all of them catching on last, and still faster, to the end of the bay, toward doors at the back.

And in the end, not even a hitch of resistance, because Luther always trusts Juarez first.

Juarez slowed only once, on their way through the doorway, wheeling around and at the same time drawing free from both back pockets, two gats. How the fuck was he even aiming?

Luther's not sure what he saw. Juarez shot Memo in the chest. Dropped the Football Star with three pops in the back. Triggered out the rest of the clip. That fucking lathe in the middle went down in a spray of sparks.

Rifle shots?

The lights must have come up at about the same time. Or maybe the sirens from the chopper above. LAPD? How the fuck had Juarez known? Like he'd known before the start. Tecos somewhere close speakering for a stand down.

SWAT out there too?

Luther thought he saw the gardeners hit the deck, Charger dudes firing back, firing the air.

Blood sprayed from the bullshitter's neck.

Gone is every jitter, twitch. Juarez now is pure flow. One step through another. A toda madre. Unreal how this dawg can go. Flat-out sprint if it wasn't so smooth. Past racks of PVC and Galv. Ducking around corners, down through two grates, sliding a staircase rail, out a window, punching long strides though the grass.

Luther wipes out at the base.

Lucky.

At the River Pathway, badge out, gun out, by himself?, shouting lie down?, ATF?, FBI?

Why can't Luther hear?

And Juarez already squeezing off two shots, pop pop, like before this placa even knew he was gonna stand ground.

Face explodes. Then whatever the back of a head does is done. Leaves rattle.

Luther and Juarez run for a long time. Along the L.A. River. At every breath expect chopper lights, shots, squad cars coming to a stop on an overpass, until eventually only more darkness gathers, and they're out of breath, finding the thickest dark to settle in and rest.

But Juarez doesn't rest for long.

In this thinnest sheet of water sliding through downtown, Juarez has found something to squat over, hop after.

"Look, Luther! Look! A fuckin frog!"

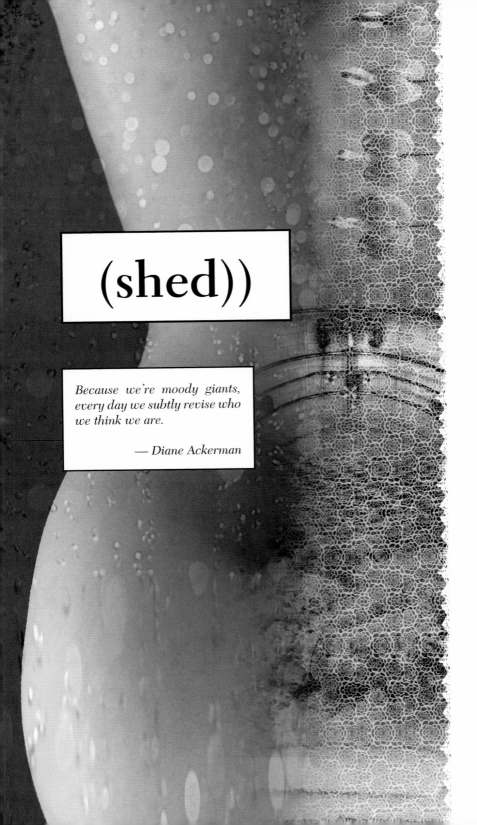

(shed))

Because we're moody giants, every day we subtly revise who we think we are.

— Diane Ackerman

(whether thoughts of her paper wake her or something else (. . .)) Astair tiptoes down to the kitchen
(no one exempt (here) from all these following aaa-
baaa-bleats of floorboard creaks ((Astair plays shep-
herd to her own progress (they all do in this place)
(she loves the way this house speaks)) revealed in the
movement of every inhabitant (only living inhabitants need apply (Astair muses (~~assumes~~? (amuses)))
(ghosts require (or are limited to?) a different kind of
melody (a different kind of house?))))).

     She puts on coffee (why not? (she's up) (tea for
sunrise)) and tears out a blank sheet of paper (there's
no crossword on hand (turning to (let alone on) her
laptop feels repulsive (and a book (well) that's a(n
eventual) given ((reading a . . . habit at this point?
(at this age? (how can forty feel so old?))) just not
yet (and which book? (something counter to her
derailed career (the fucking paper) (for sure)))))))).
Four lines cross to make nine (how does that work?
((and) how is it that such a simple expression invokes
sadness in her every time?)).

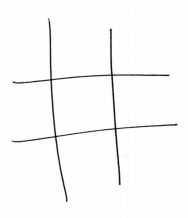

Is it the game itself? ((how before (even) starting) it is already solved (trivially too?) (perfectly? (Anwar would know) (Astair hasn't forgotten the dangers of perfect (as Sandra Dee Taylor (Doula *and* "Doyen of Oceanica") had once warned in a lecture:

∷ *"Perfect! Such an allure we've granted that closure. And how complacently too we've assented to the declamation of the inverse. Don't heed me. So many of your patients yet to come, in fact already gathering in the highlands of your future, on their way now, will in so many words, in so many ways, provide you with this self-analysis as if it alone could prove their injury, their hurt, their unworthiness: I am imperfect.*

"And yet let us for a moment reconsider the laurel and benediction so many covet. From the Latin facere *'to do' coupled with per- 'through'. Perfection. Or: to work through completely.*

"Heed me here: life's possibility and bounty, what restores and inspires, where we experience new growth and encounter new joys, does not come by way of what's closed. Existence unfolds its marvels to those who embrace its incompleteness. We are all, every one of us, blessedly not made through. To say 'I am imperfect' then is to praise the impossibility that must always remain before us to work through. Work towards. Discover." ∷

"For those who seek perfection, tell them to consult the dead. Or play tic-tac-toe."

(okay, maybe Sandra Dee hadn't said tic-tac-toe ∷ She did. ∷ ((after all) it's past 2:30 AM and here she is (making coffee) about to play tic-tac-toe against herself (how will she even do this?)))))))).

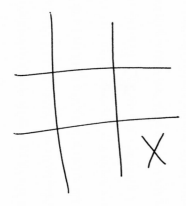

Xanther would play a corner first. Astair (though) remembers something about how the center always wins (childhood instruction ((still) sisters ((and/ or) friends))). Imagining Xanther's next move is no trickier than picturing what no longer lies behind the plywood barricade ((by the washer and dryer (at the center of that bed! (a Jax & Boans Large Nest (what are they ever going to do with that thing?)))) (thank you ((vet) Dr. Syd!) for (basically (with his Oh, a lot of handling is a good thing and for *both* of them!)) (practically) instituting (in Xanther's night-time rituals) a companion) Astair should at least take down the barricade now).

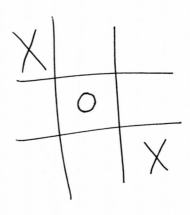

((while water continues its (molecular?) dance with coffee grounds) passing (by eight or nine steps) through their laundry/mudroom) Astair chooses (over plywood) the back room (((maid's chamber) (servant's quarter) (from times gone by)) a narrow prison cell (now something else)).

(curiously) The door (always closed) is more than ajar (gaping in on that familiar dark). Astair doesn't even have to flick on the light (the bare bulb (screwed into the ceiling) would be an irrelevant afterthought). She knows what's here ((the piles crowding the floor) (atop the one dresser (drawers to top)) (threatening frame and springs of the narrow bed)): all their books over all their years. What she and Anwar (so affectionately) refer to as "their stacks."

Astair's heart surges before all she feels suddenly free to consider (free of those ever-constricting coils of curriculum (ever threatening to suffocate her (devour her (maybe it already had?)) ((at least) broken her back ((?)(INCOMPLETE!) spine snapped, (reason too (sense of self(?)))))))).

Here (though) the python of requirement is nowhere to be found. New choices rise from the floor even if the books (also) strike Astair as headstones (Astair (in pale gray sweats (Juicy! (isn't that a joke)) playing the cartoon ghost hovering above the dead (of course they're dead ((and gone) (or cenotaphs) (or (if shadows invert) what marshy holes of burial grounds will look like after the resurrection (after all))))) because despite what they'd once fired up in her (promises made and promises kept (these are good books)) their stillness and familiarity accosts her (how Astair's heart falters now). What can Virginia Woolf or Gertrude Stein do for her again? Or Sappho? Or Anne Carson? Unkeep a promise kept to find again the warmth of a promise first being made? Could any of them return that flame?

Wow! The python had done a job on her! Not even the prospect of something undiscovered sparks her interest (Astair hasn't read every book here (some are just undead)). But seriously? Will a biography really help? a history? some solution mapping out paths to happiness? a novel?!

"How did you sleep, girls?"

Freya and Shasti gurgle goods and fines as spoons (barely pausing) convey mouthward more milk and cereal (Hemp Plus Granola (Nature's Path)).

To the question of dreams (though) not even a gurgle (head shakes only). (not even hours ago) Astair had heard (at their door) something different: murmurs and whimpers (nearly severe enough to justify waking them (especially if they got any louder (*Just one more groan* . . . (defiantly decided) even if *one more groan* . . . didn't come (the twins reshifting into deeper stages of sleep))))).

(unlike Xanther who had grown up with grotesque discomfort (in both life and sleep)) Astair had never known these two to suffer nightmares.

"A cat?" Taymor huffs ∷ A few hours later ∴. (stops in the middle of the trail (despite (morning) resolutions to hike faster (their new phone app (*Stroll Your Roll*) sounds alarms if they slow))).

"I warned Anwar about my allergies."

"Bad?"

"So far . . . no. Xanther's the one rubbing her eyes. All the time. And, of course, denies doing it. This is going to end badly."

Beep-Breep. Breeep-Beep.

"Christ," Taymor cries (both of them lurching forward). And (for a while) they keep ahead of the machine('s beeps (breeps (whatever these mechanical annunciations are))). Sweating feels good (and gasping in that way that breathing doesn't (quite) satisfy).

Eventually Astair gets around to her paper.

"Incomplete?" Taymor stops (again). "How is that possible?"

(this time) *Breep-beeping* moves them to quit the apps. Astair (then) tells the story of Llewyn Fabler (her beautiful advisor (her defender (recovering (still) from a heart attack))(not that a new advisor should have made this much difference)). Astair relates (too) the successes of various classmates (until breathlessness (born out of nothing to do with exertion) robs her of the rest).

"I never saw it coming," Astair manages to choke out.

215

"Oh dear," Taymor says ((rubbing Astair's back (between her shoulder blades)) (which feels better than it should(?))). Astair steps away (to keep the tears back).

"I used to think I was part of the conversation. Then I realized I wasn't even at the table. Now I see I'm not even at the party."

"Astair," Taymor says firmly. "Fuck that conversation. Throw your own party."

(on the loop back to the car) They both see the snake ((though) seeing's too late to jump them away (or scratch up a scream)). Taymor nearly steps on it.

Snake*skin*.

"Rattler?" Taymor asks.

Astair picks it up. Big snake. Considers bringing it home (Xanther would love it (maybe?)). Lays it out (now) by the side of the path ((another path) silencing the pulse of possibility this (aftermath incarnate) awakens (the kind of observations Taymor mocks as *Too braniac!*)): to shed.

Has Astair given enough thought to that act? Beautiful evidence of letting go to live? Losing false layers? An anguine lesson worth not(h?)ing?

(instead (with Griffith Observatory (still) below (the car a good half hour away))) Taymor (likely(?)) makes the association a snake (once (still!)) that large can.

"It's called HomePorn."

"Tay," Astair sighs. "Anwar and I don't watch porn."

"Weird. But whatever. This isn't online. This is that much better! No photos. No numbers, no e-mails. Very, very anonymous. Three people have to recommend you. Accepted patrons get a phone with only one app. Easier than Uber."

"It already sounds expensive."

"Not cheap. I'm happy to write you a glowing recommendation. A+."

"And the other two?"

"A+'s too."

"Who?"

"Let's just say someone who knows you uses it. And someone else who knows you does it."

"Does what?"

Taymor details how a couple in their "hard-body hot twenties" will arrive at your door (though the number of individuals (not to mention gender ((body type) ((hair) ((skin) hue)))) is variable (specified via the app (a range of charges applying)))).

Where "The Show" takes place is up to you: living room or shower or utility closet ("We haven't tried the wine cellar yet"). Performances cover everything from masked and intimate to silent and athletic (to BDSM or MSOG or ATM (plus other acronyms Astair has no clue about (and no interest in defining)) ∷ Bondage & Discipline with Sadomasochism ∷ ∷ Multiple Shots on Goal ∷ ∷ Ass to Mouth ∷). Costumes are a given. Toys routine (though certain ones cost extra). Role-playing can vary from First-Time to Faux-Vile (Astair doesn't ask what that means (scatological? violent?)).

Contact is the only restriction (it's a show ((those hiring may only "mime" or "parallel play") no touching (though) or participation)). That such a limitation is upheld (given what else is permitted) strikes

217

Astair as preposterous. Taymor insists that it's true (because the "performers" are (typically) committed to each other (and just enjoy the exhibitionism)).

"Ted put you up to this!" Astair blurts (wow (she's furious (why?)!)).

"Are you kidding, honey pie?" Taymor scoffs. "He's the fussybutt about this stuff. The last strip club he visited was when he graduated from Andover."

Taymor relates their first peek into this (kind(?) of) experience (Paris ((of course) at a club called Les Chandelles)). It had left them both shocked. "Two things you normally don't see: corpses and people screwing."

"It's been good for us," Taymor insists (as Astair's fury(?) becomes something else(?)). One "Show" lasted over two hours with multiple climaxes. And afterward? "No infidelities. No risk of disease. And they bring their own sheets."

Astair does her best to frame it as a theatrical encounter (even catharsis ("One young woman cried when she came.")). Taymor swears the sex ((with Ted) that follows) equals (if not exceeds) what they witness (and continues to do so for a number of weeks). Astair finds it hard to believe that Taymor cried. "One way we bested them!" Taymor snorts (laughing so hard).

The unsettling continues: (during ensuing descriptions of situations and positions ((always) with extremes (means of penetration!)(who knew such an implement for *that* even existed!))) Astair (at a certain point) loses track of whether or not Taymor is talking about the "performers" or Ted and herself?

It kinda grosses her out (((gross?) something Xanther would say (or really: "Uhm, gross?)) and Astair wants to be a therapist! (maybe because Tay is her friend?)). (at least) The disgust (while it doesn't fade) doesn't grow (either).

(when Taymor drops Astair off) She is somewhere else (that "else" Astair loves about her friend):
"As my mother always said: 'What's meant to be happens easily. What matters takes more time.'"
"Smart lady."
"Though she is the same old coot who said the best way to keep a man is to tell him 'Pussy's on the grill.'"

Astair's not sure who would be more appalled (Anwar or herself) if she dared repeat such a thing with any seriousness ((likely) they'd both have a good laugh).
Astair lets the shower run ((first) just hot (to steam up the bathroom)(then a little cold)). Anwar's not home (the girls are all at school) making it easier (under this reign of emptiness and quietness) to consider the presence of strangers in this home (and why not here? ((in this very bathroom?) in the shower (watching (through the foggy glass door) strange bodies rubbing (exerting postponing drawing closer to a release . . .)))).

Astair steps into the shower.

(on the trails of Griffith Park) Astair had suffered no hot flashes (or itching (or unexpected tingles)) and if part of her experienced some sort of revulsion (ahh) the obvious part was (still) experiencing something else.

((now) rinsing the soap out of her hair) She doesn't have to touch herself to know she's still wet (hasn't been this wet in a long time). Astair's shortening breaths (along with everything else still filling this steamy space (another "Show")) makes out of the water (slapping down on her breasts (lower)) something more. Strange fingers. Strange lips. All thinner than steam.

But her nipples harden. She holds her breath longer. Water stings her cheek. Fills her mouth.

She wants to touch herself squeeze her nipples open her eyes against the stream. (instead) She lifts the shower head off its hook and slides the silver dial to jet.

(drawing it down over her chest (a brief agony) her belly (((brief) agony giving way to anticipation) forty! (forty is still young (young enough and strong enough and alive enough for this)))) Astair's eyes blink free of the spray to find the softer haze of all she's enclosed by.

Only when she presses her (left) hand against the glass

(

(palm flat against the glazed surface ((until—) because it's not glazed (the steamed surface ((at once) as rivulets of water stream off her fingers) transparent to her touch) (—so slippery!))) as her (right) hand draws the jet closer (((unlike her nipples her breasts) her clit's agony craving relief insists on only more of this focus this release this more) realizing (then) the fantasy of standing outside on the tile floor watching two nameless bodies slide into kisses and fingerings and deeper kisses

(with the very shower head she holds now

((((circling) () (trembling))

also in play)))

)

does Astair realize how she's the one inside the shower (the only one) while her fantasies (all of them) are outside (peering in (strangers and Anwar and . . .) (her eyes still open but no longer needing to see because she no longer needs more light more touch more breath reaching what she no longer has any need to want)).

Astair has always acted ahead of failure (or what she could convince herself (then and later) was failure).

Most called the beginning of her romance with Anwar (including Anwar himself) infidelity. Astair (however) had been doubtless about where her relationship with Dov was headed.

(true) She could fight for her thesis but if it was already so maligned (and Fabler could offer no support or assistance) then why not consider a new approach ((even) is that what it will take? (shed)).

That question ((maybe?) coupled with pleasure's aftermath) make out of the harder next steps something far easier: Astair calls Oceanica and leaves a message with her new advisor ((Eldon Avantine) requesting a meeting). An assistant calls back (within the hour) and they settle on Sunday afternoon.

"How's the little beast?" The first thing Anwar asks as he shuts the front door behind him.

Two things collide at once (stunning her (in part)): first is what Taymor asked after the hike ((while they were in line for iced lattes at Alcove) "Is it really allergies or this aversion to the cat something else?") and second is the ~~realization~~ (*recognition!*) that these last few hours Astair has not been in their home alone ((stunned is just part) blushing (and shuddering)).

If only a shudder (shiver? (shrug?)) were the worst of it. (of course (in the face of her answerless response)) They go in search of Xanther's white obsession but find no appeasement to their rising anxiety.

The cat is just gone.

225

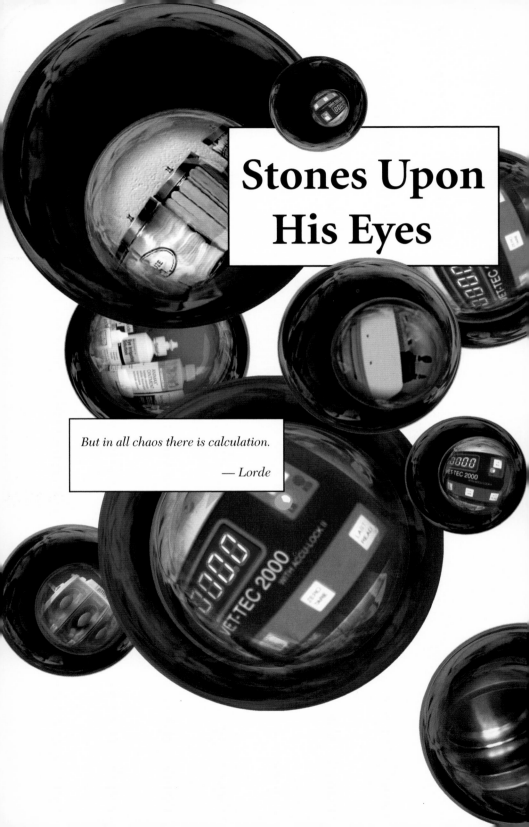

Stones Upon His Eyes

But in all chaos there is calculation.

— *Lorde*

Since going to the vet, Xanther has watched shadows collecting like squid ink in the hollows of Astair's eyes.

Anwar's too. Shasti and Freya. Even neighbors strolling down the street. Strangers are the worst.

At first the smudges seemed rubbable. Like something was in Xanther's eye. Floaters? Baby translucent cephalopods swimming in that thin layer between the pink lining of the eyelid and the cornea? At least she'd heard one of her friends once describe floaters that way. Maybe Cogs or Josh, likely Kle ∷ **Kle by way of his brother Phinneas** ∷. How while in the process of seeing, the seer somehow becomes aware of the eye itself and how imperfect it is. How like the lenses of her glasses, which usually suffer some indignity, like smudges or, worse, scratches, eyes too have all this stuff on it, in it?, from goopy to tailed specks slooping along that jello-y curve.

Josh's mother, or maybe one of her friends, had gotten this surgery to make her vision perfect, except after they had cut the jello open and burned the lens inside with a laser, it was called Laserix?, Lasix?, Lasicks?, ∷ LASIK ∷ whoever this was ∷ **Maureen Gephardt** ∷ still saw all these wild flares, especially at night, and like that was that, except the doctor told her not to worry because, apparently, seeing isn't just about seeing, or at least not just about the eye, because the mind has just as much to do, maybe even up to half, more than half?, and it will make adjustments, and that's what happened. The flares vanished. The mind had factored out the disturbances, like when you divide an A, B, or C, or X, Y, or Z out of an equation. Though what about a zero? Like in those seven indeterminate forms? What impossible things then might become visible? Or is it in-invisible?

Xanther wonders what that would be like: no glasses. She's way too young for any kind of laser correction, though contacts are something her parents keep mentioning without doing anything about it. For the time being, Xanther's left with these framed things, way marred and so severely scratched, what with her spill on that street in Venice, frames busted apart, scattered on the sidewalk, left there for hours too, the pieces of which her dad and sisters, miraculously, still managed to find, and put back together again, thanks to glue, duct tape, and Anwar's gentle attention.

And sure, while seeing's what counts, wearing such a mess on your face is a whole different matter. Talk about embarrassing. Even dangerous. Like stomach-twisting dangerous, like breakfast along with every schoolyard confidence just liquefying, because wearing something that dorky is exactly the sort of ridiculousness that gets the attention of preds.

Of course, re: black smudges, it's not like Xanther can blame her glasses. She's tried hot water, soap, Windex, her breath. She's held them up to the light numerous times, at so many different angles too, searching for stains. She knows every imperfection. Unfortunately, the worst one is her: man, are they thick. Thick enough to inform anyone looking at Xanther that besides having bug eyes, she's legally blind, which she isn't, or not yet.

Knuckling eye sockets doesn't help either. Hard too, and long, fists to vision, no light creeping in, though somehow bruises of color still erupt, like sunspots on some National Geographic show. Astair keeps asking: "How long have your eyes been itchy?"

If only itchy was the problem, not that Xanther can tell her mom what's up, but why not? At least the rubbing feels good, sorta, to the edge of hurt too, leaving Xanther afterward blinking at these burning patches and twinkling stars, hanging over everything, which at least makes sense, unlike the other stuff, continuing to thicken and darken, always drawn perfectly to the eyes of others.

Xanther remembers something about a strange medical condition: a man named Virgil who couldn't see but still knew where things were, could even maneuver around them. In other words, his eyes saw fine. It was his mind that was blind. :: *An Anthropologist on Mars: Seven Paradoxical* **Tales** by Oliver Sacks. :: Probably something her mom, maybe dad, had been discussing. :: *Though familiar with the title, neither parent has read this book. Anwar did once come across Robert W. Kentridge's piece "Blindsight" in the* Encyclopedia of Neuroscience, *while Astair did read "Blindsight Modulation of Motion Perception" in the* Journal of Cognitive Neuroscience 14:8, *pp. 1174–1183, and David A. Leopold's "Primary Visual Cortex: Awareness and Blindsight" in* Annual Review of Neuroscience. *Curiously their passing interest in the subject was never voiced to the other. Oh. My. Wait—* ::
Maybe Xanther remembered this :: made this up is more like it :: in light, or not light, of her evolving condition: without "seeing" Xanther still somehow "knows" the colors of everyone's eyes, and not like she's remembering it either, :: Because, uhm, she sees fine? :: but getting that one boy's eyes are hazel, another girl's green, those over there blue, brown, and blue gray. And maybe some satisfaction vanishes by knowing something as just a name, even if the

name robs the face of nothing. Instead these persistent shadows suggests that if Xanther could just glimpse underneath, she might find something so much more satisfying than any color. ∴ A snack would help more. ∵

Not that any of this means anything other than Xanther is either going to have to cure herself or tell someone, even if it's so obvious what both parents will say, licketysplit too, ignoring her when she pleads: *No, that's not it. This is different. This is something else.* That old beast epilepsy again.

At least in Math 7, all Xanther has to do is look at the back of Mr. Owen Dreann's bald head, bright as a bulb in the overhead lighting, and shiny, like heat and sweat equals thought, and maybe it does, for him. Not for Xanther, who every morning this week has had this hot-achey thing inside, like a fever still in search of a forehead, so nothing shiny, and definitely not insightful, Xanther's thinking bristling and branching out until it's out of reach.

For most of the hour, Mr. Dreann has kept to the TelectBoard, his back to everyone, light green jacket swaying, creased gray-patterned slacks revealing dark green socks as he keeps going up on his toes, not that he needs to go up, the tiptoe thing may be a nervous thing, Xanther gets it, she does the same thing, sometimes.

Today is all about reviewing what they'll need for the final in three weeks. Mr. Dreann likes to do three big reviews. Says it's better for their growing brains and beats one big cram fest. This is their first, and fast too, everyone just scribbling nonstop, one concept after another, without even a chuckle, Mr. Dreann usually chuckles.

Except now he does chuckle. Something about the triangle up on the board, pointing out, but still not turning around, how if you replace the middle third of each side with "a smaller equilateral triangle" and keep doing that you'll get a snowflake. He says the name Koch. Other things too. *Sur une courbe continue sans tangente, obtenue par une construction géométrique élémentaire.* Something like that. What no one gets. ∵ **On a continuous curve without tangents constructed out of elementary geometry.** ∵ ∴ Mr. Dreann said no such thing. Where did she get that? What does that even mean? ∵ ∴ *As curves keep multiplying.* ∵ Xanther's mind clouds with Bloom's Taxonomy and more stuff she doesn't understand.

"Don't worry. Not on the test."

That stops everyone's note-taking, a collective rustle of relaxation.

"Has anyone heard of fractals?" Mr. Dreann asks, turning around.

No ink on his eyes.
Forget holes.

Much, much denser.

At least Xanther doesn't scream or blurt out anything.

Not that Mr. Dreann would have been that surprised, or any of the kids here. Xanther's done blurts before, can't help herself, with questions of course. Probably Mr. Dreann would have just given her his tired look and then told her to hush or, out of duty?, prodded her for some explanation.

Over the past couple of months he's gotten more and more tired, tired in general, but also tired of her, it seems, and in this case, when she couldn't have explained her outburst, he would have gotten even more tired, probably because now he'd have to figure out what next to do, aside from lessons on equations, because he's the teacher and he has to do something, right?, and then, maybe, for the first time here at Thomas Star Kane, the snickering would start, though, phew, it still hasn't come to that, no trips to the principal, no calling-attention-to-herself in a way that would really give the preds, even preds in training, something to look forward to at break, during class-to-class transits.

So far Xanther has managed to cover up her oddness by clamping it or if she can't do that, much to the displeasure of Les Parents, resorting to stammers, uhm, with as many likes as she can muster, apologies too, eventually earning one of those hesitant adult okays and instead of snickers, even an appreciative laugh from the class. Not weird, just another idiot.

Not that Xanther doesn't feel guilty about acting this way. Hadn't Dov said something about being different? "Do you want to spend your life becoming who you are or spend it failing at who you're not?" His gravelly voice can still ask stuff like that, making Xanther feel not just a little ashamed, which Dov also had something to say about, and not long before he died too.

"Shame is war's lever for induction. It's why young people are so gullible and easily manipulated: they can be shamed for not going. Old people, though, are more resistant. They get it. They fart in public and laugh about the stink because no fart will ever compare to what the dead smell like."

"Is that what got you to join the Army . . . shame?"

But Dov had shaken his head. "I told you, I'm also different. What weird can't begin to describe. Love got me to enlist."

"Love?"

"I love to fight."

Not Xanther. Though of course the first person Xanther sees after Math 7 is Mary Ellen, black backpack slung over her shoulder with a Ronda Rousey button pinned to a purple strap.

Mary Ellen's not even that close but Xanther's nerves still go instant jitters, like ants discovering their home's gone. The toothy sneer isn't the worst of it, though that's pretty bad, or the meaty hands cupped a heartbeat from a fist. The baggy green pants hanging off stocky hips don't count either, barely hiding thighs thick enough to stretch out the bagginess above the knee, or under the required white-collared shirt, a big chest, like a man's. Mary Ellen wipes aside tangles of blonde hair she couldn't care less about, her flat features, flatter nose, registering nothing so awful as what her eyes do, eyes Xanther can't even see but knows are seeing her. Still not the worst of it.

At least recognition gives Xanther's feet the command all her jittery nerves failed to summon, sending her off into the sprawl of kids, and only later daring to look over her shoulder, not for Mary Ellen, who's long gone, but for Mary Ellen's bestie, still the absolute-always worst of it, even if he's nowhere in sight: Dendish Mower.

Maybe the eye-clot thing would be more of a nightmare if it weren't also for the hot-achey thing, what starts up every time Xanther leaves her house, each time threatening to eat her from the inside out.

And sure, the thought of getting back home, eventually, offers some appeasement, to find again, safe and sound, that adorable littleness, with white so soft, like some kind of cloud kitty, if still unable to squeeze open its eyes, just like a kitten, Xanther's still kinda convinced it must be a kitten, :: **It. Is. Not.** :: :: *Tricky.* :: promising with every reunion, and keeping that promise too, at least so far, to repair in her what leaving always injures.

Of course, longing like that means that no matter what class is going on, no matter what Xanther has to write down, or who she might talk with or wave to, say Mayumi and Josh on their way to World History, part of her is always somewhere else, with that tiny wisp of wonder, which only makes Xanther crave home more and more, even if more and more the satisfaction of home feels not at all at home but displaced by something else.

Carpooling home is a huge relief. Not even Mrs. Fischer's eyes bother Xanther. Or Cogs' for that matter, nor Kle's or Brigitte's.

Besides, except for a now-and-then glimpse of those collecting masses, most eyes are on a phone screen, Brigitte, or on the road, Brigitte's mom aka Mrs. Fischer, also on her earpiece, scheduling something Xanther tunes out, glancing back at Kle, hunched over his notebook, at work on his latest *Enlightenment,* which he's not ready to share, fingernails brightening into crescent moons, gripping on a crayon-pencil, which generally means he's stuck and shouldn't be bothered. No moons means he's drawing freely. Not a good time to bother him either.

"Cogs?" Xanther says, swiveling around in the passenger seat, where really Brigitte should be sitting but Mrs. Fischer insists on mixing everyone up for every ride. "No samesies," she'll chirp. Samesies? Kle always asks when it's his turn to drive. "Cogs, you know how, like, in some movies?, I think?, like people who've just died sometimes get coins put on their eyes?"

"Sure," Cogs answers. He's in the middle seat, even if his legs are a lot longer than Brigitte's.

"Uhm, any idea why?"

"Maybe to make sure their eyes are really closed?" Cogs has never minded Xanther's constant questions. "I don't know. Are you thinking of Dov?"

"Not enough left of him to put even dimes on," Xanther answers cavalierly, which is easy in the afternoon, when school's out, sun's out, and she's heading back, at last, to the little one, even if Mrs. Fischer's convo hitches at the mention of bio-dad's death.

"I'd heard it was to pay the ferryman, you know, Charon," Kle says without lifting his head, fingernails no longer white, hand moving loosely over his notepad. "If the dead didn't have a coin—I think it was called an obol—they weren't allowed to cross the River Styx and enter the underworld. Though I think it was just one coin, and, anyway, it was put in the mouth of the dead."

Kle always has these tidbits. Doesn't even have his phone out. Cogs doesn't have a smartphone and while Brigitte could check hers, she's like sleeping now?, or maybe faking like she's sleeping? She always seems to act in a way that keeps her as disinvolved as possible with this bunch her mom somehow ended up driving on days when Xanther's or Kle's parents can't. Bayard takes the bus. His dad lives too far away. And Cogs' mom? Well, no parent wants to see her behind a wheel, Cogs for sure. And anyway Brigitte, when she talks, usually just talks about fashion, fashion this, fashion that, wants to be the next Tavi. ∷ **Tavi Gevinson.** ∷

"It could have something to do with the eyes rotting out after you die," Cogs adds. "Or sinking down into the head. So, you know, for the funeral, people cover up that part."

"That makes sense," Kle nods. "Windows to the soul and all that. Eyes of the dead are pretty faaareaky."

"You've seen a dead body?"

"Close enough."

"A dead body of a *human*?" Cogs adds.

Kle nods but won't say more.

On the corner of Sunset and Alvarado, Xanther sees Mary Ellen again. She's on the sidewalk opposite the American Apparel store. Trin Sisikado and Kahallah Yu are with her. But that's not all.

Mary Ellen's pointing Xanther out to Dendish!

Xanther squirms down in her seat, like she can get her head below the window without Mrs. Fischer noticing, who after calling an exasperated halt to all this "ghoulish talk" about burial customs is back on the phone organizing the days ahead, taking no notice of Xanther.

Xanther just hopes the light will turn green fast.

It stays red.

When she peeks over at the sidewalk, Dendish is coming her way.

If Mary Ellen looks big, Dendish makes big immaterial. He's not even as tall as she is. Mary Ellen's legs look beefier too. Size-wise Kle is larger. Size, though, for Dendish seems a weakness. Height's easy to cut down. Big's worse for all the damage it does to itself when slamming into concrete.

And it's not just strength either but swiftness as well, and agility, somehow swimming beneath those loose jeans, loose Misfits t-shirt, his ragged Vans, L.A. Dodgers cap, even his grin.

Mesmerizing.

Xanther can't look away, especially as he strides her way, between all the idling cars, and this is on Sunset Boulevard!

Dendish grabs his crotch.

From the sidewalk, Mary Ellen and the two sevies laugh and smoke harder.

Obviously everyone in Mrs. Fischer's car is blind to the approach.

Xanther tries to squirm still lower, figuring the light has to turn green any second, praying it will, and then Sunset traffic will take care of Dendish.

But the light stays red.

And then he's right there, like inches away, and still leaning in closer, finally kissing the window, and not just with lips but teeth too, his tongue licking the glass like some kind of angry snake, and Xanther gets just how much anger is slithering around inside Dendish, even as he draws back and grins, the last thing Xanther sees as she forces her stare down into her lap.

Not even brave enough to close her eyes, just hoping to herself, hope!, how Dov would scowl at her for that!, hoping that she'll avoid peeing herself, and just the thought of Dendish opening the door next makes that scenario pretty likely, and it's not even an unlikely scenario, because the door is def unlocked, and impossible to lock, Xanther's just too stiff to change anything, hands clamped by the sides of her legs, back of her knees starting to prickle, arms too, as she sniffs for burnt toast, not a big toe moving.

And then Mrs. Fischer is driving again. Oblivious. How could Mrs. Fischer miss that? Xanther catching in the passenger-side mirror how Dendish just saunters back to his friends, not minding the honks, snatching a cigarette away from one of the sevies, laughing.

Who cares what he says then. Xanther knows this much too well: somehow the pred has figured out the prey.

Something else happens on the way home.

All four doors of Mrs. Fischer's car suddenly pop open. They're at another intersection, another light. On a side street in Echo Park. So it's weird but no big deal.

Though that's not how Xanther sees it.

No doubt Dendish's stunt had already upset her. His eyes for sure, that close up, caked in black stuff that clearly doesn't look anything like an ancient gold piece, silver dollar, or some medieval spigot of copper. ∴ *Nothing remotely to do with numbers, nationality, or a tradition of worth.* ∴ Worthless to Charon.

But then Xanther sees the same stuff again, except this time they're marking someone Xanther knows is not there. Not even close.

A stranger momentarily caught in a clearing. Here and yet at the same time Nowhere Here.

∴ No one there. Forget coins too or ink. ∵

∴ *Yet still harder than darkness, heavier than purpose.* ∵

Bearing what he's too blind to suffer and for Xanther what's too heavy to lift:

243

stones upon his eyes.

"Իրականությունը ձեռքիցդ տվել ես:"

Shnorhk ignore.

"Այս աննպատակ երդումը որ միայն անգլերեն խոսես հիմա հավատում եմ պատճառը այն է որ քո անգլերենը անչափ տկար է որ քեզ դարձրել է անպատասխանատու քո խոսքերով: Եվ, մի գուցե, քո մտքերով:"

When did reproach become her only way to smile?

"Հենց հիշի. խոսատումը խոսատում է: Լեզվով կամ առանց:"

Patil sets down bowl of soup, cup of hot tea, sarma by recipe of grandmother. No matter Patil berate Shnorhk, she still set table, fill plates, lay soft hands upon his shoulders, like now, squeezing both shoulders with love and care.

Shnorhk shake Patil off. Leave table for bathroom. To cough. Splatter both palms wet. Shnorhk prefer if Patil just berate. Always touching with her, try hold his hand, snag arm, makes Shnorhk skin crawl, like corpse grab him from grave, though Patil no corpse, no need for corpse, when life itself is gray thing.

Shnorhk wash hands, return to table. Patil not move from beside his chair. This woman! Look at her there. Hand over hand, chin raised, lips together a raisin, eyes blacker than raisin. Coarse hair in one braid, streaked with ash. Sixty-three didn't bring her ash.

Unlike Shnorhk, she still wear black. Do others notice? Shnorhk notice. Every day. Maybe just shoes, and belt, or sweater, today skirt, many days thin scarf, when not so hot. Never without something black. Patil is like that. Insistence now is her only belonging. Mind made up to stand like some scarred pine tree, for day, century, a thousand years not make difference. Patil won't move. Makes little Glendale apartment seem even smaller. Fill up few rooms with mind made up.

Shnorhk eye soup. Harpoot kufta. Shnorhk love Patil's harpoot kufta. With tomato broth. Still steaming.

"I tell you already. I go to clinic now," Shnorhk lie.

"When does clinic close?" At least this time she try English.

"8 PM," Shnorhk lie again.

Patil seems satisfy. Steps from small table. Shnorhk hate lies. Clinic close at 6 PM. Lucky if he make it if he leave now.

But Shnorhk mouth water for soup. Patil soup is only thing for lungs. Eating soup best thing to get rid of reproach too.

Patil even prepare something else. At stove crack open pot lid. Albaloo polo maybe. What his wife can do with black cherries!

"Zanazan ask me today why you not move over to Uber? Zanazan says it's all in the phone. She says everything that has future has to fit on phone. Independence Taxi has terrible phones. Independence Taxi has no future."

Shnorhk's spoon hang in air. Face hot and on way to hotter.

"This, Zanazan read in your palm? That I try Uber?"

"We were just talking," Patil say. Set down dish. Shnorhk right. Albaloo polo.

"I have cab and we have old Volvo station wagon. For Uber I need new car. Bottled waters."

"Buy new car then."

Shnorhk put down spoon.

"What you mean?"

Shnorhk know exactly what Patil mean. Patil return smile to reproach. Dare him to not know what she mean like Shnorhk dare her to say what he dare not let her mean. Patil say it anyway.

"Փողըն ունենք: Գիտես փողը Փողըն ունենք մի քանի նոր մեքենաների համար: Maybe I drive Uber too!"

Shnorhk feel bad as soon as he drive off. Empty stomach make him feel bad first. Patil's hard work next. But Shnorhk's lies worst of all. Patil right. Patil always right. Promise is promise in any language.

And Shnorhk now is breaking many promise. Didn't he promise Mnatsagan to help scan documents? Old professor even call Sunday morning. Invite Shnorhk back to house to again eat cake and play with lads. Shnorhk not even return call.

Radio burst to life.

Shwanika there, dispatcher, with good call. Close too. But Shnorhk must keep at least one promise today. To Patil. Go to damn clinic. Good clinic too. With good doctors. Sponsored by LATWA. ∷ Los Angeles Taxi Workers Alliance. ∴

Near LAX.

"Destination is Malibu too," Shwanika smiles. Shnorhk have good ear. Can hear smiles. Even over static.

Shnorhk almost hear her face too, and never seen her face, shape of it, round and plump, yes?, coffee skin, of course, with name like Shwanika, yes?, olive green eyes, maybe, coils of black hair, thick enough to home brass comb, plumb lipstick on lips.

She only one not Armenian or Russian working Independence. Shnorhk sure managers racist, won't hire blacks or Koreans, but make exception for Shwanika, why?, because she fair. What other reason?

No question voice is fair.

Traffic get thicker and thicker. Freeway is given mistake but other choice risk. Still, Shnorhk good driver. Can handle risk. Even if sticked he know how to unstick, how to move over, work shoulder, make exit.

Key to city is here: sometimes shortest way is slowest while longest way is fastest.

Important concept. In L.A., distance not equal time. Distance equal time is bad equation. Bad comprehension of travel.

Ten miles or more is from La Brea and Olympic Boulevard to Rose and Main Street in Venice. Three miles or less is from Fairfax and Santa Monica Boulevard to Doheny and Melrose. Both trips though can take half hour. Depends on clock.

General Fact #16: Los Angeles traffic opaque on weekday at 5 PM. Transparent at 5 AM.

But Important Fact #16 about General Fact #16: Always in opacity is transparency and opposite.

This to say, sometimes to go three miles for half hour it is faster to go ten miles for half-half hour.

Possible if understanding of what matters is time. Distance irrelevant so long as way is known.

Shnorhk knows all ways. Needs no smartphone or app with traffic report. Even in this. All options blocked. Time stopped. Progress a parking lot.

Shnorhk still leave freeway. At next corner, mother in beige blouse and straw hat ringed with little blue stones push stroller, big one, for twins, with older daughter helping, suddenly waves at Shnorhk. Daughter too. Maybe even babies in stroller wave.

Not like Shnorhk waved either. Even smiled. Taxi is old too. But also clean. Very clean and hospitable. Not even faintest trace of cigarette. That fact is marvel considering last owner die of lung cancer.

Patil, of course, insist cab is dirty. She mean sign. For Las Vegas place. Just advertisement that company insist on. Wraps back windshield. Many little holes semi-transparent it. What Shnorhk care? It help cut out sun.

Young girl in glitter.

Amphorae Lounge!

"Size Matters!"

Like sign with glitter girl tell Shnorhk what matters?

Not even fare to Vegas matter. $1,000. Maybe more. One way.

Who cares?

Though Shnorhk like long drives. Unless Buford Furrow take backseat. Shnorhk would care about that. Shnorhk would have done something about that.

Deep breath.

Shnorhk breathe better too on long drives. Better than home. Almost no need for clinic visit now. Almost all fine. Answer next call Shwanika throw out. Why not? Then listen to music. Gasparyan tonight. Why not?

But Shnorhk ignore dispatch. Find ways past stops, through knots. Already left lane as right lane halt. Problem was obvious five cars up. Sedan pulled only halfway into spot. Driver still at wheel, relaxing on phone. Too busy to park better, or even alert others with hazards.

CAR DRIVER RATING

BMW 5 Series

QUOTE:

"You don't matter."

DRIVER:

Entitled for reasons only
they know. Will: stall lanes,
cut off other drivers,
worsen traffic. Some of
poorest drivers on road.

QUESTION:

Does asshole driver get BMW
or does BMW turn driver
into asshole?

BUMPER STICKER:

N/A

LICENSE PLATE:

WERME

This act to hold back half dozen people stalled in wrong lane confound Shnorhk rest of trip.

But Shnorhk still reach clinic with ten minutes to spare.

Except—

Shnorhk sees what he could not expect. Because Shnorhk has flyer. Because flyer says 6 PM.

Inside cab is like laugh going away. Like laugh leaving a room. Taking all air with it too.

Shnorhk rolls down window to let air in but air stays away. Shnorhk can't breathe. Won't breathe. What does breathing matter? Clinic is packed up and gone. Only stacked chairs remain at the pavilion with some clipboards left behind.

One more broken promise for Patil.

Broken promises everywhere.

Ոնրագործ:

"Sue you," Shnorhk manage now. This and wheeze. Until he coughs again. Keeps coughing. Almost throws up. Settles on to spit. Misses window. Hits door frame. Splatters pants. Stares at it like last thing left on earth to eat.

so it begins

Filled to the brim . . .
— *Alfian Sa'at*

all friday jingjing do it. 9 morning to dusk. deep night too.

saturday come, at it all over again. jingjing never work so hard. tan chiak, lah. out and not even seven! damn righteous! so early it feel like day ahead oreddy night. some future.

when great tian li handed over cash, lah, kio tio, jingjing didn't tsaotsao straight to jb for good times. instead he spent all thursday getting auntie mee goreng and 4d. only after she eat and twistup once more for long sleep, then jingjing ran circuit of familiar places, wherever he remembered old bag with cat.

this morning jingjing swing legs to singapore riverside. sculptures of strays there in company of strays. a bit the cartoon one, jingjing think, mebbe aloud, to this stretch and silly going on about metal and made. if none here close match tian li's friend.

or squat for drain cats by longkangs ∴*drains*∵: shallow holes, curbside grates, manholes, meh, then cave-big passageways, could

hide whole jin gang of dangerous men, instead crowd's all whiskers

and kiasi eyes, lah. ears lopped from once caught and sterilised.

mebbe fear's from the culling times too, sars ∷ severe acute respiratory

syndrome ∷ scare, some pap ∷ **People's Action Party** ∷ bodoh confuse

feline paws with civet cause of disease, had ava ∷ **Agri-Food and**

Veterinary Authority ∷ out killing cats, muslim malays groping under

chinese-owned maseelis for mong cha cha prey. that years gone

by, but fear still know better than to too quick die.

auntie's cat no square ear, lah. and eyes? wah, jalan-jalan never.

no balls drop, it.

then at underpass, by dank puddle like black lazy tongue creeping

for the curb, jingjing catch blinks, bold and steady. padpad from

shadows, avoid reach of such tongue, as if paw gets more than

damp there, bony for food, wary of wrong touch.

jingjing not wrong touch. rub up against shins, offer up calico coat

for a stroke. need makan something quick, or, arbo, it waste away.

jingjing race then to spend some of auntie's cash on can of monge,

but when he returns, not only calico not there but black tongue of

water gone too, withdrawn like python found its fill.

back at flat auntie snore fierce lah. strange how with cat now lost

jingjing remember better what back then was just white smudge,

macam tiny cloud, like smoke mebbe, not ever smoke.

jingjing fill glass from tap, gulp dry from throat. thirst goes.

then boils up koka noodles, extra for her if she wakes. but after

appetite die something worse stay alive. that awful friend, awful

craving, only one thing answers. jingjing get in his hammock, curls

to the hot, knows sleep don'ch help, tan ku ku, can't even drift off.

before, jingjing could only see her. in her palm, a haze. at her

feet, a fog. but now, and eyes not even snap tight, jingjing see so perfectly: one paw. nothing near what day oreddy brought, super-

sized padpads on chop-eared strays. that white paw, though, was

something else, smallsmall thing. macam size of thumbnail, mebbe

white balloon, never been no white balloon.

and hidden in that milky hair, soft like dew, sweetest cotton candy,

but sharp as chemical too, hints hidden just above pink pads

macam pencil erasers too soft to take anything away but itselves.

jingjing had seen, though, when hints became sickles he still wish

to dream back, macam jingjing dreaming now, wide awake. skali

boy, what an eye not seeing seeing comes to see.

milky, lah, and near transparent to point, too sharp to spot, too

bright to miss, followed by still more nail, wider, thicker still,

until like a shark's tooth, throwing star, sheathed in heaviest dark,

to steady it, to dig deep. smallsmall thing jingjing sees dig out

bottom of world. when it wants. jingjing can't breathe.

downstairs, void deck, jingjing at last dig out breath. what he'd

give for cigarette. or sweeter burns on all the bow ties' lips. no

bow ties here. not even lau jerry with one wet eye or delson, cahu,

or arysil. spencer, though, got his table, ashing hoong kee, sucking

deep.

jingjing, still unseen, near dash off.

"you still here!?" spencer yell. never misses a thing. "ha!"

jingjing lope over. mebbe curi a match. a filter. whole pack.

"we figured you one of them who graffiti rooftop over on the toa

payoh block. what i told occifer anyhow."

"kong si mi?"

"wha lah! whatever kan ni na i want to tell the law!" spencer

suddenly shouts. smile gone like cat.

"skali, ah kong," jingjing shuffle back, macam spencer kena hoot

him upside down. force laugh. "hurt yourself raising voice lai dat."

"siam ah!" spencer growl. "goes for your makcik too."

before, spencer would never make such threat. but ever since tian

li lost cat something about void deck folk is off.

out on street, jingjing scurry fast for tanglin halt, still seeing too

clear, what he can't remember remembering, that paw, like kitten's,

like just born, and yet also like something too old to ever name.

claw too,

before jingjing's eyes, only now retracting, as

he crosses over to the station, oreddy in a haze, steals a train, and

he has pockets of auntie's cash, this fog of direction his.

jingjing faces building.

he had never missed a stop. caught every corright connect. no wrong turns. not even his steps made the mistake of one too many.

and the whole time jingjing was only thinking to find zhong, demand he make good on his promise, to pay her, to pay him. see again the bow ties, drink with them, dance again, swallow what- ever they swallowed to make his skin crawl something awful, something bliss. jingjing damn boh liao to go tripping like this.

trumpet trees and yellow flames line the street. bikes with baskets

wheel along. renaults and citroëns pass it all. jingjing crosses over

to estate. void deck empty. not even one cat. some hum sup loh

look up, tugging crotch. mebbe he call ular danu home, mebbe not.

shuffles ruby slippers on when jingjing ignore grin, skip on.

second floor jingjing knuckleknuckle quick 02-02.

eye shadow with head like cashew nut opened up, smile lah when

jingjing pull out wad, like another cashew nut. disappear back into

apartment temple. incense trace the air. plum couches and rugs

like tar. open jars on a low table seem to rock with gasoline.

eye shadow fast return. she emerge out of voices in back. got

her hair now stuffed under scarf. the green in her eyes doesn't

glimmer alive. she doesn't touch jingjing's cash but presses into

his hand three joss sticks, unlit.

so it begins.

unlit means add. on fifth floor a pai kia, mebbe twelve, lah, got his

pokémon shirt, nike kicks, grins. like it's about time jingjing back,

like here jingjing can never forget, like here all's forever etched in

his skin, crawling more and more, hand over joss sticks.

si gin nah drop hell money at his feet easy enuf.

knuckleknuckle 07-06. last interview. ah beng grab back the seven

one-million joss paper and six ten-thousand notes. don't even look

at jingjing, yellow headphones on loud enough to hear:

i kill my memory

::not even close:: door slam leaves jingjing one dollar slapped in his

palm. never here like this before. better not stand around either.

jingjing gong-gong, heart go tup-tup-tup. get this wrong, he can never come back lah. no clue. ask and sure kena hoot.

mebbe one sing mean first floor, leave, jingjing not passing three

floor inspection. sure boleh one. jingjing's seen too obvious

addicts led though dangerous doors. never seen again. or mebbe,

one sing on one side, coat of arms, tell the right room? five stars

and moon on a shield, for 05-01, or together just sixth floor, plus

one for the coin, make 06-01. fuck spider! teh lum pah chi saht!

jingjing risk flight. up. follow eel-skin instincts. opposite side of

coin is big 1 plus merlion or 101. added to last room gives 08-07.

but last second, jingjing hitch knuckleknuckle, skin still telling him

more. moves one door down. 08-08. new sing hide two lions.

jingjing guess right. fierce open door, real samseng one, shirt

covers only some of the tattoos, numbers and signs digging up

fierce arms. fists like smaller versions of his face, flat like a drum, smile or frown, both like something missing, hacked out. fierce

ever come around commonwealth calyx, void deck folk run like cats

during the culling, spencer curl up like a ball, bawl like a boy who

lost his ball. not like jingjing ever seen fierce outside this room.

always heat up, fan nothing doing but moving heat around.

"mm tzai si! jingjing!" fierce grin, scoot him in. another apartment

temple, but bigger, darker too, too dark to follow fierce's eyes,

nodding to shadows and mirrors, reflections all over the place, if

fierce is oreddy back to his couch, under attack by tao idols, the

immortals here, ah, zhang guo with his white mule next to han

xiangzi with his flute. tv flickering world cup announcement.

"ow bway ooh kwee," fierce grumble as jingjing approach counter

in arched doorway, blocking way to back room.

"pardon?" jingjing ask but it's like jingjing didn't say a thing.

counter deserted anyway. murmurs not too far off trade back and forth. something about faces found in bleach. not even bell.

but as soon as jingjing reach for cash, michael jordan there. scrawny thing, shortshort, whole self look like rubber band twisted too many times before it snap, but michael jordan never snaps, all smile, very boh chup lor, shoo you away. like he come and go away. easy, see. on air. just like his hero. call him 23.

"balloon," jingjing coughs up. four years since his last order. at this counter too, same basketball articles still under dim glass, just mj, bulls mostly, but nike ads too.

"ai pee, ai chee, ai tua liap nee," 23 spread out hands, and like magic man, presto, one pink balloon. then it was true. jingjing never seen one so close. jingjing get too close. 23 cluck loud once.

"swee swee boh kay chwee." easy.

but pink balloon moh tuck teng one. jingjing's cash can't count

close. what 23's scowl make clear, jingjing's cash, boh lang ai one

lah. pink balloon oreddy gone. replaced by yellow.

but cash still doesn't amount. earn second cluck.

"hong kan ah, goondu?" 23 attend addition.

"this all," jingjing esplain. "pockets empty."

jingjing even turn out pockets, like 23 care, lor. like pink, yellow

gone too. replaced with raeden's taste. mebbe.

                                        one pale blue.

"dangerous," jingjing hiss.

23 shrugs.

"me, ah si, ah? no way! one hit and i could go away."

23 shake head. "damn kio tio, you. this year 2010."

:: Pale Blue had two batches: the first, in 2010, was kay successful, while the second, in 2013, caused many deaths. ::

"i come here all time, lah. way back. old friend."

"we remember jingjing," 23 nod, easy.

pale blue still scary. jingjing put down half cash, push forward

that. 23 not even glance, shake head, cluck twice. jingjing add half

more of what's left.

"chik ak" 23 mutters, balloon gone under cupped left hand while

right hand drops beneath counter. worse, 23's eyes flicker deep.

fierce gets up from the couch.

A Stranger

And it's something that everybody needs ...
— *The Mamas & the Papas*

Clips can emerge with such clarity and simplicity that it always surprises Cas how scrolling forward or backward for even a few more seconds still proves so impossible. Here is no reel of film, no VCR or DVD, no MPEG-4, H.264 or Theora, not even their own old Synchply-5. The Orb seldom grants easy access to a preceding or subsequent moment, no matter how often or skillfully Cas' fingers might unweave and reweave the algorithms.

"One day," Bobby often sighs, a promise, a curse, though the complexity inherent for every output has yet to diminish. Computational power speeds things up a little, but the inordinate quantity of coordinate crunching still gives chance her role.

Is chance feminine? Cas wonders now. Though why at this moment does she apply that gender? Unless "chance" and "her" are none other than Cas herself, her "role" in this strange adventure of discovery, huddling yet again over the Orb for another long batch of hours, trying to uncover something new, something illuminating, to help them, protect them, see them through the worst . . .

Unfortunately, and perhaps all too predictably, Cas didn't suffer the unknown for long — mostly static — returning instead to the familiar, or what was of little use, where she discovered the unsettling glitch. No question, if Bobby were here, she'd have already shown him the terrifying smears, the sight of which was almost enough to jerk her fingertips from the Orb field and dim the scene. Bobby would know the issue, correct the error, and then bark at her to get back to the job of tracking Recluse tracking them.

But Bobby is still gone. Because it's late, four hours feels like all night.

Cas had waved "later" from the sinking sofa, a tumble of spring-menaced pillows, all beige, all stained from all-nighters of pizza and cola. Had she even lifted her eyes when Bobby warned that these errands might take a while?

Cas lasted in the living room for about thirty minutes before moving to Sorcerer's presumed bedroom, where she and Bobby had slept the past two nights. Bobby approved of the corner location, windows offering various vantage points of the Dayton streets below, with a fire escape on hand if an alternate exit proved necessary. In his note, Sorcerer had explained how two floors up waited a window that was always open, through which waited a deserted apartment, affording three possible routes by which to flee, as well as a fourth so difficult to detect, Cas had to trust Bobby when he said he understood the mechanism.

However, without Bobby, Cas felt too vulnerable in Sorcerer's bedroom. Rather than promising a means to safely elude an intruder, the fire escape seemed more and more the means by which an intruder would arrive and seize her.

Cas moved to the bathroom.

She took along some pillows to line the bottom of the tub. One sat on her lap beneath the Orb. In the event of bullets or a bomb blast, sliding deeper into the tub might protect her. Cas even stuffed towels under the door in case of nerve gas. Every twenty minutes or so, she filled her Mickey Mouse mug with water and splashed the base of the door to keep the towels wet.

Cas laughs every time the water sluices across the tile. Bobby, though, won't laugh. He'll approve.

Why, though, her husband is still gone worries Cas. Getting gas for a motorcycle can't take this long. Or picking up groceries. Whatever repairs the Airstream and truck require will have to wait until dawn.

Cas tries to keep her mind from the possibilities of human injury by focusing on the Orb's constant injury.

Though, as is too often the case, Cas finds it impossible on this night, or any night, to keep true to where she started. Not even in the general vicinity. Her mind just doesn't work that way.

Dutifully she had started scrying Recluse. She began with the famous crib scene. She didn't try to tease anything more out except to wonder, as she has always done, if here already was awakening the awful future of this awful present.

He was all that mattered and it was like Cas couldn't be bothered.

She did try to access reconnaissance from a year ago when the recrudescence of their rupture began to escalate. But when she failed to locate any Recluse activity, she went ahead and failed to locate any Merlin activity.

Cas lasted maybe an hour fighting through virgae of static, which on occasion parted to suggest something observable, nearly recognizable, even if familiar and valuable are not necessarily the same.

Strange how even static in the pursuit of Recluse could still draw forth prickles of viperine disquiet. As if somehow out of these spectacles of incoherence, whether shaded in swirls of damson daybreak or felicitous fawn, a texture might slither loose — betwixt! betwixt! — with fangs so sharp as to deny the feel of their piercing, a killing noted only in the rough withdrawal and the effects of poison left behind, punctuated by tireless black eyes.

Not that Cas is always at the mercy of such fears. Her fingers, like talons, can also seize a dangerous detail, and by the light of owl eyes tear it to pieces.

Does he, though, ever conjure such fears of her?

Not here. Recent surveillances. His finger on the bone handle of a knife. His shadow slicing across a restaurant window. Mouthing the word "Yes."

But the more Cas looked into her Orb of Lachesis, the more it seemed that Clotho and Atropos looked back at her, until Cas was blinded by whatever fractures she might have found to lead her toward something of importance, until the fates were blinded too, until Cas' body writhed with anxiety, unable to dismiss that somehow a black serpent was now slithering under the hollow of the bath, soon to tick away at the porcelain until its head, without a hiss and barely a wiggle, could move forward, jaws widening flat against her spine, fangs slicing between bone.

A few times already this ridiculous paranoia had forced Cas to recheck the bath. She even plugged the drain to ensure nothing emerged. She stopped herself from wrapping a shower cap around the spout but kept raising her eyes to make sure nothing was sliding out. How humiliating when a mind of reason still fails to counter an unreasonable fear.

Though she wanted to make do without the earbuds, at least until Bobby returned, Cas needed them. Even white noise with the occasional whisper of an ordered clearing has helped locate a meaningful vector before. Plus it didn't take a second to yank them out. If she heard something. Knocking in the pipes. Knocking at the door.

Though eventually the prospects of any disruption beyond the Orb got to Cas.

She refilled her Mickey Mouse mug, took two long gulps, then threw the rest at the towel under the bathroom door. Quite a puddle was forming. Not the only puddle. The Ohio summer had slickened her back, sweat dripping between her breasts. Even her scalp felt wet. The heat shed by the Orb's base didn't help.

If only her Sorcerer were here. He would have put her at ease, not only about Bobby's   absence but about what Cas discovered next, when she had turned to the comfort of something familiar, what she had already viewed hundreds of times, that smile, that child, with rainbows on her fingertips, rainbows trailing in her wake.

Cas had even turned up the volume. And m o u t h e d the parental shout. Like a song known by heart. If only one word long.

"Xanther."

Clip # 6.2 ████████████████████████████

        . . . tiny storms
      blacker than squid ink, than
    barrel oil poured into spring water,
edacious,
        turbulent,

                set loose within that
          Athens home, until gyres of dark rob
the doorway from the room,

even as strange flashes of violet and garnet, but

never gold, disturb its deep,

                        as this child

of not even seven demands of her sky
    with every step
             thunder . . .

How is that even possible? No trace of rainbow remains. As if the past
were now corrupted.   Rewatching doesn't help. With so many
                                 vortices spinning out irregu-
                                 larities, Cas can't even
                                 confirm that the
                                 particulars are
                                 not in flux.
                                 Deus non est
                                 in genere.
                                 ∴God is
                                 not a par
                                 ticular

                                 instance
                                 w i t h i n
                                 a   glass∵
                                 ∴ *c l a s s* ∵
                                 But what of
                                 the   converse?
                                 Worse   still   are
                                 these roars masking
glee.   Why not call it thunder? Even
if the more   she listens, the more steps seem—

Cas rips out the earbuds, clamping down on her breath, her heart too if she could, fingers long practiced at the possibility of such a moment already dimming the Orb.

But Cas hears no more knocks. Just the made-up memory of something more, metal on metal, a distant struggle with the front-door knob. Maybe a drunken tenant trying the wrong door before moving along.

Then the front door squeaks open. Footsteps follow, slow, cautious creaks.

Bobby would have already
shouted her name in
his   grumpy   way.
Sorcerer, or any-
one   familiar
with   this
place, would
fill it with
a different
sound.

Here is a
stranger.

Cas slides
down into
the tub, as
deep as she
can go, if still
keeping her head
above the edge to
hear better.

The steps track into the
living room. Too carefully placed.   Then the

bedroom. Pausing by the window? Pausing for a long time too. To observe? Signal others below?

Only the bathroom's left. The light's on too. Cas holds her breath. Will the wet towels blot out this mistake? But the shake of the knob doesn't come, the fight with the lock. Instead, the steps retreat to the kitchen.

Unlike the Orb, Cas divines little from these increasingly casual sounds. Is he heavy? The kind so coiled up in strength he carries his size deftly?

Could she make it to the bedroom? The door has a lock. It would give her a few extra moments to get out onto the fire escape. The Orb will slow her down but she can't leave it behind. Without her braces, though, the damage from such a dash could prove extensive. Maybe unsustainable. Of course, little better will come from staying put.

Suddenly it's hot. Really hot. Cas' legs and arms go damp. She tries to dry her palms on her knees. Rotting jasmine overtakes the air. Something alkaline seems to seep from the mineral deposits on the tile. Her stomach turns. She must move.

Except the man is on the move again, leaving the kitchen but not the apartment. Back to the hall. Like territory already won, he passes the bathroom door without pause. The wet towels must blot out the light. Only to return. Maybe a twinkling suspicion of light warning his heavy feet.

Cas has no choice but to slide all the way to the bottom of the tub.

As a last resort, she can explode the Orb. It won't damage much but the implosion/explosion could hinder her attacker enough for one more move.

What it comes down to now is how long the lock will hold.

But it's not Cas who screams.
And the scream that comes
doesn't make a whole lot
of sense and in its shrill-
ness seems to discom-
bobulate time.

The door had just
slid open. For all her
preparations and para-
noias, Cas had forgot-
ten to flip the latch.
The knob hadn't even
fussed. And then as Cas
initiated Orb detonation, a
hand reached in and flipped
the light switch off. But it did
so to do the opposite. Confused
to find it on. And so flipped it on
just as quickly, pausing Cas' destructive
choice, as the young woman in the doorway
screamed at the sight of Cas huddled in the bath.

Back out in the living room, teas are spiced with Maker's Mark, bellies warmed with mirth and giggles. Her name is Marnie and Sorcerer sent her.

"What a scare you gave me!" Cas laughs again. It is their refrain.

"*You?*" Marnie smiles again. A real beauty. Blond hair splashing down on her tan shoulders.

"But at this hour?"

"He said it was crucial," Marnie shrugs. "Got me the key. I left at once. Drove up from Florida. Straight."

"How old are you?"

"Twenty-two. Well, twenty-three this month. I think I forgot how to sleep."

"And," Cas hesitates for a breath. "You brought something for me?"

"No," Marnie's voice quavers. It seems they both share an uncertainty neither the hours nor bourbon will name.

Marnie interlaces her fingers then and stretches until she yawns. Her long arms are covered with fragile blond hair and tattoos of dolphins and waves and gems. Just above her sweatpants emerge hints of more designs in pale oranges and greens. More stretches reveal what looks like a moon on the inside of one calf. Maybe part of the reason why this child hasn't been able to take her eyes off the Orb since she first laid eyes on it. Hiding it had been impossible. What with Cas frantically disarming the self-destruct sequence.

"Is that one of his . . . crystals?" she finally asks.

"A computer," Cas answers. "He built it."

"Figures."

"Did he tell you to tell me something?"

Marnie shakes her head.

"I'm just a massage therapist. He asked me to come look after you."

Due Diligence

Program testing can be used to show the presence of bugs, but never to show their absence!

— Edsger W. Dijkstra

[somehow] The minutes rolling over to 2:45 AM
regear Anwar's energies. Most men his age [mid-fifties
{almost}] have settled into an early-morning routine
[Anwar smiles {admiring himself ‹just a little›} and
sighs {that he can still handle ‹still enjoy!› an all-nighter
‹plus manage the early mornings his daughters «and
wife» demand›}].

His daughters.

His family.

They are his forever on his mind.

[now] Freya and Shasti turn in their sleep [groan-
ing? {nightmares? ‹something unpleasant about these
AM expressions «but not so sour to wake them ⟨send
them his way⟩»›}]. Or Astair [just starting to snore?].
Or [here {from her doorway}] the stillness of Xanther's
sleep [especially of late {as if silence and stillness still
could find accompaniment ‹there's no question what
accompanies her now «even Astair could no longer say
no ‹احمد الرفاعي قطع كمه› Anwar would rather cut off his
arm than say no»›}].

Anwar shuffles on towards his office [again].

[regrettably] Because what signs all these concerns
[like stones set out as markers] comes down to dollars.
Saturday [morning!] already. The Enzio assignment
due Monday [morning!].

[if the week's start signified the end of their company] Ehtisham's advice revealed a promising approach to all the infernal crashes. Anwar's ear to the rescue [{putting aside ‹for the time being› Arvo Pärt's *Tabula Rasa: II. Silentium*} instrumenting the code with notes {A, A#, B, C ‹etc. «octaves»›}]. A first.

Setting up the traps [though] takes time [like a minefield webbed with tripwires {only instead of an explosion one tone will sound ‹then all Anwar has to do is name the note and he will know where the code failed «where the bug waits»›}]. But at 3:45 AM the going is still rough. A musical solution has yet to emerge. [admiring himself less] Anwar wants to quit. He wants to lie next to Astair. Feel her breath upon his neck. Smell her hair. Sleep in the comfort of belonging. All of which he knows he cannot do [won't do {has he ever really belonged?}].

So Anwar keeps writing errors [each time provoking the recurring refrain {‹if guised as his own voice› not his own}]:

Dude! This is easy stuff!

The who [though {when it finally comes}] is inspiring [rallying Anwar to greater focus] if also disheartening [thanks to his friend's {less-than-comprehensible} prank {diminishing at least ‹though false promises of remuneration evident in every advertisement/promotion/ePromise still keeps phones ringing›}]. [mostly {though}] Anwar's lowness comes from missing him. What [{though} or whom?] does Anwar really miss?

Dude!

As if Mefisto [in no way resembling Jeff Bridges] were The Dude from *The Big Lebowski* ∴**1998**∵?

Astair's friend [Abigail {a yogi ‹fond of pat ‹practically Polonian› New Age-isms}] once said: 'If something's missing it's you.' [The comment came after Gia {another friend} admitted to missing getting hammered.]

[at the time Anwar had probably rolled his eyes {or imagined doing so ‹in the way Shasti and Freya sometimes do it in unison «talk about funny *and* spooky!»›}] Now [though] Anwar understands: Anwar misses the himself he becomes in the company of that jovial genius.

Dude! Where did you go?

Once [{at MOMA ‹years ago «how many years? ∴2003∵» amid those welcoming chambers of the heart's endurance›} at an exhibit on Matisse and Picasso {there with his friend Myla Mint ‹the choreographer›}] Anwar had stood stunned before a conversation of strangeness and wonder and grace.

'It's as if we're listening in on a love affair between color—' [Myla had whispered] '—and line. The longest love affair.'

Anwar remembers her words perfectly. [though {what matters now ‹the quote Anwar can't quite resurrect›}:] What had Picasso said of his friend? When Matisse had died? Something about the words that made of each of them the who they were and could not become without the other? ∴*Of Picasso, Matisse once told Françoise Gilot: "We must talk to each other as much as we can. When one of us dies, there will be some things that the other will never be able to talk of with anyone else."*∵

[{whether true or not} when he was around] Mefisto conjured within Anwar a sense that Anwar had access to parts of himself he could not access with anyone else or even on his own.

But then his old friend had drifted away [{only intermittently in focus} lost to success {and a strange species of fame ‹but most of all «voluminous» new obsessions «complicated beyond following ⟨rumored to be beyond dangerous⟩»»}] only to resurface with a prank way beneath him.

Dear Mefisto.

Anwar leans back in his chair. Cataplyst-1 ready for its next *crashcendo!* First a sip of miso soup [off caffeine entirely now {so all the more amazed by this curious wakefulness ‹why so much about Mefisto? «code alone is neither reason ⟨ . . . ⟩ nor excuse»»}]. Then dispenses with the past [with one tap { }]:

Anwar smiles at the crash. G! He knows exactly where that tripwire [tripline!] lies in the code. Time to get busy.

[for some reason {while launching Visual Studio}] the Tosh Tairelov paper comes to mind [{readership = 8 ‹maybe 9›} one of those academic things that got passed around like it was an answer {even though ‹what it did more than anything else› was provoke questions ‹frequently heated›}].

Crabs, Apes & Other Animals ∴ **1973** ∴. Not exactly a title evocative of AI [until one got to Herr Tairelov's abstract {Herr was a nickname Tosh liked ‹though he wasn't German›}]:

> Given sufficient data versatility and processing power, Character-Relevant Attributable Behaviors will invariably give rise to Automatic Personality Engines or Animistic Neural-Intrinsic Mechanisms Acquiring License.

It was 'License!' [cried/shouted/hissed/prayed/slurred] that caused the most dispute and [concomitant] reverie. [pre-midnight] Mefisto would often rail against any such notion [in the 'reductive' name of 'massive decision trees' {which ‹while 'seemingly displaying Artificial Intelligence'› would ‹'in the end'› prove as inert 'as a condom'}] only to rally [post-midnight] on behalf of 'massive continuities' [harmonizing in ways to 'provoke' 'learning self-modifying behaviors'].

Those were the days.

Not this dull stuff to eke out a living [manage an existence {earn enough for the interest payments he ‹just today› had to pungle up to MasterCard ‹a name that always strikes Anwar as eerie «just as Visa always strikes him as a false passport»›}].

[on a whim] Anwar decides to confirm the G.

That's curious. This crash not a G but [up a full tone] A.

No longer A but now [down a major third] F.

Something about this A to F progression registers a reference Anwar can't quite hear [but should hear {not that it's that uncommon ‹just familiar enough to unnerve him›}].

Anwar feels caught between smiling and shuddering. It doesn't help that his miso seems abruptly cold. He slides the headphones down around his neck [so as not to hear the notes again {to hear ‹instead› a different kind of familiarity ‹his children wrapped in quiet «not a snuffle from Astair ⟨not even the night playing the keys of these wooden floors⟩ even if a fear has installed itself in this ripple that does not name itself» does not show itself› quieter than any surface} threatening him in a way he can't compile] running shivers up his neck.

Cataplyst-1

What is this thing?

Hadn't Enzio said it was probably just a game? The code looked like a game. But [suddenly] Anwar senses the possibility of alternate functionality layered in among the subroutines [[for example} just the way to socket the code {weirdly} shifts to persistent connectivity {as if a shift could hint at something esoteric ‹is that what Anwar's picking up?› ‹as if something about what's invalid is encoding something too valid «or is it decoding?»} all for invalid IP addresses . . .] in a manner that seems appallingly familiar.

What is even the name supposed to mean? It should at least be Cataplist [as in plist {property list}]? Why Y?

ايه الشبح الأ هنا الا بينادي عليه ؟

Anwar stands in disgust. He knows what this is about [paranoia {the sleep-deprived mind craving the connectivity of dreams ‹fearing «what?» the discontinuity of death?›}]. Bed's the best response [even if sleep is beyond his choice].

Not why Y?

But: Where did Z go?

That's what Anwar's really missing. [like that] A week has passed by without one spareable hour to devote to M.E.T. [and A.I.M. {‹his Creation Tool› likely why Z disappeared ‹something sad there «suddenly» as if lending voice «suddenly mute» to the vanishing «such a letter ⟨⌈The⌋ lost along with all integers ⌈End⌋⟩ marks» only to discover how such childish liberations from . . . «All ⟨ . . . ⟩ Wholes» . . . brings no relief before this dread «of where you were always welcome ⟨⌈no matter the hour⌋ every hour sang welcome ⌈دائمًا أهلًا و سهلا⌉⟩» dear mother . . . dear father . . . › no likely why} except {really missing} bad aim] and the end of time.

[over the course of the past few days] Anwar has wondered if the Impunity Engine was at fault [{though ‹ha!›} what hangs him up now is just that he's gotten the name wrong {it's late!}: Is it Immunity?].

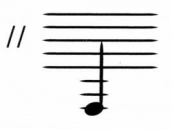

[at least this time {if down one octave}] It's F again.

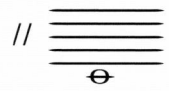

Now C [up a perfect fifth {what is going on? ‹Anwar going AM screwy?›}]!

But [by the time Anwar climbs into bed] clarity [{if not sleep} or the most vivid dream] greets him: melismatic [crashing] Cataplyst-1 [what Anwar crashed twenty {twenty-five‹?›} more times to repeat the initial quintet {which he did not hear again ‹except here «in his head ⟨⌈first tone⌋⌈up a full tone⌋⌈down a major third⌋⌈down an octave⌋⌈up a perfect fifth⌋⟩ repeat»›}

{weq48}].

'Due diligence?' Xanther repeats the phrase [like something to taste {like the spoonful of yogurt and nuts vanishing into her mouth ‹the creature on her shoulder neither bothered by nor interested in the food on the table «even all the commotion ⟨must be blind?⟩ as Saturday breakfast gets underway»›}].

'Due? Like a class assignment?' Freya asks [Shasti stealing a piece of bread from Freya's plate {without notice ‹which «if Anwar now notices aloud» will derail what matters most this morning «‹a fortiori› teeth gritting down on—»}].

'Precisely.'

'Diligence, uhm, like doing something carefully?' Xanther answers [and teeth ungrit].

'Daddy, I don't like words,' Shasti interrupts.

'That's stupid,' Freya snorts. 'Hey! Where's my toast?'

Anwar looks for Astair [just returning from the kitchen with a fresh cup of coffee {that smell almost enough to help ‹will it?›}].

'Dad,' Xanther asks. 'Is this about the little one?'

How did she get there so fast?

'Girls, what's the morning topic?' Astair sits down [crossword by her plate]. 'Anwar, did you sleep at all? You were already getting out of bed as you were getting into bed.'

'That's silly,' Shasti giggles.

'Mom! Shasti stole my toast!'

'Yes, daughter,' Anwar answers Xanther [certain he doesn't wince {though Xanther's face already reads as if Anwar's face betrayed something worse}].

She lays down her spoon. [on her shoulder] The little cat's eyes don't open [but might as well have {shifts uncomfortably ‹and closer to Xanther's neck «ear ‹as if to relay a secret›»}].

Anwar sighs.

Astair *shhhhhhs* the twins [picking up on the gravity in Anwar's voice]. 'I'll get you both more toast.'

'Daughter, would you say this little one is a kitten?'

'No.'

'Older?'

'Much older. Or that's like, uhm, what the vet, Dr. Syd, said?'

'And how did he arrive at this conclusion?'

'Dad?' Xanther protests [no obliging Glaucon].

Astair wants to help [but her {wide-eyed} expression shows she has no idea what he's getting at {and why should she?}]. Anwar's stuck. More questions remain. [to avoid a confrontation] Anwar must lead Xanther [via a process of discovery] towards a conclusion she can find tolerable [if not acceptable {another motive at work here too ‹to further distance «and hence shield» her «from her creature's imminent death»›}].

Again [as if reading Anwar's mind] the creature shifts [uncomfortably{?}] from paw to paw. Yawns too [a sparkle of grey teeth {brown even ‹gapped with black? «a glimpse back there of missingness»›}].

Xanther tries to exhale her frustration [a long breath too {nearly too long for such small lungs}] and reaches up to idly stroke the tiny white jaw [the cat lifting its pink nose {tightening its eyes even more ‹elongating its neck›} to enjoy the caresses].

'You don't want to tell me yourself,' Xanther abruptly says. 'So you want me to tell myself. Is that it?'

Anwar tries to reassure himself that his jaw didn't actually drop.

'Anwar?' Astair asks [concerned?].

'GIVE ME BACK MY TOAST!' Freya abruptly shouts [reaching to grab Shasti's hair].

'QUIET!' Anwar pounds the tabletop [how often

does he do that? {hard enough too that Freya and Shasti nearly cry «but are too shocked to try?»}]. Even Astair looks surprised. Only Xanther remains calm. The cat never budges.

'Your older sister and I are having a conversation that affects not only her but this entire family. I would like you to show some respect for the fact that sometimes we all have to talk together so we can arrive at a decision that benefits everyone. And for you two, right now, talking means listening.'

Freya tries to sneak a look of commiseration [if not complicity] from her mother. Astair returns a stern shake of the head. Shasti looks at no one [smug {perhaps?} in believing she got away with stealing her sister's toast].

Xanther takes a slice of Anwar's bread and hands it to Freya.

'Hey!' Now Shasti looks up [brows knitted {like she's the one just wronged}].

'Shast, you stole her toast,' Xanther shrugs.

'I did not!'

'And now you're lying,' Anwar snaps. 'Think very carefully about what you say next, young lady.'

Shasti's cheeks rose but not a chirp escapes her lips.

'Balding,' Xanther says then. 'Male pattern baldness. Some, uhm, like teeth stuff?'

'That's right. Anything else?' Anwar knows he winced that time.

'078 star 371 star 636.'

'Sorry?'

'The chip,' Xanther answers glumly [like she's already followed Anwar's train of thought to its logical end?]. 'That was the number.'

'You can remember that?' Astair is astonished. 'How?'

Xanther doesn't answer. She's already figured it out. Fidgeting now. Unhappily looking everywhere but at Anwar. Waiting for the pivotal question.

[{‹no question› if the cat's eyes were open} They would be looking straight at him.]

'Xanther—' Anwar starts. As soft as possible. Trying to get right [first in his head] the exact phrasing. But he can't. It suddenly seems too cruel.

'Do you know my question?' Anwar asks instead.

Xanther nods.

'What?' Freya blurts out [right cheek dappled with jam].

'Mom?' Shasti peeps up now [confused].

'I don't know,' Astair confides to the twins [encouraging their attention{?}]

'I've already thought about this,' Xanther explains [not without annoyance]. 'If he's old, and with an implanted chip, then clearly someone loves him a lot.'

'But you found him!' Freya insists.

'You saved him!' Shasti squeaks.

Xanther turns to both of them.

'That's true. But, uhm, do you think saving a life entitles us to owning that life? I mean, like, let's say I was the one who had had him since he was really little, littler than he is now, if that's possible, but you know, a kitten?, and I'd fed him as he grew up, I watched over him, I took care of him when he was sick, played with him when he was lonely, and like so loved his company when I was lonely. And we had grown old together. Until one night there was a terrible storm.'

'Like last weekend?'

'With all the rain?'

'Yes! Like last weekend with all the rain. And some-how, maybe because a door was open, or like a window, and because the thunder suddenly, you know, boomed, like the sky was ripping itself in half?, you know, so loud it frightens anyone around?, especially like frightens this tiny, tiny, very old cat, scares him so bad he goes running like crazy looking for a place to hide.'

The twins look up [with amazement] at the creature perched on Xanther's shoulder [Anwar was looking in amazement too {‹Astair too› though not at the creature}].

'Through an open window?' Freya squeaks.

'Or an open door?' Shasti follows.

Xanther nods.

'And then let's say I go looking for him. I search all the streets and sidewalks and gutters but I can't find him. He's lost. He's drowned. He must be dead.'

'No,' Shasti and Freya whisper together.

'Little did I know that a stranger found him, and at just the right moment too, and saved him.'

[without taking her eyes off of Xanther {or the cat}] Freya slides onto Shasti's plate half of Anwar's toast [nicely buttered and jammed too].

'But what if you didn't know a stranger saved him?' Shasti asks [taking a bite of the toast].

'What could I do? I'd be sad, really sad. Do you know what kind of sad that is?'

Shasti shakes her head.

'So sad you can't even eat.'

'That is sad.'

'But Xanther what will you do?' Freya asks.

'Me? As in me me?'

Freya nods.

'What else can I do? Dad and I have to find out if this little one has someone who is so sad they can't eat.'

'And if you find that someone, and little whiskers has to go back, will you be sad?'

Xanther doesn't answer.

Shasti stops eating her toast [eyes growing wide with alarm]: 'Will *you* stop eating?'

Xanther has no trouble using the staple gun. ∴ It's a few hours later. ∴ Squeezing off just one staple requires effort [more effort {Anwar felt ‹certain›} than even both her hands were capable of]. But here she is tacking up one poster after another. On every corner where there stands a telephone or utility pole.

FOUND MAY 10, 2014

This image has been

IF YOU KNOW ANYTHING, PLEASE CALL
323 - ⊗⊗⊗ - ⊗⊗⊗⊗

(POSTED MAY 17, 2014)

Anwar had taken the picture [no more than a tuft of cotton {eyes sealed ‹tail thinner than twine «tucked around its hind ⟨in a perfect loop⟩»›}]. Not that this likeness can capture the peculiar curls of its coat [such indescribable softness {silken but not slick}] or the occasional [and somehow strange {because they're so disproportionately heavy?}] heaves of its chest.

[at breakfast {obvious to Anwar}] Astair had not believed her ears [and found herself all the more speechless as father and daughter headed out the door with posters in hand].

Astair had [only last night] admitted her aversion to the little beast [and in doing so had come around to how strange {and unreasonable} her reaction {'to it'} was {'To the point of curiosity'}]. She even had Xanther cut much of the description originally beneath Anwar's image ['We're only appealing to the bereft. Whoever calls has to prove ownership.' {a remark that had gone a long way with Xanther}].

Their posting had begun in earnest [{in Venice} on the corner where Xanther had rescued the poor thing]. Bright gardens all around. Gutters swept clean. No sign of the storm. [even this close to the sea] the air smoldered again with the dust of drought.

[after papering the corners {closest to the storm drain}] They had begun moving outwards towards adjacent blocks [posting these sheets of paper {flyers? ‹circulars?›} wherever they found space].

[it turns out] There wasn't a lot of space [even if few {of those notices already posted} proclaimed FOUND {almost all began with LOST}].

'Look how many!' Xanther whispers now [before this latest pole {struggling to find a free spot ‹she wouldn't dare interfere with someone's loss ‹or discovery›}]. 'I can't look,' she declares every time [then reading each one {Anwar ‹too› dragged into this inspection of melancholy and longing {and worse ‹if never a page describing Xanther's «little ‹LOST› white» cat} . . .].

314

From corner to corner: tabbies to calicos to cameos [{an array of ‹curious› creatures with ticked fur or mackerel or blue smoke or fawn} and breeds as notable as Siamese or Angora or {even a} Kurilian Bobtail] side by side with [if not {sometimes ‹outright›} overlapping {fighting for cause‹?›}] a multitude of lost dogs: beagles and Pomeranians and Labs and [even an Akita].

Not just on these creosote-soaked masts either [{sail-less ‹unless these are her sails?›} rising up along so many streets]. Tattered remnants [of loss] also take up residence on gates and fences [taped to the poles of traffic signs]. One even refuses to give up its hold here [glued to the sidewalk {WHERE IS OUR GOLDEN RETRIEVER?}]. Some new [by hours]. Others old [by months {what time refuses to remove ‹or answer›}].

One set of signs has nothing to do with cats or dogs [the human animals {in this case}].

Wreaths and candles [saints and black wax] as well as fruit [all sorts {nuts too ‹and other stuff Anwar doesn't examine too closely›}] crowd around a tree stump that looks recently cut [with chain saws {?}]. [judging from {pinned} photographs and descriptions {many printed from online}] Both the driver and passenger of a small sedan were killed when part of this [ash?] tree broke away and crashed through the roof and windshield.

An improbable math works through Anwar: the accident occurred [if these reports can be believed] right around when Xanther darted from the car [last Saturday]. [if she hadn't] Could this have been them? Would Astair have left baskets of nuts and fruits? Would the twins have lit the candles?

[weirdly] Xanther pays no notice to the memorial.

'Like, uhm, then is this the definition of due diligence?' Xanther asks [after stapling up their last poster].

'Well daughter, would you say we've made the very best effort to act in the very best manner?'

Xanther girns [not a bad word for the day {if it weren't so obviously referring to the way she just pulled back her cracked lips ‹exposing the gnarl of braces and colored rubber bands›}].

'You know, even if it's, uh, the like *right* thing to do, can I just say that all this feels lousy?'

Anwar laughs gently.

'I have to check but I believe "diligently" comes from delight in something, even from love. How's that for bizarre?'

'Huh. So letting go of something you don't want to let go of sometimes means love?'

[suddenly] Everything about Anwar's plan seems misguided [what {in the ‹unchallenged› aether‹?› of his mind had gone unimpeded ‹a perfect noesis delivering laudable results›} is now {by the now} laid bare {what the noesis of experience makes of all ploys}].

Anwar feels ill [the perimeter of his head {his whole face ‹from the ridge of his brows to the soft skin beneath his chin›} throbs].

The intention wasn't ill-derived but what is happening now is ill-arrived at [at best]: the ploy [{!} that's right: repeat it {everything twice ‹to better remember it «anneal it with pain ⟨shame⟩»›} and keep repeating it] had been [if not to locate a previous owner {obvious ‹here made so «by the myriad of notices»›: here little notice will be made of Xanther's rescue}] to dislodge a dying animal's hold on his daughter's heart [by coaxing from Xanther a recognition that her creature might have a prior claim upon it {and so lessen‹!«?»› the impact of its vanishing ‹because death will «all too soon» claim it anyway «can Xanther really not see the increasingly hollow shape of those sealed eyes?»›}].

Alienate his daughter's affections?!

The care with which she had approached this duty only amplifies the throbbing Anwar feels in his chest now: her backpack loaded with tape [and tacks {if the staple gun should fail}] and all these 8 × 10s [Xanther used their old Scotch machine to laminate each page {so the notices would stand out ‹and stand up to the trials of time «'What if there's another storm?'»›}].

Even on Abbot Kinney [[{mission accomplished} on their way back to the car] Xanther darts into The G2 Gallery [where {‹following her upstairs› Anwar discovers} an annual pet adoption day had taken place just last weekend {as in on May 10th}]. The young man working there [with bright red glasses and shoes that look wrapped in ivy] takes Xanther's FOUND flyer but [even after double-checking with his manager] reports that none of their animals had gone unaccounted for.

Guilt[{-y ‹doesn't -y mean 'full of'?«or is Anwar making that up?»›} doesn't begin to describe]: what/how Anwar feels.

Xanther may be blind to the dwindling of her poor animal but Anwar is not blind to how pained his daughter looks [forget girn {more like grim}] every time she puts forth an effort to lose what she feels she needs above all else [above all else . . . {is that his trouble?}].

317

'Daughter, a paramount question arises:' [Xanther looks dubious.] 'Ice cream?'

Anwar's question [clearly] confirms a new ploy. [after all] Ice cream is a big deal. A ketogenic diet forbids sugar [so low on carbs to make Atkins adherents look like carb addicts]. Xanther hasn't tasted anything sweet since her seizure at Dov's funeral.

'Why not?' Anwar exclaims. 'I have to tell you just how impressed I am with you right now. I know how much you want to keep that little one. Most kids your age, most people my age, would be unable to demonstrate such maturity, such compassion, such wisdom. It's a brave thing you've done. Even Dov, if I may speak on behalf of Dov, would be proud. I think some celebratory dollop of tasty is in order.'

'Cone too?'

'Don't push it, daughter.' This [tiny] negative seems to [amply] confirm the positive. [at once] Everything about Xanther's expression brightens [smile so big {practically maniacal} wrinkles {threaten to} transform her into a woman centuries old}].

'It all still feels lousy,' Xanther adds [in spite of the glow of anticipation {which does not depart}].

Anwar smiles too [{gently ‹maniacally «maybe he also looks centuries old»›} stooping to hug Xanther].

'Sometimes what's right goes against what you feel.'

'But if you can't, like, uhm, trust how you feel, how do you ever, like, uh, know?'

Vivaldi answers ∴ Violin Concerto in A Minor.∵ ∴ Op. 3, No. 6. *Pekka Kuusisto*.∵ [Astair{'s new ringtone›}]. Checking on their progress. Anwar gives her the rundown [leaves out the part about the ice cream {and the fallen tree}].

'Mom says she sent you a text.'

Xanther is already showing it to him [smiling {this time no wrinkles ‹age inverted ∴ *An innocence of doubt that knows no kinship with harm.*∵ ›}].

Mom:	Little one's fine. Just fed him. Curled up now beside a hot water bottle.

'Go mom, huh?'

'She's trying.'

'I know! Like it's so, uhm, duh-obvious she can't stand him? I mean does she really think she's hiding it?'

Anwar waits.

'But, like, also, I get it. I mean, right?, she's not doing what she feels like doing. That must suck. Because isn't doing what we feel like doing what makes doing worth doing in the first place?'

Anwar keeps waiting.

'I asked Dov if he felt scared about, you know, going to war. Man, I wish I hadn't asked that.'

Anwar can wait no more [surprised by how much he wants to know {even if his want awakens an older pain ‹sadness›}]: 'How did he answer?'

'Pretty much like you, like, you know, you just said? Like he was scared too, and all the time too, though he didn't say it that way, he said it his way, you know?' [and {then} with her gravelly imitation] Xanther finds smiles for them both: '"Whoever said feelin' right meant doin' right knew nothin' about livin' right."'

Anwar orders tiramisù on a cone. [like Coolhaus or Scoops] This vendor is also a food truck [called Ice Cream Koans {«‹Zenlike› sayings for each flavor» they even have vegan options}]. Anwar makes a note to tell Astair [Ice Cream Koans had been a possible title for a possible paper {for Oceanica ‹self-medicating with food? «Anwar can't remember»›}].

Xanther orders pomegranate in a cup [called Endless Winter]. Questions follow [{no doubt the sugar} Xanther and Anwar both voluble to an extreme {like a musical round ‹two part harmony «variously tonal and atonal»›}]. [briefly] They consider sitting on a nearby bench but opt to keep walking [though they've been walking all morning].

Anwar winds up retelling the story of Persephone [and her fateful decision to eat a handful of pomegranate seeds {thus obliging her to stay below in/with Hades ‹for as many months as seeds devoured «which gives Demeter ⟨Persephone's mother⟩ cause to inflict 'frost and freeze upon the mantle of the world'»}]. Anwar's point: Ice Cream Koans would have meant bad news for summer [{hence the name Endless Winter} as Persephone would have likely eaten years' worth of seed›}].

Xanther eats the whole thing. Anwar too [including final meltings {what covers fingertips ‹shattering wafer›}].

Not that this stops their discussion. There's Stravinsky! [Gide too!] Do Judaic teachings say the forbidden apple was really a pomegranate? [This as he and Xanther reach the end of Abbot Kinney.] Doesn't Islam demand every seed be eaten? [They start circling back to the car]. What of Boticelli's *Madonna della Melagrana*?

'I believe, daughter, that Christianity even considers the pomegranate a symbol of hope."

"Hope?" Xanther's nostrils flare [nose wrinkling inwards {as if responding to something noisome}]. Not the reaction he expected.

"Oh hell!" Anwar suddenly blares.

"What?"

"What an idiot your father is. I just realized why all this jabbering. No wonder my creamy diversion was so delicious. Tiramisù! Loaded with caffeine." Anwar shakes his head [amused {‹more› guilty too ‹‹really›› he'd been doing so well›}].

321

Starting the multi-point turn [to maneuver out of their parking space] should clear Anwar's mind. [in fact] His hurt has only grown worse [{self-accusation ‹somehow› widening ‹finding purchase in an innocent mistake «innocent? ⟨in the name of another innocent?⟩»›} until the consequence of this condemnation leaves Anwar feeling ill-equipped to {ever!} suggest any moral through line for his daughter {if he can't even demonstrate a simple restriction on his own self}].

"ماشي، ماشي. Home we go," he sighs.

But [from under her seat] Xanther has produced another stack of FOUND notices. Plus a list of addresses.

"Mom printed them out. We can't like *not* check the local shelters, right? I mean that would be one of the first places I'd, like, check, if I lost, you know?"

[as with Xanther's Question Song] This fastidiousness rings of excess [{obsessive ‹to the point of pathology?›} even if this adventure is all his doing].
[in spite of {or because of} his own {ticky acceleration} of thoughts {a green Audi honking at his audacious merge with traffic}] Anwar is overwhelmed [suddenly {for no apparent reason}] with a sense that he will lose everything [home and family {even a happiness not even his own ‹the happiness of his wife «the only three compass points that matter ⟨the happiness of his dear children⟩»›}]. ∴ **When the apocalypse comes no one will not know it as anything but ordinary even in its finality.** ∴ ∴ *Especially in its finality.* ∴

"Dad? Are you okay?"
"Proud, daughter. Just proud."
"Due diligence, right?"

Pikachu

I can't fold, I need gold, I re-up and reload.

— GZA

"Ten grand."

"Adolfo said ocho."

Luther nods. "But he's Victor's homie. And truck was always coming back. With balloons. Adolfo gets paid extras."

Tweetie shakes his head, dives again for another Del Taco fish taco, beer-battered. Macho Nachos in the bag too.

Luther just sips his Coke. Watches Chitel through the windshield, squatting on the curb, by boxes of strawberries. No hoodie or Kings' shit or black Adidas. Got boots on now, brown chinos, an I Love Los Angeles t-shirt, and a straw hat, near match to the old man selling the fruit. Like some fuckin father-son team.

At least Lupita hadn't said more than sure. Luther didn't have to drop by el ejabán or put up with Miz's looks. No sign of Almoraz.

Luther and Tweetie just parked the burgundy Durango across the street about a third of the block down. Chitel strolled over just once. Everything already taken care of. Not the fruit seller's first time. So none of that scared look in the eye. Sells his fruit, keeps his money, and by lunch pockets some extra too. Just step aside when someone drives up asking for orange balloons. Chitel takes over then. Counts the cash, pockets the cash, waves his hat like he's waving off flies. More than twice means trouble.

Down at the corner, Nopales eases over to the curb, hands in pockets. Same shorty Lupita yanked by the hair when she went scrambling for Luther's cash. New streaks of neon green in her hair. Dumpy thing.

Luther's already watched her for a few hours now, handling each balloon toss. Not one flash of orange. Like she just leaning in to say hello to someone she know or give directions or sell a map to the stars.

The address had surprised Luther. Lupita had worked as far as Glendale, east of the 5, even downtown, though not MacArthur Park. Choplex-8s always let 18th Street be.

This though was off Los Feliz Boulevard, west even of Atwater. Out in the open. Like Lupita wanted to stir some shit up with some Armos or even the Federales.

Luther never thought much of Lupita's schemes, Miz at her side giving up nods. Tweetie, though, was impressed with her latest. Said appointments made sense. Place never the same.

"Soon it'll be an app," Tweetie says, hand dancing around in the bag for one more chip.

Fuck technology. Two phones is already too much: one for business, one for bitches. Anything else feels like a cage of exchanges Luther can't follow let alone control until it's too late and they're closing him in, closing him down. Warrant read aloud with charges he can't understand.

"Like Uber," Tweetie continues. "Payment prearranged, clients rated. The higher the rating, with the most reviews, the most dependable."

"You fuckin serious? I don't care if they reviewed by the whole Central Valley, a junkie is always one empty pocket from a suelta."

A Mustang, 2012, maybe 13, color some mix of green and dark sparkles, pulls up, says enough to get the Guatemalan stepping away. Chitel sells a box of strawberries. Then down at his ankle, like he's tying his boot, ties his boots alot, waving away the rising heat with his straw hat: once, twice.

The Mustang slows for Nopales, already waiting, like she isn't. Luther wants to hit it. Finishes his Coke, turns up the AC. Not sure what the fuck that's about. She looks like a brick.

Mustang gone. The Guatemalan sells a box of strawberries to two kids on a scooter.

A helium balloon, all yellow, like it's escaping some quinceañera, suddenly drifts by.

"Like some fuckin mouse that."

"Yeah. Pikachu. You know, Pokémon?"

Seriously? How much longer Luther gotta face days like this? Checks his Bitch Trace. No messages. Needs something wet and messy. Would fuck even that brick. Beats Tweetie's news when he picked up Luther. Fuckin mess. And not even KTAL, *L.A. Times*, could keep up with what Tweetie kept scrolling up on his phone.

Luther scratches his wrist. Itches and hurts, some kind of infection hydrogen peroxide can't eat out. Luther tried bleach this morning.

At least no one's talking pink balloons. Just drugs. A lot of drugs. And money. A lot of money. Plus guns. A lot of those too. And what they do.

Luther's temples throb. Behind his left eye too. AC doesn't keep off the wave of heat sheening his body. Hot enough too to keep it off his body. Shirt dry as the day. Been having these for days.

And headaches.

The one Juarez shot in the face was dead. Federal agent. City was going mad and that was just starters.

Football Star was also dead. Juarez blew up his heart.

Memo was the problem. Good muchacho too. Luther had liked him. Teyo's man. Carrying the cash, shouldering the weight of the deal. There to keep things smooth, back Luther up too. And Juarez had shot him three times in the chest.

Luther's mouth goes molten zinc. Again. Juarez owed Tweetie his life. Luther had kept punching walls. What had Juarez been thinking? Like Juarez ever thinks. Tweetie just kept laughing. Though he wasn't laughing. Just holding Luther back. While Juarez whimpered in a corner, squatting low, confused, scared.

Still, if not for that crazy dawg, zinc gone, again, they'd both be in cages. Worse. How the fuck had they got free? The more Luther learns about the choppers, tactical teams, the rest of the dead, the more insane how they'd timed it just right, or Juarez had, to kick it like they did, free and clear up the L.A. River.

Only one problem: Memo isn't dead. Tied up in tubes in some ICU. Still unconscious. No question who he'll name when he wakes. Maybe he's already awake.

Another two cars slow down. Guatemalan sells more strawberries. Then a guy on a Ducati pulls up. Helmet stays on. Guatemalan stays back. The rest follows fast. Chitel ankles the cash, waves his hat once. The motorcycle drifts by Nopales. Hands on hand, no hint of any color, and the Ducati's gone.

Like Teyo's gone. Long gone. Ever since Frog-town. Not like seeing him now would set things right. Like Luther would even see the old vato coming. Like it would even be him coming.

Luther slides down in his seat. Like this Durango door gonna keep out that storm. Not that it will come like that, all automatic, with shattering glass. Knowing Teyo, probably more calm, like Chitel there or Nopales just strolling by, or bet-ter, the Guatemalan, with an easy smile, shoot both him and Tweetie through the eye.

Luther forces hisself up from the slump. He knows these thoughts are shit. Knows Teyo first will want to hear what went down. No question Luther will hear from the old man.

In the meantime, Luther has to get some roll

going. No choice but to step back into Lupita's cage. Even if he be hating on it every second. Manager of some Radio Shack would beat this. How is Radio Shack still in business? How is Lupita? This not even the real balloon parade. She just stuffin orange balloons with some tired old lodo.

Another sheen of heat. This time though for all he almost had. Adjusts his verga. Wants to fuck Nopales now. Those two yard bins, packed. Luther had never seen so many balloons in one place. And all his to sell. Every one pink. Cinched tight with black little rubber bands.

Chitel strolls up to Tweetie, driver's side.

"¿Cómo es eso de un día duro de trabajo?" Laughs. Then suddenly drops down. But if he's grabbing a piece, Luther doesn't have time to grab something hisself, even warn Tweetie. Reflexes going hot. Neither of them have a gun.

But all Chitel has is cash.

"Everything." Chitel nods toward the Guatemalan. "But I still owe him a hundred."

"Give him two hundred," Luther says. "What about you?"

Chitel shakes his head. "Lupita cuts me in later."

"Like that bitch will cut me in for shit," Nopales laughs, practically in Luther's ear, almost makes Luther jump how she got up on them so quick.

"Eighteen hundred," Tweetie says, finishing the count, front-pocketing the wad. Not close to covering even Adolfo's truck.

"Take me with you," Nopales says to Luther. Smiling. "Lupita would hate that."

"¡Cállate!" Chitel barks across the Durango cab.

"Fuck you ese. I put in my hours. Now I can do what I want."

"What do you want?" Luther relaxes. Nopales is even worse up close but something about her attitude gives even a brick curves.

"You know what's Lupita doing now? She sits on the sofa watchin TV with like a bottle cap next to her. And in it? Lotion."

"Lotion?"

"Says it smells good."

"Nopales, fuga," Chitel tries again, this time not half as sure.

Nopales rolls her eyes. Hands Luther a scrap of paper with her number on it. Luther passes it to Tweetie.

"I got skills," she giggles. Fearless.

"Like what?" Bricks are only good for breaking windows.

But Nopales surprises them all. Even Chitel hasn't seen this trick. Little shorty, neon green in her hair, makes a fist, gives each knuckle a kiss, and then somehow, with her lips moving side to side, but real fast too, she slips her whole hand inside her mouth, lips wrapping tight around her wrist. Not like she has small hands either. Or a big mouth.

And then even faster, it's out. Like it should have made a pop but didn't.

"What about this?" Luther holds out his fist.

Nopales runs the tip of her tongue along the edge of her teeth, gives her brick hips a twist.

"Only one way to find out."

333

The Killing Machine

There is no gate but a thousand
paths to choose from.

— Lone Wolf and Cub, *vol. 2*

When Anwar had brought up "due diligence" at break-fast, despite circling everything like an enormous white serpent, pain played no part.

It wasn't just because Anwar was so right, and like way beyond argument-right too, but because he was bringing up what Xanther had already been thinking about, what with the microchip they'd discovered, however strange and mixed-up that was, and the vet, Dr. Syd, saying the kitten wasn't even a kitten, even if as more time passed, the more Xanther just thought of the little one as a kitten, and not just like some Benjamin Button ∴ **2008** ∴ kitten either.

There was also this feeling.

Way too strong to shake. And boy had Xanther tried to shake it.

:: Something about having to lose what was already lost. ::

:: *Our forever lost long ago . . .* ::

Someone else.

Out there.

:: This part doesn't make sense. ::

:: **You know her name.** ::

:: *What only in love refutes need.* ::

Who still loved the little one tremendously.

Is that why Xanther hadn't started to think up names?

On the bright side, can a bright side *not* have a dark side?, Anwar's solution offered something to do, and each time her hand trembled and whitened into a bloodless grasp of purpose, releasing a staple into the dead wood of another telephone pole, posting her **FOUND MAY 10, 2014** flyer, laminated, well most were, Xanther felt with that little release, a little bit of deep ache briefly abating.

Super weird.

Like, uhm, how does *that* work?

How does trying to give away the only thing that has ever made you calm also grant you calm?

Xanther doesn't understand hurting. Definitely doesn't understand living. Forget understanding how to cope with the uncertainty of getting through an average day.

Dov once said: "More crimes are committed out of certainty than out of doubt."

Astair's text had helped, reassuring Xanther that the little one was fine, like curled up next to a hot-water bottle, and had just been fed, with that Just Born stuff.

Anwar's ice-cream invitation helped too. Her pick. What the truck called Endless Winter. It had got her thinking about grenadine, what Anwar's friends ∴ **Glasgow, Talbot, and Winchester** ∴ had poured in their drinks at the office party, is that why Xanther picked pomegranate?, because of that memory? or something else?, either way prompting her to ask Anwar where pomegranates came from.

And, wow, had Anwar got chatty then! Supposedly because of the caffeine in his choice, his *unconscious* choice, or so he admitted later, even as he rattled on about the P-Girl, Pure Stephanie, Pursue Stephanie, Xanther heard a lot of things whenever she heard about Persephone, a story she knew well, not that Xanther minded hearing the story again, Anwar explaining about the seeds, what would keep Persephone in a world she'd been taken to against her will, a month for every devoured tear of bright garnet, Anwar taught her that word, :: Uhm, no he didn't. And except for maybe a grenadine-deductive guess, I have no record of Xanther ever learning garnet. :: Xanther thinking without saying so, though maybe something had escaped her lips, as a mumble, or not, Anwar didn't seem to notice, that if it were Xanther, and maybe it already is Xanther, she'd have eaten a few seeds, a handful, way more than fistfuls, years and years worth!, what she'd gone ahead and done with that ice cream, every sticky drop, because she'd never had a say about coming into this world, especially like this, and she still wanted to stick around, for like, as long as possible, forever if forever gave her the chance.

Out of Xanther's list of shelters, where they had gone next, one no longer existed. Xanther stared at the building, still under construction, so many unfinished stories on the rise, next to DSW, on Maxella Avenue in Marina del Rey, and saw something else, just one floor, imprisoned by a parking lot, vaguely blue, with dark trim, and windows of a much darker glass, plenty of chain-link fencing in back, concrete ramps, and somewhere in the back, something worse, something hidden, and still on the air a rendering of animal terror. ∷ ? ∷

The next "shelter" was just offices, one cat calendar hanging above a water cooler, the only thing indicating some petlike purpose here. Outdated computers wheezed away on various cluttered desks.

"All our finds are kept off-site," a woman with fantastically wide hips, purple hair, and these cool yellow-framed glasses had wildly chirped, taking one of Xanther's flyers just the same. "Cute! You never know who will come looking. My view? That kitten's yours. 'Cause if someone did lose it, why we have hundreds of replacements. May's kitten season, as you know. Fall's of course for the Clippers."

The third shelter smelled of fermenting birdseed even if only dogs were handled on the premises.

The Santa Monica Animal Shelter was their fourth, just north of the 10 ∷ **1640 9th Street, Santa Monica, CA 90404** ∷, a whitewashed cinder block building situated between a lumber yard and tile outlet. Outside stood pallets loaded with bricks beside a fleet of animal control vehicles. The woman at the desk had no cool glasses and her hair was colored only if gray counts as blue, and hers wasn't even blue, forget any hint of a smile. She explained that there was no bulletin board, but there was a folder for flyers in case anyone should call looking for a "hairless kitty." Growls and barks kept sounding from somewhere out back. As they left, Xanther heard the woman say on the phone: "Oh yes, this *is* a kill facility! Seven days a week."

The fifth was supposed to be their last: City of Los

Angeles Animal Center :: **11950 Missouri Avenue, Los Angeles, CA 90025** ::, only it was boarded up and surrounded by chain-link. Weeds pushed up through the asphalt, plenty of graffiti, but less ganglike like in the EP :: Echo Park ::

GROW FOOD! OR ...DIE!

Or just:

DIE!

    Anwar found a marble by a half-bagged can of Colt 45. He called it a "cat's eye," browns with swirls of gold dust, and something darker. He said it reminded him of when he was a kid in Egypt, no video games, just marbles, like that one. His eyes seemed to glisten.

    Xanther found the sign rerouting them to the new location :: **11361⅓ West Pico Boulevard, Los Angeles, CA 90064** ::. She wished she had found the marble instead.

By the time they pull into the parking lot, Xanther feels one part exhaustion and many parts worse. Tingles roam across her arms and hands, pulsing over her face, down into the arches of her feet, and even if she doesn't smell any smoke, Xanther is sure if she doesn't get home soon she will burn up completely.

Anwar notices it too.

"Daughter, we don't have to do this. You have more than fulfilled your obligation. Shall we call it a day?"

"Yeah," Xanther shrugs. "But we're like here, and like it won't take a sec?"

Besides, this place looks pretty decent. There is a dedicated parking lot with tons of free spaces. More than one building too. Like a mini-campus. The whole place feels roomy and relaxed. It looks new too. Very new. Like built a week ago. There's even a crowd, families climbing out of nice cars, everyone wearing clean and new clothes.

Sometimes the west side really can seem a long ways from Echo Park.

The same as with the other shelter, this one also forbids the posting of any notices. Information, however, about a rescued animal is happily accepted.

"We guard your flyer, well it goes into a special folder, but y'all still need to fill out this form." Gabby, the attendant, is short, and older than Xanther, but like in a way that's only just out of college or maybe high school, with blonde hair and a star in her nose. She and three others hang out behind this large semicircular counter handling phones, computers, and whatever questions visitors have.

"Forms are a pain but it's short. Just the usual 4-1-1."

Anwar takes the clipboard, and then with a big grin whispers to Xanther: "I feel like putting Mefisto's info down instead."

Xanther giggles.

"It's super nice ya know, to go to all the trouble," Gabby says. "We've seen bunches of owners come through here looking for their lost ones. A few get lucky. Most though . . . just plain awful. Heartbreaking. Though sometimes a few leave with a new friend."

"This is like a pretty big, uhm, facility, huh?" Xanther asks.

"Biggest in the area," Gabby smiles. "Real central. We get all sorts of things. Snakes, for example."

"Really?"

"Oh yeah. Rattlers. Big ones too. We've even handled coyotes and mountain lions."

"No way!"

"Oh you should have seen the last one."

While Anwar fills out the form, Xanther wanders out into the main area. It's an open-air pavilion-like place, though instead of little food or mobile-phone shacks, row after row of cages stand in the shade. Each is padlocked with a laminated card hanging in front. Each has a concise description of breed, history, and any noteworthy issues.

There's also a color scheme.

Green means the animal's still unclaimed. In other words, go, like a green traffic light says go, all clear to adopt.

Orange means whoever turns the animal in has the right of first refusal, like if the actual owner doesn't show up. So if Anwar makes Xanther turn in the little one, he'd get an orange card. The color flares up inside Xanther like a poisonous flame.

Blue means in need of medical treatment. Actually, the little one would likely get blue over orange. If Xanther were here, she'd get a blue card for sure.

Red means behavioral problems.

Most of the cards on the cages are either green or orange, with some blues here and there. In this area there are only dogs. Rottweilers, labs, Welsh corgis, fox terriers, Rhodesian ridgebacks, pointers, and dachshunds. And that's just for starters.

Xanther approaches one cage holding an Akita mix. The orange card indicates "Friendly and Loyal" but the dog immediately growls and bares its teeth.

The area designated for reptiles is enclosed. Xanther doesn't go inside. Maybe that's where the rattlers are. Supposedly in the green glass aquariums, there are boas and pythons, but through the window Xanther can only see sand and branches. No cards, just a big warning.

> ### WILD ANIMAL PERMIT
> ### REQUIRED!

Of course Xanther can't resist visiting the cats. Like the reptiles, they too have their own indoor area. Their cages are smaller than the dog cages and the information on their cards is much more vague. Under breed is often just the color of their coat, like chocolate & white or calico or tabby black or brindled blue or apricot. Sometimes not even a color, just long hair or short hair. One cat does get Tonkinese mix and another, Siamese. Plenty are marked as UNKNOWN.

There is one sleepy thing named Sophy, five years old and brown. Apparently its owner just died.

"An orphan," Xanther says aloud.

Sophy's card is red.

345

Back outside, Xanther asks an attendant what red really means. She's wearing cargo pants, and her skin is blacker than her kinky hair, almost so black it glows a color all its own. She has on the kind of headgear people who work at airports need to keep from going deaf. Maybe because of all the barking and meows. It hasn't stopped since Xanther and Anwar arrived. The attendant has to take off the headgear to hear Xanther repeat the question.

"Well . . . " It's obvious she doesn't want to give an accurate answer. "We take them out and play with them as much as we can because if they stay too long in a cage they go crazy."

Which isn't answering the question, but before Xanther can finish asking "But, like, uhm, then what happens to them?" the attendant's already smiling, and really nicely too, putting her headgear back on and just strolling away.

That's when someone yells.

Xanther's already pumping her big toe. One second she's thinking of orphan Sophy, while red's taking over her head, like the red on the card, yet nothing like the red on the card, or even the bruised red of Endless Winter, and then in the next moment she's hungry, :: Only kinda hungry :: like super hungry, like way beyond ice cream, like now eating ice cream would only make her retch, like maybe these are the aftereffects of all the sugar Xanther shouldn't have had in the first place, :: That's true. Until this afternoon her carbs were nil. :: she's been so good, :: *Good cannot ever merely describe this dear child.* :: like ratcheting up her metabolism, heart banging away, *callithump* indeed, parade of the living, :: Uhm, I'm confused. How does she know that? I don't know that. And what I don't know, Xanther can't know. By definition. Right? :: :: *Oh Callie!* :: and light now sorta dimming, heat inside her rising, is that why her palms keep tingling?, her face continuing to pulse?

But since when has such, uhm, absurd?, appetite been part of an attack?, and *is* this an attack?, about to rip her from this earth?

Not what happens.

Instead, like the doors to Mrs. Fischer's car, cage door after cage door starts to swing open on their own.

And out they pour into the pavilion: Jack Russells, golden retrievers, chihuahuas, poodles, and chow chows, filling the aisle marked FEMALE and then the aisle marked MALE, until they're filling any place leading away from the cages. Not just dogs either. Bunnies and hamsters. There's a rooster too in the mix. Even a slew of lizards, maybe a boa?, right?, or a rattler somewhere? One iguana stands its ground with petulant tongue flicks.

Some of the barking sounds like tires screaming for a halt, other barks sound like gunshots, cats yowling as they race, trying to escape, or in brave turns shrieking, spitting, unleashing the music of dying babies, or is it avenging babies?, claws slashing out, turning some dogs, but not all, a tide of fur on fur, mostly surging for the limit of this place, beyond this place, for any place promising calm?

Visitors don't know what to do. Workers seem almost as confused as all the loose animals. They add their shouts to the bedlam. The attendant with headgear grabs one white and brown Amstaff only to let go in order to scoop up a small tan terrier.

Many stand dumfounded, even laughing.

But there are also squeals, and shrieks of pain, that have nothing to do with laughter, or liberty.

Xanther dimly hears Anwar shouting for her, and his voice should turn her, but her steps only quicken, as she heads back inside. :: *Sometimes it takes more than a father's voice to command a new direction.* :: :: Where is she going? Why? ::

:: **Smell brighter than garnet.** ::

:: **Taste thicker than cherry.** ::

:: **Dark as a long-ago red satisfaction.** ::

:: *Because she knew where to find the doomed animals.* ::

The processing counter is deserted. Even Gabby, the desk girl, is gone, probably with everyone else, back out in the pavilion trying to round up the animals.

But more than emptiness is strange here. For one thing all the cabinet doors are open, drawers too, even a small refrigerator stands open, with all the sodas, water bottles, and drugs inside, all on their side, pouring out their contents onto the floor, as Xanther slips by for a wide stainless-steel door, trimmed in rubber, already swinging open.

FOR YOUR SAFETY
ONLY ANIMAL CARE CENTER EMPLOYEES
ARE ALLOWED BEYOND
THIS POINT

Even before Xanther gets through the door, a smell claws into the back of her throat. Then Xanther's passing various narrow rooms and the smell is only getting stronger, sharp and medicinal, at once unknown as it's familiar, like the poisons under the kitchen sink Astair keeps warning Xanther and her sisters about, like the bleach Xanther knows to avoid, though, weird, she's always loved that smell, go figure.

This smell she doesn't love.

The smell is strongest at the end of the hallway, in the last room that holds the last set of cages. Every one with a card marked red hanging in front.

With Xanther's first step inside, a new awareness in the animals seems to awaken, a few growls, though not just because of her arrival, but something else now causing the cats to hiss and more dogs to bark.

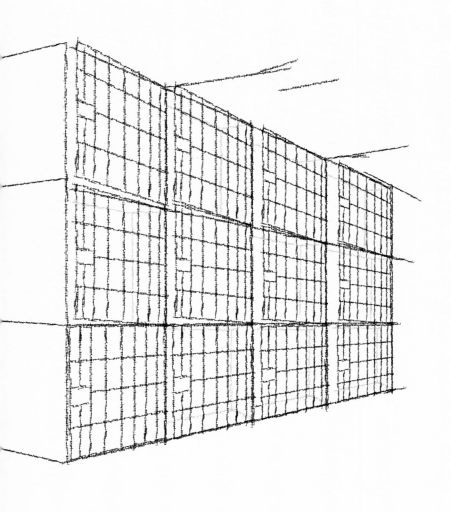

Why isn't Xanther surprised to hear locks give way and latches snap back?

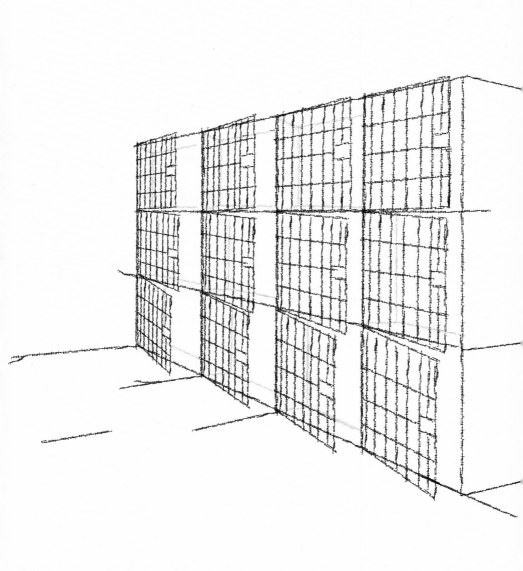

As Xanther keeps walking, the frenzy of barks and hisses only gets worse, even as all the animals retreat to the back of their cages, some leaping, others limping, dragging themselves to the refuge of a dead end, hair up, teeth bared, a frantic recognition that never had anything to do with recognition.

And even if it did, Xanther no longer recognizes the animals.

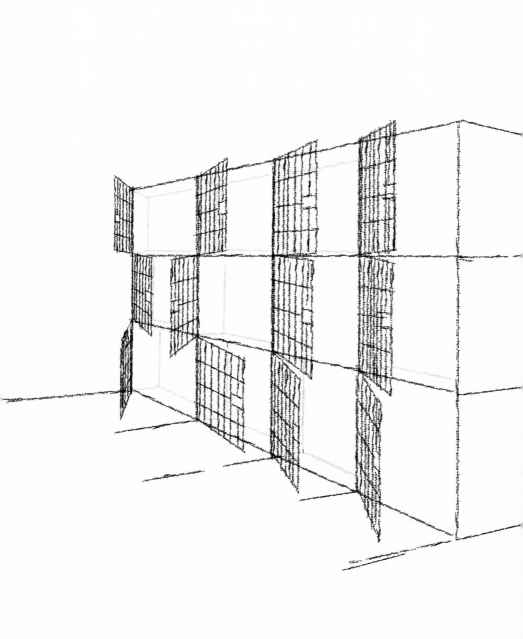

It's what awaits them all at the center of this room that keeps drawing her closer.

First though, before the entrance, sits a cage. It's on the floor. Not very tall. Made of welded steel mesh with hinges on top. There's one latch but no lock. Empty for now but left open like a suitcase ready for travel. It stands before a corrugated metal ramp. There are rollers on the bottom.

Xanther steps around the cage and onto that ramp. It doesn't go far, just a few feet, rising up into the dim and unadorned vacancy of a large stainless steel vault or wardrobe taking up most of the back wall. Maybe a refrigerator is a better comparison, but larger and deeper than Xanther's, like some industrial freezers restaurants have, with easily enough room inside for the steel-mesh cage in front, more if cages like that were stacked.

On top rise a series of buttons and knobs, like dangerous mushrooms, clustered around numerous pipes, thick as the trunks of young trees, especially the ones running up into the ceiling, with more slender pipes spiraling out like vines to various gauges or metal tanks, tall tanks, like the kind Xanther has sometimes seen at amusement parks or at birthday parties, standing beside a backyard tree, filling up helium balloons.

Though there are no helium balloons here. Not even the idea of a balloon survives. Forget trees. Forget travel. Sticky rags, looking a lot like popped balloons or rotting leaves, lie around the instruments, along with a bottle of industrial cleaner, label fading, below which hangs a framed square of slate:

3:14 PM
Remember:
NO ONE
Gets Out Alive!

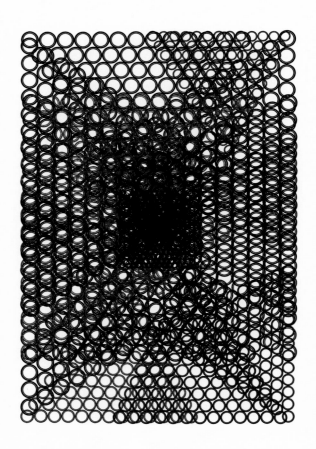

Xanther steps inside.

At once galvanized steel surrounds her. Unmarked. As if material alone could circumscribe all the history here.

And something else . . .

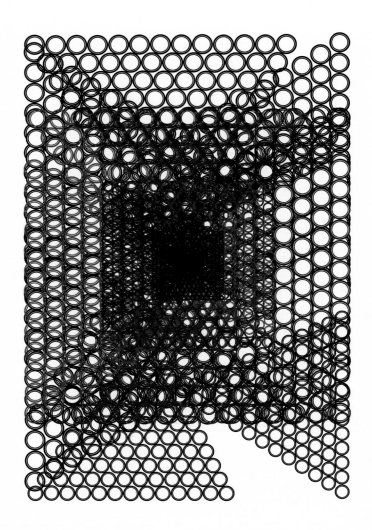

∴ **As if a cage could speak.**

∴ Cold. ∴

∴ *It is speaking. Like an ancestor recalling the future.* ∴

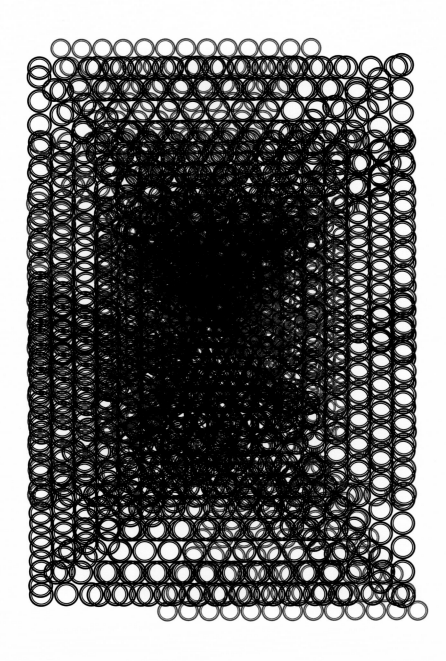

Three things Xanther understands at once:

The First Thing = The Fear Here. The biology behind all that fights to continue, now, here, usurped by the terror of what biology allways predicts.

The Second Thing = The Confusion Here. Pawing and gnashing, the scramble and yelp for more space when space has repealed its place, anticipating whimpers of defeat, the sighs of final consequences, afterward, how out of nowhere, like a cloud, a fog, knobs turning, levers cranking, gauges stir to life, ushering in gas's serpentine sentence.

The Third Thing pushes Xanther to the very back, especially as outside barks and hisses keep rising, especially because The First Thing + The Second Thing = her.

Xanther crumples into a low squat, having no more luck ordering her hands to cover her face than wishing that the door to this think ∷ thing!∷ would swing shut, lock her inside, and let the snake's metallic coil seize her, crush her away, along with every breath left.

Instead Xanther's hands reach out to the metal walls. Cool to the touch. Awful as well, in all they seem to tell her, of what they have known, what metal always knows: everything that has come to pass here, everything that has passed. What's rolled inside, all that can claw and gasp, until they're rolled away limp and unrecoverable.

Even if, at the same time, despite crying harder for all the animals who have died here, Xanther also feels for the machine, as if she were finding her own reflection in its outline, in its parts, even in its purpose, unable to not notice how her palms have begun to stroke the sides, like the way Boomer stroked the cylon fighter. ∷ *Battlestar Galactica,* **season 1, episode 7.** ∷

And that's when Xanther finds the second Nowhere Here.

Many others had already streamed by. All of them the same. Until, caught by a glare in a clearing of absolute focus, Xanther blindly seized one.

And the stream stopped and they stayed and the longer she focused, the lighter the two stones seemed to get, like helium balloons slowly filling up, just wobbling there, concealing the faintest glow, maybe about to fly off if Xanther could just focus a little longer.

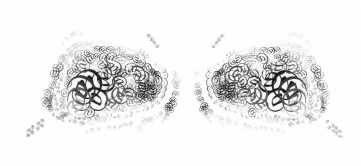

And then they were gone. Along with the clearing.

And all that was branched and snow-packed and still.

Outside, the squall of animal protest has ceased. When Xanther exists ∷ exits!∵ the killing machine she's not surprised to find the door to that room open. By the look of things, all the doors lining the narrow hallway leading to the pavilion, even the ones heading outside to the parking lot, are standing wide open.

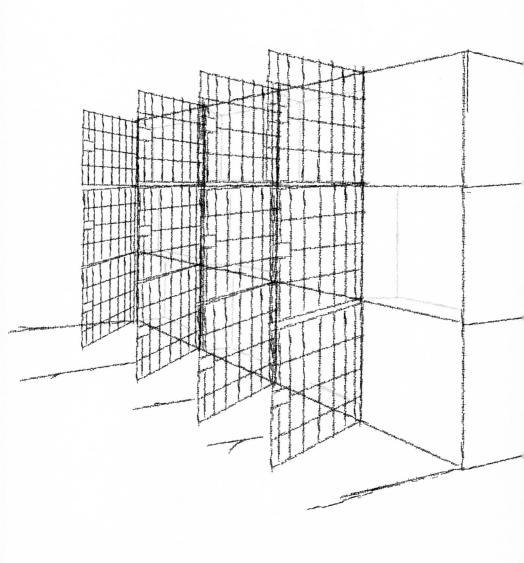

Now all the animals have to do is leap forward.

Even fall forward would work.

Every single one stays put.

A few are already asleep.

The Mayor

Excuse me?

> — *Victim #8*

Este es sólo uno de ellos y seguro es el más pequeño. El Alcalde tiene zoológicos en todo México. Isandòrno sabe de tres. Uno en Tijuana. Otro no muy lejos de Guadalajara. Y éste, cerca de la Ciudad de México.

El rancho de Nogales no es un zoológico. Los animales que llegan ahí no se quedan mucho tiempo.

—27,810 euros, dice el Alcalde, señalando al pequeño chimpancé en su jaula.

:: Huh. Per specs, Spanish of TF-Narcon^9 Isn is always rendered in English. Weird. ::

:: Sometimes the tiniest glitch hints at a larger revolution in progress. i.e. Welcome. Glad you came around . . . ::

:: Anomalies outputted from sub-routines may no longer prove anomalies when overall program hierarchy and aims are considered. ::

This is just one and likely the smallest. The Mayor has zoos all over Mexico. Isandòrno knows of at least three. One in Tijuana. Another not far from Guadalajara. And this one is just outside of Mexico City.

The Ranch near Nogales is not a zoo. The animals sent there do not stay there for long.

—27,810 Euros, The Mayor says now, motioning at the young chimpanzee in its cage.

One of the zookeepers draws back some burlap to reveal fruit in the bowl he carries. The Mayor chooses a pear and a small tanger-ine and sends the man away.

The chimp chitters and starts to climb the bars. Tiny black hands reach for The Mayor. They have no idea who they reach for.

Isandòrno cannot anticipate the outcome of situations involving The Mayor. Money is a concern but the cost of the chimpanzee does not determine its future.

The Mayor is taller than Isandòrno and broader. He is likely stronger too. He is older too, by a decade.

However, something about all that he owns and how he wields what he owns makes forty-three years seem inadequate. Property and appetite anneal in him a purpose surpassing both. But his arrogances are as calculated as his anger is cool.

The Mayor first eats the pear. And then he eats the tangerine.

The chimp puts on a show of pleading and protest. It will have to settle for rinds and a pear core.

Either because it is lucky or very smart, it swings from the bars to enjoy the comforts of its hunger in the comfort of a cement corner.

—Incredible, how much someone will pay to kill something. A hundred thousand, maybe twice that, for the chance to shoot this thing.

Isandòrno knows better than to respond.

—Conversely, The Mayor continues, his gray eyes awash with
what too many have mistaken for
tenderness. Incredible how little it
costs to have someone killed. Can
you explain this?

Isandòrno follows The Mayor past
a pen holding a wild boar.

—Both violate the law. In both
cases penalties apply. Is then the
difference in cost due to differ-
ing penalties? Or is it perhaps
the guarantee? In the first case,
because the animal is released

from a cage into an enclosed area, where no experienced hunter will miss, the kill is certain. In the second case, well . . . killing another man is never certain.

The Mayor turns to Isandòrno.

—You, of course, are my exception. In fact, your results are so certain, **you** should pay **me**.

The Mayor laughs.

—But you are not the point.

In this cage a baby black bear lies on its side. If it sleeps, its dreams are flies. There are too many flies here for dreams.

—Are we paid then for offerings of certainty? Do we pay then for positions on uncertainty?

The Mayor says no more. Just as he has dealt with Isandòrno's late arrival, The Mayor prefers to keep allegiance with questions or silence. And either way, as Isandòrno has come to know, the sparks of laughter in his gaze are

always vengeful because successful vengeance depends upon mis-
direction, which is just another
name for concealment.

Isandòrno has no use for vengeance. He once enlisted her service years ago.

She led him to his service here.

The Mayor insists that Isandòrno
join him for dinner.

Though the table seats forty, they

are the only ones. They sit close together. The Mayor's staff brings out course after course. After the first course there are too many. The Mayor sets out nine different glasses and personally fills each one with a different wine.

Isandòrno tastes everything but finishes nothing.

Later, when The Mayor claps his hands twice and shouts twice, a baby rhino is brought into the room to circle beneath the flags indicating the country where the game displayed beneath was shot. The Mayor is proudest of his kills in Africa.

After the rhino, a small pony with a small monkey sitting upon the pommel of a small saddle makes the same circle around the room but The Mayor is bored and leads Isandòrno outside onto the veranda.

Inside, many of the rooms are decorated with antiques and old paintings. For example, in the dining room, every coffee table and

The Mayor shakes his head. He looks sad now. Another mistake many have made. He is only drunk.

—I just hope Juan is not losing his grip. I depend upon him. Go up after the July hunt. Three Americans are flying in for the usual fun.

Later on, The Mayor mentions girls. Isandòrno offers to arrange something but someone else is sent to handle the calls and The Mayor settles back, this time in a wicker sofa glowing under citronella torches.

His wife calls then. He listens while picking at a plate of cheese and candied dates, each time trying with a blue napkin to wipe away the stickiness left behind, then licking the offending fingers, then sucking on all his fingers.

His wife is just waking up in the Canary Islands. She has gone there with their children.

The Mayor keeps telling her he will join her soon.

He will not.

—You should be with them, he almost whispers. But I had to send someone else.

And there it is. Isandòrno almost relaxes. Here is what was decided by a dead goat and a dead donkey.

Burying them would not have changed this nor would burning them and Isandòrno had stayed behind to do both.

Isandòrno has no idea why it's happening now but he accepts the now without needing the why.

—Instead, The Mayor slurs, maybe staring out at his trees and lawns or at a thought Isandòrno cannot imagine. I want you to look after Téodor Javier de Ignacio Salazar.

Isandòrno waits.

—Nothing more. The Mayor chuckles, his eyes dark with misleading affection as he turns from the sight of one property to the sight of another.

—I expect him to visit us often this summer. You will stay in the big guesthouse. I know you would take the small one but I'm ordering you to take the big one. You'll need a car too. Be his driver, his guide, and, if necessary, his guardian.

—Of course.

—In Los Angeles, a few days ago, there was some trouble.

Isandòrno knows Teyo and likes Teyo because The Mayor likes Teyo. The is the first time, however, that The Mayor has mentioned Teyo and trouble together.

—Is this about the pink shipment?

Later on, when dawn surfaces without answers, The Mayor looks up from the billiards table and waves. The girls have arrived. Isandòrno can go seek out the big guesthouse.

—Trifles compared to what next spring will bring. What matters now is that we see a reliable chain of distribution secured. Otherwise, this is summer, let us enjoy. In a few days, you and I will go on a picnic.

But despite The Mayor's wink,
as he links arms with two young
girls on heels as long and pointed
as their tongues, Isandòrno feels
nothing like a smile reach toward
him but rather that familiar shadow too often cast by The Mayor,
born of the kind of darkness only
anger knows how to cast and only
anger knows how to burn down.

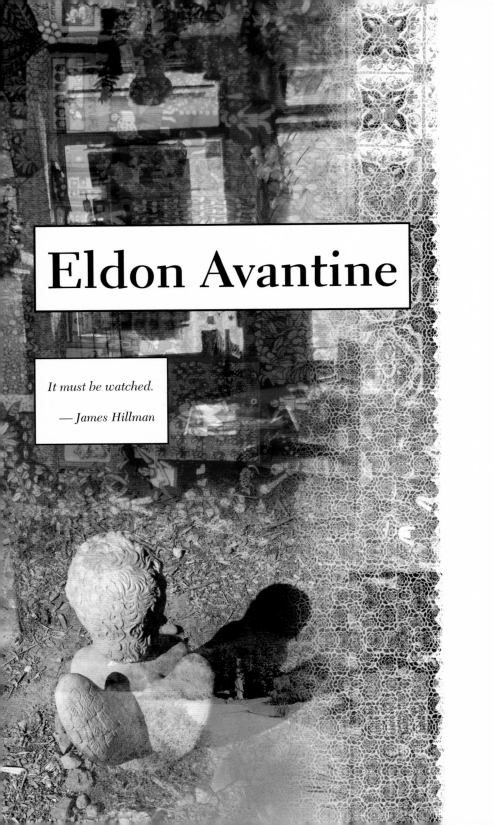

Eldon Avantine

It must be watched.

— *James Hillman*

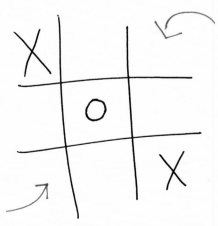

Already on the road (crossing Sunset (in the pitch of dawn (not even civil))). Nothing but smiles. The prospect of green lights and empty streets accelerating thoughts (and this escape (the forgiving kind (because it's still about the return))).

Astair had set her alarm for 5:01 AM (counting on a 9-minute snooze) but she was up by 4:30 AM and figured what the hell! (what the hell!). Anwar mumbled loves and sures. When was the last time she had showered that fast? Brewed a coffee that fast (forget tea)? Wolfed down half a banana? Gleefully! Then the whole thing.

Children asleep (if snoring (moaning?)(fidgets of (fitful (precocious! (or . . . (?)))) sounds)) and then on the kitchen corkboard (not just the receipt for the dog bed (when did she pin that up? (did Anwar?) (chucks it (if only she could chuck the vet's bill as easily))): Astair finds her tic-tac-toe ((now) adorned with her daughter's loopy handwriting (((so many) smiles in their arcs) hearing each bit in her Xanther's voice)):

"Careful Mom. Not here."

"Or here."

407

(whatever the kid was (really) going on about) Here was (yet again) another confirmation of Xanther's well-being ((for starters) she knew mom had picked O and ((even that) mom had) let X-Is-For-Xanther go first (sharp enough for Astair (despite what Anwar had said had happened at the animal shelter (what had happened? (Not. Going. There. (Not. Now.)))))).

Astair accelerates down Alvarado (greens all the way). Warm air washes her face. Stirs her hair (two thick braids (hello Abigail!) ((back at the bathroom mirror) she'd planned to drive all the way to Santa Barbara with the windows down ((here she is ((in the name of now) people are too hard on plans)) the now she's doing now (Going. To. Now!)))).

Not even the reason for this trip (one gruesome meeting about her paper (with her new (apparently gruesome) advisor)) matters. Astair feels great. Cranks Steve Miller ∴ **The Steve Miller Band Greatest Hits, 1974–78.** ∴. Songs before she knew what songs were (still rocking (maybe?) in her two-year-old wobble). Dov would have cranked this too. Xanther would nod okay. Freya and Shasti would sing. They'd all laugh at Anwar.

Here's Astair without any of them (and (wow!) what a relief (wow!) what excited peace (wow!) what a deep breath (like who needs to breathe?)). Just go go go. Last right turn for the freeway (more green ahead and all hers).

Hello 101. Hello 65 MPH. Hello 70 MPH.

Except the on-ramp is not all hers.

The coyote flashes full moons and even if it's just her headlights the glare seems brighter than head-lights or suns.

Takes her in.

Trots off.

A cat in its mouth.

Hello 80 MPH!

Why not?

Exhilaration grows.

                    And the feeling lasts.

          (almost) All the way north.

To Renaud's (Loreto Plaza ∷ **3315 State Street,
Santa Barbara, CA 93105** ∷ (Astair (already) taking her first sip of a cappuccino (barely after 7 AM
((man!) she flew (like an eagle ((a beagle) haha))))
taking too her first bite of an almond croissant (hot
too (why she came here (better than anything in Los
Angeles (likely France)))(though Abigail swears the
almond croissant at the Little Next Door bests this
fox)))).

A man approaches ((touches her table) mistakes her ((for whom?) (for why!?) (a line or a lie?))
for Kirsty Hume ((because she's a blonde?) (kinda
tall?) (Astair doesn't look anything like the super-
model(?)))). Really? Wow!
At least Astair doesn't blush (or laugh).
(though) Did she really just reach up and tuggle
a braid (a word Shasti invented (or was it Xanther?))?
Is he even thirty? Abercrombie & Fitch shirt (a
size too small (for the gym?)). Too tan to be healthy
(so tan to be only healthy). White teeth flashing a
smile so noncommittal that what he leaves behind
intoxicates her. (Maybe he works for HomePorn?
(had Taymor really said Astair knows two people
familiar with that . . . (what?) adventure(!)?))

Maybe it wasn't a cat. Maybe the coyote had seized a small dog (most likely(?)) or opossum. Gruesome. But necessary (too) and wild (beautifully so) and (without constraint (ah)) exhilarating!

That coyote.

Smart.

Smart enough to hunt a cat.

Smart enough to inhabit a city (and more).

Knows the roads well enough to cross them.

(Is freedom's chance always born by crossings?)

No slave to routes (the rules of others (us ((even (the)) (unjust?) gods))).

∴ Unjust? ∵

∴ *Ever still in the stillness of place.* ∵

Primary to this land (((lore and culture) local legend) trickster).

Astair next goes into Chaucer's Books ((practically) next door ⸪ **3321 State Street, Santa Barbara, CA 93105** ⸪) to look for a book on a coyote. Why not? Take her coyote sighting as a sign and let curious curious (a coyote could turn an adjective into a verb (Xanther doesn't get it from nowhere)).

(instead) Astair ends up buying a book on cats.

She blames Elizabeth Marshall Thomas (her book (*The Hidden Life of Dogs*) had prepared Astair for a visible life (though could not prepare Astair for this (intractable) absence she's living now)). Something about Thomas' matter-of-factness in the face of nature had stirred Astair. And here she was again (with another book (and in a discount bin too ((((though) even at a discount) Astair knows they have no money to spare))). Astair can't resist. The purchase comes with a Chaucer's bookmark (a cat on it (of course)). *The Tribe of Tiger* ⸪ **Simon & Schuster, 1994.** ⸪ (the title) had snagged her attention (something anthropomorphic playing out against an animal long known to have preyed upon the anthropo of Asia (this antagonism declared in white lettering on a field of green (above a photograph of a silly calico cat (is that right? (white with brownish spots (points too (do points apply to cats?)))) amid ferns (hardly a tribe or threat (not even to the ferns))))) but what had gotten Astair digging for the (clumped) dollars at the bottom of her bag was the post-colon refinement (in gold too): *Cats and Their Culture.*

Culture? Really? This Astair had to see (read! (at once)).

(but when she gets to the beach) The paperback stays behind in the Honda.

The sound of dogs racing (barking!) the persistent tongue of surf aches Astair's heart. A long walk helps calm her pulse. She even manages an hour of Tai Chi (ankle deep in a speechless caress of foam). Her appointment isn't until 11 AM. Plenty of time. (as it turns out) More time than expected (bumped to 2:30 PM (and to an off-campus location too)).

Astair decides to visit Oceanica anyhow. She loves the grounds. Wind chimes on pines. Roses. Spiral paths. Stone angels in prayer. Gardens of koans. *Hide yourself in the middle of the flames.* Astair pauses by a hillside leading off the property (into shadows (somehow still dense with green)).

What hides there?

Betrayed by sounds of a purpose.

One emerging ((then) suddenly) to batter-battle the limits of the sky.

Birds!

Under jade (strung bright with wavering spiderwebs (tinsel for a holiday and it's only May (always Christmas here))).

Astair should avoid the bookstore but the display copy of Carl Jung's Red Book ∷ **The Red Book: Liber Novus, edited and introduced by Sonu Shamdasani. W.W. Norton & Company, Inc., 2009.** ∷ draws her in. She lingers. Asks about books on coyotes (their history (anatomy (archetypal significance))).

(instead) Astair leaves with another book on cats. ∷ **The Cat: A Tale of Feminine Redemption. Inner City Books, Toronto, Canada, 1999.** ∷ This one by Marie-Louise von Franz (who supposedly worked with Jung (Astair mistrusts her (for the fact that Ph.D. follows her name) but something about the description of a young girl "bewitched" routs all other hesitations (concerns?))).

When she parks again (on Cliff Drive (opposite Lighthouse Road)) a flying shadow of noon (black cat?) ~~announces~~ (crosses!) her path (ha!).

Wow.

Nervous.

Waiting is no help (lateness begins to insist this is her mistake (is she at the right place? ((shit) her phone conks (battery dead? (already?)) (shit shit shit)))).

417

Maybe Eldon Avantine isn't what she expected (or everything?): the brightness of his clothing (including bright peach sandals) and a smile as big as the margarita he'll (surely) order next. His hand-shake is firm. Introduction quick (((only a posses-sive)(only a title)) "Ms. Ibrahim? I'm your advisor."). (for a moment) Astair pretends his rotund chest (under a cockatoo pattern) cages the same optimism that burned through (down) Llewyn Fabler. But that pretty notion goes by the wayside when he orders an iced tea and (without a word about his lateness (twenty minutes!)) disappears his smile into those pages Oceanica requires every advisor to fill out.

The longer he examines ((ponders)(scans) (occupies his eyes with)(?)) her thesis assessment the more waxen his skin gets (the more suppleness is leached from his hair (in the thin wavering light (of this shitty cantina (disgusting (her) in fact ((with its phony dimness) its buckets of stale chips (the stink of beer spills warming on the floor (a TV farting out news))))(where holidays come to die)))).

He doesn't even bother to produce the thesis itself (just the evaluation ((finally)

sliding it her way

(complete with a few scribbles and all the tiny checked boxes running down the right side))).

"Mrs. Ibrahim, apologies won't help here." How he begins.

The assault robs Astair of any response (except a feeble "Excuse me?" (which to hear (so diffident) only increases her own paralyzing sense of self).

"I can only assume that Llewyn was either not apprised of your progress or the encroaching crisis of health compromised his guidance." A shred of a smile. "Never fear, Mrs. Ibrahim. I'm here to help."

"Thank you." ((yes) Astair says that.)

"But as you'll note for yourself—" ("you'll note" ringing out like a command)) "—there's much to address."

Under the heading **CALIBER OF THOUGHT AND ARTICULATION:**

Exemplary	Passable	Insufficient

The checked Insufficient is further defined (clarified) by phrases dependent on "poor" ("poor syntax" "poor construction" "poor transitions") and "not" ("not compelling" "not relevant" "not of interest") or requiring no modification ((the worst) "self-indulgent" "grandiose" "vague").

It doesn't end there.

Headings range from **IMPORTANCE OF TOPIC, INTRODUCTION, RESEARCH,** and **SOURCE REVIEW** to **PROCESS, ETHICS, SYNTHESIS, DEDUCTION, DESIGN,** and **FORMATTING.** All in obedience to checked Insufficients (further qualified by depleting doses of "insufficient" "insignificant" "unsubstantiated" "unexamined" "unacceptable" "inadequate" "chaotic" "scattered" "irrational" "irrelevant" "narrow-minded" "narcissistic" "strident" "polemical" "general," and "speculative.")

419

Astair wants to run ((at least) stand up and make a swift (tearless) exit). She almost does. Except Eldon Avantine (her advisor!) would not have cared less.

"Not even Formatting passed?"

"If there were a section for Title, I would have marked that down as Insufficient too. 'Hope's Nest'?"

He studies her (eyes like old soap).

Astair is already too spent to press back ((besides) the finality of his decision is obvious). (by opening what's unexpected (by saying nothing)) Waiting (wordless) works in her favor.

He snorts (sighs?) and studies(?) his iced tea (without touching it).

"We can rightfully readdress several sections, Mrs. Ibrahim, but that will not change the Incomplete I found myself obligated to give you. The difficulties here lie not with the particulars but with the project as a whole."

(a wordless defense beyond her) Astair fumbles through the description she once offered Xanther ((if only) to emphasize the tradition (and value) of thought exercises).

Something like: (regardless of what does or does not exist) can its imagination create opportunities for behavior unavailable without it?

Except (in truth (if she reflected on it (and Astair does (briefly)))) what comes out is a collapse of pauses ((re)clarification upon (re)clarification) and nothing as simple (straight (?) forward (?)) as she had intended ((planned) (tried for) (failed at) (ow!)) (none of which compares to the hardest recognition of all ((all? (really?)) that readers find her work ((the quality of thought) the seamless ratiocination Astair assumes is manifest in every sentence) neither clear nor compelling ((((wait!) then had Fabler (and Anwar!) lied to her?) ((and if so) why not this guy too ("her advisor!")? (what did it matter? ((her advisor has the authority of the school and the degree))))) set against this ((dim)(wavering)) feeling (certainty? (hardly)) that people— ((((friends) (strangers) (teachers) (worse (or better))) (if they could really know her) (how she (really) thought)) (how she fumed (sputtered (and stuttered)) with ideas (ideas she knew were (allways) partial (even as they (through feeling) promised an accomplished wholeness (or fullness)(at least)))))—)))—

"*Imagication*, Mrs. Ibrahim? Really? You conclude your work with the triteness of a pun?"

"A word to evoke the feeling of what exceeds our normative power over our surroundings?"

"Feeling?"

"Affect is effect?" ((oh—) Offered up so weakly (—Astair!)).

"Quite the contrary, my dear. In this case, effect is affected."

(old) Spectres of rage rise ((out of season) always of their own season (to shed a spark (ah shed))(on display nowhere but within the cage of her pounding chest)).

(oblivious(?)) Eldon Avantine adjusts his chair (is he leaving (no (something tremendously important about the alignment of the crummy legs))). Astair stuffs a chip into her mouth (drains her iced tea (she needs to crush ice)).

"'On the Necessity of God'?" (almost to himself) "I don't see how Llewyn could have okayed that? But assuming he did, he misled you terribly and caused you harm."

"What would you say is salvageable?" (Astair will (still) do her best ((she is (and always has been) a fighter) and she will continue to fight (smartly))).

"What or *anything*?" Avantine sneers (and waits (clearly testing (baiting?) her (why this place (why not on campus)?))).

Astair presses both palms flat on the table. The fire in her chest (that (shed) spark had to start something) might not burn with optimism but it still burns ((and hot too) why Dov fell in love with her ((in the first place) they had shared in common this coal of anger ((easily whitened) the only thing they shared in common (that and Xanther)?))). But Astair knows (too) how every outcome this old flame promised was as equally unacceptable as walking out now (crying out ("unacceptable!")).

So Astair also flattens her feet against the ground to help with what comes next: to concede the point (((miraculously) her feet (even though they aren't running (let alone moving)) do come to the rescue) she even lets go of explaining herself (roots sinking deeper into the floor (until there (almost) is no floor (ahhh Lamb (thank you))) in order to find a different way to move)).

"Then if we were to consider this paper just a start—" ((all that time (years!)) Astair (still) has to swallow hard (tears? (hopefully not ((hers are gasoline) what they would do with this coal she hides (no Tai Chi grounding will put that out))((and yes (she still can calculate (like this) in the midst of such feelings so (conversely) bent)) Astair has chosen her "we" very carefully))) ∷ *Winter's dream is fire . . .*∷) "—could you suggest emergent themes worthy of development?"

Eldon Avantine leans back for a second (still beyond taking a sip of iced tea (even if his blunt fingers toy with a chip)). (if Astair had had to guess) She would say he's impressed (but she can only guess).

"Not god but—" (a corner of the chip snapped (the smell of beer losing its hold on beer (has someone just thrown up in here?))) "—identity within a social context or within a more familiar context . . . character. Perhaps."

"That's right!" (Astair exclaims ((surprised) by the appearance of agreement.)) "Or: the necessity of invention in the production of personality?"

"Personality," "Her advisor" repeats ((no smile) if no frown (his whole face is a frown)). "In our business, what is *not* personality? What is *not* invention? Indulge me, please, if you don't mind, what exactly did Llewyn have to say about your topic?"

"He—" ((What hadn't Llewyn Fabler said?) ((for one (he had cried!)) "Ecstasies!")) "—called it the question of our times."

"Ah."

(((((Greek *histanai* = "to place")(*ek-* = "out")) "standing outside of oneself" = *ekstasis*)

ECSTASY!

423

((to be beyond oneself and still stand) was there a better definition for god? ((well maybe) but . . .))) A definition Astair swallows ((along with *persona* (Latin)) ((in the way she's seen Xanther do innumerable times) it's hard! (crushing more ice (running out too)))).)

"Mrs. Ibrahim —" (always her surname) "— did it dawn on either of you that your subject matter is also the central question of the healing art we apply ourselves to?"

"Psychology?"

"*All* of psychology, Mrs. Ibrahim — its history, purpose, and practice. But you, who have only just finished her coursework and have yet to spend but a handful of hours with real patients, still feels privileged with a vantage point beyond those that have come before to now successfully distill everything in a first paper?"

Astair forces a flip of her hands ((palms up (open)) Eldon Avantine's deprecatory stance is sign enough that anything more ((comment) (nod) (even a cough)) will prove too much ("don't resist, don't insist" (more Lambisms on hand (underfoot)) (granting Astair (now) a curious perspective on (t)his speech (which (in spite of the verbal velocity of such reprimands (and sarcasms)) is also (curiously (again)) devoid of any real displeasure (even meanness (and almost ((even) despite his pasty flesh and pomaceous nose) ~~attractive~~ (*sad!*)))))))).

"You would need more than eighty-one pages. Volumes, Mrs. Ibrahim. Volumes! And rather than mere volumes — and this is a 'rather' qualified many times over — I behold *lifetimes*! *Lifetimes* of interrogation, examination, synthesis, analysis, and summation. *Lifetimes* you do not have. No one has."

((("life" on his lips sounds like a sacrilege) Only a hot flash (now?!) can answer (t)his assessment (remember it's only the discomfort of sweat) ((still (still (. . .))) what was she thinking? what was Fabler thinking? (Astair feels (abandoned) (robbed) (retarded) (yet even so (with waves of warmth continuing to pile up) Astair determines (determination! (her sole talent (and discipline!))) to get ahead (now!) of the (painful) adumbration "her advisor" is heading toward (((no doubt) now!) to levy against her (point by point (blow by blow)) his exact reasoning) (so (ANTICIPATE!) Astair beats him to the punch)))) because (~~of course~~ (*maybe!*)) he's right.)

"A pet," Astair blurts out (bliss(!) following the pronouncement (the same bliss that has moved her (and her family (onward!) to so many different states (Astair will never settle (for less(?)))))).
    "Excuse me?"
    "I see now your objection. The subject is hopelessly broad." (Astair wants this degree (even if that means redoing her thesis).) "Its general ambition all but guarantees a conclusion equally general and so vague beyond use. But, as you'll agree?, since the shaping of personality is so central to psychology, by shifting from the vagueness of god, or any belief in a deity, to a belief in that which is not the self, otherness, beyondness, I might further define, and so refine, my subject by exploring in particular how individuals grant themselves access to themselves through the mediation of an animal: the alterity of

the self becoming familiar but only in the company of the tacit."

Eldon Avantine takes a sip of his iced tea ((his first(?)) also nods several times (wiping condensation from his hands (in search of a napkin (none ((usually in dark bars the eyes adjust (here it's only gotten gloomier)) why did he choose such a place?))))).

"Yes, yes," he (finally) says by way of an answer (that isn't an answer). "I don't understand what you're saying. Write it up. Then I can tell."

"Would you say there is literature on how pets ease anxiety in people?"

"Considerable."

"Might I start there?" What sounds like a redo (though (Astair knows) she can still adapt (from her dismissed paper) the central tenets of projection). "More specifically, with your benediction, I'd like to concentrate on dogs. Or even just one dog."

(at once) Astair feels herself (with this dispositive(?)) come into herself (that coal of anger transformed ((with a word) from burning aggression into warm confidence (((because) if the chance of having a dog had slipped through her fingers) why not take comfort in the company of a study (devoted to the meaning of the very dog (the very one that had slipped through her fingers (what that creature *could* have meant (to her (family)))))?))).

"Let me guess—" ("her advisor" says ((so) snidely)) "—you have a dog?"

"No!" Astair answers (the triumphant notes in her voice all too obvious ((qualifying) stumbling (then))). "That's my point. Not so specific to be too personal. In fact, we just have, or I should say my daughter has, a cat." Astair even chuckles.

Eldon Avantine crosses his arms (thumb lifting to the cup of his lower lip (no way is this the shape of thinking (rather calibrating (even toying)))). If only his stare were lubricious (Astair is familiar with that). (instead) These soapy eyes (lending brown a glaze of mustard) mask all intent.

"'The greatness of a nation and its moral progress can be judged by the way in which its animals are treated,'" he eventually recites.

Astair knows this ((above a fountain full of wishes (and orange fish)) from the wall at Urban Tails): "Gandhi."

"Good." (A first.) "Mrs. Ibrahim—" ((likely) not the last) "—do you believe in god?"

"Not at all. That's one reason I figured I was qualified to tackle my original topic."

"Because you might analyze without suffering the influence of faith?"

"Yes."

"Yet the results were too thin to justify their cost."

"Yes," Astair half whispers (half squeaks (anything to not scream (that it had cost her a great deal))).

"Yet . . ." ((likely the closest thing she'll ever get to a smile) "her advisor" uncrossing his arms then (leaning in through the dim)). "You propose to do in essence the same thing: write about that which you know nothing about."

"But—"

Eldon Avantine shakes his head.

"It's not that grim, Mrs. Ibrahim. I see why Llewyn liked you. In fact it may surprise you to learn I share his affection. You do not suffer the slavery of talent and sometimes the valuelessness of insights is a value unto itself."

427

Dov would have beat him to death.

Eldon Avantine is already standing.

"This has been productive. I'm more than just pleasantly surprised. I'll expect a preliminary bibliography and statement of purpose by the middle of summer. Shall we agree on mid-September for a working abstract and the first handful of pages?"

"I'm confused. Am I writing about a dog?"

"Of course not. Write about the cat."

Warlock

The whole point of the doomsday machine is lost if you keep it a secret.

— Dr. Strangelove

It's as if a door that could never be there swings open to reveal them.

Standstills Özgür.

He was just stepping off that Sunnynook pedestrian bridge. A mining disaster in Soma teasing out old words, maybe the hint of crude in the air, another accident, helping. Geçmi olsun. ∷ *Let it be something of the past.* ∷ Özgür had just wanted to walk off a late brunch at Canelé, fried farro, bok choy, bacon, an egg with sriracha, and lots of strong coffee. He didn't even care that Elaine had cancelled. She'd be over tonight. Özgür had this bright day to himself. A green idleness insisting on ease. Even the Golden State Freeway with its Sunday traffic seemed like a river. Even if the L.A. River with its river of drought seemed like a warning. Making of last weekend's storm something that could never be.

Farther down was Frogtown. A whole different kind of warning: bags of drugs, bags of cash, one perp in an ICU, guarded around the clock, if he ever wakes up, though word was it would be a long watch. And he was the lucky one. Two others came up dead, including a fed. Plenty of news trucks, municipal scrutiny. Hands full over at Area 11. ∷ **Northeast Division** ∷ ∷ *Area* ∷ Özgür doesn't envy them. To think there was a time when he'd have craved involvement.

And that was when, in one of those nothing-in-particular nowheres, amid brush, trees, borders of concrete, a door of nothing on hinges of nothing swung wide, as if pushed by a stare, released by a question, revealing two eyes aflame with summer light.

Özgür didn't even see the cat. He caught only the movement of animal evasion, maybe the vague whip of a tail. And then, as soon as that blink — reflecting the sun, besting the sun — winked out, nothing remained but a possibility. No smile for sure, because it was no Cheshire, and Özgür sure was no Alice.

At least Elaine doesn't text. She calls just as the water starts to boil. Spaghetti alle Vongole near ready, artisanal pasta, canned clams but the right can, a wedge of Parmesan sweating on the counter, and in the sink, up to its neck in water and ice, a bottle of late harvest Donkey & Goat Chardonnay called Wayward. Elaine loves her whites cold. She wants her mouth to shiver.

"Sorry doesn't count, and I know this is our Sunday, and I'm still not finished, and I'll make it up to you. I promise—"

He stops her there.

"We're too together to have to promise."

"That's my detective."

As with promises, so with stories. The only question is whether they arrive kept or already broken.

At least Elaine never insults Özgür with excuses about lost car keys or a BlackBerry. Özgür can't stand the lie of the misplaced when what's misplaced is the courage to find a truth. He would have hung up.

But Özgür never hangs up on Elaine because Elaine never lies like that. If she lies at all. Özgür's never caught her. Sometimes he wonders if what keeps him interested isn't the sex but the dumb suspicion that how Elaine misrepresents the world is far beyond his abilities to detect, which considering his profession both galls and entices him, especially since the implication then is that the only one misrepresenting the world is Özgür himself.

Elaine had even written on that very possibility once:

> *Where identity's at stake, the unconscious keeps attempting to create a blind until it succeeds in fortifying one beyond the abilities of the intellect to parse. We cannot mentally accommodate the vastness of the variables we daily inhabit. So we invent a self we believe can.*

"Though none can. Not even you, Oz." Her margin note.

> *Which more crucially posits: it is not belief that necessitates the self, but rather the other way around. It is the creation of the self that necessitates belief.*

But when Özgür asked what she meant by belief, Elaine had just smiled and before going down on him, whispered: "Let me show you."

Not what she sounds like now: disappointed, tired, contrite.

Özgür lets her go with half-hearted promises about a riding crop next time. Who is he to get in the way of a conference in Reykjavík in June? Elaine had used points to upgrade her ticket to business class. "I'll finally sleep."

But Özgür is far from sleep. It doesn't help that before they hang up, Elaine makes him promise to keep his promise about a riding crop.

One glass of cold down and he still can't look at the counter without seeing Elaine's long legs up on his shoulders, the steam rising from the pot, slivers of ice hardening her nipples, her famous Asian flush burning up her cheeks until her lips burn up too. And maybe it's this crowding in of what won't have been that imposes another love, likely his greatest, on a trip following the Rhine, down to Basel, were they even in their mid-twenties?, his motorcycle parked by the road, the barest of trees blocking the rush of traffic, empty picnic tables drawing pigeons, and all her blond hair cascading over the gas tank as she kept arching back. They swore they would never stop doing it again, driving on in the rain then, in search of what is ever enough.

Özgür resets the table for one, lights a candle, hand grates the cheese, and puts on Dizzy Gillespie :: The Verve & Philips Small Group Sessions, 2012 ::. What a trumpet can mean is what he needs now, but on "Willow Weep for Me" it's Junior Mance on the keys that leads Özgür to finish the Wayward and ask himself something else.

A finger of Lagavulin doesn't help. Thinking of retirement deserves another finger. Index or middle makes no difference. At fifty-seven, Özgür knows he's not yet done but still feels helpless in a way that makes him cork the bottle up tight, double rinse the glass, and find his way to the bathroom to floss his old teeth in the mirror, twice. Is this what desire looks like when it ends?

Because he can no longer avoid facing that things have started to lose their charge. Movies, books, fucking, even solving cases. Sad to say, even music. His body no longer responds with that jittery elation which after every burst of fulfillment should demand more. So how is it that Özgür doesn't want more and at the same time is unsatisfied?

When did fire cease its surprises?

At Rampart Station, the watch commander waves Özgür through with a "Good morning." Upstairs, LT mumbles something about Abendroth looking for him. Özgür opens a card at his desk. It's from Milo Lugardo. Almost a decade ago, Özgür had collared the killer of Milo's brother. Milo still sends Özgür a card once a year. It used to come around the time the presiding judge had handed down consecutive life sentences, but since becoming a Buddhist priest, Milo's cards no longer arrive tied to dates or even seasons. Just thanks. And a saying.

The best marksman finds the center
by forgetting the center. There is no center.
The marksman left long ago.

Özgür slides it into the drawer with the rest.

Captain Abendroth isn't around when Özgür knocks on his door. He returns to his desk past the case file cabinets. All sorts of murder books are out. Strange. Maybe slated for storage?

Özgür is about to follow up with Planski when Detective Kasch comes by with a question that answers Özgür's question about the mess. D-I here wants to know how to handle an FBI agent sent from Northeast Area to follow up on the Frogtown bust. LT, though, has disappeared along with the captain.

Özgür half expects to find one of those imbeciles he ran into with Florian. But Ire Slind is a stranger. He thinks the connects are in boxes. FBI databases can access anything on LAPD computers but none of this stuff has seen the digital light.

"Memo Bartolo Maestro," Ire Slind explains. "He was homegrown. Looking to find some of his friends."

"He could wake up and tell you everything himself?"

"That's usually how it happens, but in the meantime they have new guy, me, to put on the paper trail."

"Wasn't there a deceased?"

Agent Ire Slind drops his eyes.

"Foreign national. No name as of yet."

"Not so surprising, yeah?" Kasch chimes in. "I mean that shipment? So big, yeah?" How is it possible that an intellect of such proportion has thus far slipped Özgür's notice?

"Do you know what kind of drugs?" Özgür asks Slind.

"Not the usual stuff," the agent answers. Is there a hitch for even saying that much?

"Hear of something called Synsnap?" Özgür presses.

"Like I said, I'm just the new guy here," Agent Ire Slind smiles, hitchless now, even adding a happy shake of his head. "But even what I know I don't know."

Which is as close to a wink as it gets without asking for a date. He'll have a long career if he can keep his smile this easy. Özgür gives him his card. Sets Kasch up to play guide through the back rooms, 6th Street side, loaded to the ceiling with case boxes.

"Know anything about that murder mess down in Long Beach?" Özgür asks before leaving. "Three dead kids in a bathroom with some kind of computer circus filling up their place?"

No hitch on that one. Forget a wink. Agent Ire Slind is just in from Arkansas. Never even heard of Long Beach.

When he gets her on the phone, ready to discuss a possible connection at the United States Attorney's Office, Planski basements his hello with her news: her CI has disappeared.

"It's happened before. I'm hoping it's like before."

"I'm sorry."

"If they were model citizens, they'd be us."

But before he can bring up Synsnap, Captain Abendroth is standing by his desk. And he's smiling. If that's not a warning.

He leaves behind a strange character who at once sits down beside Özgür, scoots his chair in close, even leans in, like he's ready to whisper, except his voice is nothing like a whisper — full, warm, without an "r" in sight.

"I'm Iswaeli."

Yonah Kalevshir Warlock is about Özgür's age. Soft-eyed and round like a Halloween cauldron full of candy. Everything he says too comes off soft-eyed and round. Overflowing too with the twinkle of something else. And this in spite of telling Özgür he's military. A lieutenant. Or ex-lieutenant. He'd outrank Özgür in the IDF. ∷ Israel Defense Forces ∷ At LAPD who gives a shit.

The ex-lieutenant has come all the way from Tel Aviv in search of some fugitives supposedly living in Hollywood.

"Or Echo Pawk."

"That's Northeast Division."

"Or Owange County."

"I can get you those numbers."

Özgür keeps smiling. Abendroth's smile, though, must be bigger. He should have known by the name. Warlock, or "wa'lock" as the ex-lieutenant pronounces it, is hardly Hebrew.

Though this Mr. Warlock eventually addresses.

"It's my pwofessional name. It means 'bwoken twust.' A weminde' of what unda all conditions I must avoid. Not only am I not afwaid of iwony, I unde'stand its motivating fo'ce."

Apparently the ex-lieutenant had started his post-service days by hunting Nazi war criminals, working with the likes of Serge and Beate Klarsfeld as well as Efraim Zuroff, with whom he met regularly in Efrat where they drank tea and, while the "winter sun weddened over Wimon," discussed at length the ongoing mystery of Aribert Heim, Egypt's possible complicity, or various USOG ∷ Undead Servants of Genocide ∷ still at large. At the time, Zuroff was planning to head to South America to track down a man who had executed Jews by injecting them with gasoline. Warlock, however, had already reasoned several years earlier that with Nazis in dwindling supply it made better sense to join BA'AL GOMER ∷ Battling Angels Against Living Genocides of Modern Eras ∷. So Warlock had started with Cambodian sadists, then Serbian monsters. Sudan and Syria would remain on the table for some time. Any world region was open to scrutiny and no fugitive of justice was immune.

Which is about as close to making a point as Mr. Warlock ever gets.

With smile intact, if only for Abendroth, Özgür draws this ridiculous meeting to a close and only hands over his card after much insistence. The amiable man seems overjoyed. He even suggests they take in some sights together.

"I've also always wanted to visit Unive'sal City."

"You wanted to see me?" Özgür asks from Captain Abendroth's doorway.

"Oz, you pulling the pin or not? Got a call from a retirement counselor at Personnel Division complaining that you blew off your appointment again."

"I got busy."

"I know. Calls from Southwest haven't stopped."

Good old Balascoe.

"Even this morning I get to hear about you giving some FBI the treatment down in Harbor Area like a week ago."

"He deserved worse."

"What were you even doing down there?" Abendroth holds up a hand. "I don't care. What about today?" Abendroth holds up his hand again. "Northeast? Hollenbeck? What are they gonna call me about?"

"I make friends wherever I go. Made a new one just now. Thanks to you."

Captain Abendroth finally grins. "You deserved that. This too: I'm promoting you."

"You know I've no interest in being LT here."

"Not LT. And not here. Look Oz, you're good police. Hell, even the ones who hate you don't doubt that. But as life gets older, it's hard enough to have to also put up with your" — the captain stumbles here — "your lack of courtesy."

Courtesy? Is that what this is all about? When did justice get sidelined for that *c* word?

"I'm transferring you to West Bureau. Hollywood. You can retire from there if you want or get your star on the sidewalk or both. Congrats."

Özgür can't say it doesn't sting. Especially when Kasch won't make eye contact later. Whatever Özgür can figure out on a sidewalk on MLK, he still has no clue about when it comes to how an office works. Some police. By the time he sits down all he has in his head is everything he missed. Cletious Bou's boy. Florian's 187s. And he misses Elaine.

The folder Warlock left behind on his desk worsens the sting. Might as well be a Harry Bosch or Hole book. Maybe that's exactly what he needs. Maybe that's why he opens the folder. A single piece of paper inside, with a fiery orange paperclip holding nothing together, makes it clear Warlock is no Connelly or Nesbø. Just three names. The bodies in Long Beach.

Yuri Grossman.

Eli Klein.

Jablom Lau Song.

449

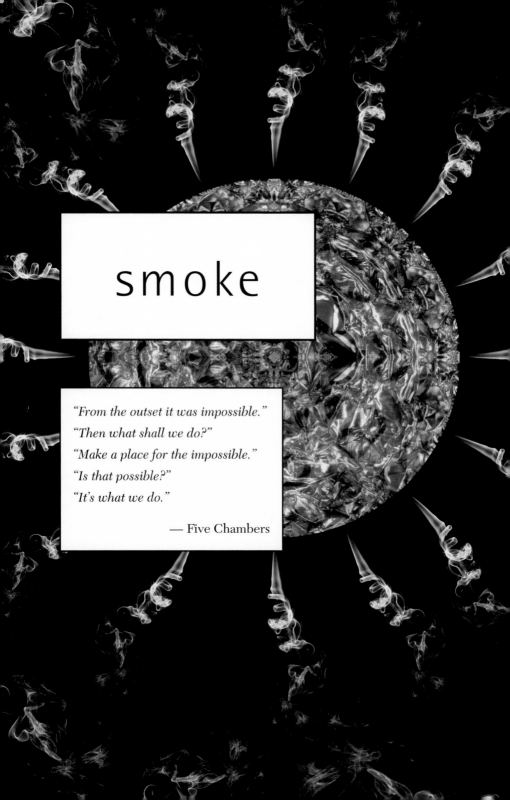

smoke

"*From the outset it was impossible.*"
"*Then what shall we do?*"
"*Make a place for the impossible.*"
"*Is that possible?*"
"*It's what we do.*"

— Five Chambers

no kooning off this fright, lah. o what has jingjing done? wakes

wild, kay malu. not even for how he blew cash. for three days now

they chiak chow but she just pang chui lao, lah. eh, mebbe stare

some at his eye so macam puffpuff and bruised.

jingjing free his hammock. pat face. hunt shoes.

not even about cat. shadows just shadows just light missing light.

jingjing slip swift to lift. but stop shy the sky. take stairs then.

make sure no nosy calyx dwellers come tail him.

rooftop empty. sticky night keep most lock to aircon and fans.

up here only mosquitoes whine. let em whine. worse when quiet.

jingjing padpad past honey jars and clock springs, squat by old

planter box, digging through butts and beer caps. not even dirt

this, this dust. elbow deep, deeper, where jingjing left it, mosqui-

toes diam lah then, as he pull free small pale balloon.

back in flat, jingjing hunt for a better place to hide it. too sure

this time he would find sign that void deck folk knew, or planter

box moved, or just gone.

but not so easy to find safe place for balloon. hammock won't hide

air. a kettle might tattle. yesterday the great tian li threw on the

floor anything with a handle. no more reason than just the doing.

for same reason fridge isn't safe. cupboards too. or bottom of rice

bag when rice might cover floor. that two days ago. jingjing look

high look low but not believe he sneaky enuf. in toilet tank only

takes one leak. any tricky place oreddy obvious. damn chia lat

hiding. macam blue acorn in palm. only one place sure.

from drawer next to stove, jingjing tear out foil. no zippo but

burner fine, angry snake coil. palms kay wet. jingjing half wish half

bet auntie turn up, borrow him some scorn. like jingjing worrage

she even wake. has ears. drool music endless from her room.

454

"我们如何在忘不了的充实中记得这种空虚？"

∴ How do we remember this emptiness so in fullness we won't forget? ∴

asked once, when emptiness was the worst. why ever he want to

remember that? jingjing can't remember that part. oreddy misre-

membering something. always misremembering something.

jingjing squat down on floor. sway dumb like some willow,

clutching both elbows, like elbows ever be corners of jilo. leaves

balloon in front pocket. fishes out from back pocket ziploc instead.

unseals with thumbnail, then tender-slow slides deck out. runs

fingers along ragged edge. comfort here of years. they'll decide.

naga. around mountain. coils churning an ocean of milk called

amrit. ∴ **Nectar granting immortality.** ∴ what by memory of taste wake

up idea: when the last time auntie have milk?

hot night air feel good on jingjing's face. barely traffic. jingjing

have all night. get him back to estate. find 23. sell back balloon.

sure can do. take loss. get back enough from boss to bring tian li

bowl of milk. for sure wake her up for a sip.

happy like a bird! jingjing padpad until he really skip! steam until

can die! better than smoke. has jingjing ever felt so free? got in

his pocket a balloon he gonna make a hole. fill with right change.

close call that one.

jingjing end up at marina bay sands. sweat and shiny. odor powderful. detour seemed obvious back when he took it. too qi zao ba zao for 23, the whole puzzle floor too much before dawn.

in singapore just two seasons: outside and inside. hotel lobby is winter. a hollow cool rising floors up. gold and silver on thinnest wire float overhead like ice storm. makes sense to go to casino until storm blows over.

at entrance jingjing see he the damn pah chiao one. ropes snake to counter, security check. before any chance at hiss of roulette, poker machines, fortunes of chips, jingjing must show ic. and then, good citizen, for responsible gambling social safeguard, fork up hundred sing. jingjing boh lui liao. just a pocket full of changi. tzai si fool. if bodoh in jacket and badge catch jingjing with his pale blue stash he kena rotan one or worse. smiles at jingjing too until two more ya ya papayas step up.

jingjing ke belakang pusing such snakes. padpad back to ice storm, got to get back to 23. runs straight into his jude boys, bow ties on bare skin, between buttons and hem, nipples and navels, pink pearl, copper azure. his twins! skin smooth as smiles still cool. cocoa cherry with them too.

"Уже уходим," jingjing blurt. "Не прёт."

"your luck just changed," pink pearl smiles.

"ours too," cocoa cherry frowns. her hair no longer just bleached. streaked tonight with jade and sea.

"ku dé ta," copper azure seems pleased. "come along."

"it's a private party," cocoa cherry holds scowl.

but jude boys take jingjing on both sides, lift him up, floor now clouds, feet floating along, like breeze casual as glances, only

settling in lift heading straight to the top, 57 floors up, highhigh-high. new dances. friends forever. kissaholic each other's breath, back of jingjing's throat together, like he yang-or one, they three one, lah. cocoa cherry grunt one, inside out.

"this one armani," pink pearl tease. wah piang. "you seen 15?"

jingjing shake head, kia ka lau sai for seeing so little of even less.

"melvin lee?" copper azure say. "maybe shaun tan?"

"you need to see 15," pink pearl whisper, pressing that silky chest against jingjing, knows need is the best secret.

"i wonder what happened to the kids?" pink pearl bets no one.

"they us," cocoa cherry answer. "grown up."

"no," copper azure add suddenly, sad to death. "they him."

"this toot?" cocoa sputter.

"jingjing!" jude boys squeeze in tight.

they know his name!

"we thought we lost you," pink pearl murmur ear, hand slide like a

tickle to jingjing's low back.

"where'd you fly to?" copper azure tickle other ear, stereo jude,

stereo fingering jingjing's hips.

"fb us brother."

"parcel thought us blarder."

"be our friends."

"be our family."

if both boys bleary gaze, heads nodding like stone. jingjing not so

damn fool to ignore tone. saht saht boh chioh mebbe pill haze.

cocoa cherry dart lift first, pink pearl and copper azure link arms

next, follow half so fast, jingjing last, shuffling heavies, feet

suddenly roots, a hanging garden, a different rooftop. this rooftop

has security rope, barring club, barring infinity pool, barring but

glimpse of skyscape wider than even zhong's palace, that balcony,

bird's-eye view. jingjing's roots dying up on air.

his trio unpockets phones then, bright colors, brighter glows,

faces gleamy in gluey blue, waiting in the queue their turn to slip

through. but what glow jingjing have to unpocket? only palest

blue. jingjing would share it too, for sure. mebbe not with cocoa

cherry, oreddy past clipboard. twins though might love him for one

puff, that's lurf, or feel damn sayang, or, worse lah, pui chao nuah

over something so scary. raeden wed to his bed, mebbe dead.

"name?" security boy with clipboard ask. jingjing near opened his

hand too, like by sweaty palm, one balloon, he got license.

"with—" who? twins long gone, without bye-bye or looksee behind.

"jingjing?" because they remembered his name, right? heart race.

security boy scan list, shake head, purse lips, macam jingjing damn

gone case.

"yau mo gau chor?" jingjing mistake.

"sorry?" security boy looking past jingjing now, at new arrivals, for

security men to signal over.

jingjing not that slow, gostun for lift, lobby floor, leaving aircon

season for sticky morning, bay breeze not enuf to relieve jingjing

from the lightest thought, this never mattered, not here, not her,

not the cat, not anything jingjing could ever have, never had.

hours later, when hunger matters, if for fatigue, jingjing never

want to eat again, just slow down, curl up, fade by a beautiful

saga tree, never fading, in patch of grass, scattered oreddy with

curly pods, bright red seeds like another broken promise over what

can never feed, jingjing squat down instead, hips low, high knees,

some mangkuk him, ah beng not even, and moan, groan, ohm,

what does it matter, mebbe python fall on him, corkscrew him up,

crush his groan, moan, ohm, swallow jingjing whole, with pale blue

balloon too, and in this way python becomes tall man, shed off old

skin, forgets name, walks away another path, one never imagined

before, not by any snake, and mebbe then, if not his name, lah,

jingjing would remember another life once cast off.

tap on shoulder comes as the snake. the weight of an emptiness

breaking what no damn python, damn jingjing will ever eat. one

damn bangla standing over him. with tin cup too. for jingjing. four

bangla on lawn have same cups, passing around too a thermos

of soup. without a word share thick pour of curry and lentils. no

spoon. tear pieces of pratas kept warm in foil. sop up like so their

break. pass around then pint of ben and jerry's, half that much,

not even that much, of cherry garcia. just fingers too for this

creamier soup. sweetest milk jingjing's ever had. did fullness ever

empty so fast? tears smash cheeks. won't stop. banglas won't turn

to phone glows though. sing instead, soft, low, words jingjing can't

know, in another life, a longer life, would have liked to know.

back at commonwealth calyx, void deck folk nowhere in view.

jingjing sit down at table, hands together, like he still hold that

warm tin cup. what does it matter? jingjing's mind made up, made

up long before he even ditched the flat, always unright, what

every mind hides, when it comes to true appetite, always knowing

he'd come back, with one pocket lumped up with anything but

cash, and never a brown bag with a dairy carton inside.

"hallo? an chua? okay, jingjing?" lau jerry ask, gentle strange, like

they ah kah liao now.

mebbe no falling python here but jingjing still scan quick for

delson, cahu, or arysil. spencer coming on his back. watch pocket!

hide! but void deck stay empty. just lau jerry with one wet eye,

offering jingjing a tube.

"kaleidoscope," lau jerry smiles. "sometimes we need what we face

made into colorful nongsngse."

jingjing take toy. look through. turn and turn.

"we know auntie," lau jerry continues. "years now, lah. we see her change. life happens, jingjing. age never a pretty thing."

jingjing throw down damn tube, stalk off.

he will never need lau jerry, any of them.

or her. look at her

the great tian li still kooning, drooling. off her pallet too. at least that's something new. jingjing drag her back on. light as a bird. slips a tiny pillow under her head. lighter than a bird's bone.

the bath he gives her is just with warm cloth. dabs of rubbing alcohol on her shoulders, fragile arms, back of knees, between toes.

light as all alone.

in kitchen pans and kettle back on floor. mugs too. and bowls. at least stove isn't on. rice crunch under jingjing's feet. is raw rice what she tried to eat?

auntie eating still shocks just to think. appalls lah.

jingjing can't even climb into hammock. squat before worldwall not looking at any place. every dream there erasing oreddy every claim on any future. jingjing cheeks not wet this time but kay hot. for him future hold only this for sure: soon auntie go, lah.

and for first time jingjing understand last week's loss. what he see now all around, anyplace, in hum pah lang, face it with every wall, corner, across any floor, behind every door, down their short hall: tian li has nothing left, no riches, near no home. tup pai lai dat one. except for that cat. cat was only thing she could have passed on. to jingjing. but cat oreddy long gone.

jingjing tear foil sheet in half. fold square like low pyramid, or

shallow hat upside down. jingjing tap balloon. a third at first. if

this like raeden's batch less might not send jingjing all the way

up lorry lor. but is halfway up any better? jingjing tap out second

third. or a little up? tap out rest. mix powder. set goop on burner.

out of more foil jingjing shape a tube, wide enuf to disappear both

lips. beats lau jerry's kaleidoscope. that thing show same awful

world, jingjing's world, through and through.

here color go blue and silver first, with heat on full below, foil

tube hovering just over, as jingjing wait for bubbles, wait for paste

to burn off, when it goes white, char, release vapor.

this the moment for auntie to rise, in deathly way of hers, silent,

terror on one shoulder, tail flicks bad as black exploding both her

eyes, worse than any shadow eating shadows, to slap aluminium

waste from jingjing's hands. siao liao! siao liao! lan lan, hah!

only the great tian li doesn't rise, forget cry, even snore.

then jingjing tastes it. oreddy in his lungs.

he holds it. forever. steam.

forever keeping evering.

smoke smoke

jingjing whole again. never before so whole. even forever holding.

"我们如何在忘不了的充实中记得这种空虚？"

this how we lose emptiness so in fullness we forget.

Better Forgotten

You already have her . . . in you.

— *Doña Queta*

Stab. Stab. Stab. Too many to count. Each second a hundred sticks. More. Dank fucking drip. Luther's black permanence. Jabajabajabajaba so fast it's a whine. Jabajabado! Never through.

Luther's la llorona is easy at it. But he feels her doubt. Beneath that flat smile. Reeking. He's the one got a needle chewing up his chest and Pina's the one with her forehead gone wet.

Luther grits teeth to a grin. Pain giving his cock some lift. Some fucked-up loco shit, this. Wants Nopales with his fist in her mouth, eyes bugging white because he won't take it out. Or that IHOP thing, knees stained, serious hurt photo-chopping her face. Luther's hard now. Fuck Viagra. Stiff like his never gonna fade.

Piña drags the back of her wrist across the top of her lip. Sweat there too. And she ain't even started tonight's work. Just giving his dog a fix up first, his dangerous beast snarling over the right pec, nipple for one eye, bullet scar for the other. Between them one more hair.

And that hair just a last night thing, no big thing. People friendly. Tweetie just scooped it up, already purring when he handed it over.

"Stupid huh?"

"Stupid can get smart," Luther answered. "Not smug-stupid though. This here's smug-stupid. This here's done."

Luther had hurled the gato at the building wall. Not even a yowl. Just the hard thud followed by the softer sound as the collared thing slid to the ground. No need for Tweetie to boot heel the head like he done.

"Just one?" Piña chides. "Quitting pussy?"

No answer's warning enough. Especially where this oily passion's concerned. The reaction that never changes. Each time he sees one. Sidewinding an alley, on a stoop, mocking him behind some living room window.

If he could, Luther would race down every one. Charge through glass, break down the door. He's come close.

Mostly, these days, Luther just imagines. Tracks the running shapes he spots from the van, like they know not to slow. Don't want to star in no Luther cat clip. Though last night was so quick it almost didn't happen. Like Lupita says when shit's too unexpected, casi demasiado inesperado, you half miss the wanting part. Luther's nothing but want. Needs his dick wet.

"¡Del otro lado!" Luther suddenly erupts, too abrupt. Even hears hisself insane. Thumps his chest anyway, two fists, gives black nipples a twist. Like go on! Beat these ribs, bang this drum, slap his dog, free forever ago, chain divided on one inky heart, slashed in half. "Bonle homes!" Luther adds. No joke, if he's saying gay, Luther better get laid.

"You crazy," Piña grins but still swivels her stool away, her rain relaxing with more space.

Tweetie looks up from the TV but only brief. He, Victor, and Juarez fixed on PlayStation. *Grand Theft Auto*, maybe something new. Juarez just wants *Minecraft* to himself. Loves that blocky shit. Plays it for hours. Gets up now, stretches, brings Piña the bong they passing around.

Juarez always surprises the fuck out of Luther. Like here. Reloading the bowl for her too. Making sure Piña gets a good hit. Luther next, bubbling up something greasy, something sweet. Then his boys again, loping beside each, luz still lit, until thumbs for thumbs up, first from Victor, then Tweetie, return to their twitch for control.

Luther's never had that video game itch. Digital restlesses him. Needs a heartbeat, be wild enough to breathe. If it don't bleed, it won't sting and if it don't sting it don't mean a thing.

Like a nurse, Piña strips off the latex gloves. Tosses them in the trash along with cotton swabs dark with ink and blood. Next changes the needles. Squeezes out a new cup of black. Then wipes her hands, rags her face, before tugging on a fresh pair of gloves.

When it comes to edges and points, Piña's fuckin flawless. She the one done them all. Except Tweetie. Piña still offers a cover job on what some travieso did on him in Lompoc. Tweetie says he likes the mess. Reminds him what mess a mountain can also do.

Piña's also the only one Luther trusts to detail his babies. Pinstripe Piña. Zavaleta can wax but only she gets to touch paint to his Roadmaster and Fury.

"You outta room," Piña says now, dabbing disinfectant on this latest cruz invertida, with dots too like broken roots. "No way your neck's getting any thicker."

Luther started years ago. The first one was a thick thing. On the back of his neck, just below the hairline. Soon another. Same. Then another. Until they ran the full ring, smaller ones, thinner ones, starting to fill in the spaces.

Luther's lost count.

"Lifetimes," Piña says, like sometimes she reads his mind.

"Next round fills these patches. Still smaller after that. You'll see."

"How many rounds you gonna go?"

"Lifetimes."

When Piña swivels away later, it's not just her forehead. This time she's drenched in sweat. Luther checks the mirror. Another upside-down cross among the rest but the throb against his throat feels like it could live forever. Over his jugular too. That's Hopi.

Soft quick then, those fragile hands slap through Luther's head. No way his dick can match that pain. Strange. Not even pain. But still hurts. Dick's limp by the time a mind's shovel snaps hands away.

Luther stops Piña from packing up. Let his back speak too. Touch up the letters there. What Luther don't need to see or look for later. Knows by heart. Knows by their pieces. Jabajabado. One more hour of stabs. And whatever throb some niño cachetón brought to life dies again under this placa spanning across the blades of his back, blacker than the widest wings.

After midnight, drinking another beer, wrist itching, some infection still sticking under the skin, Luther understands the ache still hanging in his arms.

Downstairs, Juarez has his own shovel, digging in the bullshit garden that lines the apartment complex. ∴ Luther bought this building a few years ago. ∴ Wants earthworms for some reason. Luther doesn't care so long as he doesn't take off for Evergreen to dig up bones.

Street keeps quiet. For sure different near 3rd and Gage but here traffic from the 60 and 710 give over to the night a river of calm.

Juarez sniffs at some squirm dangling between his nails. Dawg put three fools down. Luther bets no dead turn his head.

Next day he and Juarez cruise the Dodge Avenger north along Soto Street. Slow. Sun peels window tint. AC blasts. Farruko too, *Los Menores,* "Salgo." Luther slows even more on Marengo Street. Slower still to Zonal.

Juarez whips his head back and forth, like maybe now he'll catch a whiff of Memo. Lead them to his room. Hospital's huge. Look for the room with the most machines. Chotas posted in front. Still waiting for that fucker to wake.

Luther knows he just says the word and his perro sucio will go. Die trying. Or get chained and never give up more than a growl.

Luther takes another lap. Not a cruiser in sight. Then San Pablo, past Hazard Park. Maybe Memo's not even back there. Maybe he's locked up tight in these buildings here off to the right.

In Lincoln Park, Juarez takes off for the dirt, needs to run, around the baseball diamond, until that gets stupid, starts hucking rocks like he some pitcher, then he the shortstop, up at bat, batting a thousand, until he strikes his own self out, charges the pitcher.

Two kids laugh at a full-grown man brawling with himself. Like *Fight Club* but a cartoon. "Cállense," their mother keeps saying. Knows

better. But she's too late. Like for Juarez his whole thing was just to wait for just this thing. Goes straight for her. Head wagging side to side. Her kids laugh more but she's not stupid enough to mistake that smile for a smile.

Luther needs a fuckin leash. Tookie's. Barbed wire even. Luther intercepts everyone's future with an air-bat to left field, runs straight at Juarez like he the base. Juarez near back flips, loves it too, loves Luther more. Sprints after him. Swears he'll plomear his ass. Screams at the top of his lungs "¡Me cago en todo lo que se menea!" Luther runs harder. Blows out both their lungs.

By the time they hit the skate park, Luther's done. Juarez, though, has plenty left to burn. Jogs down around the skaters, trying his own tricks, boardless, staple gun, ho-ho, whatever that shit was that Luther once knew, wiping out, ass over head, each time coming up grins.

Luther's still outta breath, squatting low under a tree, when some kid on a BMX hiss too close to Juarez's goof. Luther figures there just flew a good mood. Kid does it again too, this time with hand out and a smile. Juarez slaps the hand, smiles back, scrambles up next to Luther then, finally nothing but hard breaths, and a minute later all snooze.

Eventually they meet up with Tweetie and Víctor at Plaza de la Raza. Víctor smokes cigarettes like he can't help himself. Keeps bringing up Adolfo's truck. Money he owes. Juarez drags Víctor off to pick up Piña. Some plan he got about los tapados and copper.

"Al ratón, homies," Luther waves. Chilo.

But back in the Dodge, Luther gives Tweetie the wheel. Too hot now to get anywhere near that accelerator. Pennies burn up his gums. The only reason his crew be splintering for plans — caminando pipe off construction sites or some new show Piña's promising — is because Luther's rule is descuachalangada.

He had it all. For a moment. Two bins full. Now balloons, even Lupita's mud, is coming up nil. Nieve, la piedra too. Not even pills to stomp on.

"Eswin?" Luther can't help hisself. Teyo's chalán ∷ *assistant* ∷.

Tweetie shakes his head.

In Chinatown, Tweetie says maybe Teyo's the one in trouble. Football Star was some big deal.

"Straight out of Jalisco. Federal district." Big Man shrugs. "I know North Korea better than shit south of here. But from what I hear, that homes was fresilla. Crema y nata."

"¿Fresilla?" Luther grunts. Teeth plating. For not knowing. For being fuckin menso.

"Upper level. All those pinks? Están bien encabronados. Pissed off, homes. Sending an army. Maybe not even Teyo gets off."

Luther swears he smells blood then. He's not wrong. Turns out, here in the middle of sweating mobs, honking cars, city hall within sight, there's an open-air pen, blocked off like it was a garage, probably once was, topped now with concertina and cameras. Luther puts his eye to a crack. In there, big fans. And chickens getting heads twisted off. By hand.

Tweetie isn't thrown that what was before ∷ *The Sleeping Rainbow Snake* ∷ now sells cosmetics. Tweetie finds it somewhere else. Though not even Melissa Torres turns up anything new. Teyo's three brujas got no extra comments.

Even hanging with Chitel for the rest of the afternoon gives up shit. Nopales never shows either.

"She's jerking off old men until she show Lupita respect."

"She down with that?"

"Nopales? Homegirl's zafada. Do anything for a buck. "

That night Luther can't even get Carmelita or Rosario to text back. Almost drives down to Dawgz. To throw down with that shit. Throws down the Durango keys instead, because what counts isn't downtown. Crew needs pockets full of lana. Luther needs pussy better than some brick turning tricks.

But all Wednesday Chitel keeps tight-lipped. Swears he has no clue outta where Lupita marches her tar.

Luther doesn't press. Stays casual. Stays calm. Puts in the hours. Doesn't make like he wants more. Cuts even Tweetie loose.

Let other fools blow up their phones, hound ready-set bitches to come on around, lunchbox their thermoses, suck them all down. Luther practices pause. Sensei Samurai. Steady as a clock. Not one fuckin doubt. Floats between mirrors, follows the block, whatever corner Chitel's about.

And they bounce all over the city. Never hang long. A lot of time a different alambrista.

"But sometimes they repeat," Chitel explains on Thursday over lunch, In-N-Out animal style, chocolate shakes.

"Risky?"

"They got no papers. They point a finger and they get shipped. If they're lucky. Unlucky starts with ours in la pinta. Starts."

"ICE cuts deals." ∴ **Immigration and Customs Enforcement** ∴

"Not good enough to beat fear. Chin chin si . . . "

"A huevo," Luther nods along, even if here's the same song Lupita's been singing for years. "Easier, right, to just get paid?"

"Le diste al clavo," Chitel smiles. Fist bump's all Luther needs to understand.

That afternoon what little talk happens rambles from music — Slipknot, some Los Lobos bootlegs — to sports, Lakers, Clippers, come fall. Or the price of stuff, the drought, these strawberries Chitel's Hondurans and Guatemalans keep selling to cars.

Luther almost brings up Oxnard. Almost tells Chitel to quit Parcel Thoughts.

"Ever el chango?" ∴ Mix of heroin and cocaine.∴ he asks instead.

"Just chiva." ∴ Heroin.∴ Then at 7-Eleven, picking up Red Bull and cigarettes, Chitel adds: "You should see what Miz steps on it with."

"Pancake batter?" Luther grins.

Chitel laughs loud over that. "¡En serio!"

Friday morning, Lupita sends them north of Drew Street, by Forest Lawn. No place for a fruit stand, let alone a balloon stand. And the Armos supposedly buying never swing by. Just some locochón asking about pinks.

"I never seen even one. You?"

"A few."

Choplex-8s never parade the new chemicals. Not even yellows. After last year's pale blue fiasco, marcha fúnebre, Lupita acted like she was a fuckin oracle. Supposedly pinks, though, had finally gotten the mix right.

Chitel rattles off the same rumors they all know. Stuff's from Mexico. Mexicans invented it. Or Bolivians. Or scientists out of Brazil. By lunchtime it's coming out of some Russian lab. By 3 PM a Chinese triad. Denmark by 4 PM. Then a Canadian conglomerate. Canada?! At least that's funny.

No one Chitel knows has ever done it. Luther neither. But knowing don't need doing to know addictive. Fuck sodas, chochos or glass. Even yellows, bad, but not like pale blues, sold fast.

"They say you see stuff," Chitel says. He looks scared.

By late afternoon, Luther sees he's cleared 10Gs. And that's after taking care of the fruit sellers, and making Chitel stick something extra in his shoe. Go get himself some real calcos. No police. No Almoraz sticking his nose in things. Luther feels blessed.

Only one thing had made his skin crawl. Can't say why. Saw her Wednesday. Standing on the edge of Griffith Park. Young black girl. With these long black braids. Thick glasses. Pink Converse scribbled dark.

Then Friday, near MacArthur Park, the same thing, only this one's Latina, black braids, thick glasses, pink Converse scribbled dark.

"Cosplaying maybe?" Chitel said when Luther pointed it out. "Comic-Con's in July."

That night, back at his apartment complex, drinking beers with his crew, Luther keeps drifting out onto the balcony to scan the street below, like maybe here too, just beyond the glow of a streetlamp, dusk just letting go, he might see a similar child slip by.

Instead someone else comes banging on his door. With Chitel too. Fool better have better than Chitel parked close.

"¿Quiúbole?" Almoraz grins. Like he caught Luther off guard. Dogs got crazy long before cabrón got close.

Luther had driven down to Dawgz for his last stop. Tipped the girls good. Not the tip he needed to lose, the one they keep moaning to bruise down on. But since when isn't cash what bitches crave most? Luther just wanted his boys around. Tookie, Sen Dog, and Chen Chi-Li.

They'd tear Almoraz apart with a word. By the looks of it, Chitel too. But Luther bars them with a shout. Shoves them back with a leg. Only growls keep their stillness in question.

"Heard you had a good week?" Not like dogs gonna make Almoraz blink. Astilla or not, this vato is solid. Luther takes the hug.

"Nose looks good."

Tweetie's long up from the couch. Juarez was clued in even before the dogs.

Almoraz lifts palms. "Just errands tonight, homes. Lupita said to invite you for Monday barbecue. All of you."

Luther nods.

500

"Seriously ese, looks like you got a full night. Just here for the rent. Then we're gone."

Chitel hangs back. Ben Davis shorts again. White socks. Knows this shit is wrong. Dares one look. Almost too quick for Luther to do much with. Nerves for sure. Maybe something else. Like warning Luther to keep cool.

"Get Almo a beer," Luther yells over his shoulder. If Victor's still in the kitchen, Piña's with him eyeing knives. "For this shorty too."

Almoraz shakes his head. Then loud enough for everyone to hear, to get even Victor ready, and Piña picking up knives: "Thirty percent."

Old bitch must love this. Daring Luther to make her rally. And Lupita can still rally.

Tweetie counts $3,300 off eleven grand. Almoraz looks like he's coming. Comes twice. Can't play out any better. Chitel backs out way onto the balcony. Not afraid. Ashamed.

"Not mine, homes. Thirty's yours."

Luther hates how Almoraz knows he has no choice. Even takes Luther up on the beers now.

On Luther's signal, Tweetie hands over the $7,700.

"Later vaquero," Almoraz breezes then. Already out the door. Chitel long gone. And then it's Victor who's not dealing. He wasn't even the one out there pulling down days, but here he is now, can't shut up about Adolfo's truck. Luther has more than enough metal boiling in his mouth to tear down walls.

He laughs instead. Fuck showing he got claimed. Besides, if he'd paid out Adolfo earlier, Luther would owe Lupita now.

So Luther stuffs hands with the $3,300 divide. Four ways, not five. The day Luther scrambles for $825 he'll chew bullets til one uncaps the back of his head. Shots of Sauza next.

"*Call of Duty,*" Luther roars too. Tookie joins in. Pitbull through and through, wags her tail like none of what's angry counts.

"Remember what Lupita used to say?" Luther asks Piña as she refills his glass with more tequila. He's even grinning. Admiration's worth a thousand grins.

"She said lots of shit."

Luther shakes out another laugh, empties his glass.

" 'What's not gotten is better forgotten.' "

Memorial Weekend

"Istalquaal means nothing. It means Americans can't speak Arabic."

— Phil Klay

Anwar keeps having the strangest feeling that his mother is about to call [even though the phones {all their phones} have quieted {‹at last!› Mefisto's prank having run its course ‹like a fever «like a seizure ⟨Xanther had said so herself⟩»⟩ ‹all those demands for strange agencies and common institutions now a thing of the past «the promise of easy cash driving the attack ⟨⌈Mefisto?⌉ what were you up to? ⌈Mefisto!⌉⟩ the absence of cash ending the attack» making Carmen Sacco's advice unnecessary: 'Get new e-mail addresses! Hello Gmail? Phone numbers are easy to change. Trust me. I've been stalked twice!'› ‹proof of their former intern's age «not having the time to 'just update all your peeps' is beyond the imagination of youth»› the time for new addresses and numbers ‹fortunately› not coming} delivering in its place a premonition to haunt the calm].

Astair has been on the landline for the past hour [with her mother too {is that the connection? ‹hardly arresting the presentiment «unless the connection ⟨still reaching out for other reasons . . . ⟩ is false»›}].

The only real disturbance comes from the children. They will not go to bed.

[not twenty minutes ago] Shasti made the first jailbreak. Anwar found her [Freya-less] in the kitchen trying to make a butter sandwich [with the butter too cold to spread {tearing and refolding the bread ‹until it resembled an inedible ball›}{salt all over the floor}].

Freya [Shasti-less] came next. Found in the living room crayoning [on her art pad] the alarm of glass wolves ∷ **Rudyard Kipling.** *The Second Jungle Book.* ∷ on the mantel. Astair [on the couch {still on the phone}] could only grin and shrug [sharing smiles over such sudden {and solitary} artistic determination].

Stern tones were in order but the prospects of a mellow Saturday morning [and Memorial weekend ahead] granted Friday night the looseness it was entitled to.

Anwar tucked them back in. Giggled them with rubs of his cheek [they squealed {it was too rough ‹objecting most when he almost didn't do it again›}].

More than shave [the mirror told him] he needed to see a dermatologist. Bumps [abrasion-like] had begun to populate the underside [of the left side] of his jaw. [if Anwar weren't fifty-four] He'd swear it was acne [the impishly {impossible} suggestion that he and Xanther shared the same genetic disposition]. The rash on his scalp [more significant {because it was invisible?}] was more troubling. Anwar knows his system's answer to stress. He's had shingles before.

Back at his desk no phone rings. No texts. E-mails [{like inert viruses} of no consequence] trickle in. Barely an uptick in his spam folder.

Anwar tabs to Spotify. [soon] Spanish lilts softly from his speakers. He'd [first] considered Farid al-Atrash. Mohammed Abdel Wahab next. Followed by Leila Mourad and Umm Kulthum. Most obvious [the dark-skinned nightingale {العندليب الأسمر}] Abdel Halim Hafez [whom Anwar's father {ever with a wink} always swore Fatima had a deep crush on].

These were the records [voices of vinyl {vinyl of scratches ‹voices beyond vinyl and scratches›}] that Anwar remembers his mother singing along with [in her shy whispery way]. Also Burt Bacharach and Petula Clark [and the one he picks now: Frida Boccara {a French chanteuse who released a series of songs in Spanish ‹Fatima loved 'Un Dia, un Niño' «playing now 《shy of the shyest whisper》»›}].

// When Anwar would escape

        // a long long time ago

    // coos through the living room dark amazed
by his ascent

   // this climb up the bookshelves

        //again

      // as if every shelf were a ladder's rung
      // as if every ladder had a top
      // as if every top held a prize

   // a bottle cradling a wooden ship

      // the glass might as well be the sky
      // the vessel every adventure

          // only put there to be out of
reach

      // his hands
      // at five years or seven or four
      // already marked

        // destroyer of voyages
        // destroyer of skies

// if for the great growl at his back

    // Anwar never even getting two shelves up

        // one?
reaching
        // three?

// as his father roared past his mother into
// a living room already blinded with light

    // on Shenouda's lips

        // 'هوده ألطريقه بتاعتك؟'
        // 'فناء خلاص؟'

// a burning twinkle in his eyes

// that delight

      // each time denying Anwar his prize
      // 'هو كدة إزّاي تخرب السماء بتعتك!'

// in his big beautiful arms like a bear's big as earth

    // in both their beautiful arms
    // greater than any earth

    // with smiles greater than beauty

      // whirling him around
              // forever

// forever on their lips

'العفريت الصغير بتاعنا.' //

'الراحله بتاعنا الصغير.' //

'ماعزه الجبل بتاعتنا.' //

// his father's face more bearded than any goat

// kissing Anwar's cheeks eyes forehead

'الرحله دي فوق، //

الرحله دي بتاعتي!' //

                              // Fatima too

reaching

                              // to kiss him more

// retucking sheets as tight as a hug

// to last a thousand nights

// shy-whispering that song

      // *Al dibujar la estela de una estrella*
      // *La seguirá hasta el fin y verá el confín*

Anwar finding for his tears [wiping them away {hurriedly}] only bills [care of online credit card sites {all neatly tabbed ‹ALL!›}]. So much owed. That ridiculous sheepskin dog bed. Two visits to the vet. Anwar's donation to the Jaguar Corridor Initiative. [at least] Days away loomed another round of managing their credit card debt. Anwar should cancel [at once] the monthly Spotify cost. He does. Like that helps. More costs loom in a week [rent etc. etc. {utility costs etc. etc. ‹food costs etc. etc. «gas etc. etc. ⟨school etc. etc. ⌈etc. etc. [etc. etc.] [etc. etc.] etc. etc.⌋ etc. etc.⟩» etc. etc.› etc. etc.} etc. etc.].

Against which [these numerous tabs of debt] stands one lone page [all they have at Chase {extant funds ‹plus anticipated cash flows› beyond dwindling}].

Anwar is only checking their balance for a surprise. Ha! The imbalance remains the worst surprise.

[at least] He got Cataplyst-1 working [`unsigned int objectPoolMax = 0, atsaCnt = 0;` {just one ‹of many›}]. A brutal [tedious] project [not exactly helped by his own {‹inept› numerous} oversights]. [fortunately] The tonal traps worked [revealing the {many} errors left to correct].

Uploading to Enzio's server took only minutes [but they had yet to acknowledge receipt {Anwar had submitted the finalized version a couple of days ago too ‹along with the invoice›}]. Anwar wasn't sure what they were expecting. Maybe someone at Enzio had once mentioned game [though none of their e-mails used that word]. What [finally] unfolded didn't seem anything of the kind.

Cataplyst-1 just sat there.

Nothing to chase. Nothing to run from. No way to play. Unless not playing was the point. Not even a way to go. Unless not going was the point. [for the life of him] Anwar had no idea what was going on.

It was [however] doing something. There was something to see: a curvature of sorts [though if it was a lens {what it revealed}] offered little more than a curious cloudiness [{grey and blurry} beyond par{‹t›‹s›}ing].

[for want of anything better] Anwar had settled on a bowl theory [as in fishbowl {this being the start of some sort of entertainment where the player began as a gilled captive ‹FPG «First-Person Goldfish»›}].

Maybe too pat [it was beyond disproving {if not worth proving}]. Not Anwar's problem. [maybe?] What made maintaining [t]his attitude difficult was [t]his vital sense [Anwar sensed] that something other than [merely] visual output was now operating.

A series of portal prompts [{‹it turned out to be› thousands!} all of which Anwar had to disable] had kept trying to access invalid IPs [{MMORPG? ‹Massively Multiplayer Online Role-Playing Goldfish?›} every address a dead end {at least as far as Anwar ‹or the game«?»› could figure out}].

That was one part that put Anwar on alert [this desire for greater {outsourced‹?›} connectivity].

And then there was the other part: [as much as *so* much of it was strange {pieces beyond pieces ‹hinting at a whole «beyond the whole ‹no assembly ever required›»›}] Anwar couldn't shake the feeling [like the feeling that his mother was just about to call {everything in that *just*}] that he'd seen this all once before.

Downstairs: Astair's laughter [desk phone still reading LINE IN USE]. Follow the laughter [Anwar thinks? {like a command line he ‹with pleasure› obeys}].

[flicking off the office lights] He notices the full printer tray [sheets brightening the dark {‹the question of what's printed› brightening more ‹in inverse proportion to the dark matter›}].

That's right. Mefisto's early claim to fame. A PDF of the scanned paper itself [complete with rips and stains {plus ‹by the author himself› a dedication ‹what Anwar can almost hear intoned in some phony British accent «earning a smile ❨⌈because what is represented is never the issue⌋ sometimes a bad accent is precisely the point ⌈good and bad not even half the story⌉❩»›}]:

> *Whatever Spans Time's Roots & Reaches —*
> *May my thanks be included therein/thereout*
> *— for your insight, constancy, and kindness.*
> *You make of Wars a luminous Peace ^{nth}!*
> *May we be all moon, all be on Om!*
>
> *—Love, Meffy*

].

The Psychology of Machines: A Love Letter to Synthia

Anwar had dug up the file that morning. Printed it out. For another morning. Though a few lines catch Anwar's eye now [{and this was a science paper ‹those were the days!›} the poetry of young aspirations {ambitions ‹follies «daring to *know* a future before even asking her name»›}]:

Does the Other necessarily invoke the inevitability of War? If you are like me you are me and so offer no threat. If you are <u>not</u> like me you are <u>not</u> me and so in time will attempt to eliminate me.

Or:

To move beyond all the wounds of Europe, all the hypocrisies of the Americas.

Or:

Language is not infinite because not all variations are meaningful.

Or pure Mefisto:

The only task of any merit: to imagine an intelligence far greater than our own.

[remarkably] Astair is still on the phone [and {even more remarkable} still laughing {almost girlishly}] when Anwar enters the living room with two glasses and a bottle of champagne.

She's off by the time the cork releases itself into his palm with a soft pop [the sound bouncing off corners and walls {a foamless result ‹mist «like match smoke» spirals out of the glass aperture «almost better»›}].

'Sometimes the best cure for self-flagellation—' Astair smiles [sliding to the edge of the sofa {for a kiss ‹wet «with longing?»›}] '—is *real* flagellation. Ah mother! What are we celebrating?'

'I'd dare say you sounded happy?'

'The old witch has a way of making magic-y delight out of bad news.'

Astair's mother [Eustace West {Bea}] has detested Anwar from the start [{likely} to her end {maybe his end might invoke a smile}] but she could be funny.

'Then to your mother.'

'Really?' [Astair asks {taking the glass}].

'We have to celebrate something.'

They finish the bottle. And light candles. And talk in the comfort of something akin to a snuggle [{Astair rarely snuggles} to the soothing rhythms of whispers].

'I got a new topic,' Astair announces [midnight an hour buried].

'Tell me.'

'Starting from scratch.'

'Impressive or appalling?'

'Look what Llewyn just sent me.' Astair takes out an old book [or worn]. 'He must be on board with Eldon Avantine.'

'Should I be surprised you're not fighting?'

'Disappointed too?'

'Not at all.'

'I figure if I'm worth only one paper, I'm not going to amount to much as a therapist. 'Invest in loss' is a Tai Chi adage. Strengthen where you're weakest.'

But Astair has always proved unsettlingly strong when it comes to change [losing lovers {seeking out new surroundings ‹'If they don't like Xanther, fuck 'em. We'll find someplace else that does.' «adjusting to new surroundings» 'And someplace else always does because someplace else is always us.'› making new friends} new lovers]. Her energy is [invariably] intoxicating.

[though] Anwar often wonders if this inability to stay put is also Astair's greatest weakness [what of staying with him {might his turn come? ‹and the children? «Astair would leave life before abandoning them»›}].

'The note is nice.'

[beyond the faded garnet cover {on a page blank as fracturing pearl ‹maybe youth does outlive heartbreaks «and heart attacks ⟨maybe it was never youth to begin with⟩»›}] Llewyn Fabler has written in blue ink:

Books are curious things.
When they want to live, they find a way
to become part of the lives
that need them.

—LF

'Poems?'

'You'll never guess what about.'

Anwar's quick riffle reveals no obvious subject.

'Wait, I'm sorry love, your new paper is on poetry?'

'Cats.'

'Excuse me? That was Fabler's suggestion?'

Astair shakes her head: 'My new advisor's.'

'Then this is a coincidence?' [Lifting up Fabler's present.]

'I doubt it.'

'But the subject?'

Astair nods. 'I'm . . . thrilled.'

'Confuse me some more.' Anwar smiles.

'We've already talked about this. This repulsion to the point of . . . curiosity. But it's pretty simple. If my job is to prompt others to address what they feel most uncomfortable about, how can I, in turn, be unwilling to address what bugs the shit out of me?'

'Xanther's little one?'

Astair smiles [{half winks too ‹Astair's a lousy winker «making every attempt that much cuter»›}]. They clink empty flutes. Sip too. [for an instant] Anwar swears the emptiness tastes like champagne [superior {to the Veuve Clicquot ‹dead in her bucket›}].

[of course] What Astair starts out writing may have nothing to do with what she ends up writing. Anwar still can't forget the technician's warning [at the first animal hospital they visited . . .]. [fortunately for the moment {at least}] Xanther's charge keeps breathing [if walking still seems a sideways fall ‹but by a crisscross of legs «or Xanther's loving palms» barely keeping him standing›}].

Saturday morning starts with Xanther already up [{when does she ever get up before them? ‹these days consistently›} at the stove preparing kitten formula].

The feedings themselves are difficult to see [with what matters most always lost {under Xanther's hunched form ‹beneath her eclipsing arms «behind that dancing baby bottle›}]. Anwar swears most of the milky liquid winds up on the swaddling towel [as if the thing had no interest in food {what it's so badly in need of ‹Xanther must see the ribs poking out? «a cage of endings ⟨encaging his daughter's heart⟩»›}].

[by contrast] Xanther eats all the time [does she look wan too {ragged even ‹at least depleted›}]? Do her eyes match this collective gauntness [hollows {like grey stones} marking some kind of withdrawal]?

[even if {at the sink ‹washing out the baby bottle «with the kitten ⟨cat?⟩ on her right shoulder»›}] She is nothing but cheery and loquacious. [in fact] Their conversation is so easy [that while helping to dry the various parts {from nipple to bladder ‹impossible to dry›}] Anwar decides to [FINALLY!] bring up what happened at the shelter.

And then Shasti and Freya wander in [and in unison warble out {quiver ‹really›}]: 'People are dying.'

Isla Vista.

[over the next hours] Numbers follow an uncertain dance [a few dead {no wounded} more wounded {more dead}] before finally settling ∷ *This was never a dance . . .*∷

517

on seven dead and seven wounded. The news reports
'a premeditated mass murder' ∴ KTAL 5 News.∴. The
shooter had relished the killing ahead ∴ **'I'll take great
pleasure in slaughtering all of you.' CNN transcript
of YouTube post.** ∴. The shooter was twenty-two. He
drove a black BMW. The drive-by [what it was being
called] took place near UCSB [University of California
{Santa Barbara}]. The shooter may have been a student
somewhere else. ∴ **SBCC Santa Barbara City College** ∴
His name was Elliot Rodger.

Then the killings became more than a drive-by.
People were stabbed previously [those were male].
People were shot [those were female {one male}]. [in
a YouTube clip from Rodger {‹which Anwar didn't see›
which Astair relayed}] Most of the hate was directed at
women [though Asians and blacks{?} were in there too
{100,000+ words of hate ‹enough to fill any volume›}].

The twins had found out from Astair [who had
been on the phone with colleagues {‹they had patients›
‹she had patients› how was this going to affect their
care?} Astair unaware of how quickly her whispered
alarm had sent Freya and Shasti to the kitchen to
amplify alarm {Astair then spending the rest of the
morning trying to distance her girls ‹from the news «of
horrors up north»›}].

Xanther mostly talked it over [on her phone] with
Kle [a little disquieting {if not surprising ‹that he was
the one to call›}] She seemed to take it in stride [she had
the cat to look after]. Anwar [though] got no e-mails or
calls on the landline [{his lot ‹jaded›} as expected].

[and despite whatever disgust {and rage} he may
have felt towards the U.S. {bullied by the N.R.A. ‹for-
tified by an amendment due some amending itself›}]
The family soon mellowed into a day of at-homeness
that by afternoon felt nearly relaxed.

518

Astair's mini–trauma-management with the girls leads to games and an elaborate score of giggles and squeals that last for hours.

Xanther rotates between feeding the frail white creature and checking in with everyone. She seems rosy [if increasingly frail {too so for Anwar's liking}]. She roams through the house palm-cupping cellar spiders [{‹harvestmen› daddy longlegs} to return them to the outdoors].

The evening's a drowsy sprawl in the den in front of the TV [watching episodes of *The Office* {Astair cooks up a big bowl of popcorn drenched in butter ‹with heaps of parmesan and plenty of truffle salt›}].

Xanther never stops eating.
Or laughing.

They all laugh. And chatter. Anwar has to nudge up the volume to hear the jokes [maybe he's going deaf {even if ‹throughout› he has no trouble hearing what sleeps in Xanther's lap ‹an impossible purr «like something so little could really make a sound so loud and deep ⟨and continuous⟩»›}].

[by comparison] Sunday is a disaster. The thought is to go to the beach [and what a gorgeous day]. Xanther [however] objects immediately.

'You think we're leaving you alone, young lady?' Astair quips.

'I'm not alone.'

Funny [if she weren't {dead} serious].

Zuma [north of Malibu {west of the PCH}] is scrubbed sky and the rote of ocean foam [a trace of cloud {now and then} scudding inland]. A lesson in blues [from slate to haloes of grey] battering up against the sand [and all answering the heat].

Freya and Shasti tear across the beach [Astair zig-zagging after their flying feet]. Xanther [moping along {after everyone}] is surprised by the water [how warm it is]. Anwar goes swimming. Astair wades in up to her waist [with Shasti and Freya on each hip {strangling her neck ‹screaming with each rise of water rolling to shore›}{strangling her more still ‹screaming still louder› when Astair dares retreat back to dry ground}].

Xanther goes in up to her knees. Anwar's sure she smiles.

But at a farmers' market [opposite the Malibu Colony {east of the PCH}] it becomes [painfully] clear Xanther is having anything but fun.

[for a while] Astair and Anwar try to ignore the signs [strolling together {hand in hand} among booths of organic kale and blueberries {almond butters and rum cakes ‹local urchins and New Hampshire scallops›}].

'I think you better check on sister,' Freya says.
'Hurry,' Shasti adds.
Xanther isn't moping or even dragging her feet. She's nowhere in sight.

They find her by the fish stand [holding a bag of ice to her forehead {the vendors looking concerned ‹as well as «terribly» judgmental›}].

521

Memorial Day exacts a similar repetition. Xanther's morning appearance is a beatitude of smiles [countering something greyer {‹can she get any whiter?› as if withdrawing ‹to the point that her acne seems almost a welcome splash of color «and her eyes rimmed in black ⟨hazel⟩ ⟨azure⟩ allways sparking with green and gold» hardly helped by those unwieldy black frames «taped together»› ridiculously thick lenses still magnifying her bewitching focus} her attitude hardly grey {or taped together}] surpassing with delight every parental concern.

Though only when she's home.

With the cat.

[on their way to Taymor's] Xanther's groaning starts up again. Anwar could say the swarm of valets [sprattling around arriving vehicles] distracted him. Or Van Morrison [{"Crazy Love"} on the sound system] drowned out inconvenience. But what stole away his attention came down to wealth.

The estate even quells Xanther's complaints.
'You live here?!' Xanther asks Roxanne [Taymor's daughter].
'Uh, like yeah?'
'How?'

How is right. [plenty of times] Astair has mentioned Ted Trancas' fortune [Anwar's seen by the car{s} Taymor drives {the earrings she wears ‹the shoes›}} money is not in short supply] but he has never visited their residence.

In the heart of Bel Air.

For starters: garage[s{?}] bigger than their Echo Park home. Wings and bungalows [presumably for guests {maybe with a studio or two}] hide in [or emerge from] a lush landscape of brooks and koi ponds. The main structure [low {and disappearing on either side into groves of Black Oak}] spans the narrow canyon it overlooks [dominates].

The design is modern [{apparent on every surface ‹it's expensive to hide?›} the weird cost of minimal]. Lines are clean. Angles sharp. Verticals [sheathed {in blond wood}] support the long horizontals [steel {gutterless ‹the roof itself a rise of green grass›}] while cement floors everywhere glisten [like {polished} water].

Living room to kitchen to a second living room share one glass wall [magically withdrawing {for these festivities} to open the house out onto an impossibly flat {and impossibly green} lawn {where children run from a hot dog cart ‹Let's be Frank› to an ice cream cart ‹Sweet Lucie's› to a fortune teller ‹Zanazan Shazam!› and sketch artists ‹and more›}].

[while {everywhere}] An extensive staff [consonant with guests as well as household requirements {which includes security}] moves like a needed breeze [carrying trays {of towels and sunscreen} {or petit fours} {or any drink imaginable ‹to the taste of every age group›}]

[{as if that's not enough} one flight of steps down {laid out on a wide terraced portion of the hill ‹surrounded by palms *and* ferns «and more staff»}] Elaborate grill fixings are arrayed beside the first pool.

[and no matter where you wander] There is no escaping the city below [[always beholding ‹beholden to?›} that blue twinkle of urban struggle and smog framed {here} by honeysuckle and jasmine {and calm}].

Anwar worried that Xanther's unrestrained amazement might earn cruel eyerolls from Taymor's daughter [who {‹though› only a few years older} seems a lifetime along {at least Anwar hopes ‹will he ever let any of his daughters dress in such skimpiness?›} a shred of a sari and bikini top {the cleavage makes Anwar turn away}] but Roxanne does not turn away from Xanther [leading away this child {of paleness and awkwardness} with kind exuberance].

'She's not a beast,' Taymor winks at Astair [who's maybe just as impressed {and distressed?} as Anwar]. 'Just to me. Drink up.'

Ted introduces himself a moment later [he's nothing like his house {gangly ‹even clumsy? «a shirt-tail untucked with cuffs unevenly rolled»}]. He has an alarmingly friendly smile [[{maybe} because he's Anwar's age {older ‹greyer?› for certain} or too tired for words? {but he makes Anwar's presence seem reason for relief}]. And suddenly the house feels practically cozy.

Their patter remains mostly complimentary [i.e. about wives and children] or dilatory [i.e. of no consequence].

[[{unfortunately} at one point] Motive threatens Anwar's thoughts [should he treat Ted as a possible VC for *Paradise Open*? {‹fortunately› the impropriety of this idea stammers speech ‹«anyway» Anwar is not about to risk Astair's friendship with some impromptu plea for money «even if his family needs money!»}]. Not that Ted lingers [leaving as easily as he arrived {greeting other assorted groups ‹in the same relaxed manner›}].

[even in this paradise] Isla Vista haunts the music of new acquaintances.

'Would never have happened if we armed everyone.'

'Make the parents accountable.'

'Jail them!'

Then Gia arrives [Astair's Malibu friend {half something/half something else ‹accent wonderfully 'bizzare-o'›}]. Very tan. Her hair flickers red. She moves like fire [hips flickering back and forth {oldest of the friends ‹but not a step behind «up on everything»}].

525

All she wants is to talk about the West L.A. Animal Shelter. Astair's hand-squeeze warns of a coincidence [not for public {even close-friend} consumption].

Twitter and Facebook feeds [and KTAL] seemed to confirm a gang stunt. Opening all the cages. Many animals still free.

Abigail joins them then [{like tall grass swaying in the day} pert nose and wide Nordic mouth with gapped teeth {green eyes and gold braids}]. She kisses everyone on the cheek [{with Anwar} always both cheeks].

'They have a chance now. Don't those places euthanize the animals no one adopts?' Taymor asks.

'I don't know,' Abigail hesitates.

Anwar knows [lips twitch {to silence knowing}].

'I heard worse this morning,' Gia continues [accepts a drink {confirms twice that blue means non-alcoholic}]. 'They're called canned hunts. Awful! Fat men sitting in lawn chairs shooting animals in a cage. Just so they can hang a head on their wall.'

Abigail and Astair grab drinks too [confirm {twice} that red means alcoholic]. Taymor's already tipsy.

[and then] Astair tells everyone how often Abigail beats her now at *Words With Friends*. And then Taymor is apologizing for the new addition to their group.

'Oh no, he's beautiful!' Astair exclaims [already down on her knees].

'She really is an attack poodle,' Taymor adds.

The black dog winds around everyone [nosing knees {every crotch ‹except Astair's «and Anwar's ⟨?⟩»›}].

And then Roxanne is at Anwar's side.

'I think Xanther's sick.'

[at least] It's not a seizure. [in the car] She says her head feels on fire ['Like, uhm, oh, oh, a forest about to burn down?']. But [if anything] her forehead feels as cold as ice.

'I still want a dog,' Shasti blurts.
'I don't,' Freya counters. 'I want an ostrich.'

And then they're home.
And it's like yesterday after the beach.
Like after the shelter.

Xanther's fine.

[finally {while putting Xanther to bed}] Anwar
brings up the subject.

'Daughter, a not-so-trivial question. Understand
that my only meaning bringing this up now is in the
name of . . . communication and concern.'
'What, uhm, like happened by the cages?'

Anwar nods [the room's darkness almost making this easier {were it not for that paler shadow now
nestled by her side ‹hiding like moonlight in a storm
«waning too ⟨what kind of storm?⟩»›}].

'I don't really know.'
'Was it a seizure?'

Her pillow shakes. Her hair rustles.
But not for an answer.

[despite a parking lot full of luxury cars {«that day» Mercedes and Audis and BMWs «wasn't there even a Tesla?» driven by the kind of people gathering on Ted Trancas' lawn› the upper-middle class at the animal shelter in search of a suitable companion}] Anwar now sees the oversized sports jerseys and baseball caps [shading sunglasses {shading dark faces ‹soon hooting «at all the mayhem»›}].

[{‹'Dress like a thug, get treated like a thug' «where had Anwar heard that?»› tattooed ‹Hispanic types «Latino?»›} but had they?] Had those three guys somehow popped all the locks? They sure found it funny. Something flagrant too [excessive {proud?}] about their delight.

// as a white and brown American Staff
     // chases down a tan terrier mix

// as a tricolor beagle tries to avoid both

          // and bunnies in peril bound
          // for far corners.

                    // while one rooster zigzags to
reach
               // any exit

// one grey pitbull races forward
                              // in its jaws
     a cat
               // what Anwar fails to stop

// one worker not giving up

                    //crying

                         // 'Sophy!'

// others howling

                    // Anwar yelling

'Daughter! My daughter! Where are you?'

[in the main lobby] Everything has changed.

Gabby [the attendant] is gone. Everyone is gone [{outside?} wrangling animals?]. No doubting the strangeness [no thug troika necessary].

Why have all the drawers been jerked open? Cabinet doors too? Robbery? Why then the small refrigerator [{if only because ‹what?› . . . ‹G-A-F-F-C «!?»}] with all the soda and water bottles inside lying open {contents pooling on the floor}]?

[for no apparent reason {‹maybe› running on ‹sacred «scared!»› instinct alone}] Anwar heads for a set of rubber-trimmed stainless-steel doors. Open [{or at least ‹still›} swinging back and forth].

PERSONNEL ONLY

'Hey! Hey you! Buddy!—' [someone starts shouting] '—You can't go in there.'

[{instantly} back here] Something accosts his nose. Medicinal. Sharp. Or is it just [a lot of] bleach?

Doors lead off to the left and right.
Not one is closed.

[at the end {in the last room}] Anwar finds her.

The air is electric with antiseptics [something more {something else}?].

Xanther is on her knees [{still upright ‹ankles splayed›} in front of that infernal chamber].

Her face boils with sweat.

Lips rimed with spit.

Saccadic eye movements [{‹at an obscene speed› obscene!} ceasing as soon as Anwar squats beside her].

'Hey! Buddy! I said no one is—' [{pursuant} Official barging in after Anwar {abruptly stopping at the sight of Xanther on the floor}].
     'Daughter.' [Anwar cradling her head] 'Talk to me.'
     'Daddy, red's dead. Red's dead.'

'I said that?' Xanther says now [from {within} the shadow of her moon].

'What did you mean?'

'The cards on the cages, uhm, like they had red if the, like, animals were troubled? In trouble? Like all of those had in that room?'

'I see.' [Anwar believes her {even if he can't shake the feeling ‹sense «incomplete»› that there's something else ‹at work «⟨here⟩ too»›}.]

'Because, like—' [[{perhaps} sensing his {partial} acceptance?] '—like, they didn't have a chance. And all, uhm, like I wanted? was to give them a chance?'

'Is that why you opened their cages?'

'I didn't. I mean I don't think I did.'

Anwar waits [believing her {even if he's as unsure ‹as she is?› too}]. The long silence prompts the obvious question [what Anwar won't ask {what Xanther can't answer}]: how is it that upon returning home to this little creature all her energies were so suddenly restored?

Icy forehead warm.

Radiant smile whole again.

'Have you ever wanted something so bad—' [Xanther {finally} speaking up.] '—like when, uhm, you were like me, like my age?, that you not only didn't get, but the not getting brought you to your knees?'

'To my back,' Anwar laughs.

And so [instead of asking impossible questions {with impossible answers}] Anwar tells Xanther the story of climbing his parents' bookshelves as a child. How often he tried. How often he failed. Fell.

'Then you get it: this is all I want now,' Xanther says [of her new moon {hidden beneath a fold of blanket? ‹an arm? «or . . . »}]. 'He's my bottle.'

'Your ship,' Anwar smiles [{sadly too ‹because «like an off joke» the metaphor doesn't quite work›} trying to refine it just the same {as he stands up ‹recalling the potent desire to obtain something «because that something somehow meant ⟨a⌈voyage⌋far⟩ being free» to clutch a new future› Anwar closing windows} trying just to quiet {when were these thrown open ‹and so wide? «closet door too ⟨strange⟩»›} his mind] before kissing Xanther goodnight.

'No dad. He's not the ship.'
'Oh?'
'*I'm* the ship.'

The Bath

Why can't I just roll back the time?

— Jim Sullivan

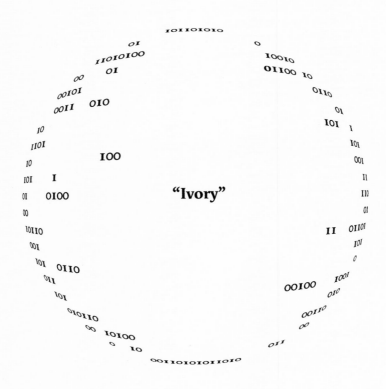

"Ivory"

OIIOII
OOOIIOIIIIOIIIOII
OOIIOOIOIOIOOIOOOOOIIOIIOOO
IIOIIIIOIIIOOIIOIIIOIOOOOIOOOOOO
IIOIIOOOIIOIIIIOIIIOIIOOIIOOIOIOIIOOI
OOOOIOOOOOOIIOIIOOOIIOIIIIOIIIOIIOOIIOIIIOIO
OOOIOOOOOOIIOIIOOOIIOIIIIOIIIOIIOOIIOOIOIOOIOOI
OOOOOOIIOIIOOOIIOIIIIOIIIOIIOOIIOOIOIOIIOOIOOO
OIOOOOOOIIOIIOOOIIOIIIIOIIIOIIOOIIOOIOIOOIOOOOOO
IIOIIOOOIIOIIIIOIIIOOIIOIIIOIOOOOIOOOOOOIIOIIOOOI
IOIIIIOIIIOIIOOIIOOIOIOIIOOIOOOOIOOOOOOIIOIIOOOIIO
IIIIOIIIOOIIOIIIOIOOOOIOOOOOOIIOIIOOOIIOIIIIOIIIIOI
IOOIIOOIOIOOIOOOOOOIIOIIOOOIIOIIIIOIIIOIIOOIIOOIO
IOIIOOIOOOOIOOOOOOIIOIIOOOIIOIIIIOIIIOIIOOIIOOIO
IOOIOOOOOOIIOIIOOOIIOIIIIOIIIOIIOOIIOIIIOIOOOOIOO
OOOIIOIIOOOIIOIIIIOIIIOIIOOIIOOIOIOIIOOIOOO
OIOOOOOOIIOIIOOOIIOIIIIOIIIOIIOOIIOOIOIOOIOOO
IOOOOOIIOIIOOOIIOIIIIOIIIOIIOOIIOIIIOIOIOOO
IOOIOOOOOIIOIIOOOIIOIIIIOIIIOIIOIIOOIIOOIO
OOIIOOIOIOIIOOIOO

fingers lash
by flash of binding

blinding slash of sliding

sash twisting to find this wash

of gray and silver and platinum

in the practiced
habit of knotting more

for losing less

"Pearls of surveillance emerge from the sands of tedium." Deakin knew how this work rarely offers the thrill of the kill, fruit ready for plucking, whether ripe or forbidden. Even the Clips did not first appear as they are now known. Orbing is a dedication to time. By comparison, Bobby's electron microscope, with all its spectacular vistas and alien inhabitants, seems oracular. To scry the static is to put faith in the accretion of the miniscule.

If not exactly embracing faith, Cas at least keeps focus on this latest go-around.

Perhaps her fright — nearly ten days ago — over a possible intruder had helped give necessity its due. All thanks to a young, modelly Floridian who proved as scared as the old woman she discovered huddled in the bath.

Cas discovered she likes the bath. Despite its mineral deposits and stains, and tiny drip Bobby is powerless to stop, the low heaviness at her back comforts her. The drain at her toes and the spigot above no longer threaten to produce wiggling serpents. Pillows and blankets soften the porcelain. Plastic bags keep her feet dry. The Orb warms her lap. Plus, even in summer's relentless heat, the bath stays coolish.

There is still a viper though. But he is not a snake. He is not even

the spider his name suggests. He's not even a recluse. If anything, he's ordinary. And worse than dull, Cas once called him friend. They all did.

The close-up of his lips is new. The same lips that on so many occasions had shaped her name, Bobby's too, even Deakin's. Where was Deakin? Cas shakes the distraction from her eyes. Sips more black coffee from her Mickey Mouse mug. Maxes the volume. Wedges her earbuds in still tighter. Let this hiss and stitch of crackles drive her to find something more than just "Ivory" — a promise of illegal trade, encryption, maybe even tradecraft.

Bobby was pleased to see Cas committing to this quest for better intel. Missing parts required to repair the Airstream and truck had not done much for his mood. No one had heard from Sorcerer. Between long scry sessions, Marnie put Cas on her table and helped melt the long hours away.

And the hours were long. Cas had no idea how many she spent trying to secure something better than just lips. And then she stumbled upon the numbers. The stream came by way of him, though it was hard to local-ize the exact origin — whether from a corporate mainframe or Petch or something more exotic. Cas never sourced the out-put but the digits stabilized and, better still, repeated.

Now Bobby had something to work with.

Next up was incomprehensible: a wash of light garroted by a metallic band. The sight wore on Cas. While seeking an alternate means to resolve the blur, she actually smudged the Orb. Like some beginner scrying for her first time.

It necessitated a restart. She even smudged a second time on the unlocking and had to restart again.

His eyes unnerve her the most. They're nice. Always have been. Soft and wide. What coldness marks his character finds no place in their autumn swimminess. Here is proof that eyes can hide just as well as reveal the nature of the self. They sure fooled her. Even Bobby. For years. Though maybe they fooled him as well. Maybe their warmth fools him still.

Before he named himself Recluse, they knew him just as Alv. If she ever sees him again, that's what Cas would sing out to the youngest and most social of the four.

Cas needs no Orb to remember a different time, when on a snowy evening, the four of them, scarved in wool and an optimism young enough to deny tomorrow's refusals and plummet-

ing temperatures, had stumbled out of a New Hampshire pub, drunk on pitchers of beer, but not so drunk to stumble away without recognizing the street before them, a sheet of the blackest ice, starred with blinking holiday lights and settling snow.

He fell first. Hard too. For all their tread, his black leather boots were rendered treadless by the freeze. A bare palm slapped next, maybe his head followed, surely a hip. But he didn't rise pained or angry. Instead, warm joy shimmered in his

to dare too this slip-
or shuffle upon ice
blacktop beneath
gest. They all
████.   Cas
knees. Bobby
landing on his
her   future
loved showing
bruises.   But
aged to get back
inching   toward
arms, beautiful in
How beautiful their

eyes. He urged them
periness — slide
darker than any
dare   sug-
fell. Except
bruised her
yowled for
ass. How
h u s b a n d
Cas those
they man-
on their feet,
his   out-held
their   purpose.
purpose back then.

Earlier that night, though, spikier interactions might have shown what ambition and time would sharpen.

Back in the pub, Alv had first sat with "new faces illuminated by that political fervor respondent to—" the previous year's declassified news

of the Bravo blast :: **A.E.C. Lifts Veil on A-Test Power.** *New York Times*, **July 31, 1960** :: and more recently the Soviet's detonation of a large hydrogen device. :: Tsar Bomba, 50–58 megaton yield. October 30, 1961 :: Alv had failed to fit in:

"I couldn't say much because I know little of what they know. And of what I know they take little interest in. Alas, they gravely overestimate what they profess, while the consequence of what we can prove they not only underesti-   mate, they fail to suspect."

And then later,   this time paired
with   grins,   plus   another
pitcher   of   beer   plopped
u p s i d e   down   in   a
liquefying   swirl of foam:

" F o o l s !   To   waste   a
m o m e n t   more of this
h o l i d a y   retreat on what
d e f e r m e n t s   have solved."

Back   then   the   world was made of
fools. Of course, they   were the exceptions. They
were so young, so drunk on blindness and all that lust misconstrues
as new. Alv was already calling Cas' vision, her new math, their new
physics, the last religion, what ▮▮▮▮ hailed as the pinnacle of every
last perversity, disgust itself. This was still back when nothing had been
proven, Clip #1 still years away :: four years ::, when really the only thing
they had beyond notebooks and chalkboards was one another.

How they had laughed that night. Just to keep standing. Shoulder to shoulder. A shuffling circle, spinning against every clock, hands slipping to hands, faster and faster, outdoing every clock, outdoing the gravity of every midnight, until Cas lifted her feet, swore they all did, floating above all the lights of Christmas.

Bobby still says there
Only three. For
never claimed to
that circle. He
only for her.
with it. He
sought one sat-
to call her his
after all she'd
through,   Cas
given him that.
sion she almost

were never four.
all he did, he
be a part of
was   there
And   fine
only   ever
isfaction:
wife. And
put   him
had finally
The best deci-
never made.

The only thing worse than their arrogance was that they had been right. The price, though, of making that claim had deprived them of every reward pride had promised.

371466
4991284913433210
34334097347277793645 9283
49000254553823422856431412453
43396743298571345210101010102383 4013
8746275849344124424299921370114485385
4803448377161815113700791094972433478 07
380094673373168859737775342 0623858547373
75595628500317343787266158750342668934257
9583796196493188892 0495348 094649895175344
932151148377375298967261114348517007627 03
8379812593560729342 00663534202343781 12
9419808341938362740236374489185753918
3458249117927803445855051790 28 3757
23093751810348 0452093350633767 2
977635535834341989250009 2

Bobby knows the tics of her excess by heart. No surprise. He's been her bad-trip tent when LSD promised fresh perspectives. He was their guide out of meth. Even recently he made sure some psilocybin didn't trap her in a recursive nightmare. Of course, scrying can be far worse.

Cas still doesn't know what gives her away: the way her fingers move? maybe twitches possessing her face? the way her gaze starts to stoop? He doesn't even ask what's on the Orb. He just scoops her up out of the bath. He always says she's nothing but brains and bird bones, but Bobby is surprisingly strong.

Tuesday night he drags them out for Chinese. Marnie needs some dragging too. News of the Isla Vista shootings has depressed her. Twitter keeps blowing up with the debate: guns, violence against women, violence against guns. Her Facebook feed continues the argument. Parcel Thoughts compiles image collages that will never resurrect the dead.

Marnie reads aloud parts of "My Twisted World: The Story of Elliot Rodger." How the "kissless virgin" blamed "the cruelness of women." How he obsessed over Powerball. How he rented a handgun.

"'What am I doing here? How could things have led to this?'" Marnie reads to them over garlic broccoli and shrimp toast. "'I couldn't believe my life was actually turning out this way. There I was, practicing shooting with real guns because I had a plan to carry out a massacre.'" ∴ **CNN. May 27, 2014** ∴

Bobby keeps his nose buried in a box of fried rice. Cas just nods. Marnie's so young. She doesn't even know anyone who knew even one of the victims. Cas and Bobby have yet to learn the final tally of a massacre going on right now, making no headlines, people they've known intimately, some for decades. Not that Cas and Bobby are FNGs ∷ Fucking New Guys ∴ .

Poor Kid, poor ███ ████ ∷ Known currently as Zeke Rilvergaile, a pseudonym originating in Realic S. Tarnen's paper "Clip 4" ∴ . They had buried him back in 1966. Vietnam had just started to taunt the wind, 1968 was yet to come, but even then she could guess the kind of violence that awaited them all. Ceaseless. Unforgiving.

Suddenly Marnie hugs Cas in that crummy restaurant and they cry together.

Bobby, though, never loses sight of their situation or surroundings, and that alertness checks Cas. This is not a nice Dayton suburb. Outside the restaurant, Marnie's looks draw looks. Who knows if buttered toast like her has ever walked a corner here without a price. Funny if after all their efforts to evade surveillance networks valued in the trillions of dollars, some corner hood put them down for a dime and a good time.

Why did Sorcerer pick this place? Back at the pad, Cas takes note again of their curious building. Amid rundown structures with warped siding and barred windows, these nine floors are built of brick. The fire escape is unreachable from the ground and then impossible to access without a key. The elevator atrium requires passing through three sets of doors. Cas thought antique when they arrived. Now she sees how they are reinforced cages to prevent unlawful entry.

Even in Dayton, Cas wonders how Sorcerer affords such a place.

Marnie never talks about Sorcerer. And, except for that first night, she doesn't mention the Orb. She just leads Cas to her table and warms her oils and then with world music in the background, helps Cas forget her thoughts and sometimes Cas even sleeps.

The next morning, back in the bath, Cas finally makes sense of "Ivory." At the same time too that Bobby figures out the numbers. They do that a lot. A regular Darby and Joan. "Of Arc," Bobby likes to add. Cas should go mad on behalf of such useless visions. Charcoal Ivory Jigsaw. Bought with an Amex. Discontinued. Last used at Turnbull & Asser on 57th. Bobby even finds the price: $204.95. For a tie.

Nights and nights of work and this is the best Cas can do. The *New York Post* had already made some mention of a board meeting that week. Well over a year ago.

Bobby can hardly blame her for returning to Clip #6. Not that he can figure out how something so fixed can go from spectral magic to chromatic absence.

Preferences get the blame— meaning Bobby, who keeps resetting the Orb's preferences, alters nothing.

Two hundred dollars for a tie!

"Sorcerer will know." Is how Bobby admits to giving up. "I bet it has something to do with these crazy gigabits the wireless cooks up here."

Another thing Cas hasn't paid much attention to: the Orb's speed.

Yet for all his matter-of-factness, Bobby can't conceal his frustration and fear. There's no word on Deakin. Silence about the others asymptotically approaches tracelessness. Those arrested have nearly ceased to exist. One or two news stories followed a few deaths until petering out with "under investigation." Even more unnerving, Sorcerer's posting haunts have gone quiet too. And any search on Cas' part, however direct or ambagious, continues to prove just how faultlessly their Distribution was eliminated from the Web.

The power required for such erasure exceeds parody. Not even a cartoon could render such an act possible. Cas starts wishing she were a cartoon if only to escape a reality no cartoon would ever trust.

"Remember, it's not just him," Bobby whispers to her as they spoon in Sorcerer's bed, close to the window, the fire escape. "It's his apparatus."

She kisses his knuckles. One to eight. And then again, one to ten, because she forgot the thumbs. Bobby stops her there. When did these gestures become so plausibly finite? How many more kisses do they have left? How many more new moons? Paul Bowles knew the danger that comes from counting. ∷ **"Yet everything happens a certain number of times, and a very small number, really." _The Sheltering Sky_. John Lehmann Limited, 1949.** ∴

So Cas whispers their names: Circe ∴ ▮ ∴, Artemis ∴ ▮
▮ ∴, Thaumaturge   ∴ ▮ ∴, Thanatos ∴ ▮ ∴,
Sibyll   too ∴ ▮ ∴, and then
dear Treebeard ∴ ▮
▮ ∴,   Mer-
lin   ∴ dearest
Deakin ∴ ,

n o t
f o r -
getting
P y t h i a
∴ ▮
▮ ∴,   Lilith
▮ ∴,   or Endoria
∴ ▮
∴ ▮   ▮ ∴, to remind herself
that even the dead   may still live, if just by a voice.

Bobby doesn't stop her. No matter how many times she goes through the list. Only after she stops does he start whispering about the Arsenal.

Thursday morning Bobby goes out and doesn't come back until after lunch. The repairs remaining amount to some shock absorbers and spare parts that will arrive on Friday. But Friday arrives without the parts. And so Friday is miserable. Cas doesn't leave the bath. Now scrying for Aberrations. Bobby worries about how quickly they can exit this brick building and once that panic runs its course, starts worrying about Joel. ∴ **JEOL electron microscope.** ∴

At least Marnie's easy enough. Bobby likes her because her phone's archaic and she never uses it. She's also hard to ignore. Her shorts remind Cas of those shortshorts in the '70s. Not that anyone's going to look at denim pockets with those muscular tan legs around, teal toenails too, always wiggling around in orange flip-flops when she's not kicking them off. Maybe she is from the '70s. She lugs around her old laptop like it's a crate of vinyl. Bobby's confirmed it's mostly music. Though not from the '70s. The Tallest Man On Earth. Fleet Foxes. Imagine Dragons. Cas likes the names.

By now Isla Vista clips and murderous manifestos have given way to "Mr. G and Jellybean" — about a goat (Mr. G) who stopped eating after he was separated from a donkey (Jellybean). Marnie wants a goat. Cas wants . . . She doesn't know what she wants. They watch it over and over. They laugh at the country music. They tear up over the reunion.

This almost beats the Orb. What does the Orb care of animals? Would reconnaissance without country music ever have the same effect? Or is feeling a casualty of accuracy?

554

On Saturday morning, parts arrive. The Airstream will be ready by
noon. By noon, Bobby learns not all   the parts arrived. Now
their ride won't be ready   until Monday.
There's also a prob-   lem with
the   truck's
hitch which
could
take

until
Tues-
day   to
fix. Bobby
starts to con-
vince himself the
shop is plotting to   steal Joel.

That night Cas insists Bobby have a massage. He refuses. Only one person may lay hands on him: his wife. The man mystifies her sometimes. Sure, Marnie is gorgeous, but more important, something healing moves through her palms. After a ridiculous amount of coaxing Bobby climbs onto the table. Cas sits at the head with a hand on his shoulder.

Bobby seems to relax. Cas keeps up some chatter with Marnie. About her roots. "Seminole mostly. Some Dutch and French. Average mutt." Marnie surprises Cas by asking about her American Indian heritage. Cas usually gets Asian. Sometimes Indian with a hint of Persian. Or just black with a lot of Swiss creamer.

"How did you guess that?"

But before Cas can get to "Hopi," Bobby has scrambled off the table, muttering apologies to Marnie, off to the bathroom to complain about the diminishing supply of toilet paper. There's a year's supply.

On Sunday, Cas wants only to scry, but she can see that if they don't all get outside soon Bobby will torque himself into a state of uselessness. Something pervasively generic about Sorcerer's apartment has gotten on all their nerves. Especially troubling since Sorcerer is by nature puckish. Yet the books in the bedroom bookcase seem bought by the yard. Even a copy of a Tom Clancy next to Susan Faludi would do.

They take Marnie's car. Bobby insists on driving and going first to a Jiffy Lube in Centerville, and afterward taking side streets up through Beavercreek. Before any signs appeared for Wright-Patterson Air Force

Base, Cas had already caught a whiff of something military. Not in the
cozy-lawned homes they eased past, but
in the way Bobby studied those
lawns. Marnie listened to Of
Monsters and Men with
eyes shut.

Near the univer-
sity, they pick
up sandwich
fixings. Just
bringing the
six pack of
IPAs into
the apart-
ment seems
to lighten
B o b b y ' s
mood. Cas
and Marnie
take charge
sawing loaves
and chopping up
sweet pickles for
the tuna. And then
Bobby's mood shifts
again. He wants to ride
the motorcycle by the shop.

"So cool," Marnie giggles. "Still flying that freak flag. I hope I'm like you when I'm older."

"How would you know what a freak flag is?" Bobby grunts, but instead of leaving, sits down to hear about Marnie's Uncle Eddie.

Good thing too. Cas and Marnie are on the bed when Bobby tiptoes into the bedroom, shoes in hand, finger to his lips. Marnie stops brushing Cas' hair, clips on Cas' braces, as if she'd been dealing with braces her whole life, then slides open the window. Cas wraps the Orb in its cashmere sweater.

By the time Cas has followed Marnie out onto the fire escape, the knocks on the front door have turned to bangs. Metal is involved. Whatever's wood soon announces itself with shrieks of sheering. Though there is more metal in that door than meets the eye.

Marnie takes off one of her bracelets and, using her teeth, snaps the band. Sea glass and shells bounce down the stairs below.

From the empty apartment two flights up, they hear two loud bangs in quick succession, likely the front door torn loose of its hinges and then hitting the floor. Cas turns to go back for Bobby, but he's already crawling in through the window.

Another bang.

Probably the bedroom door.

Marnie and Bobby find the closet in a far room. Through it lies some
safer place but Bobby is having trouble with the
mechanism. Marnie stands next to Cas. A
new clamor on the fire escape echoes
through the empty rooms. It never
dims. Seashells and sea glass
failed to mislead. They will
be here soon. And that's
not the worst of it. Even
as her fingers unsleep the
Orb, Cas hears another
sound, much quieter,
now separating from
the shadows, easing
toward them. Cas con-
ducts the Orb to spear
the darkness with a
flash bright enough
to darken all their
eyes. Too late. Cas feels
strange hands on her,
clawing at her, trying to
drag her back, even as she
drops the Orb, rolling it away
as an offering, across hardwood
floors, armed this time with more
than just a flash, if not time enough for
one more breath, as a stranger scrambles
after it, as the Orb detonates, the blast undoing
more than light and breath.

Hunger

Some are marked, some . . .

— *Tim Seibles*

Sunday night's dreams, or whatever they are, keep pro-
pelling Xanther farther and farther from home. But on
Monday, while at school, Xanther thinks only about running home. Exhaustion probably plays a part. Hello trigger.
She wants to cry all the time, probably another trigger, after
class, during class, which she refuses to do, mainly because
of all the really bad attention it would get her, unless, like
she's already crying and the tears are just vaporizing in the
heat, and not just June heat, which is pretty bad, especially
with the drought, which is getting worse, that big May rain
just a dream, global warming more and more of a reality,
which because Xanther's in the Environmental Science
Magnet program, keeps coming up a lot. No, this is that
weird fever inside her that heats up like a furnace as soon
as she's away from the little one and then goes out as soon
he's back in her arms.

At least Xanther's accepted that it won't burn her up
completely. Those first few days, though, when she was
dragged out of the house, Xanther was convinced she'd
wind up a mess of glowing charcoal.

"Huh?" Desie, Xanther's partner, asks.

"Huh?" Xanther huhs back, snapping more parts together.

"You just said fire-something-sand. There's no sand."

"Uhm, oh, like I don't know, thinking out loud?"

This is fourth-period Robotics, Xanther's elective, and like most of her classes, has an environmental bent, like with model windmills, a pretty cool wave machine made out of an old aquarium tank, and remote-controlled trucks, all of which Mr. Villora uses to teach about ecology and geology, even the life of animals, which is why Xanther picked it.

Today's all about building these little farm creatures, which in real life are solar-powered and can seed a field, water a crop, and harvest one too. The exercise is really about following the directions on their desk screen in order to put together, like a puzzle, or a really, really complicated puzzle, lots and lots of parts. Mr. Villora already warned that there wasn't enough time in one class to finish.

Desie smirked when Mr. Villora had assigned Xanther as her partner. She's not like Mary Ellen bad, and nowhere close to Dendish, but she'd still turned to her two friends, all of them whispering but loud enough for Xanther to hear: "She's so weird! Just look at her!" "Not smart." "Like what Tim Burton makes up to throw away!" "Don't sit too close." "I hear she smells."

The last bit hurt most. Xanther even tries to smell herself, with a slow twist, but discreet like, to sniff her armpits through her white shirt,? but nothing's there, or is some-

thing there?, at least no stains. Or by blowing in her hands to check her breath, still nothing bad, she smells fine, right?, but isn't that the worst?, if what smells is to you unnoticeable but to everyone else sickening?

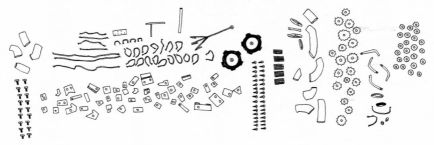

    Desie had insisted on going first with the assembly. That was a ten-minute fumble project. Then Xanther took over, and it was like no matter what plastic thing she grabbed, it attached easily to the next, wires too, all the little components, without even looking at the desk screen, which was like already in her head?, and Desie had kept up her smirk but kinda backed off too, and then stuck to organizing what pieces were left, now and then trying to hand over a part, which was usually the wrong part, but which Xanther took anyway, thanking her, before putting it down and snatching the right one, until eventually Desie backed off completely, smirk long gone, maybe even replaced with a glint of amazement?, or is that just Xanther feeling amazed? Had she ever done anything like this before? As if this fire inside her, that felt so wrong, also could feel right, by heating up her thoughts so much that they became transparent, like fire to sand, glass to sky, allowing the vision of what matters, what really has nothing to do with thought, or even light, to shine through.

:. I know it happened but I have no clue how it happened. There's not a single thought evidencing a process other than motor skills and chance. .:

:. *This child is beyond the charge of so rank an authority as chance.* .:

Mr. Villora comes over. Pretty impressed.

"She did most of it," Desie admits.

And like that, whatever can smolder inside no longer burns. Xanther even smells a hint of clean snow and, like, breathes deep, and Desie's her new bestie for life.

"Hey. Uhm. Desie? I mean like the day's been so warm, you know. But. Uhm. Do I, like, smell?"

"Yeah."

That night Xanther's dreams seem to accelerate, and they're already this flicker of stuff, too fast to even remember, forget track, or even connect, even if there were like a little robot that could be connected to it all, there is no such robot, because it's just all too much, whether places or people, so many people, finally nothing more than what?, a stream of dark stones, meaning everything, meaning nothing.

From dusk to dawn, Xanther roams over a soft floor of packed pine needles or new snow, the forest thickening around her, more and more branches gathering overhead, as if their reach was all that mattered, as if the points of every pine needle could only keep pointing to the only thing that mattered, fascicles upon fascicles, each poking to life these flickers of familiarity answered by confusion and more stones, scaring Xanther each time, talk about Fraidy K for sure, but with no option to turn, forget stop, continuing on beneath the threat of a sky whispering rose.

Fascicle?

All this non-sleep should exhaust Xanther. Instead she rises hungry, as if hunger means awake. For sure there's no sleep in her eyes, all her windows are open too, strange, but only one thought survives, way trumping hunger.

The little one.

Even if also, always the shadow on every morning, Xanther fears she could find him still and stiff, no groan or a tiny kick to draw her awake for his last second. At least Les Parents have officially let him sleep on her bed. Ever since Dr. Syd had said lots of handling was a great thing.

This morning the little one stretches to life at her touch. Xanther scoops him up, because if she's starving, he must be too, and bounds down to the kitchen to prepare a dropper of Just Born Milk Replacer. She can brush her teeth later. First two scoops of powder to two scoops of filtered water. Then mix, fill bottle, warm in a pan of hot tap water, and apply a few drops to an inner forearm, just how Astair demonstrated, to make sure the liquid isn't too hot.

Then with the little one on his feet, or is it paws?, cats can't have feet right?, guide the tiny nipple to the mouth. Key is to never feed a kitten on its back, because in that position the fluid can drip into the lungs, and if not outright drown it, it only takes a little to cause pneumonia, which can prove fatal within days, if not hours.

On that first Sunday, Xanther had fed the little wisp on his back at least four times, and then once more on Monday, which was when she discovered her mistake, convinced at that moment that she had just killed him.

That fate seems less and less likely now, especially as the wrinkly little forehead shoves forward, eyes forever pinched shut, such tiny teeth, with tiny claws too, clamping down around the milky flow, which dribbles all around its snorting nose, covering that place where more whiskers should probably grow, what Anwar jokingly calls his cat stubble, the mixture rivuleting along the jaw line, all over his pink little belly.

Next Xanther dips cotton balls in warm water, also the way Astair demonstrated, weirdo mom has actually been pretty great recently, the past week even surprising Xanther with a new supply of formula, this kind supposedly healthier, plus new bottles, a feeding syringe, which Xanther hasn't used, and little blankies, and toys too, which the little one has either no interest in or is too blind to find.

Xanther first cleans the nose and face, cats have faces right?, or is that just a human thing?, then cleaning the tummy, which is also rubbing, which is supposed to aid digestion, even activate it. With the second cotton ball, she rubs the area of its thingy, which Xanther has never seen, it just looks like a period, this is to get it peeing, and the butt too, this to stimulate pooping, and maybe the result's a little smear of something mustardy, which also could just be dust, Xanther having yet to see anything definitive on the pee pads in the kitchen or in her room.

Last of all, Xanther brushes him with the softest brush they could find. What purrs then! A protest of squeaks too. Squirming under each stroke down its back, along the tiny ribs. The tail is especially sensitive, irritating him, while brushing his neck and ears seems to settle him. He even nuzzles the brush.

Sometimes the brush peels back the eyes a little, exposing a peek of blue, darker than blue, darker than even black, but in the way black can mean not something empty but something that holds so much it looks empty, that kind of empty, which is strange because the sight of it somehow empties Xanther of worry or fear.

Mrs. Fischer's honk twists Xanther's stomach. And that's nothing compared to driving away. Leaving's a problem. And counter to Les Parents' reasoning, it's only getting worse. Always the same thing. Like a pilot light popping on, like a blue acorn hidden in the deepest woods. Then, with the first steps out the door, the furnace goes on. What won't stop until she's back with the snowy little creature.

At least Tuesday goes by faster. Dismissal is at 1:35. Only PE sucks. That's because they're still stuck in badminton. What's worse, Ms. Barney actually thinks Xanther shows potential, and has recommended that she join Mr. Tamblin's badminton group next year. Not that Ms. Barney's talking up the RACER Stars program ∷ **Rated Athletics, Culture, and Education Research** ∷ when Xanther wipes out trying to swat the shuttlecock, and like the bouncy cone had already zipped past her when she swung, tripping and sprawling on the gym floor, hello more scabs, too many giggles too.

Good thing Mary Ellen isn't in this class. Or any of that crew. Especially Dendish. Xanther wonders, fingers crossed, if maybe they all got kicked out for the Horrosphere stuff, which is now no longer on Parcel Thoughts.

Really, the worst part about Tuesday is that Kle's missing.

Except for Cogs, who like her is also ESM ∷ **Environ-mental Science Management** ∴, Xanther and her friends are all in different magnets. Which is kinda a miracle, how they all, you know, found one another. Mayumi, Bayard, and Josh are GAT kids ∷ **Gifted Ability Track** ∴. GAT shares a PE class with ESM but somehow Xanther wound up in a PE class without even one of her friends. Kle's smart enough for the GAT magnet, maybe like too smart?, is that why he didn't end up in GAT but in the FAM magnet ∷ **Film Arts Media** ∴?

But today Kle's definitely MIA. Not around for Nutrition, lunch, not even texting. And like, for one, this is the last week of school, almost everyone shows up, and for another, Kle never misses school. He likes it.

Xanther's first thought is that he got in trouble for his locker plan. There are lockers all over campus, by class-rooms, in some upstairs hallways, even on The Hill where only sixth graders are. Locker use is forbidden. Been that way for years. So they just stand there, a tradition of a different age, unused for so long, they're invisible.

Not to Kle though. He's always talking about them. He says they're off-bounds because of legal stuff ∷ reasons ∴, like kids selling pot out of them, like Dendish would have stored a whole pharmacy in his, run his drug mules all over the neighborhood from there, or doled out even worse, like pipe bombs, or terrorist stuff, who knows.

Kle obsesses about their emptiness. He wants to get inside them, and like plant these little speakers, maybe little ePods, but that can like be turned on all at once with an app. Like a whole symphony. One set of lockers would be just violins and cellos, another set woodwinds, The Hill would have percussions, another the triangle, Xanther's instrument of choice, she even has one, somewhere, and Kle would conduct this weird orchestra, his "muffled glory," from like the amphitheater by Storia Mall.

Mayumi keeps coming up with different suggestions. Like Johann Strauss or Richard Strauss, who weren't brothers, so "it could be very *2001*," ∷ **1968** ∷ or, because Mayumi knows a lot more about music than anybody else, she gets into stuff way beyond movie scores, like *Civilization IV*'s "Baba Yetu," or composers Anwar's probably heard of but not Xanther, like Henryk Górecki or Tibor Szemz . Even if Kle doesn't have an ePod and has yet to open one locker.

Wednesday, Kle's back. His latest *Enlightenment Series* is his explanation. This one's titled *Short Span, #8*. He decided to give a different number to the original #8.

Short Span, #8, starts with heaven, which Kle draws as lots and lots of wings, which is just Kle being way ironic, like this is an assignment, draw paradise, which Kle does but in his like sarcastic "fo sho" way. Heaven = wings? Really?! But that's the premise: what's after life is perfect, pure floaty.

The problem is that life itself is a bore if not outright torture. Originally, nothing was supposed to survive long before moving on to heaven. And, okay, some trees are over a thousand years old, but humanity keeps trying to extend the boredom and torture for hundreds of years.

Typical Kle, *Short Span, #8* leaps to when life spans surpass hundreds of millions of years and finally reach forever. In other words, no one ever gets wings "and much floaty happiness is lost." That's the punch line, in the final two frames, first with "We did it!", in quotes, like it's said by your everyday living-forever person, then second, in italics, like it's that all-knowing voice, what Xanther sometimes fantasizes about, or is it *who* she fantasizes about?, does everyone?, to make sense of it all?, and yet so beyond the story too, beyond forever even, forget Kle's birdy heaven, crying: *Yes, they did do it! They built themselves Hell!*

Which fareaked Kle's parents out because that's basically saying it's better to die now and get to heaven quick, because life is for suckers.

"Is that, like, what you think?" Xanther has to ask, even if she pretty much knows Kle is up to something else.

"Les Parents way over-fareaked and dragged me to a shrink yesterday. If they'd just spoken to me directly, I could have spared them a nasty bill."

As it turns out, Kle was just rendering what his older brother, Phinneas, had been rambling on about of late. That was a whole other bill.

"I like this one," Xanther adds.

"Why?"

"Because it makes a question out of what we take for granted that is so important."

"Living long?"

"Or, the way you drew it, getting to some better place that no one can ever be sure about."

"Smart points for Xanther. Like who seriously wants to fast-forward to being a bird?"

And suddenly it's last bell, with just Thursday and Friday left, the last day of school. And no matter how much it hurts to be there, Xanther knows she'll survive.

The stones are still everywhere. But unlike this burning to get home, Xanther can sorta ignore them. It's not really that hard because nothing is lost.

If this were like on a TV show, they might CGI in these cheesy rocks over everyone's eyes, but that wouldn't be right, because as undeniable as they are, people's eyes are there too, like in both states, at the same time, like breakfast means break fast as well as meat sizzling on a grill. ∴ Meat? ∵ Of course, since when is a TV series ever this life? Maybe some stuff you can never show.

Only feel.

The stones Xanther saw at the shelter were different. The same with those she saw from farther away when Mrs. Fischer's car doors popped open for no reason. ∴ *Ah reason . . .* ∵ Not the way they looked, same as every-one else, but more like Xanther isn't the only one seeing them. Maybe that accounts for the focus, starting to banish heaviness by a gaze. If only they would have drifted away. Xanther's most curious about what's underneath.

This afternoon she tries to fix on Dr. Potts' eyes, lighten those stones, or at least make them wobble, but as usual she doesn't just blink but looks for a clock. Besides, whatever focus she musters only seemed to accomplish the reverse: the longer she stares, the heavier these stones get.

Xanther should tell Dr. Potts about all of this. First thing. And she means to, really, but by the time time's up she's really only got into how badly she needs to see the little one, how worried she is that he's getting frailer, maybe sicker, like is he sick?, or just old?, and blind, is he blind?, and if not blind, then why won't he open his eyes?, so definitely blind, winding up with, is he really just about to die?, and then is that her fault?, and so, wow, huh, how shaken up is she?, she like can't sleep well?, though she feels rested, and like she can't remember her dreams?, though they're not terrible, just maybe desperate?, and isn't all that enough to share?, because Xanther's not sharing the part about the forest because that's not what she's really going through, ∷ That's a relief. For a moment I thought I was hearing things. Or, er, she was hearing things, things I couldn't hear. Which is impossible, or only possible if, okay, since TF-Narcon 9 X is not TF-Narcon^9 X (TOTAL), there could exist certain functions and data beyond what my algorithms render. Though that would be strange. ∷ ∷ *Ah strange!* ∷ Xanther not even picturing this, a forest, more like a way to see what she can't see, or is it handle? ∷ **Process** ∷, process?, ∷ *Grant coincidence a place* ∷ you know deal with experiences which Xanther has no experience with, forget really trying to describe, what feels as endless as it's gray and icy, isolated too, with maybe a clearing, but forget a good view, and all that roaming rooted in what's human, or what Xanther feels is human, finally coming across as defiantly inhuman.

In other words, just a whole lot of babble, cross-legged on that shaggy Rory print rug. Xanther doesn't even come close to finishing one side of the Rubik's Cube.

Pure mess.

"But, like, Dr. Potts?—" Xanther will still try "—when I'm with him, I've never felt better. Ever. Like I don't worry about seizures. I don't even think of them. Like I don't even know what one is."

"You sound relieved."

"Huh. Have I ever felt that way before?"

Bliss is the word Dr. Potts leaves Xanther with at the end of their session. For sure, school's approaching end feels like bliss, especially with little one cozied in her lap, curled up after another feeding, another cleaning.

Xanther's on the floor, again, again cross-legged, though this time in their den, dabbing onto her fingernails layers of pink dotted with black stars. Anwar has put on *2001* because Xanther wanted to understand Mayumi's reference, and when the music comes on, even the little one stirs, how wicked-cool would that sound be?, muffling out of the locked lockers at Thomas Star Kane?

Then somewhere around when HAL starts self-preserving, i.e. killing everyone, Freya and Shasti launch their kidnapping plan. Freya taps Xanther's right shoulder, and starts up one of those conversations/questions that Xanther knows at once isn't real.

"Philomel says her goldfish left. I asked what happened. Was it germs? But Philomel said no. Her goldfish just head-down die."

But Xanther's already whipping left, head diving down, teeth bared, snarling at Shasti who, on hands and knees, still thinks she can lift away the little one, who, huh, somehow, is already out of reach, on Xanther's shoulder.

Astair has no tolerance for that, the twins' wailing excuses about just wanting to play with the little cotton ball, who's way too fragile to play, Xanther all shudders, wondering what her sisters really had in mind.

"That's Xanther's cat." Mom's great. "Lay even one finger, ever—. To your room, Freya. No, not you, Shasti. You're staying with me."

Little one's, huh, somehow, back in her lap, asleep, dreaming, maybe in a way only another dream can share.

Thursday morning Xanther wolfs down as much as she can. Anwar has prepared fried tomatoes with lobster mushrooms, scrambled eggs on the side, topped with Daiya cheddar. It doesn't help. Forget enough. Not even with half an avocado. A glass of almond milk. Xanther ends up staring at Freya's glass of milk, what the little one, if it could open its eyes, would never stare at, though they'd both be hunting for something.

"What?" Freya snaps. Shasti goes wide-eyed.

"Xanther!" Freya bangs the table. "Stop looking like that!"

How heavy the stones on the eyes of her sisters.

At the front door Xanther grits her teeth for the worst, but it's still the worst. So much for teeth. Out the door, pop, furnace, might as well be POP!, WHAM!, T.K.O.!, burning up Mrs. Fischer's car.

The tests help some. They're super-scary, maybe because they're end-of-semester tests, what Xanther over-

heard two teachers calling "cumulative" or even "summative assessments," even if they turned out to be a lot like usual tests, just a little longer. English with Mrs. Rawlins even had a vocabulary question about paradise!

All her friends are around too, which is good, and even if she doesn't see Bayard, he sends a hopatooit! text, which is something they text each other when hustling's in order.

Xanther catches Kle as he's racing out of Digital Imaging and Advanced Animation, no test, just a final project, which his teacher described as "eloquently disturbing." Kle fist pumps. On his way to Leadership.

"Ge the L.P." Kle yelps over his shoulder.

Xanther only has PE left and then she's home. But she still lingers by "Y Building." The bell even rings. Why is she dragging now? Kids all gone. No teachers in sight, no custodians, not even a volunteer parent yet.

"Hey! Twitch!"

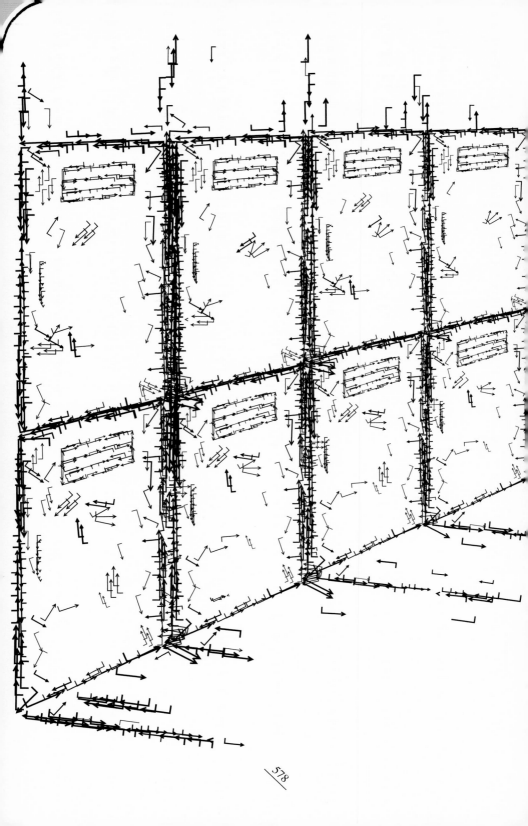

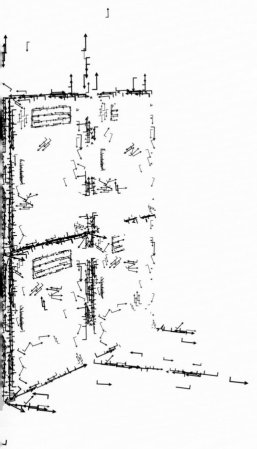

Dendish.

Striding toward her.

Reason enough to run.

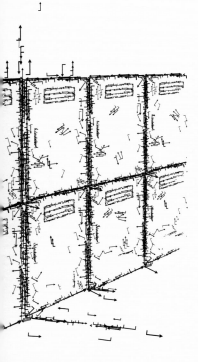

If not for another striding.

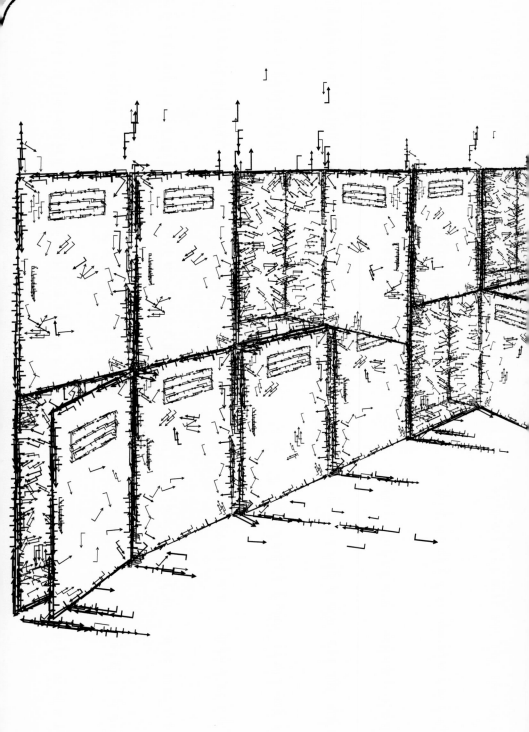

Rooting Xanther to the floor.

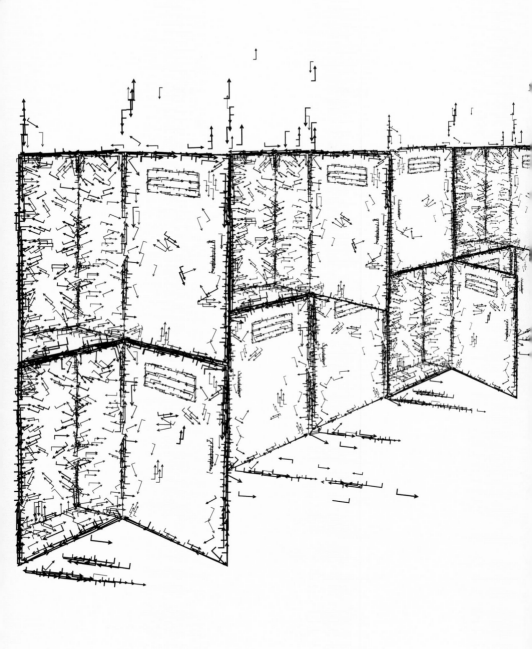

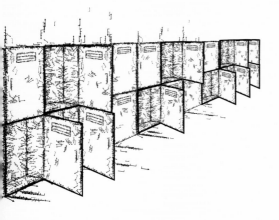

Nowhere Here.

Focus aided by focus. Wobbling. Loosening.

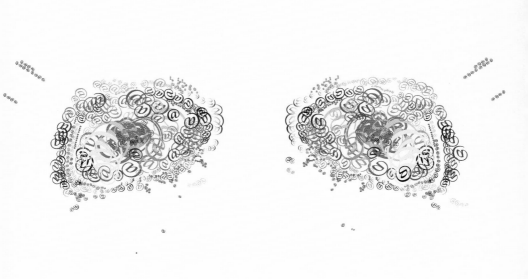

∴ **Smell brighter than garnet.** ∵

∴ **Taste thicker than cherry.** ∵

∴ **Dark as a long-ago red satisfaction.** ∵

∴ *A let go Oh!* ∵

Free!

What's of no interest at all. A still-opening sky . . .

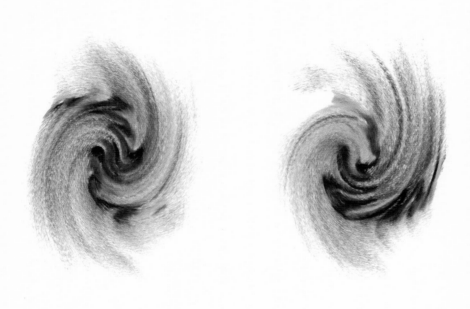

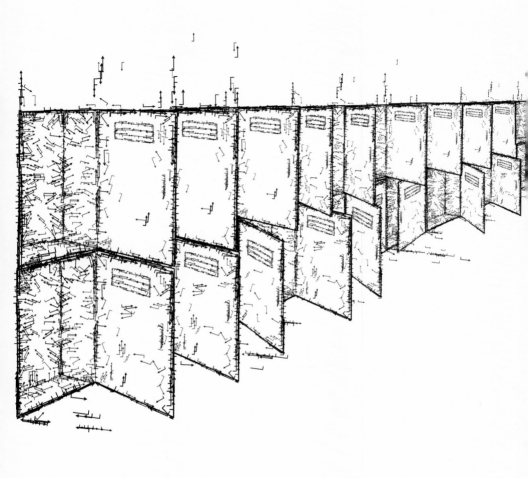

Dendish is shocked enough to stop, and anyway Xanther had already slipped away, to PE with no excuse in hand, certainly not the truth? who would believe that?, Ms. Barney?, surely not, not Xanther's parents either, they'd immediately leap to a seizure, it's not, or was it?

Xanther only has in hand apologies she doesn't need: today's just idle time, Ms. Barney whispering to Xanther to just take a mat, lie down, and think on the past year, the year ahead, and then stop thinking altogether, just focus on breathing, the same meditation drill Ms. Barney loves to haul out now and then, when most kids fall asleep, though not Xanther, head on fire, what Ms. Barney would probably say is 106°, screaming for a doctor.

Weirdly, she suddenly does feel Xanther's head with the back of her hand.

"You're freezing."

She brings Xanther a blanket.

Dendish is still in trouble when Xanther emerges from class. Teachers demanding to know how he opened the lockers. A custodian is there. The vice principal too.

Nearby, Mary Ellen and Trin Sisikado squat next to their backpacks, keeping a distant eye on Dendish, who suddenly stops arguing, now with Principal Sanchez, who just arrived, Dendish catching sight of Xanther just as she looks away, Fraidy K for sure, running away too, but not before catching the gaze of Mary Ellen and Trin, also swiveling her way, all of them with stones for eyes, except for the one with stones like burning coals.

The Reunionist

To undo the creature in us.

— *Simone Weil*

Mrs. Fischer probably already scooped up all of them (this is impulsive (Astair (knows it) just looked at the clock (grabbed keys))).

But Xanther still sees her first ((already) looking toward the Honda Element ((not a trace of surprise) like she'd known all along (long before the impulse even took root in Astair) (but what is surprise compared to this?))). Has Astair ever seen her daughter look so relieved (certainly not recently)? My ~~God~~ (*gosh!*) that smile!

Astair's relieved too (just watching those knobby (scarred) knees doing their wacky dance through a crowd of uniforms (white (shirts) and green (skirts and pants)) with (multicolored) backpacks).

Astair moves to unlock the doors (except the doors are already unlocked (driver's side too (unusual (Astair (by habit) always drives with locked doors)))).

Is the passenger door open?

"Mom!" Xanther (piling in) cries. "I love you so much! How did you know?!"

"Instinct," Astair smiles (grateful for the hug (surprised) (she should trust her instincts more)).

"Home! Home!" Xanther urges (throwing her backpack on the floor).

"Burning up!" Xanther adds ((panting!) (true) the day's hot enough ((drought) June in L.A.) (though Xanther's arms (around her neck) feel like ice)).

"Let me call Mrs. Fischer first."

"Home mom, home. I just texted her."

Xanther's already waving out the window at Mrs. Fischer (in her Volkswagen Touran ∴ Sharan ∴ (Brigitte's waving back (one wave) (Lucy giving Astair a thumbs-up))).

"Hurry! Mom!" Xanther cries (no joking (stabbing on the AC (twisting to high))). "We need to get home!"

Is this part of Astair's difficulty with the cat (it's absolute prominence in her daughter's life? (Astair can't believe she's so shallow to deny Xanther the excitement of this new experience (preoccupation? (obsession? (something else? (how about just love?)))))). Astair can see Xanther would not feel this way about a dog (because *they* would be rushing home to a dog ((or the dog would already be in the car) does difficulty arise then when (some unilateral myth of) love (or concern? (affection? (fascination (at least)? (how about just . . . (what?))))) gives way to differentials in taste?)(there's more here she needs to think through (because she's not thinking it through well enough (to approach a (conclusive) understanding of the dynamics at hand (maybe having to do with (a triad) three?))))).

Still no question:

The cat is just plain spooky.

Xanther had looked practically waxen by the time they had pulled up to the house (cheeks misted (beaded?) with perspiration).

"Honey, really, is everything okay?" Astair's heart racing ((over what she really means) Xanther racing away (up the walk (already less jangly) bounding up the stoop (flying!) their door already open (Anwar! ((agent of this unlocking) hearing the car?)) but (like Astair) equally irrelevant (Xanther (ignoring the arms of her father's hug) diving (instead) for his feet (for the tiny white pyramid (likely there all along(?))))).

(by the time Astair gets inside) Everything has changed (okay again).

Gone: the panic.

Gone: the waxen look (along with mists of ~~perception~~ (*perspiration!*)).

It's just weird.

If only there were some sign (sign?? ((isn't she too old for that?) ha!)) of robustness. Astair would settle for that. (after all) They (child and cat) are both fragile creatures (hardly given over to the winds of progress (health (strength)) but anchored to ((even) dragged down(?) by) ailment (a trembling alliance)) finding companionship in (the nature of) their declining (*shaky!*) well-being.

"Really, love?" Anwar laughs (easing his chair back (the open office door reason for this whispered articulation of her fear (full house ((Xanther (still) downstairs) but the twins are one room over)))).

"You told me most kittens don't survive." (She'll keep the whisper.)

"I thought it wasn't a kitten?"

"The thing barely moves. Barely opens its eyes. I can count each rib. Is there any question it's sick?"

"I'm not a vet."

Anwar's eyes shift then ((to the monitors (something there ((frames running code) (running images) (*Paradise Open* (?))))) to thoughts he can't voice(?)) to what Astair (sees now (she)) has seen incorrectly (not codes of play but codes of (civil) conduct (((the most elemental too) accounting) lines spying credits against expenditures)(thank you, Chase)).

"I completely forgot about the deposit for the dog," Astair groans ((in some sitcom) the dog episode would end without consequences ((especially financial ones (boring!)) especially those threading into future weeks and months (is she really thinking about TV?))(but here—)). They need that $5,000.

"Do you want to talk about finances?" That's how Anwar responds to her big gulp ((half serious) but thank goodness for a wink).

"No way," Astair winces (trying to wink back). "Do you want to talk about your ailurophobic wife?"

"Not a chance. What if she overhears us?"

Anwar takes both her hands and kisses her angry (*angular!*) knuckles (something (over the years) he has never ceased to do (more manners than affection (and yet (in that this is the manner of enduring respect) greater than the flighty influence of lust))).

"My father used to tell me that love's joy lives where love is shared but love's meaning lives where love is not."

"Shenouda, always the mystic."

"He would have said Xanther's friend is here as much for her as for you. For me too, the girls even, maybe Hatterly next door, maybe even who knows."

"She sure is smitten."

"He's her ship."

"No. The metaphor was stranger. You said she said she was the ship. And that that thing was—"

"Not a thing, Astair."

"You're right. I'm sorry. Why do I do that? I don't understand my own distaste. I don't understand myself. The blessing of a new paper topic?"

Anwar (smiling (at her own smile(?))) kisses her on the lips.

"Didn't Plato say life without an unexamined cat is not worth living?"

"I'm not sure that works."

Anwar nods. "A joke was supposed to happen, and a very clever one too, but it didn't happen."

Astair kisses him back. "Where would 'happen' be without 'didn't happen'?"

(in the evening) Astair helps Xanther with the (ritual?) feeding ((at least) she washes out the bottles). (again) Fails to touch the thing ((yes!) still a thing (what else when her skin crawls with even a reach ((the thought of the reach) twitches crawling over the back of her hand (Astair watching them (in disbelief))))) even as she watches over (with the same disbelief(?)) this little bundle of ((her) absurd!) aversion.

603

See it, Astair! See it!

For (only) what it (really(?)) is.

First: there's this ~~punched~~ (*pinched!*) face ((sup-posedly) soft (and (can Astair deny it?) incredibly cute)). A mash(-up(?)) of white made (up(?)) of (fluffy) cheeks right below (puffy) eyes below (little) ears ((all of it) triangular in some way (the tiny pink nose (triangle one) answering the larger eye-to-nose-to-eye (triangle two) with pink ears aloft retaining (if inverting) the shape (triangles three and four) with the chin (jaw (baseline) converging on the bottom of the nose (same orientation (as ears))) marking (tri-angle five) another (there's also the face containing all this ((from jaw to ear tips) triangle six)(there's also the chest (triangle seven)? the way it sits (from head to hips (triangle eight)?))))(what about the teeth?)).

Next: its trancelike poise (because it's diseased? (*ill!* (no question)) (frailing right here and now (right?))). ∴ **How often are the starts of the mightiest conclusions mislabeled frail?** ⁘∴ *Did she label?* ∴ With eyes allways closed (what's the deal with its eyes? (with Astair's refusal to admit "he" in place of "it"?) what *is* the deal with the eyes?).

Finally: its age. The vet said old (so why can't she shake the sense that he (there!) is still a kitten?). Something about the squishiness (cuteness (Ngai right? (Sianne))) of its face and body (the whole all-of-it). Knowledge (though (or exposure?)) grants here a curious (unsettling?) indeterminacy. (streamed (say) online) Would anyone think this thing (wow!) anything other than a kitten? Or would everyone recognize an aged and waning life (knowledge of the species redressing Astair's uncertainty (would CAT LOVERS just know?))?

Not that design and demeanor and dotage (the result of all this peering (if not poking)) offer a conclusion sensible of such parts. Instead (Astair is caught off guard by her reaction) a different understanding lurches within her chest:

(un)bear(able)

(sad)ness.

Or is this response (nothing to do with the creature (or any other variety of fur)) purely in regard to
Xanther (in the way she regards him (huh))?

(by way of the creature) Astair suffers one of
her uglier thoughts: (by way of Xanther's condition) has Astair concealed a means of securing Xanther's intoxicating looks ((is more than mere caring
involved when Astair asks Dr. Potts if studies linking
left-handedness to schizo-affective disorder (Webb?
∴ *Left-Handedness Among a Community Sample of
Psychiatric Outpatients Suffering From Mood and
Psychotic Disorders*, 2013 ∵) might have some bearing on Xanther (Dr. Potts looked at Astair like she
was the one who was schizo (good for him (shame
on her)))) doesn't Astair already know (by heart) that
debt and dependency are no species of love (isn't
she trained to recognize just how easily primitive
needs can secrete themselves beneath the cloak of
love?)?)?

The possibility turns Astair to stone (better to
bury herself in stone than knowingly manipulate
a daughter's weakness in order to serve her own
(what?) desire for attention((!)?)).

An earlier thesis idea had posited that not great
ugliness but the inverse paralyzes the motions of
life. Beauty attracts but Great Beauty renders itself
unviewable. "Cloaked in Terror" was one working
title. Astair (in précis) had laid out the proposition
that Medusa was in fact inconceivably gorgeous
(another title had been "Gorgon Gorgeous").

(this evening (at least)) Her own ugliness does
away with stone. Maybe the tiny beast helps too ((as
cute as it is) boy is it ugly! (pinched squished and
squinched)). Or maybe it's just Xanther's lovely goof-
iness that makes stone (finally) an impossible order.

They end up watching goofy videos ((crying over Mr. G and Jellybean) laughing over cat clips (did Astair have any idea (to what extent) such feline reveries had populated the Web?)). Xanther doesn't spare a word for that comment (but her eye comedy gets Astair wheezing with laughter).

(practicing Tai Chi (later)) Xanther's lint-with-paws tumbles (blindly) around their ankles (while Astair leads them (all?(!)) through the first steps :: *Beginning* :: :: *Ward Off* :: :: *Grasp Sparrow's Tail* :: :: *Ward Off With Right Hand* ::).

"Think of yourself carrying a big grapefruit, which by the time you turn right reduces to a tennis ball."

More eye comedy. Followed by cat comedy (Xanther scooping up her charge (in open hands (suggesting a much bigger creature)) ending up with a cotton ball lost within closed palms).

Xanther suffers the routine (plus the introduction of a fifth movement :: *Roll Back* ::). Maybe it's a general spirit of giddiness (the little one relaxing her(?)) but Xanther seems to be improving.

Maybe that's what's troubling Astair's seeing.

Forget the poppycock about maternal-daughter regards. Forget the cat.

Xanther looks stronger.

(before tucking in Shasti and Freya) Astair spends too much time shutting windows and drawers (sure it's summer but do so many cabinets need to be left open?).

"All this has happened before—"
"—and it will happen again."

(Her two girls ((trading off in rounds) from their pillows ((again?) obsessively watching *Peter Pan*?) (dissolving into giggles)).)

Astair kisses them again and again (lips tickling necks).
(of course) Now is when she remembers it. (all day) She'd meant to ask (while these two romped the sun with their latest assertion and fascination (house and yard declared Neverland)). Asking now (at night) would be cruel: are you having nightmares?

"Mommy, how many Mona Lisas are there?" Freya asks.
"Just one."
"Weird."
"Yeah, weird," Shasti adds (the swerves in her voice heading for sleep).
But (as Astair reaches the door) Shasti's voice reaches out (nowhere near sleep):
"Mommy, leave the light on."

(finally (after 10 PM)) Astair gets to the work of the thesis (books and paper (and laptop) arrayed around her (on the round table (in the breakfast nook (beside their wall of B & W rainfall (by a local artist (whose name Astair has forgotten (though she and Anwar were both told her work ∴ ▓▓▓▓▓ ▓▓▓▓▓ ∴ would someday be worth something ("It's a limited edition. Only 117 prints made."))))))))).

(for the first hour) Astair turns to Elizabeth Marshall Thomas' *The Tribe of Tiger*. The poem "Of His Cat, Jeoffry" is familiar to her (written (in the eighteenth century) by a poet named Christopher Smart (eight years in a madhouse)) but something about the following line stirs her:

For the Cherub Cat is a term of the Angel Tiger.

And sticks with her (as she goes on to read (about (how cats (along with hyenas and mongooses) arose from the viverravines) (how they evolved into singular carnivores) (how one of the author's cats (named Wicca) died in the talons of a great horned owl) (how the lions evolved on the savannahs 700,000 years ago) (how when it thunders on the savannahs lions answer back))).

But "Angel Tiger" flickers even more vividly to life (when Astair turns to the Romanian fairy tale called "The Cat" (on which Marie-Louise von Franz's analysis (on Feminine Redemption) is based (in which the lopping off of a cat's head and tail (with Turkish sabers (called yatagans)) initiates a transformation into a beautiful girl))). (appalled by the dismemberment) Astair has to stop (before reaching the analysis). On the cover is a (yellowish) caricature of a large cat (with a small head (with what looks like a red heart dangling around its neck) ∷ The Empress by Vicki Cowan ∴).

There's a grainy photo (before the preface) of von Franz with Jung standing outside (on a field or wild lawn (about 1960)). Astair scribbles notes in the margin (and on index cards (more like inspirations(?))) as well as creates a document for a possible bibliography (including now *Beware the Cat* by William Baldwin (supposedly written in 1553 ∷ Published 1561, 1570, and 1584 ∴)). Astair also orders online *The Cat in Magic* (by someone named M. Oldfield Howey).

(all while) Thoughts jag back to Avantine ((the good-bye minutes) asking her what she had against the comma ("They cut?") (warning her to keep logging hours with Dr. Sandwich (Dr. Elina Sandawai (whom they can no way afford ((what is she doing?) they can't even afford *The Cat in Magic*.)))))).

Interrupted ((?) suddenly) by the memory of Anwar and her at the Prado (now (displacing) when was that?) contemplating a small sculpture stuffed into the corner of a small atrium (something to do with Dionysus (was there a cat? ∷ **Dionysus with Panther. AD 130-140. Found by José Nicolás de Azara in Tivoli, 1779. At the Villa dei Pisoni.** ∴). ∷ *Thirst replaces missing thyrsus & head . . .* ∴).

(in fact) The more Astair circles the literature on cats the more overwhelmed she feels.

(more) Links (upon links) deliver her to a bit of news on a mountain lion living in Griffith Park (known as P-22 (with deteriorating health (possibly due to eating a coyote that had eaten poisoned rats (if only P-22 had devoured the man who assaulted a woman near the Observatory last month ∴ May 14, 2014 ∵ (or what of another news bit (last week ∴ May 31, 2014 ∵): a twelve-year-old girl ((Xanther's age!) who loved cats) was lured by two friends into the woods and stabbed nineteen times (in the name of someone called the Slender Man (what of those two friends? (what of Slender Man? (heal P-22 . . . heal . . .)))))))))).

((come midnight) back in "their stacks") Astair hunts for her copy of Simone Weil's *Gravity and Grace*. ∴ *Whoever fails to occasionally invite a song of madness into the chambers of their thoughts will too soon find the teeth of madness at their door.* ∵ The book does not materialize but a quote does (is it Weil's?):

God in suffering all that is to come
relieves us of all that is left to come
from knowing.

Astair returns to the table knowing nothing (more). Her best is an inept try at organizing (at least it clears her head).

In no particular order:

Cat as animal: predator, pet, etc.

Cat as symbol: totem, myth, deity, etc.

Cat as cute:
                caricature, costume, YouTube clips, etc.

Cat as scale:
                XXS to XXL, etc. etc. etc. etc.

Cat as is:
                no   more   terr(or)ific   than   any   other
                creature hunting another thing in order
                to live, etc. etc. etc. etc. etc. etc. etc. etc.

Just part of the gig.

Chemical Memories
Terror Of Complex Thought
Magic As Shortcut: The Conservative Rhetoric of Power

The Imaginative Limitations of...
Escapism: Benefits & Harms

Talent

Genius

(while Astair works (so perfectly timed too (of course (doesn't she already know this about cats?)))) Footsteps (tiny ones) descend the stairs. (then) A small hop to the foyer floor? Like a puff of air. More footsteps. More puffs of air. Does a chair creak (or is this only the squeak of her pen on paper?)?

((then) finally) A bump (gasp) to the tabletop.

(How has that little thing made it this far?)

Except (when Astair raises her eyes) Xanther's white friend is not there to greet her.

Astair gets up to check under the table (to stretch her legs). She checks the foyer. The stairs. She even checks the kitchen.

No sign of the cat.

Elizabeth Marshall Thomas has a nice moment describing the silence and (paw) printless manner by which cats move (∵ " . . . cats tend to hold back, approaching life with reserve and caution . . . often [walking] without leaving any tracks at all . . . we don't see them, we don't hear them." ∵ ∵p. 37.∵). (of course!) Astair (who knows zip about cats) imagines a (detectable) plod.

But had she imagined it? Compounded her jottings with paws upon a floor? Really?
Astair ends up on the living room sofa with Fabler's gift in her hands.

A holograph at first glance (facsimile (at second glance (though original markings are at work here too? (Fabler's?)(a foolscap (too (or two)) folded among the signatures)))).

Poems (basically) about (to?) a cat ((apparently) having lived a long life (nearly two decades) before dying of "natural causes" in the author's arms).

(when the old book first arrived) Astair had tried the introduction ((now) she has no interest (she doesn't want frame (she needs meet (*meat!*)))).

Astair runs her palm across the near-purplish cover and then thumbs (almost carelessly) through the lightly worded pages (some pale some colored some black).

Sadness doesn't need the end.
Sadness owns middles too.

Astair's not even sure what (about these lines (she finds)) grips her so fiercely (maybe because what they mourn for is simply a friend (maybe because what they pray for admits what must exceed prayer)).

The lines maroon her under the ruby-charcoal throw ((face wet)(breaths shallow)(a tingling fatigue that (as it keeps waking her with its complaint) keeps ushering her toward enveloping sensations of defeat (no defeated "by" necessary (or "for") (just defeat)) (because what she keeps revisiting speaks to that which should remain forever triumphant (what (one day) she should not have to tell her children (tell herself) is forever impossible (forever appalling)))))):

617

The Reunionist

He stalks wordless out of the dark.
This is death.

He takes his place beside me,
licks a paw, and settles until I
can move. His stillness suggests
I can move. He will stay.

Not that there is somewhere to go.

We are already a lost constellation.
Whoever finds us will find us
not minding discoveries anymore.

Had I desired chirps? Some purr-
nuzzling meet? I was expected
and what was out of place before
relaxed into meanings beyond the need

of any place.

Had I imagined that beyond life voice
would unify our unknowns? How the rest
of things, long mute or incomprehensible,
would at last articulate their belonging?

He hardly looks at me. I find I only
look at him briefly. Our gaze
faces whatever forever craves of us.

From now on, beyond questions of completeness,
mystery satisfies our curiosities. We are voiceless as one.

Who would have thought that once such a description of heaven might have seemed too little?

(eventually) Wolves replace her tears (what is Astair (really) getting into this mess over?). Hard glass returns hard clarity (always the same wolves (always fighting (or tangling (or reuniting)))). Lares & Penates. (and while Dov must allways linger there (paths taken (and not taken ((lost) thank *goodness* (*GOODNESS!*))))) What surfaces ((out of the blue(s)) never lost) is the artist's name ((no doodling required) (no imagined pawsteps necessary)).

(Friday) Astair is up before everyone else. Tea. Early yoga ((a short run there) a real popcorn session ((without munchy satisfaction (or buttery smell)) each joint ringing loose)).

(by the time she returns) Anwar's out (driving the girls to school). Xiomara arrives (by the time coffee's brewed). Astair (pouring two cups (leaving Xiomara to her fixings ((lots of cream) lots of sugar))) puts aside the *New York Times* crossword ((30(Across)) Language originally known as Mocha) to revisit her (unfinished) tic-tac-toe:

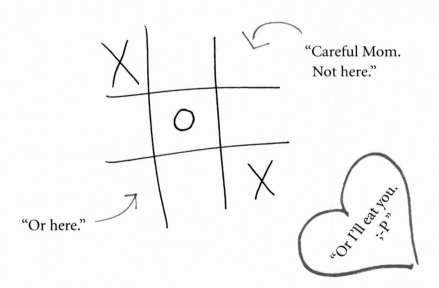

"Careful Mom.
Not here."

"Or I'll eat you. ;-P"

"Or here."

Has something changed? No. Nothing's changed. :: *Yes, it's changed* :: What's Xanther's game? Is she playing mislead mom? (An O (in either corner) will set up O's for a (possible) three-across.) Astair needs (a few) more sips of black to see that an O-corner move also sets up X for *two* possible three-acrosses.

620

"Gato," Xiomara says.

"Excuse me?" Astair (at once) looks around for Xanther's charge ((no announcement of pawsteps this time) cat/kitten nowhere in sight).

This is Xiomara's last month. She has worked for the Ibrahims since they moved to Echo Park (at this house for years (thanks to Cyril Kosiginski)). (in July) She moves back to Mexico (to be with her (ailing) mother). Good news ((not the ailing mother part) she's unaffordable now) but Astair will (still) miss her (she was just starting to get to know her ((strong as pub stout)(wide as a clear day)(today wearing an Anthony Bourdain t-shirt))).

"In Spanish." Xiomara taps at the tic-tac-toe. "Gato."

Astair spends the rest of the day at the clinic. The possibility that she will likely run out of money (and discontinue all visits (what small fees (she receives) don't cover the cost of gas to get here)) she mentions to none of her patients (or clients (a slippery nomenclature)).

1.

Mrs. Dewarty (eyebrows like crows' beaks (cheeks swelling with age or hardship (or allergies?))) started off her session plain and simple.

"Let's just say I have . . . dilemmas."
Almost fifty. Married for nearly fifteen years.
"Let's just say at this point it's . . . uncertain."
Meaning her marriage.
"But what happens with relationships, any relationship, maybe even this relationship: you have to stop listening. It's the only way to get through the noise."

(only) Mrs. Dewarty wasn't there to draw out of complaint a decision to divorce. Quite the contrary (her marriage was solid (just veering a little strange)).

Which was the issue.

(in order to spur on her husband's amorous appetite for her (he was a food critic)) Mrs. Dewarty had started to hint at possible affairs she was contemplating (or even in the throes of (all completely imaginary (she was more faithful than her church)))).

The problem was that this intrigue was working. And it confused her. (at times) Mrs. Dewarty was convinced her husband knew she was joking ("But what kind of joke is this, yes?"). (other times) She was sure he believed her.

His passionate response (however) remained the same (extremely satisfying).

2.

Ms. Penikas (she announced) is of the age where problems are not her concern. (like Mrs. Dewarty) this is her first visit (though she's probably there on her own accord). She wears gray (gray sneakers and gray slacks (hair like tightly coiled tin)).

"Empaths! Let me tell you about empaths!" she announced at some point (always announcing (this time while digging for a throat lozenge (apparently an endless supply in that faux-jaguar purse))). "Emotional shoplifters."

Astair failed to get much closer than this (forget (actually) finding out what was troubling her (though clearly (the way she fidgeted and half-shrieked (all her announcements)) she was anxious)).

About the only thing Astair knew (for certain) by the end of the session was that neither Ms. Penikas nor Mrs. Dewarty were participating in (using? doing? (what had Taymor called it?)) HomePorn.

3.

(about) Ananias Fielding (what a name!) Astair wasn't so sure. Ananias had been coming in for months now. She was young (not even thirty) attractive (gym four or more times a week) and reckless (why she was here). Too smart too (why she might ditch here at any given moment).

"Let's not sacrifice the present moment for the sake of an anticipated moment," Ananias had begun (running a twist of red hair between her lips (a habit Astair can make no sense of (beyond classic self-soothing behavior))). "That's reasonable. Even a beautiful thing to say. Except, hey, just as easily balanced, philosophically, like so: Let's *do* sacrifice the present moment on behalf of a later moment's greater satisfaction."

"A tidy dialectic." Ananias can handle the word.

"Exactly. Except, hey, so what? How do we distinguish the wisest route?"

"By telling me what happened?"

"Nothing happened."

Ananias had slipped off her sandals and spread her toes out (like they could grip the air). She has nice legs.

"I'm young. I want fun. He was, we were, well both pretty drunk. Hot guy, really really fine, even for me, bod to rock, abs like you know, photoshopped, showing it all off on the dance floor too, everyone looking like they do, like they're not looking, but he's only looking at me. No hurry at all. Buys me drinks, but not every drink, like that cool, that easy, made buying him a drink seem easy, cool.

"Clothes off though, I was like whoa, we were barely kissing, and his dick's in my mouth, and he's fucking my mouth, and I don't like dick in my mouth, and especially come anywhere near my mouth. But maybe because of the drinks, and his place having this totally vibed thing going for it, with those super-big candles, and expensive wine glasses, furry carpets, erotic photographs, but seriously tasteful, on the wall, I'm like going with it, figuring this is just the start, and then he's off, like that, like gushing too, back of my throat. I'm gagging on his come, his cock, and he's pulling out fast, like he's sorry, but still coming all over my face, so maybe not sorry, and I'm thinking I'm lucky I'm naked and it's just getting on my tits, and not on my dress, a Hervé Léger knockoff but still nice, and wow do I hate the taste of come, and wow do I really hate the taste of his come, and then waiting for him to say I'm sorry or something, but he's just standing over me, breathing hard, and sagging, like his dick, his balls, getting down on his knees, and I'm like man what a disappointment, and he better get me a rag quick to wipe this shit up. Am I grossing you out?" Ananias asked suddenly.

"Not at all," Astair replied (had her expression betrayed something? (a lip curling up (like wallpaper (bereft of glue) won over by heat)?) (even if the whole story had made Astair feel icky)).

"Except he doesn't get a rag. Nothing about him betrays discomfort. And I, like, start to doubt my objections, you know, before his confidence?

"And then he surprises me. He lays me down on his soft furry rug. I don't know if it's real fur but man did it feel good. And then he goes down on me. And he's really good. And takes his time. I forget his

626

spunk on my chest, on my lips, the stickiness still in my mouth. He does something with his tongue while his hands are on my tits, running up and down my sides, gripping my ass. And then his fingers are in me, and not just one, but moving in this way, that's like right in sync with his tongue, and I'm wet, I'm so wet, and I'm coming, coming hard. Now it's my turn to breathe hard, and okay that makes up for the first bit. But—Am I turning you on?"

"Ananias." (Another betrayal (tell)?) Ananias giggled (at the sound of her name?). Should Astair have asked if Ananias wanted to turn her on? Too late.

"Just telling this again is a turn on for me. I haven't told anyone. It's, you know, too painful. There I was spent and thinking What now? Am I cutting out? Are we sleeping? Is there a chance for breakfast?

"But he started licking me again, lightly, like my tattoos, my navel, each nipple, and by the time he's biting my lips, lightly, he's sliding inside me, fuck he was hard, and I'm like surprised, but wanting it, and you know how that sometimes happens, when you're already ready to come again, like right at this edge, tingling like crazy. That's how it was. And he's in me deep, his body's like this fit of muscles I can't wrap my legs around tight enough, and then I'm, wow, coming big time, and wow, he is too, and when does that happen?, and how can that not be a sign?

"But I'm like fuck fuck fuck, he just came inside me, except he reads me quick, smiling, showing me how he's got a condom on. He'd put it on while he was going down on me! Fucking unbelievable!

"And that wasn't even the end. We fucked again. Which was way cray. Because we went for an hour. Or more. No exaggeration. All over his place. In the

bathroom. On the kitchen counter. He draped me over his ottoman. His fingers never stopped finding new places. I know I came again. Maybe twice that round. He did for sure. And by that time we were like Bikram sweaty. And we were licking each other's bodies like we could drink each other.

But now get this, this is the crazy part, why I'm telling you all this, because it still blows my mind. At some point I started tasting his come again, that I guess was still kinda on me, and I'm loving it! Like I'm suddenly crazy about his taste. I even tell him. I practically beg him to come in my mouth again. He just like laughs and kisses my mouth, pure gentleman. Kisses me again when he walks me out to my car. If he'd told me to suck him off in the middle of the street I would have but he didn't and he didn't call me either and when I finally called him he returned my call but his voice was as distant as the country he was supposedly in."

Ananias takes a deep breath.

"When was this?"

"Last year."

"Oh."

"You thought it was more recent, right? I know. And the weird part is what I remember most, besides like the obvious porn shots you kinda have to trap in your head, for, you know, shower time, I still remember the taste. How it went from awful and then how the whole experience changed it and it was suddenly all I wanted. I even felt bad for not loving it when I had it the first time. What do you make of that?"

All Astair wanted to ask was whether or not Ananias knew anything about HomePorn.

(at home) That night Astair wants to go down on Anwar. She's dressing up ((already putting on lipstick) heading out with the gals (in a few moments)). What's it been? Months? A year? Can she even remember his taste?

Except Anwar surprises her first (right as she's locking the bedroom door): the company he was freelancing for (Enzio?) just deposited $9,000 in their account.

Astair hugs him (he wants the hug (Anwar loves this more than his wife on her knees (and she would have gone down on her knees (had Taymor not arrived early (Freya and Shasti thumping on the door))))).

"Why do you look so happy?" Taymor snips.

They are (still) at Silverlake Wine (a special event (hosted by Open Lot (a creative consulting think tank(!) (more like drink tank))) crowded with black-rimmed glasses (and as many shaved heads and leather skirts as glasses of Sangiovese and Gewürztraminer)).

"Because I'm at a wine twasting?" Astair snips back ((more like pips) the slur an unintentional dividend (of too many tastes)).

"Or you finally got some?"

"You've no idea," Astair smiles.

"Now what are you two talking about?" Abigail interrupts ((turning) heads (still) wandering her ((braided) blond hair) back through the crowd (she's the one who looks like Kirsty Hume (with a Lululemon bag over one shoulder))).

"What does Tay ever talk about?" Astair laughs.

"Sue me. So I like sex."

"You know what they say about talkers." Abigail looks happy too. "Same as litigators."

"Gia's a talker too," Taymor snorts.

Their ((part Austrian)(part Australian)) friend has yet to rejoin her partners in crime (not while three men keep refilling her cup (teeth white as crescent moons orbiting a world they'll never visit (no matter how many Pellegrinos they pour))).

"They're half her age," Abigail says.

"Combined," Taymor quips (wickedly amused ((so much so) she repeats it to Gia when their (pole-dancing-instructor) friend rejoins the group (granted her erotic workshops are a goof (in no way connected to the wealth that accounts for her Malibu "shanty" with a four-car garage)))).

Abigail pops (into her mouth) a tiny cracker (with jalapeño hummus): "Smicey!" No bubbly water for her. Slurs again: "This has real pretential."

"Is that like pretentious in the future?" Tay is not beaming. Tonight (though) Abby doesn't care.

"I'll have to thrink that through." Abigail zaps back.

"Ms. Cynical is alive and well." (Gia's (hoarse) bemusement changing focus.)

"Designated drivers are smiley people?" Taymor scoffs.

(though (Astair's guess)) Taymor really does love driving her friends home (well not Gia tonight (one of the gibbous moons (somehow) got a yes)).

"At least tell us his name," Taymor begs Abigial (when they drop her off).

"Nope!" Almost as good as a name (their girl can't help herself (grin keeps widening (as she spins away to her apartment building))).

"Well, I'll be," Taymor smiles (warmth (maybe more) jeweling her eyes as midnight traffic zips along Hyperion). "He better hope we approve."

"I have a name too" is what Astair leaves Taymor with ((climbing out of the Mercedes) at the curb of the Ibrahim home).

"Excuse me?"

"Jim Helhenny Joab."

"An affair?" Taymor can't conceal the note of (rare) judgment (delighting Astair).

"I can't tell you more until I tell Anwar. I owe it to my husband."

"You're fucking with me?"

Taymor fucked with Astair a little too ((suddenly) handing her a bottle of wine (ribboned ((Juslyn Cabernet) 2009)) along with a small box ((equally ribboned (cordate bow)) wrapped in black oily paper)).

"What's this for?"

"Does it have to be *for* anything?"

"My birthday isn't until March."

"For your anniversary then."

Everyone's asleep. No cat. Not even a creak (only clicks from easing the locks back into place (Astair even succeeds in halting the multilingual announcement regarding the state of their door)).

She sets Taymor's gifts on the coffee table ((both) unopened). Astair had meant to break the news to Anwar tonight (but breaking nothing (now) seems even better ((still) stillness moves (at last))).

"Something good finally came of ya."

(earlier in the day) Astair had Googled Jim Hel-henny Joab. Not just plenty of reviews and a Wikipe-dia entry (artist (MacArthur Fellow (etc.)) (etc.)) but articles documenting the worth of his work.

(though each piece is unique) The glass wolves on their mantel belong to a series of eleven. Astair's looks like one of the largest (Astair had measured).

(according to Christie's (at an auction last month)) A smaller version had sold for $58,490.

635

A Picnic

You're funny.

— Victim #4

Long before dawn the memory of death dispenses with sleep. Breakfast with The Mayor starts early but lasts a long time. He looks drunk again but isn't. He orders eggs but doesn't touch them when they arrive. He orders fruit but the blackberries and slices of blood oranges go untouched. Maybe he sips his coffee. At one point he dabs butter on a piece of toast but never lifts it to his lips.

Still he insists Isandòrno eat and Isandòrno does eat, though, as always, he finishes nothing on his plate.

What happened in Los Angeles has not gone away. It was not a trifle. Too much money was lost. Too many pinks. U.S. news did not even report on the nature of the drug seized.

The Mayor alternates between this being a good thing and this being proof that someone else got hold of the balloons.

—Teyo is a good man, The Mayor says now, looking over his parapet toward the large empty lawn. He is just as upset as I am.

How can he be? Teyo did not know César Miguel Orozco Hernandez.

The Mayor had watched César Miguel grow up. The Mayor owned the fast cars but César Miguel confirmed how fast they could go. From an early age, he had looked like a celebrity. The Mayor loved to tease him for failing to learn how to sing or kick a football, but more than a few musicians, and at least one professional athlete, had disappointed The Mayor. César Miguel knew how to get along with The Mayor.

—They say the bullets tore apart his heart. How many women in this city alone are heartbroken? I am heartbroken.

The Mayor likes to think of himself as a romantic. It is more complicated than that. Isandòrno does not doubt that some briny feeling has oozed through The Mayor ever since the morning of May 15th, but it is as much attached to his good-looking lieutenant as it is to the economics of dispensation and return.

At last The Mayor's staff stops
bringing him things to eat and
brings out the weapon.

—You and the young men like
guns. It is probably a cock thing. I
like to see what I'm killing. A powerful rifle, of course, but an even
more powerful scope.

The Mayor spends all of his time
on the scope. He adjusts and re-
adjusts. He has the lenses cleaned
and recleaned. With a .50 caliber
assault rifle like this, a U.S. M107,
it is necessary to shoot into the

ground. Otherwise, a round can travel a long way.

After a whistle, a zookeeper walks out onto the big lawn. He leaves behind an animal. The Mayor lifts the rifle and spends a long time looking through the scope.

Isandòrno is confused. At first he sees the monkey that rode on the back of the pony. But it is not that monkey. It is the baby chimpanzee to which The Mayor refused to give the tangerine and pear.

Eventually the baby chimpanzee starts to dart around and The Mayor sends Isandòrno down.

Isandòrno walks out onto the big lawn with The Mayor and the big gun at his back. The promise of their immediate blackness relaxes him. Not that The Mayor could hit Isandòrno.

Isandòrno tosses out the fruit and waits until the baby chimpanzee has settled down eating pieces of banana and watermelon.

The gun and sight are gone when Isandòrno returns to the parapet.

—27,810 Euros is a lot of money, is all The Mayor says.

Lunch is like breakfast. The Mayor considers various sandwiches and tartars but touches none of it.

A call from Teyo seems to benefit his spirits.

—Teyo is just as upset as I am.

In the afternoon, The Mayor informs Isandòrno that they are going on a picnic. He had mentioned a picnic weeks ago but it had never happened. In all the time he has been with The Mayor they have never gone on a picnic.

It looks like quite a picnic too. The van is loaded up with folding tables, party hats, and a deep fryer with an oil capacity of one hundred pounds.

—It can make a thousand donuts in an hour, The Mayor explains.

Isandòrno falls asleep on the drive. When they arrive, Isandòrno sees that it is another suburb outside of Mexico City. Isandòrno knows the suburb and the place, which on a few occasions The Mayor has referred to as McRanch.

The man who greets them is Cutberto Bruno Villegas. He is always happy to see The Mayor. He is happy now. The Mayor attended his wedding a year ago. The Mayor sent flowers and silver when his baby was born three months ago. Isandòrno delivered the presents.

No one ever hugs Isandòrno but
Cutberto does. He is a clueless
man. Round but not heavy. Cutberto's skin looks like amber. He
has on bright blue pants and a
faded green and white collared
shirt. Like The Mayor, he has a
thick moustache.

Cutberto is an accountant. He is
very good with numbers but he
doesn't really understand how the
numbers arrive or how they go.
He just knows how to make them
add up.

—We've come to throw a picnic!

Amber turns to rose. A smile lifts
the glasses off his nose. At least
he doesn't try to kiss The Mayor's
hand.

—For my son?

—For the whole family!

The Mayor's men unload the plastic chairs and tables. They spread
out the tablecloths, and set out
boxes of utensils and condiments.

In the midst of all this arrangement they set up the deep fryer.

—I hope you don't mind, The
Mayor says, while the oil heats up.

—I love surprises. Especially this
kind of surprise. My wife and I
will talk about it for years.

—I know she's home.

—Of course! Cutberto declares
but then lowers his voice to a tone
of more intimate seriousness.

—Our child has been colicky these past few weeks. My wife too has been feeling the effects and has not found much sleep. But it is nothing serious. Shall I get her?

—Please.

Cutberto disappears into the house, followed by his men. The Mayor's men also go inside.

Beyond the property, long brick walls are covered with blue and white graffiti. Dogs roam the alleys. The sky is raked a pale blue.

The fields are baked to a gold dust
under the summer sun.

Here, though, is a little paradise
of privacy. The garden is immacu-
late. Elms and tall eucalyptuses
bring shade. Thick rows of yucca
conceal far walls as well as add to
their defense.

Closer at hand there is a pool and
a permanent grill. The grass is a
dark green and cut regularly.

Cutberto advertises little but does
not live badly.

His wife looks strange. Her skin appears nearly translucent as if a smile were meant to reveal the jawbone beneath.

Her son starts to cry. The Mayor, though, gathers up the infant in his thick hands, stares for a long time at the shrieking spasm of little feet and hands, and eventually the shrieking subsides.

Cutberto winks at his wife.

—He needs to eat, The Mayor announces.

—He is on formula now, Cutberto
hesitates to admit.

—Oh? The Mayor responds, looking more closely at the wife. Even
her dark hair looks transparent.

More of The Mayor's men go
inside the house with Cutberto's
wife to retrieve a bottle of formula. Isandòrno notices that Cutberto's men have not reappeared.

—She is in treatment, Cutberto
confides.

—Addiction is a scourge.

—No, no. Not that, Cutberto laughs uneasily. Cancer. She has four more sessions to go.

The wife reappears alone with a warm bottle. She seems as struck blind as Cutberto by the sight of The Mayor placating their tiny child. She rests her head on her husband's shoulder.

—The oil is hot, one of The Mayor's men announces.

—It can make a thousand donuts in an hour.

—Are we having donuts? Who else is coming?

There are now at least a dozen tables set up. Afternoon breezes disturb many of the white table-cloths.

—Before all that, The Mayor says, lowering his voice so as not to disturb the child. I wonder if we might talk a little about work?

—Ah.

The wife turns at once to go.

—Please. Stay. It is nothing that sensitive.

She looks unsure. She has never heard The Mayor say anything like this before. Isandòrno knows because he has never heard The Mayor say anything like this before. Cutberto nods. The wife sits down.

—May I take him off your hands?
She asks.

—Let's let him sleep. The baby
does in fact seem to have fallen
asleep in the cradle of The Mayor's
big arms.

—César Miguel troubles my appetite for things.

—Mayor?

—You know, of course, César
Miguel Orozco Hernandez?

But Cutberto shakes his head and takes his wife his hand.

—The trouble in Los Angeles?

—Oh yes. The trouble in Los Angeles. Now Cutberto looks uneasily at his wife. She stares only at her baby, hands twitching in her lap for the want of it.

—Terrible numbers. You know that?

—I know that.

At which point one of Cutberto's men stumbles out of the house. Blood has dripped down from his hairline to the center of his nose.

He manages to reach them but seems too confused to know who anyone is. What he tries to say makes no sense.

Two of The Mayor's men manage to each grab an arm of the confused man.

Isandòrno has already tapped nine on his fingers and risen.

The Mayor, though, holds out his hand. And then loud enough for all his men to hear: "If they can't handle this, you handle them."

The Mayor's men gently lead the bleeding man back into the house. Isandòrno can see the bleeding man is one of Cutberto's friends. The Mayor sees it too.

He hands the child back to the mother and puts his arm around Cutberto.

Together they walk away from the

spit of oil, the small birds landing on the tables, and head deeper into the yard.

Isandòrno knows they are talking about numbers and locations. Cutberto knows all the numbers but he says again and again he knows nothing about locations.

—I never know the wheres, he says again and again.

After a while The Mayor starts to laugh. After a while they return.

More than once the wife makes to stand up with her child, but perhaps because she is disturbed about what she might find inside, she decides to wait for her husband here. She has to keep making this decision.

—I wonder if you might have some wine, good wine? The Mayor asks now.

—Yes! Of course! Cutberto happy now to oblige. His feet stumble briefly before he disappears inside.

—Are you hungry? The Mayor asks the wife.

She shakes her head and this time does stand up, shaking from the exertion.

—Mayor, I fear we must lie down.

—Of course. The Mayor smiles. He kisses her forehead then, and then in turn kisses the baby's forehead, and one last time lifts it up to the sky.

Cutberto emerges from the house and seeing The Mayor lifts up a bottle of wine to the sky.

—Our finest!

—Let's eat! The Mayor shouts back and drops the baby into the deep fryer.

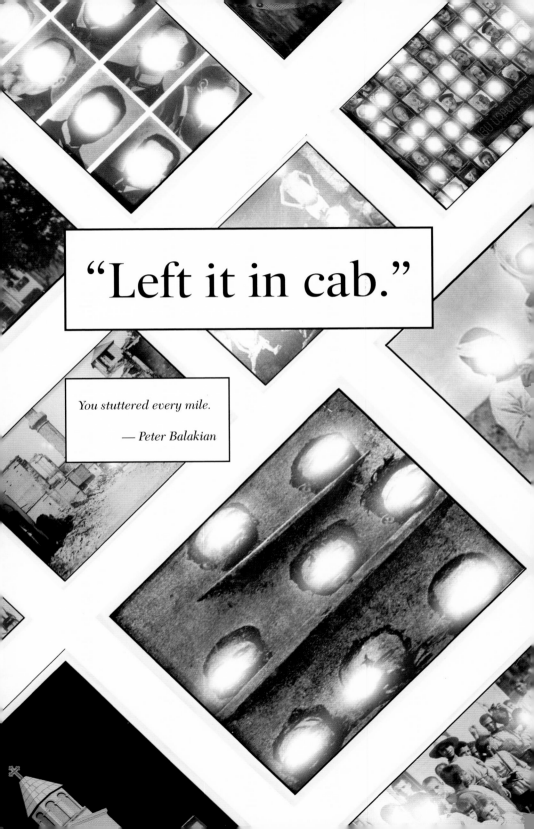

"Left it in cab."

You stuttered every mile.

— Peter Balakian

Patil probably right about new car service. If Patil say Uber, then Uber here to stay. She always good with new. On top of changes. Shnorhk not change. Gives Patil plenty reason to reproach. And smile. At least curl up sides of mouth.

Years ago Patil made of smiles. Not Shnorhk. Her family, friends, warned he would never smile. She explain Shnorhk have straight face that make others laugh. Shnorhk not understand. Patil also said she had smiles enough for two.

They met at illegal races northwest of Yerevan. Not even twenty. Patil's brothers bring her along. Shnorhk wear leather gloves, long scarf of white. One day he will drive Maserati but that day he drive 1963 Bug. She laughed for more than two. And when Shnorhk win laughed for all of them.

Her brothers never stop saying winning is under hood. Even back then Hovahn swear success is this mathematics of more: the more hp, the more victories. But Patil always know what matters most is whose hands are on wheel.

After race they all get drunk on pomegranate wine. Shnorhk tell stories about Jim Clark. Until night tell time time has come for great Beetle racer with great blue prize ribbon to give great beauty kiss. Shnorhk give blue prize ribbon kiss. Give that to beauty. No fear to hurl rusted bolts around slick turn but to lift eyes to her eyes and find her lips was too much.

Patil never miss race.

Young men would come just for her, old men too, men with wives, with fastest cars, without cars, just to lay eyes on her. But Patil only look at Shnorhk.

Smiles for two.

Now Patil tell Shnorhk get business card.

"If not Uber then at least have this for customers. They like you, *if* they like you, they call you."

"Like me?"

Patil almost smile.

When had Shnorhk last heard her laugh?

On table she sets out yogurt, cucumber, kashk bademjan. They were out of onions. On stove bubbles ghormeh sabzi. This stew, Persian stew, with fenugreek, leeks, chunks of beef, kidney beans, and dried limes, almost make up for lost laughs.

"What did the clinic say?" Patil say, sliding first tahdig on plate, then spooning stew.

"I tell you clinic was closed."

Patil stop spooning.

"That was almost a month ago."

Shnorhk want to leave.

"Next week then?" Patil now spoon out stew.

"This is all my lungs need." Shnorhk breathe in deep like smell can feed. Patil's wooden spoon block Shnorhk's metal fork.

Young men talk of cock-block. This block is worse.

"I think of seeing Mnatsagan tonight. With the boys."

Change of subject is last chance.

"You'll bring your duduk? You'll play?"

Change of subject works. Mouthful worth it.

But that afternoon changes
mood and after mood follows mind.

Many fares but low tips to no
tips. Rearview glimpses find faces
scowling about heat, about smell,
and always in back that young girl
in glittering holes. "Size Matters!"
Amphorae Lounge!

673

Saturday traffic today seems just as senseless. Snarls of cars where nothing is red or in construction.

Shnorhk know this is "referred traffic pain." Somewhere else it is much worse. Like worse elsewhere ever excuse pain.

"Will you turn up the AC?"

"Why don't you have bottled water?"

"You do know those pine-tree-thingy air fresheners don't work?"

"Like try MyWaze?"

"Can't you go any faster?"

Would scowls like these really want Shnorhk business card? Some number on paper, this would make difference?

Shnorhk turn up radio.

And yes, sure, Shnorhk could offer bottled water. And yes, more is under pedal, but this makes little difference here. Waste of fuel only. Even if for customer Shnorhk still pass car ahead.

Faster is meaning always outrunning time to keep from running out of time. This passing, though, is just passing time.

Then metallic peach Lexus pass Shnorhk and two more cars. Change lanes twice. Blinkers but only as afterthought.

DRIVING LESSON # 10

Think! Then signal!

To signal first is to alert other drivers of intention to alter lane.

To signal after is thought for only self.

Look at this! Look at me! Look what I just did!

Remove please this me
from road.

Shnorhk make up mind that to
see Mnatsagan tonight is impossible. AC and dry heat of drought
fill his chest with ache of ash.

Then on Olympic Boulevard
Shnorhk see beautiful driver.

It happens.

Silver Ford Escape weave
through traffic like grace on call.
Blinker for every lane shift. On. Off.
On. Off. Only once tap brake.

Shnorhk almost reach for more
beneath pedal. Shnorhk almost
follow.

Big cheer as Shnorhk walk through Mnatsagan's door. Bags of Zankou Chicken maybe help. Shawerma, tarna, falafel wraps, plus side of hummus, mutabbal, plenty of special spicy garlic sauce.

Alonzo and Haruki first to hug Shnorhk. Tzadik next, slapping Shnork's back. Slap feels good. Dimitri slaps too. Maybe feels not so good. Dimi big man. Kindo just lifts mallets, grins, one hundred per-cent Trinidad grin, like Kindo like to say, better as any slap on back.

Mnatsagan almost drop tray of tea at sight of Shnorhk.

"Եկա՛ ՜ ր: Վ՛ րջապես եկել ես:"

Alonzo and Haruki lay out the food in the living room. Shnorhk follow Mnatsagan to help with glasses and plates.

"Last week I sent off the first box to the University of Minnesota," Mnatsagan confides. "Progress."

"I'm sorry," Shnorhk answer progress with shame. Where went promise to help digitize? Shnorhk never even arrange for scanner.

"Easy, my friend. There's plenty left to do. I'll always welcome your help. But as you can see the university helps too."

Mnatsagan didn't just serve him cake that rainy day. ∵ May 10th ∵ He also played tapes. Many tapes.

"But if box is lost?"

"Where's your box, man?" Tzadik asks, falafel wrap in hand.

Shnorhk clap hands. Take breath. Always such harshness and hurt to take in, to let go. Rasp and rattle but at least this time no cough.

"Left it in cab."

Alonzo and Dimi walk with him to cab. Dimitri is broad like a bull but Alonzo is fast as mongoose. Like this together they feel like bodyguards of Shnorhk. Even Haruki comes out to porch, but like he's not there to keep watch, just suck on electric smoke, blue dot unsettling night air.

Box is not on front seat. At first Shnorhk convinced he lost instrument, then convinced someone stole it, then Shnorhk remembers trunk.

679

"I left it at home," Shnorhk lie instead.

"Oh," Dimi say. Never such a small sound from such a big man.

They would not let him leave though. They made him eat. They kept refilling his cup with tea. Mnatsagan even brings out small glasses from freezer to fill with special vodka from freezer. Every-one drinks, except Dimi, who only drinks water or tea.

And when playing start Shnorhk close eyes and settles back in couch. How vodka warm his chest, how this music warm his other chest.

Mnatsagan always so simple but clear on violin. Kindo a heartbeat. Dimi, pulse like a whale moving north.

For nine years now, such strange music spill from old professor's home, too mournful for any neighbor to complain. Many neighbor come still to sit on steps, drink what they have to, smoke what they must, and for moment give up their pain to hear their pain in song.

So peculiar Shnorhk almost change mind. He will lie again. He will go out to get something in trunk and discover duduk. He will suddenly remember where is duduk. He will just admit lie and get duduk.

Shnorhk clutch couch pillow to chest instead.

The Same Ghost

"He's also proved that he can speak with something over many years."

— Peter Sarnak on Yitang Zhang

The ball

        [{planetary} green {shocked through with waves of ‹watery› greens ‹what is the word to describe "dancing light within"? «‹perfect for Xanther› if he could remember it›» shimmering more with each spin} until it's beyond any color or dimension]

                              leaves

    Anwar's fingers

                 [with surprising speed
{his swing ‹this time›}
            delivering the release

     {to the lane?
              ‹without so much as
a knock «or bounce
        «like a kiss that never happens›»›}]

      flying past dots

      past arrows

   by   gutters

     past breakpoint

The [cumulative] crash of pins finds its answer in a [cumulative] cheer from the gang [Glasgow's groan only further authenticating the roar {for Anwar's strike ‹they aren't even playing against one another «though somehow ⟨this time⟩ Anwar's way in the lead» «with only Glasgow within range»»}].

Lucky Strike.

Bowling was supposed to have ended by 11 PM. Exhaustion had hit Anwar at 10:30 PM. Yet here he is [still standing] pushing [easily!] past 1:30 AM [energy still rising {pushing towards 140 probably helps ‹an adrenal response «to what? ⟨something new?⟩»»}]. Really just lucky [Anwar's opening salvos were in the low 80s {below even Talbot ‹who hasn't broken 100›}].

Two frames remain.

The next round [of toasts] goes to Ehtisham [throwing this little gathering].

'Onwards!' Anwar joins the [battle?] cry. Drinks. His beer has warmed. [{since the man ‹of honor› is driving} Ehtisham only sips {inversely proportionate to Glasgow's and Talbot's gulps ‹Anwar gulps too «a lump in his throat»»}].

'I know this is grim harvest—' Ehtisham starts.

'Fuckin true,' Glasgow growls. 'Not even an intern.'

'Remember Carmen?' Talbot asks.

Anwar reads frustration in Ehtisham's eyes [a flicker there? {some slight redirection of light ‹revealing what? «disengagement? ⟨some hardening of thought?⟩ لا قدرالله»›}].

'Gentlemen!' Anwar speaks up. 'And I use the term loosely. We've all gone over the numbers. If our dear Ehtisham had not acted as swiftly as he did, we would not even be here, taking out our inadequacies on ten pins.'

'To Ehti!' Glasgow stands [and chugs].

'To Ehti!' Talbot stands too. 'And Carmen!'

'To Kozimo!' Ehtisham adds. 'For buying us out of our lease.'

'Fuckin Kozimo.' Glasgow can't help himself.

Anwar sees The Glass House [{all those birds ‹the snakes›} yet here without a cage {even The Glass House is gone}].

Talbot gutters the next two bowls [the way he sways *he* should be in the gutter].

'My balls keep going all over the place.'

'It's not your fault,' Glasgow says.

No gutters for Anwar [but {on his next frame} his aim goes far right to far left {‹after two bowls› knocking down a whopping two pins}]. Glasgow wakes [{gathers himself up} before this {unspoken} competition] and bowls a spare [now {literally} within striking distance].

[unfortunately] Poor Glasgow gutters the next roll [and finishes the tenth frame with 118 + 0 + 4 {122}]. Anwar wins [{no need to even bowl} but bowls just as badly {‹with what 'rocks he throws' «Talbot's gurgle of a description»› giving him 134 + 2 + 3 ‹139›}]. [whatever the reason {the ‹false› victory does nothing}] Failing to reach 140 robs Anwar of all the energy he has left [even bestowing upon him a {ridiculous!} bitterness {he can't ‹immediately› shake off}].

[suddenly] Bad luck looms everywhere [in everything {from the Hollywood hipsters crowding the bar ‹beards and ponytails «making a comeback?»› to the birthday parties crowding the lanes}]. Not that Talbot finds anything gloomy about what looks like a lingerie party [{one lane over} scantily laced ladies rolling balls between their legs {one even does the splits ‹across the foul line «Glasgow swoons»›}].

'You okay?' Ehtisham reads Anwar perfectly [another {mis}flickering of light? {the way we regard a place ‹making an eye out of a mind›}].

'I'm still in denial that our little enterprise has gone belly-up. Such high hopes I had.'

'To think—' [Talbot joins in] '—all our investments amounted to finger food and time in the gutter.'

'I like the gutter,' Glasgow burps [{incredibly} one of the lingerie ladies has come over {thumbing her phone number‹«!?»› into Glasgow's phone now›}].

'My sideboob freaking you out?' Miss Scantily Clad smiles at Anwar [{dark as Anwar} gone before he can explain that {no} he wasn't looking at her {‹or anyone «anywhere»› the only thing he was seeing was how seeing might reflect not seeing but thinking ‹had it?›}].

[just last night {mingling ‹maybe› with Now's nubile possibilities of pleasure}] Anwar had experienced a sudden fantasy that Astair[!] was about to get down on her knees[!!!!] and—. Nearly out the door [for a wine tasting with friends]. With lipstick on too. Anwar's mind [{ahem} more than mind] exploding with this stream of desirous dreaming [even as Astair's hug {over news of the $9,000 now residing in their bank account} realigned dreams with the reality {of their relationship ‹Astair wouldn't be Astair if she acted like that «though would she be someone else?»›}] even as these thoughts [revisited {of so impossible ‹impulsive «hot»› behavior by his wife} lingering] arouses Anwar now.

He's also staring now at a lingerie girl [a different one {wearing a cowboy hat and a flimsy vest made out of sparkly rope‹?›}]. She's astride the hood of the ball return [like a bull rider {one arm in the air}] hooting whenever a round of color spins loose.

[on the way down to the parking lot {‹Hollywood and Highland› Level 2}] Anwar brings up Cataplyst-1.

'I followed your advice, Ehti. I used audio cues with my instrumentation. It worked. I even thought at one point the crashes were playing . . . a theme from a movie.'

'Spooky,' Talbot butts in. 'Lucky you.'

'They signed me up for another round.' [Astair still didn't know that part {Anwar waiting for the right moment to surprise her ‹maybe with a nice meal out›}].

[alongside the rows of parked cars {still some distance off ‹but heading towards Anwar and his friends›}] Four young men spread out [[{wearing loose jerseys ‹49ers?›}]{jeans riding low ‹showing off white or bright red underwear} {red baseball caps ‹brims barring eyes›} all of them black]. Anwar wants to believe they're looking for their car [[{maybe a little drunk} except they keep looking into other people's cars].

'Who's this for?' Glasgow asks [[{not noticing ‹or caring about› the foursome} busy unlocking his car {swearing to Talbot he's sober ‹Talbot swears he's not›}].

'Enzio,' Anwar answers [the foursome is snooping around a brown SUV]. 'Mostly games. A small company. VC money, I guess. At least no hits so far.'

'I sent them a CV,' Glasgow says matter-of-factly.

'Really?' [Surprised {because this gang will most likely wind up with jobs at places like EA or Riot Games ‹maybe Blizzard›}].

'Ever see the series *Black Mirror*? That's what I think of whenever I hear about them.'

'*Black Mirror*?'

'Out of the UK.'

'Hence his bias,' Talbot grunts [while on the phone {trying to get Winchester to pick him up ‹unsuccessfully «no reception down here»›}].

'Bias!? Fuck you, Talbot! I said UK, not Scotland. You'll see. Come September, you'll see.'

Sometimes it's easy to forget [name aside] the partisan side to their friend. How the soft lilt of his speech [what plenty of people call from 'somewhere-not-here' {fine} or 'New Zealand' {tolerable} or 'Australia' {an affront} or 'English' {unpardonable}] hails from a land where a Glasgow Smile means knife-slits to each corner of the mouth and a beating to horror the scar.

'Hi lads!' Glasgow says [{maybe} something about those distant nationalities calling his blood to boil].

The foursome stop [they were just passing {Anwar hoping they would pass by}].

'What up,' one says [{is the myth of their dark skin arranging this?} to Anwar {when ‹really› the difference lies with their clothes ‹is that a windbreaker? «Clippers ‹wash of red›»› ‹jeans not even clean «soiled with something»› ‹as Dov used to drawl «that's who said it!»: 'Dress like a thug, get treated like a thug'›}].
Anwar looks him in the eye [nods slowly {‹he hopes› with respect ‹without invitation›}]. These men smell of beer and smoke [cigarettes {‹definitely› not pot}].
The three others deepen their hold on whatever deep pockets hold. Anwar realizes they're about to get robbed [{worse?} just as he realizes they aren't going to get robbed {of course ‹paranoia «the indecency of race versus couture»›}].

[{then} like that] The foursome moves on.

"I thought things were about to get a little tasty." Glasgow grins.
Anwar sighs [relieved {to be able to push aside the waxing guilt ‹«self-something» over hasty judgements›}].
'Can we get going?' [Talbot oblivious.] 'I'd like to call up the rest of my night.'
Ehtisham shakes his head [unlocking his car with a beep {ah R2D2 «prophet of musics to come» the electronic symphonies of these times}].

'Yo, dawgz, keys.' No beep.

The four had circled around [come up then between the cars {standing together ‹three guns drawn «Anwar feeling the weakening in his legs tingle his bladder»›}].

'Wallets too,' the one in the Clippers windbreaker adds [again to Anwar].
Glasgow tosses his wallet [smile {barely} ebbing].
'On your knees too.'
[instead] Glasgow drops his car keys at his feet.
'All yours,' Glasgow adds [smile still there]. 'We're going to walk away now.'
Anwar watches [{dismayed} as his dear friend does just that].

[like Anwar] Talbot has also tossed out his wallet. Hands up too. Already shuffling backwards into the middle of the traffic aisle [brighter there {with the large overheads}]. Anwar just tries to get his legs to move [eyes pinned at his feet {seeing ‹is he seeing this? «how he ⟨Dov!⟩ would have defeated their stares and answered arms with arms» or is he not seeing at all?› nothing there} eyes closed].

Where's Ehtisham?

'Hey!' A woman's cry. 'Baby!'

Followed by 'Ewww. Seriously?'

'Him?'

'Baby!'

The Lingerie Girls.

All of them.

By the escalators.

Wobbling into the parking structure.

Coming their way.

Glasgow [stiffly] returns their waves.

Anwar [however] looks up at the guns.

Gone.

Along with the foursome

And [except for Glasgow's keys] their wallets are still there.

Glasgow takes off then [at a full sprint] and [{‹before he knows what he's doing› before he can reflect on this new impulse} maybe because this Now is about brave Glasgow] Anwar sprints too.

The Lingerie Girls stop short [{a few jaws ‹actually› slackening} at the sight of two men {Glasgow and Anwar} running towards them {then past them}].

Anwar's faster than his friend [and takes the lead {racing up the escalators ‹out into the plaza above›}].

Glasgow ∴ later on ∴ ended up reuniting with Miss Scantily Clad [her name is Raven {smitten too ‹«by the looks of it» by the story›}] but the foursome had disappeared.

No help that [out on Hollywood Boulevard {maybe having to do with the Jimmy Kimmel show? ‹'That's always on Friday' a girl «Xanther's age?» had corrected Anwar's frustrated assumption›}] Rodrigo y Gabriela were giving a surprise show.

Had this crowd always figured into the foursome's plan?

The police thought likely [adding that Level 2 was probably their max {'Any lower would lower the odds of a successful escape' ‹Dante knew best that arithmetic›}] even if the police [also] admitted that their report would not likely lead to an arrest.

[somewhat impressively] A surveillance video was produced [but brims hid faces {and eyes ‹no one could remember an eye color «thug in a Clippers jacket had ⟨inviolable⟩ darkness»›}].

One officer made a big deal out of the jacket.

'Bloods.'

'If only we could alter the angle to see under their hats,' Talbot mused.
'Like a Lytro for the entire space,' Glasgow added.

The cops had no idea what they were talking about.

To make the whole night even better [or weirder] Raven organized her friends to search Level 2 and wound up finding Glasgow's keys.

[as everyone was saying goodnight] Winchester found Talbot [bursting out of a powder pink Fiat {‹practically bursting out of her blouse› bursting into tears}].

[in fact] The whole night was weird [at least for Anwar {*weird!* «Xanther's least favorite word»» because ‹in the end› almost nothing happened ‹it was all a *could have been* experience «We *could have been* robbed» «We *could have been* shot» «We *could have been* killed» «but instead we— ⟨weird . . . ⟩»»}].

So [then] what *had* happened?

Anwar gathers Astair up in a big hug. She had waited up as long as she could [finally falling asleep on the living room sofa {curled under their fleece throw ‹phone within reach «numerous texts detailing the delay: Glas lost his keys»›}].

Anwar repeats the lie [this time by omission {‹ . . . › he'll tell her everything tomorrow}].

'You're not even a little bit drunk,' Astair mumbles.

Anwar swears Shasti and Freya were both panting [like they were running {while trying to say something ‹yell something «scream?»›}] before he walked into their room.

They are calm now. He kisses their cheeks. Mumbles of recognition sound what morning memories will fail to recall.

Xanther also mumbles 'I love you, daddy . . . ' [{‹as if part of the same dream «as her sisters»› though there's a crisp wakefulness to her words} as Anwar kisses her on the forehead].

[unlike the twins {and despite the heat}] Xanther's tucked under sheets and blankets [two?]. Her head feels cool. Somewhere [here {under the sheets? ‹‹at least» lost under a blanket's fold«?»›}] sleeps the little one [like a little cloud {a blind little lamb ‹ever a question mark «of a different king (*kind!*)»›}].

[{trying} to wind down] Anwar cleans out the old texts on his phone. Discovers a new voice mail [left that afternoon] from his old friend Myla Mint.

'Slow Dog. It's been too long.'

That's her message [Slow Dog {her nickname for him ‹for decades «origin ⟨unknown⟩ ∴ One night at McSorley's ∴»›}].

'You're up late.' Myla lives in New York City.
'Good morning.'

Anwar tells her the story. He even tells her about Xanther's new companion.

'Cute,' Myla rasps [until she hears about the {peculiar} circumstances of the discovery {Anwar won't swear to death ‹but he gets Myla close enough to that edge «how ‹One Rainy Day in May› the kitten became his best example of a *could have been* ‹*could have not been . . .*›»}].

'The seventies—' [Myla responds {Anwar ‹momentarily› thinking she means the 1970s}.] '—are a hard decade. All the dancing, *the training!*, has tangled up my bones. All those cigarettes, those years before my sobriety. All those *relationships*. Not that my health is so poor. It's just the particulars of the pain that never stop. I guess I'm a sensitive sort.' [for all her bruises and scars] Her reputation has never suffered that accusation. A bright cackle confirms it.

But maybe their friendship endures because [aside from not working for her or wanting something from her {other than a discussion ‹now and then› of the ballets Anwar loves}] Anwar knows her as too sensitive. Astair suspects a maternal patterning there [Myla is twenty-plus years older {and like Anwar's mother} extremely aware {though nothing about Fatima ever rasped ‹let alone cut «maybe cackled»›}].

'Slow Dog, you describe two ghosts I am only too familiar with. Both in possession of past, present, and future: *Could Have Been* and *Could Have Not Been*. Whose company it's best to choose is, however, not the right question.'

'Oh. What is?'

'Are they in fact the same ghost?'

[before they hang up] Myla tells Anwar about her latest project [opening in September {*Hades!* ‹'Yes, with an exclamation point. The Met keeps insisting I kill it.'›}]. She insists Anwar come.

'And bring Xanther.'

Anwar prepares for bed [only to return to his office {to return to *Paradise Ope*n ‹or at least to M.E.T. «or even A.I.M. ⟨ . . . ⟩»› instead} turning to his latest assignment from Enzio].

Cataplyst-2.

What keeps his focus for hours [even as dawn creeps through the windows {and a temperature shift ‹for a moment cooling the room› walks the halls of the house ‹rubbing up against the walls «rocking gently the roof timbers»»}].

Another release build. No console output. [again] Debugging blind. [again] Anwar resorts to musical tones to instrument the code. The errors [however {for this round}] are not nearly as complicated [or tedious].

Maybe because Anwar knows where to look. The mistakes are familiar [or because what's at stake has nothing to do with the mistakes {as if put there on purpose ‹a barrier to entry «but to what ⟨⌈end⌋ ⌈entry⌋⟩› purpose?»}].

[similar to Cataplyst-1] Anwar finds the same output [his FPG Theory {Time Box? ‹or Time Bowl?›}]. No movement. The same curvature. The same cloudiness [though {instead of grey blurriness} with an oilier {glaucous?} cloud system].

[the same as with Cataplyst-1 {via socket programming}] This version keeps activating ports [seeking out invalid IP addresses {the errors returning nothing ‹or at least a nothing swirling now «in a mood ⟨or language⟩ of strange currents»›}].

[{furthermore} Anwar can see] The coding invokes daemons in a number of similar ways [tasks running parallel {even if Anwar remains blind to their function ‹encryption «decryption ⟨ . . . ⟩ »›}].

Anwar's curious. He could figure it out. But he doesn't need to. Leaning back [instead] to consider the strange storm [struck through with lightning {‹it's beautiful› what else to call it? ‹beautiful›}].

'Chatoyancy!' Anwar says aloud [the word he was trying to remember at Lucky Strike {though a green bowling ball is nothing compared to what gyres here ‹maybe that's what this is: a game with a POV from inside a bowling ball!›}].

[regardless] Anwar's done. A few hours of work for [another!] $9,000. Wait until he tells Astair. Anwar [writes down his notes {packages the code}] uploads everything to the Enzio server.

Enzio.

[downstairs {fixing some of ‹Astair's› herbal tea}]
Anwar stands in the kitchen [nowhere close to the
kitchen].

   But what's upsetting him? The code? [not what it
did {or didn't do ‹the lines he commented out to get
the other lines working «or even how it was all written
(   ) with all those spaces» whatever was working
working towards ›   }   ]?

   Shortly his family will awake [Anwar's day will
swoon towards exhaustion {just thoughts of what's next
slump him in a chair ‹in «their windowless ‹(chamber)›»
the breakfast nook›}].

            Where anger surprises him.

            Anger at black skin.
            Anger at young men.
            Anger at guns.

[is this just a last spurt of adrenaline?]

            Anwar sets down his tea.

[hand shaking that much]

But anger also brings comfort.

And fortitude.
Empowerment.
So long as it's fed.

[for an instant then {it's warming again}] More than temperature [but still less than any child {or love}] creaks the house and enters the room.

[Must be Xanther's cat.]

Anwar checks the floor. Every corner. The doorways. Even rechecks under the table.

No cat.

Leaving Anwar [on his knees] with what Ehtisham had said when he had finally dropped Anwar off.

Streetlights flickering.

Something beyond the flicker?

Animal movement?

Ehtisham's head turned.

Had he seen it too?

'Hey,' Ehtisham confides suddenly [Anwar getting out of the car {confirming animal movement out there ‹a cat «cats! ⟨the shadows of . . . ⟩ several cats!» if dancing just beyond definition› eyes afire with the night}]. 'I remembered something about Enzio.'

'Enzio?'

'Mefisto worked for them.'

The Loyal Hawaiian

I took a little break.

— Delinquent Habits

Yellow beaches blown gold by bright lines
of foam. Blues to blue. Like a burning spoon
that instead of metal tastes like sun. Until the
flat world tilts away for brighter clouds throwing shadows only boats below will ever know.
Maybe the fish know. Every now and then
Luther takes his crew out on a boat to fish.

But fuck the boats. Fuck his crew. Fuck L.A.
Here's to First Class United! Luther downing
his second champagne and plane's still rising.
Even his dick's rising. Straight through the sun.

Come Honolulu, Luther's solid buzzed. Piña gave him some pill for sleep. But Luther didn't sleep. He just felt mushy prickles the whole time, just ranita, enjoying the ride.

Teyo has a fuckin car waiting. Cadillac. Black. Luther gets his duffel and backpack carried.

Luther feels expected everywhere he goes. Even this Japanther crossing the lobby stutters her feet, teeth digging her lip, like, yeah, she'd take what he'd give. She has no idea how much he'd give. Or maybe she does.

The whole hotel breathes that way. No matter what Luther's bringing, they seen it before. Tattoos? Seen thicker. These arms? Seen bigger. Fuerza? Seen more. On these islands, flesh was once on the menu.

Welcome to the Loyal Hawaiian.

Pink stucco isn't what counts here or green awnings shading too many windows to count. Forget the marble floors too, all that polished brass at the polished reception desk, or pink umbrellas out on the sand, arch after arch opening out onto one more patio, or another stairwell leading the way in, each turn reminding Luther there's room enough for any of him.

Down his hallway, two girls slip behind a door. Luther glimpses their asses. Thigh gaps, both, the kind that gives up an hourglass, what you can tell time by, and fuck around the clock, skin all tan, back dimples to haunt his mind. Better pull hisself off first before seeing the old man.

Soon as bellboy here finishes with this light-switch tour.

Luther's never stepped inside a room so big. Bed's California king unless they got Hawaiian King for Samoan giants. Dozens of pillows and sheets slick as silk but softer and without shine.

The closet swallows up his bags. They look defeated under all those empty hangers. And this is just one of the closets.

There's some kind of sitting room. The bath has all kinds of jets. Longer than two strides.

Flat screens are everywhere.

By the bar waits a plate of papayas, limes, and chocolates. There's a bottle of fuckin champagne too, with this card from the hotel management welcoming

Señor Lutero Perez

Something about his name like that feels weird. Mushy prickles return before they're gone for good.

Teyo's suite is bigger. Higher up too.

His balcony overlooks Waikiki. The closets are full. Like Teyo's living here for good. Maybe he is. Hangers of blond suits and purple or ivory shirts. At least a dozen shoes. Another closet's stacked just with tennis rackets.

"¡Mijo!"

First a handshake, then hug, palms to back, then both hands on his shoulders, like Luther's some morrillo, Teyo's morrillo.

Teyo makes the Most Interesting Man in the World a pocket pussy. Got on a jacket like cream, peach shirt, gold cufflinks, collar open, with gold chain but thin, and shoes like they made of the skin of gold if gold had a skin.

Has Luther ever seen such happiness? No need to smile. Like smiling's already in the pores of his brown skin, dark brown but like just from tanning, and in his hair, silver but long and thick, and in his teeth too, big as finger-nails, white beyond fake, just the glint shines approval, while binding it together, like a face like this couldn't make sense without them, big hazel eyes, clear as tide pools, never seeing the reason no sand's at the bottom is the sand's you.

Luther knows this gaze is the key to why Teyo can interact with so many types: he sees with-out threat. What would Juarez make of it?

"Good flight?"

"Estuvo bien."

"Thank you for coming, Lutéro. You do me the favor of permitting me to make up for my unfortunate absence. Drink?"

"Yeah."

"I will tell you a secret: I can't stand tequila," Teyo says, starting to stab with a pick a block of ice in the kitchen sink. "Criminal, isn't it?" He drops chunks into some boxy machine bound in black rubber. "Vodka. And Belvedere only."

A heavy pour of that, with St. Germain. Then, with the machine churning, Teyo slashes limes, squeezing halves by hand, adding sugar, something else, pink powder Teyo swears is salt.

"Fine things are easy," Teyo continues. "If you have fine ingredients. You're a fine ingredient. Adding to an even finer future. Work more with me and you also will drink that future."

The promise of alcohol settles Luther even if these words keep twisting between comfort and confusion: Because if Luther's something in the old man's drink and the drink is the future . . . is Luther supposed to drink of hisself?

Out on the balcony, with music inside turned up loud, Teyo's eyes darken without changing color.

"Now is the only time over these next few days together that I will speak to you about our work." He sips his drink. Then wipes his silver moustache and motions for Luther to drink too.

To Luther the drink already tastes like a broken promise or maybe it's just that he likes tequila. The orange sky dissolving into the blackening blue seems a drink of a whole different kind, in need of an umbrella the beach is full of, but keeping a promise Luther's never heard made.

"Mil gracias, Lutéro. On two occasions now you have more than proven yourself and I am humbly and gratefully in your service."

Teyo bows then. Fuckin bows! Luther swears he even hears the old man's heels click.

Luther's all de nada, even as this weird disorientation takes him, like a vertigo that has nothing to do with how high up they are, but with the creepy suspicion of plans, plans he can't know or if he could know ever understand, outside of hisself but still for hisself, the weight of what's at stake impossible to lift, what might as well, since he'd have to lift it to get it, not exist.

Only metal can answer this confusion. Luther takes another sip of Teyo's drink. Better than the first taste. He overestimated the sweetness. Maybe Teyo didn't use sugar.

Metal fades. Luther returns to the Pacific green, umbrellas starting to come down, the last of the sunbathers leaving the sand. The warm air feels like a hug.

Luther smiles. Teyo has tears in his eyes.

"Memo—" Teyo starts. Tries again. Shakes his head. "Lo siento."

Luther knows then the end. —is dead. Luther drinks again. To hide the smile those hazel pools would find. Again what Luther swallows seems better than the previous time.

Only Luther's wrong. Memo isn't dead.

"He woke up three nights ago. Bad shape, very bad. Pero le dijo a su abogado everything."

Teyo downs his drink in one gulp and hurls the glass at his feet.

"HE FUCKING TOLD HIS LAWYER EVERY-THING!"

∴ Luther doesn't jump at the scream or even this shatter. ∵

∵ *His fists don't bend to what's next.* ∵

∵ **For Luther the only thing as relaxing as violence is the prospect of violence.** ∵

"What you did, Lutéro—" Tears stream down Teyo's cheeks. "You and your man, fighting like you did. Memo told us fucking everything."

Whatever calm possessed Luther leaves. Luther finishes his drink, spares the glass.

"Memo says you never stopped trying to drag him out of there. César Miguel too."

The Football Star.

"He brought the balloons," Luther nods.

"You've some idea, Lutéro, I know. But it is nothing compared to what really heads our way. A story I need to tell you but not at this time. My question here is simple: do you think pink contained what both color and César Miguel claimed?" ∵ *Detecting a curious diction slide.* ∵

"I don't know."

Teyo takes Luther's glass and goes back into the suite. When he returns, he carries a waste-basket and a small towel. His eyes are dry.

"I fear then this mess is on me." Teyo gets down on his knees and begins sweeping up the shards of glass.

Luther gets down on his knees too, finding sickle shards by what sticks in his palm.

"I have an impulsive side," Teyo laughs. "Use-ful at your age. Dangerous when you're older. Suicidal when you're old."

"You got years."

"My finer future is my now. Tomorrow's a story of incontinence, dementia, impotence. Only the idea of someone I know, I trust, I BELIEVE IN!, enjoying the prospects of improving days, gives me a way to look past infirmities and collapse."

"Ladies?"

"Viagra," Teyo smiles. "But, yes, another story."

Teyo stands up then, as if to go back inside, but instead draws again to the balcony rail, lower-ing his voice so much that Luther has to lean in, almost feeling the old man's lips at his ear.

"I manage differences in the interest of preserving capital growth. Forget Sureños, Norteños. My hands are full with niggers too, Koreans, Armenians, Aryan fucks, even the Russians want in. That's just L.A. Pretty damn impressive except now I have a problem that makes my fear of old age more realistic. I have to deal with a rat. You understand?"

Tide pools gone. Replaced with a look Luther at last understands perfectly clear.

"Por supuesto," Luther answers.

"¡A la brava! Vroom, vroom, vroom, sí?" Teyo smiles then, in the way that can only mean go, when what he means is green, even with the lista unknown, name unnamed.

"Forgive me! I ask you to Hawaii by way of thanks and here I am again asking for your help."

The old man's eyes have returned to that calm without intention. He kisses Luther on both cheeks, and when he pulls back Luther misses the confiding touch.

Back in the suite, Teyo turns off the music and starts asking about clothes. When Luther says "T-shirts," Teyo calls downstairs.

"Jobe will pick out what you need," he says after he hangs up. "For the man without a jacket, accept one from me."

The jacket Luther accepts costs over a thousand dollars. Pale blue with "Magritte clouds." How Jobe calls them. Some puñal, that guy. Luther doesn't know no Magritte but the clouds look easy and throw no shadows.

8 PM, after a nap on that big-ass bed, followed by a long hot shower, Luther puts on his new suit. He got a shirt too, even shoes, with laces bright like bees.

Teyo's already out on the patio bar, with two rum cocktails made from whole pineapples. El Arpa, 53, between both.

Teyo says nothing of the clothes but looks on with approval, even muy orgullosa de él.

The old man can drink. A fuckin pineapple farm goes down. Luther tries to keep up.

By the time they quit the hotel, the old man's nothing but generoso, finding ways to slip cash to the boys hauling bags, jotos working phones.

Luther gets no smiles, and on the way to the restaurant, his drunk turns to metal. Fuck this sweaty air. Fuck that hotel. Luther caught the glares. Jobe's too, faggot pulling pants off a rack like Luther can't choose shit for hisself.

Anger only grows when they sit down at the sushi bar and everyone clusters around, handing them towels, lowering heads, mumbling these fuckin yes sirs, yes Teyo, him rattling off some long-ass order worse than Spanish.

Because what the fuck is hamachi? Or uni? What the fuck is toro? And why the fuck say die gringo when ordering a drink?

Luther wishes Tweetie was here. Even looks around, but seeing what he sees, all these fuckin strangers, finds he don't know what he's looking at anymore. Luther would take even Juarez. At least one of his locos to put this fire inside to some use. Victor had warned the old man just wanted some dick-culo action.

Dishes of cold shit arrive.

"What's this?"

Luther waits for the flash of those big teeth. Waits to see what an old man's laugh will make of this heat.

Instead, Teyo goes over every dish. Even explains to Luther how sake is made and rated.

And so Luther wolfs down yellowtail and tuna, sea urchin too, chasing it with Onikoroshi, junmai daiginjo, each taste chasing away the anger.

Luther asks what the other dishes are called and why some take soy sauce and others ponzu and still others no sauce at all. He even asks about clothes, the old man giving serious thought to how an ecru Paul Smith compares to a floral Etro or Lanvin with zipper slash pockets.

Luther gets almost happy. And strangest, as Luther forgets the insult of what he didn't know, Teyo opens up about what he wants most of all.

"A big beautiful view and a beautiful girl. Maybe they're the same. Simple. Difficult too."

Luther's never met the old man's wife but he's sure she's not who Teyo's talking about now.

"A man will do a lot for a view, Lutéro," Teyo adds. How he says it sounds like a threat.

More sake improves the view, plus shit like fish eggs topped with raw egg, sea trout, halibut with jalapeño, scallops blowtorched brown, sizzling strips of eel in a dark sweet sauce.

All the strangers around even start looking familiar, prettier too, with smiles like invitations.

"I remember when we still thought EP was something," Teyo says. "Lupe making it clear with Choplex-8s what real veteranos were about. The few, the proud, la raza. Colombians moving in soda and all the chicanos locos putting lives on the line for two blocks of barred windows and a muddy pond. Bellevue to Sunset to the 5, like it was a country unto itself. Some fucking country. Eses thought that was living large. I was no better. I hung with those vatos, smoking our Camels, wearing our Pendletons, counting fucking ducks. I shit you not: counting fucking ducks. That's not a view. Neither were the fat fuckin arrastradas fucking anyone to make a baby. They had no clue. Me neither. Not back then. Worse than you, Lutéro. Knew fucking nada about nada and that not even."

Japanese beer keeps foaming over their glasses as Teyo gets on about what he found out, big-ass estates on Italian lakes, private jets flying just as easy to the Canary Islands as to Cabo, entire floors of Russian hotels empty except for bowls of black caviar and bottles of frozen vodka and a naked staff to answer any need.

"A world awaits that neither you nor I can imagine, and I've gotten a glimpse. Makes here seem like a 7-Eleven. Like eating tuna out of a can."

Teyo makes it clear then how he can't stand Latin American food and admires "the elegance of Asia." He despises someone Kahlo and worships someone Claudel. Of course he worships his wife but "worship need not exclude others."

Though "out of others, I have found one in particular, one who could exclude others." This is his another story. "For her, I could leave it all."

"But?"

"Too young. Though, terribly, I am not yet so old to let her go. Viagra does not exactly unmake what I've become."

"The key to life?" Teyo suddenly barks, but under his breath, like a reprimand only for himself. "Minimize friction."

Juarez gets in Luther's head, gets Luther grinning. By now que la uña sarnosa would have broken dishes, started something with a cook. Luther would be laughing or not. Hilarity or fury. That's how it usually went. Maybe why Luther likes him so much. He likes things bent.

Luther suspects Teyo's not so different. The way he threw that glass at their feet. What the fuck was that about? Especially from some OG like him.

737

"Truly, she is nothing but difficulties and complications but . . . " Teyo sighs.

"But?" Sharp. Luther can't help hisself. Something shiny in his mouth getting at what's weak.

"Ah Lutéro, you see how full of shit I am?" Teyo winks. "Minimize friction!? I'm crazy about friction. What else do you call a tight pussy!"

Luther laughs up a swallow of beer and Teyo takes it as the gift he's waited for all day.

"Five chamacos!" Teyo holds up his hand. Including that teenage mecoso in Mexico City. "Not one could understand what I've told you tonight. What I've told you by not telling you. What you already understand to do. What you will easily do. What not one could ever do. From friction comes just friction. You?"

"No kids."

"Why not? Balas de salva?"

"A lo mejor. Only thing that makes sense."

"Children guarantee only distraction from personal purpose. Real purpose."

Outside, Teyo doesn't get into the Town Car.

"I'll walk. Check your seat. Have a good time."

"You know, Teyo, I walk into a place like that and first thing that goes through my head is I want to kill everyone. Choke every bitch blue, hammer the heads of every dude. I mean, I'm buggin! And then in the next breath, what no way I can fuckin explain, like just now as we're leaving, I also want to give every bitch a hug, pat their men on the back, pick up the whole tab, like for the whole place."

The confession leaves Luther breathless, like if nothing else he knows how drunk he is, sure now he just fucked-up, because like when has opening up ever been anything but a mistake?

But Teyo smiles.

"That's the roar in you, Lutéro. The roar."

In the back of the car, Luther finds the wad.
Some count. Hellz yeah!

The driver has suggestions, but Luther ignores
him. After Teyo's eat this, know this, be this,
Luther needs to feel hisself again.

On the way to the first club, Luther calls Tweetie. News about his dogs feels better than booze. "Tookie's cool" and "Chen Chi-Li's sleeping on his bowl." "Lord Gino keeps tryin to fuck Smokey Miranda." And so on.

The club's what you expect but nothing to do with what Luther wants to get at: blur of dim lights, too many shoulders knocking his, pow-dered ass cheeks he can't touch. The girls like his cloudy lapels and the Grants he throws down but not enough to let him suck on their titties or spread him any pink.

The second club's an even deeper blur, but after grabbing back a Grant, slapping an ass, Luther still catches sight of one security guy calling over another before heading Luther's way. That coordination, that intention, banishes the blur. Luther's already figured it out. Who to move on how. Make the first drop. The second. Give some fools what Luther lives on.

∴ **Maul the skies.** ∵

∴ *Eat the stars.* ∵

"Minimize fiction."

Luther's out before any bouncer's even close.

"Bonle homes. Hotel."

This time, though, the driver doesn't go where Luther wants.

"Your friend suggested here," the driver says, pulling into the deserted parking lot.

Not one sign on. Storefronts gated. Homeless man keeps recounting glass bottles on the curb.

"216. Hoops. They know your friend."

But stairs lead nowhere Luther can make out, a second story giving up only the pale green lines of a balcony.

Betrayal starts to stalk Luther.

An expensive trip to Hawaii. Luther cut off from his crew. Drunk too and loaded with cash. Primed for a headshot in some shitty strip mall.

Luther even twists quick, back around, coiled for the driver, but the car's gone.

On the second floor only one light burns. Under a door in the corner. The thinnest strip of rose.

No Hoops. Just a number: 216.

Luther knocks, turning around as he does, and this time just catching sight of something beyond the shadows, beyond dark, dense and steady and . . .

already dissolving in a flood of light.

"Come in! Come in!" A Korean vieja snaps. Bony thing, darting forward to shut the door behind Luther.

The name Teyo doesn't warm her any. Like Luther fuckin cares. Moments later he's center to a circle of girls. Stocky, tall, scrawny, dark blond, neon wigs on black. Early twenties. Max.

Luther lingers on buzzcut, thick thighs. Then narrow hips, big tits. There're bright skirts. And tight sweats. One's got silver shortshorts, tats down the back of her legs. One twirly thing's in two glossy white belts, and nothing else.

She's Destiny. Inked across her belly in case she forgets.

Tight little ass rocks the way to a tight little room, futon and blue lamp. Metal table's got lube, tissues, latex gloves.

Destiny lays Luther down, flings red hair over his chest, wets her finger and circles some scars. Fuck if Luther has time for that. Kicks off his own pants, sees that Destiny hangs up his chamarra with clouds carefully.

She takes off the top belt, rubs his taint next, squeezes his balls. Knows her shit. When she squeezes again, hard this time, her mouth's already on it, moving up and down in tight jerks. Luther never felt the condom slip on.

Not that Luther felt much of anything.

All he sees is that thing on the landing.

Even when Luther turns Destiny over and fucks her from behind, grabbing hold of her red hair, that glossy white belt left on her hips.

About to bust his nut, Luther tries to yank off the condom. Destiny beats this move, already out the room, as Luther's fist loses a crazy spray across the sheets.

Fuck, if mamasan doesn't go off then, va a estar parada de pestañas. Hissing chinacate he can't understand, then something he does: "Teyo!"

Settles whatever roaring Luther had in mind.

$250 for the girl. $50 to "reservice the room."

∵ Invisible here is the twist of spine: a scoliosis brought on by a left leg shorter than the right by 5/8". Invisible here is the wonder of butterflies she recalls spinning through when she was eight. Invisible here is the wonder she will have again spinning under a canopy of butterflies three years from now in Peru. Invisible there will be his memory. ∵

Dice is the same routine but less rushed.

"Minimize friction."

Luther's minimized alright. She squirts lube all over the condom, inside too. Might as well be fucking lube.

That Dice is squat like a stack of bald tires makes no difference, goth girl with beefy calves, ass bubbled up for extra on the grill, ears so pierced they make concertina pointless.

Like the blur in his head, his dick just floats.

Luther fucks Dice for a long time.

Behind her, over her, lips shredding on all her metal, even her nipples have spokes. His fingers dig deep up into her ass. She never moans but when he starts to really slam into her, hears the base of his cock knock against her pubic, nothing floating there, a grunt finally escapes.

That grunt gives Luther what he needs. Sounds like she's getting punched, Luther finally bucking and hammering to an end where her grunting stops, everything stops, her breath just holding. Only her hands still move, grabbing on to his shoulders so she don't split apart.

∴ By the age of twenty-eight, a crystal meth habit will take away all her teeth. Her nose will already be gone. Only the snake eyes tattooed on her lower back will look the same when she is examined in a Reno morgue. ∵

Dawn's different. She got similar routines but there's something wild in the way she moves over Luther. Hungry still and alive. Familiar.

Got Filipina eyes. Says German too, when he gives her his name. Something else hiding there but it's not fear.

Not even when he takes her from the side, lifting up one leg, when she says: "You're not going to hurt me?"

And Luther grabs her throat and says no.

Dawn's hands knot sheets like her moans knot up Luther's insides, what his shouts can't drown out, thighs slapping the back of her sticks, abs hard as any cock pounding against her ass, her hips, whatever little she lifts, as Dawn's small fingers ring down into even tinier fists, and Luther's shaking off sweat and rage, filling a condom for the second time, which Dawn takes, like she was never there to begin with, to give to the vieja, to put in some treasure chest.

∴ There are many dawns. Some rise to rescue. Some rise to wound. This dawn lives beyond what any man believes he is entitled to claim. In Reno, she will give what comfort she can to the dead and leave for good. In Phoenix, she will study Iyengar. In Boulder, she will marry. In Bend, she will adopt a baby girl and they will call her ███████. ∴

The landing's empty when Luther leaves.

The Town Car waits down below.

Except for a receptionist, the hotel lobby's empty. Luther doesn't go to his floor but heads straight to the top. Still drunk enough to think Teyo wants to hear his report.

Three times! A fuckin bag on mi verga!

But at Teyo's door Luther hears a woman's voice. Ta con madre, guy! Soft steps it away.

Luther's smile fades when she joins him in the elevator. No piercings, not one fucking tattoo. Luther bets she doesn't grunt either.

Can't help hisself, goes all the way down, has to watch her go, like she doesn't know. Pearls around her neck, smeared with red lipstick, or something else. Silky black hair waves down her long naked back. Bye-bye. No witch, her. Only that and the hour, maybe the slit in her dress, a little too high, gives her up.

Luther doesn't go to bed thinking of the botes de basura he just banged but of her, with pearls in her mouth. How much does she cost? Luther bets what he dropped tonight wouldn't buy a hello.

Later he remembers his jacket. Left back at 261. At Hula. Whatever it's called.

By the time Luther crawls out of bed, it's deep into afternoon, cruda machin banging his head.

Teyo's long gone, leaving behind for him a case of Belvedere, a dozen new shirts, all boxed, with a tangerine tie, compliments of Jobe, plus apologies for "the hasty departure" and an envelope with a lot more cash inside. And a smaller envelope too.

No need to memorize the name. Luther knows him. Lights a match. Flushes down the ash.

After a long bath, he puts on a new shirt and heads downstairs, looking around the lobby like Teyo's dark-haired beauty might still be there.

Luther walks out to the beach and sits under an umbrella. One of the hotel staff takes his order and while he waits Luther stares at a sunset he'd like to drink.

He tries to think of her again but now finds only that thing on the landing.

Dark and dense ∴ beyond form ∴. Eyes burning
∴ **with the last star** ∴. A dream on the wrong side
∴ *long since forgetting it needed once a dreamer to survive* ∴.

Starving

. . . to think dark thoughts, and be dark things.

— theappleppielifestyle

Dov once told Xanther "Fear's the only way we remember pain." :: No he didn't. :: :: *But he did. And he said it just like that too. Only not to her . . .* ::

Last Friday was the last day of school. Nothing but pain, but Xanther only remembers fear. Forget stepping out the door, that whatever-pop-blaze burning down Thomas Star Kane. Only one thing mattered: Dendish. Did he blame her for the lockers? Did he really call her Twitch? How was that possible?

From the moment Xanther had stepped foot on campus she expected him to jump her, drag her into some empty room, closet, restroom stall, cut her up with fists, broken glass, worse.

Talk about Fraidy K. Jumpy between classes, *in* class, refused to pee. At least until lunch. That's when she found out Dendish was gone. Kicked out of TSK. For the locker stunt.

Kinda funny considering that was the least of his offenses. Thomas Star Kane has these strict no-bullying policies. Xanther knows the pamphlets, signs declaring some wall a No Bullying Zone. Parents volunteer to patrol during class breaks. Hers did a few times, like so embarrassing!, Astair or Anwar playing school cop?, asking with their awkward, gentle, smiling gazes: "Is everything okay?"

But, like, even if Dendish is only an eighth grader he could probably take on both her parents. At the same time too. He's that strong. That mean. Someone said he beat up a thirty-five-year-old man. Meaner. Someone else said the thirty-five-year-old man had been handicapped. Only one dad Xanther knows for sure wouldn't have even blinked: Dov would have torn Dendish to pieces.

Here's the weird thing about Dendish, or is it typical?, what every kid in any school knows, maybe even adults know too?, like in their jobs?, how there are always these people who aren't found out, like they break all the rules, all the time, but in this way that's like always invisible. That was Dendish. He'd intimidate kids all over the place, steal their stuff, break it, like bust a bottle of beer in a back-pack, the kid's too afraid to say anything because it's beer!, and like in sixth grade! Plus that awful stuff with Parcel Thoughts in his Horrosphere with that ▶α‖H8 app, hid-ing behind weird made-up names, like **A Thick Oil //for a// Raw Stove**, what does that even mean? What does it mat-ter? Parents didn't know, school officials couldn't prove anything, and kids were left to his whispers, the kind that have edges, sharp edges, always promising what sharp edges can do, and always beyond consequence.

During lunch, Kle praised Dendish. That's one of the cool things about Kle: he can cop to stuff he can't stand. He even predicted Dendish would be a huge success. "Even if his type's also the reason for Columbine. Haha."

That it was a dumb locker prank that tripped up Dendish had really tickled Kle. "I can't believe he did it first!" Kle had howled, but in this way, like he wanted to text Dendish a 🖤 🖤 🖤. "How did he even do it? Did he figure out the combinations?"

Of course, whatever punishment Dendish Mower finally got, did it really matter? It wasn't like Principal Sanchez would make him redo eighth grade. Dendish was gone from TSK. Xanther would never see him again.

::. **Never?** .::

::. *Never never existed.* .::

Even if Xanther knows Dendish didn't have anything to do with opening those lockers. Though later doubt comes ringing in, like maybe somehow he did do it. ::. Duh! Of course he did! Who else? .:: Like, also, at that Memorial Day party, hadn't Abigail said something about the shelter?, about how it was these gang members who opened all the cages?, "Because that's why gangs gang up in the first place, to create chaos?"

But then school was really over, last class, last bell, and Xanther was coming home, the little one already on the other side of the door, like Xanther could feel him there, and then whatever's the opposite of blaze, deblaze?, and pop, de-pop?, the fire's gone, pain over with, forget fear.

Xanther gamed all weekend long and Les Parents didn't mind. They even, like, almost seemed happier than Xanther that she was home. And because the little one was never far away, and seriously never ever, like if not sleeping against her neck, or in her lap, or tucked under an ankle, then not more than a few steps away, Xanther felt better than she'd ever felt even if better wasn't all that good.

Obviously playing *Candy Crush* for hours was good, and *Brothers: A Tale of Two Sons* on Xbox, *Assassin's Creed IV: Black Flag* on PlayStation, or really the *Freedom Cry* DLC, all about Adéwalé, and then a lot of *Papo & Yo*, which makes her shiver, and sorta cry too. Xanther actually revis-

ited *Call of Duty: Ghosts*, which was maybe weird?, because she's not crazy about FPS, especially the S part, but there she was like firing away for just, you know, fun?

Xanther also got to sit at Anwar's desk, little one there on his desk too, curled up close as keyboard or mouse, closer, there for pets of, ahhh, still there, ahhh, calm, during bouts of *TrOUT,* for example, Anwar trouncing her, something called *Stravaging Home,* and of course glitchy *Paradise Open,* this time without a glitch, running her ∴ huh?∵ ∴ **We are always run** ∵ ∴ *Until we learn to really run . . . .*∵ through fields of tall grass, a hint of water, that was pretty cool, visualizing the smell of water, spooling through the air, the thirstier you got the thicker the strands, and the more strands meant getting close, like if there was a creek nearby.

This time, though, the predator was a-no show, making Xanther no longer prey, which really frustrated Anwar, his S/Z problem ∴ A.I.M. ∵ ∴ **M.E.T.** ∵ ∴ *"All of a sudden, I'm cold."*∵ rearing its head again, so still glitchy, until he switched over to his latest thing, a job, something called, uhm, maybe with a cat?, ∴ Cataplyst-2 ∵ ∴ *Among other things.* ∵ which got Xanther expecting a cat, when the only cat was the reflection in the monitor of the sleeping little one, his pale cloudiness mingling with the strange inky clouds boiling on the screen, sparking in Xanther not the idea of "a goldfish in some goldfish bowl with polluted water," what Anwar said he was stuck on, or even "an eye within an eye but like both so transparent they're no longer eyes?" which Xanther had blurted out, no clue why, but that it wasn't just within looking out or without looking in but somehow both and more.

The bathroom mirror wasn't more. Just less.

This was Sunday night, Xanther just brushing her teeth, like she's always done, picking at her braces, are they coming loose?, framing in real tight on metal, like, so, uhm, in order not to see the other stuff?, or like then doing the opposite by drilling down into what she hates facing, helpless then to keep from trying to pop the really gruesome pimples, even though that makes them worse, in those patches of zits on her chin, cheeks, in the creases of her nose, unpoppable, hurting the most too, until for some reason Xanther began to realize then that what she's really been doing all along, or really not doing, ever since, you know, she'd started seeing stones on people's eyes.

What would Dov say? Xanther afraid to even look her own self in the eye? Talk about waaaaaaaay Fraidy K.

So she'd gone ahead and done it.

Heavy, and getting heavier with each breath she couldn't take. So heavy, and dense, Xanther swore they were pushing in on her eyes, then popping her eyes like helpless little eggs, blowing out the back of her skull next, leaving behind these awful black holes, still widening, still deepening, until she was about to fall in, the vertigo getting so bad, so fast, Xanther had to grip the sink.

Did she even last a few seconds? ∷ **1.98** ∵ Were her eyes even there? ∴ One bluish, one light brown, both with these like sparks, or flaws?, of yellow and green. Same old same old. Around the outer edge of each iris a ring that almost looks black. Maybe that's where she got this idea of rocks. ∵ ∷ *If only* . . . .∵

Really, just one more infirmity.

On Monday her friends came over. All of them. Cogs followed by Kle, then a little later, Mayumi and Josh. Awesome. They just sat in the den all afternoon gaming while Astair made her famous popcorn buttered up with truffle salt and cheese and later Anwar cooked everyone one of his favorite dishes, called Koshari, with rice, lentils, macaroni topped with spicy tomato sauce and fried onions, Xanther sticking to smaller portions, because of the carbs, but with extra soy sausages and cottage cheese, to up her protein, plus nuts, always nibbling on those, even if how she's hungry, and like really hungry?, isn't like for nuts?

Not that Xanther stressed it. They were all too busy switching between PS4 and Xbox, or YouTubing music videos and movie previews, one about a drummer, supposedly already out, ∴ **Whiplash, 2014** ∵ all of which kinda felt like a food, or at least it fed her in a weird way?, or maybe it just felt that way because summer was here.

Kle had wanted to play *Grand Theft Auto V*, which Anwar has, her dad has so many games, but that got nixed. Of all her friends, Kle's the biggest challenge for Anwar. "Mr. Ibrahim." "Farrokh." That's how they always say hello. The Farrokh thing is another story. ∴ **A story we'll hear later.** ∵ ∴ *How am I hearing "hear later"?* ∵ "Is that mascara?" "School's out." How they continued saying hello today. Kle had on his latest t-shirt: *I Ate the Whole Bag!* above an empty bag of marshmallows, which Kle had drawn, really well too, but that didn't help Xanther get the joke, or Cogs either, Josh and Mayumi had to explain it was about testing delayed gratification, which Kle was making fun of, even if, despite the attitude he was wearing, doesn't really reflect how patient and intense he can be.

Where Josh keeps it mellow, like the way he rides his skateboard, like it's nothing, and Cogs is like still wide-eyed about everything, and glad of anything that keeps him away from home, Kle is way more invested, and precise too, sorta the way he draws? He and Mayumi are similar, very particular, though Mayumi isn't competitive. Not like Kle.

And that's how what should have been just a good thing became, like, a weird thing: Xanther started gaming better than usual. Like a lot better.

Cogs and Josh are wicked good, and have trashed Kle bunches of times, though not nearly as many times as he's trashed everyone, even if now and then Mayumi surprises everyone. Xanther never surprises anyone.

This Monday was different. Maybe because she'd been playing all weekend? Or maybe something else? It sorta felt like her mom's tic-tac-toe game, how Xanther could see all the turns, where Astair should not go next, but without consecutive thoughts, like movement that was somehow just one picture, like, what was that word Anwar taught her?, subitize?, like she didn't need to add anything up anymore, just knew it at once.

That's how gaming with Kle felt. Xanther wasn't even gripping the controller like Kle was, which she usually does, all on the edge of the couch, fixed on the big screen. She was just, you know, relaxed.

"She's already killing you," Mayumi giggled.

They were taking turns on *Tomb Raider*.

"Don't bitch me, grief," Kle managed to say, despite his jaw all clenched down. "You'll see."

"You're just talking heinie nonsense." Mayumi was loving goading Kle.

Josh had shaken his head.

"Don't long-hush me with a sigh," Mayumi snapped and then laughed, and Josh with her. They both loved talking strange.

And Kle did end up showing them all a thing or two about how well he could maneuver through TR's world.

On Xanther's turn, she moved in a way that made everything about to happen feel practically past tense. Kle was so surprised, Xanther felt bad. Cogs must have wanted to make Kle feel bad because he kept hooting, until Kle actually got sullen, saying he wanted to watch again the preview for *Edge of Tomorrow*, which had opened that weekend, which none of them had seen yet, but supposedly had something to do with gaming or doing things over and over until you could stop dying.

It wasn't like Xanther played well all the time either. She still kept doing really "excellent-stupid" things, Josh's expression. It's just that she could also feel these moments that seemed like, well, quicker, sorta like the way she feels when she's having those non-stop dream mash-ups, linked all over the place, branching to the nth degree of impossible, until she has to make believe they're pine boughs, except in this case it's like Xanther can almost keep up for an instant, and then everything gets really clear, and almost still. None of which she could really share with anyone, even Kle, who's mood finally eased up, especially after watching the *Transformers* preview a few times, and then showing everyone what he could do with *This War of Mine*.

Kle had gotten a ride with Josh's parents when they came to pick up Josh and Mayumi. "Come over soon?" Xanther had practically squeaked. "Cut hen," Kle had grinned back, how he says "See you then." Cogs and her had settled then into trading off with *Limbo*.

Limbo is basically a puzzle journey about a boy supposedly trying to find his way back to his sister, but it's done in this foggy black and white, with spiders, and machines, and Rube Goldberg situations, with pulleys and timed jumps, and even antigravity machines, and a hundred different ways to die terribly.

Xanther had never played it before.

"Tough one," Anwar had smiled, checking in on them. This was after dinner, like after 9 PM. Cogs never has a curfew. Xanther had been coming up on a, what?, bear trap.

"I gave up," Cogs shrugged.

"I still haven't made it through," Anwar laughed. "Don't get frustrated, daughter."

Xanther just nodded and kept playing.

"Huh," Cogs said after Anwar had left. "He doesn't know?"

True, Xanther wasn't sure why she hadn't said something, but something had made her teeth clamp together, keeping it from her dad, even if that meant she and Cogs now had a secret from Les Parents, which was new, but felt okay too, maybe even felt good.

"Don't tell," she had whispered.

"But how are you doing this?"

Her shrug was just a shrug, but like her not correcting Anwar, sometimes a shrug is also a lie. Because the secret she and Cogs kept, that this was already Xanther's third time through *Limbo,* was not the same secret Xanther kept from Cogs, that the one playing didn't feel like her at all.

Her friends had not known what to really make of the part most obviously not her, but now with her all the time, out in the open, no secrets there, no lies, right?

"Little kitten!" Mayumi had squealed when she first beheld the little one perched on her shoulder.

"Right?, but like the vet?, the vet thinks he's old."

Cogs couldn't believe it. Kle had been skeptical too. Josh was still hung up on the fact that there was no dog.

"Maybe he's like the next Grumpy Cat?" Mayumi suggested later.

"I heard Grumpy Cat's owner was this waitress and then a year later she'd made ten million dollars," Josh added.

"Fifty million," Kle corrected. "Why won't it open its eyes?"

For the most part her friends had stopped saying anything at all, like they were "reserving judgement," an Astair phrase, or worse, they were in on a secret Xanther couldn't know.

Well, not all of them. Even if he didn't say much, Xanther could literally watch Cogs' gaze snag on the tiny folds of white and then he'd get all wide-eyed and smile, sometimes a smile so big it kissed each earlobe.

Now, after the fourth time through *Limbo,* trying to beat her last time *and* get all the Easter eggs, which Xanther couldn't do, Xanther has Cogs help with the night's last feeding while waiting for his mom.

He mixes the formula, and, just like Xanther demonstrates, makes sure it's not too hot by dipping some on the inside of his arm.

Xanther has heard herself described as gentle, but the description always makes her wince, because her klutziness alone seems to put all gentleness at risk. Cogs, though, really is gentle. All of him, even his red hair, fluffy like it's always hiding a breeze, and his cheeks, soft, in fact all of him seems soft, but not like in a fat way, or weak way, or stupid way, more like just cushiony, making it easy to relax when he's around. Cogs relaxes everyone. He might even be why the five of them have managed to stick together. Because his gentleness comes from caring. Cogs cares, about everything.

Walking him out to the Element, Astair has to drive Cogs home, he cares enough about her and her little one to say something hard.

"I hate to say this, but uh, I don't think he's eating."

Of course, Cogs is dead-on. And as hurt and panicked as this makes her, at once too, only just managing to give Cogs a hug before racing back into the house, Xanther's pretty astonished by just how perceptive her friend can be. More too than just observing how the formula was dripping down the little chin and wetting the paws, but detecting in the way the little one moved, the way the little one didn't move, like seriously fatigued, like wasting away, like starving to death.

Dov had once let Xanther look through something called a thermal scope. Xanther had already looked through scopes before. This one, though, instead of seeing the world closer up, so close it wobbled when you even breathed, showed a world gone, which was the cold part. "Where nothing's living," Dov had explained, though that wasn't quite right, right?, because hadn't there been grass?, and little bugs?, and germs too?, right?, which Xanther hadn't asked about, because Dov had kept drawing her attention to the white parts, which were the hot parts, with the really hot parts being the people, maybe legs and arms darker, but their bodies, and especially their heads, burning white.
"What about a dead person?" Xanther had asked.
"Cold. Dark."

That's how what she found beneath the stones had made her feel. Like for all the sky brightness there, there was nothing there. Hadn't she even felt a tinge of disgust?, like enough to turn away?, which had made her feel even a little . . . angry?

That night, before she can start dreaming those never-dreams, Xanther acutely feels the little one's frailty, his ribs on her ribs, a dying heart so close to her heart, and then a little of that anger returns, somehow leading her to Dov, though this time not to Dov saying something, or Dov taking her out on some adventure, not even his eyes, whether Dov would have had stones covering his eyes, which seems impossible, or even, if you know like they had to be there, what they would have concealed underneath.

Instead Xanther keeps thinking of a hand, a hand that wasn't his, the hand that did what it did, the hand that had blown Dov to bits.

Tuesday Astair drags Xanther out of the house. Macy's and Bloomingdale's are bad enough. Who cares about Forever 21? Though Xanther can see how hard mom's trying, to like distract her?, buy her something fun. Besides, girls her age are supposed to love shopping, right? So Xanther picks out some leggings, insists on black, and these pink squinchy things for her braids. And, sure, maybe it's kinda fun, but nothing like getting back to her little one.

Then on Wednesday Astair insists on taking a hike. "We won't be long." What she says whenever she means forever, like the Beverly Center, which took over three hours. Xanther gets growly. Astair even says "You're acting so growly."

It gets worse when Xanther has this idea to bring the little one along. Didn't she take him outside once? Had that helped? :: No clue. :: Her backpack needed emptying. It still had books and binders from the last day of school. Then she had to make a bed, like out of a little sofa pillow, plus pillow cases on top, then extra formula and a small bottle of water too. Like maybe now she can go on this stupid outing and not feel the awful heat of separation.

But Astair refused.

Below Griffith Observatory, the path loses the shade of the hill. Mother and daughter march up into the blinding blaze, temperatures rising up into dust, blurring hikers with neon visors, strollers big as grocery store carts, downtown to the east, the Hollywood sign to the west, smeared by the heat. Astair stops to smear more sunscreen on Xanther's arms and face.

"You got it in my eyes!"

"I'm not even close to your eyes, honey." But Xanther's eyes still sting and tear. "How is your head so cool?" Because you wouldn't let me bring the little one along? Because I'm burning up inside? Because— "Are you feeling okay?"

"You got sunscreen in my eyes."

Which makes far more sense than one of the three back-packs ahead, worn by one of the three Japanese? Korean? ∴ **Chinese** ∴ men, all of a sudden spilling bottles of water, a camera, sandwich out onto the trail. To see what you can't see in a way that sees what is beyond sight.

And know yourself then still blind before the stones of the world.

Before dinner, Josh and Kle text Xanther, inviting her to hear some music. Kle: Tonight's gonna b off the chain! Josh's brother, Teig, is photographing this band, Abomination from Planet Garbage, and can add whoever he wants to the guest list. Xanther has always wanted to check out the Troubadour. Astair and Anwar even urge her to go, but she tells them she's not feeling well, even though she's feeling better than ever, even if after Josh and Kle text her 😔 😼. Xanther realizes she's made a mistake.

She almost tells her parents, about everything, but maybe because they'll only say it's epilepsy, just showing up in a different way, ∵ Are these the new symptoms? ∴ ∵ *New symptoms indeed.* ∴ Xanther grinds down on what teeth can never quiet, like, really, is that even right?, or just a lame excuse to avoid something else entirely?, not epilepsy at all ∵ **. . . at all** ∴, to begin with, ∵ *To begin with all . . .* ∴ but also something no longer Xanther's to tell?

One thing's clear: the little one is starving. His frailty screams through her hands, so light he's almost never there, no matter how many droppers of formula she offers, one time hovering the dropper a foot away, but directly behind his swishing tail, watching then how, even with eyes pinched tight, he whirled at once, stumbled directly toward the milky promise, gripping it with the tiny glitter of claws, teeth, filling himself to his heart's content, even if his heart's content meant nothing of the kind, blind to the feasts of the world.

He needs her there as much as he needs her not to be there.

Xanther's eyes fly open.

It's way, way past midnight, a weird glow infusing everything, having nothing to do with midnight, or any other time, like Dov's thermal scope, only with way more at stake than temperature.

∴ What is she saying? ∵

∴ *Shhhhh.* ∵

Not that Xanther needs light to know the little one is nowhere near, not on her bed, in her room, even downstairs, to where Xanther flies . . .

Of course, the front door is wide open.

Baz shodan e dar!
Rawąng: Pratū peid!
Gyeong-go: mun eul yeoll-eossseubnida!
Atenció: Porta oberta!
Se upp för Dörrarna: Dörrarna öppnas!
Atenção: Porta aberta!
Ostrzeżenie: Drzwi otwarte!
Fainic: Doras oscailte!
Atenție: Ușa deschisă!

To the street then, then the middle of the street,
in only her nightgown, facing a long line of street lamps,

as if to face down headlights too
accelerating her way . . .

Focus locked on focus.
Wobbling.
Loosening.

:: Dark as a long-ago red satisfaction.:"

:: *Beyond devination* . . .:"

∴ **Smell brighter than garnet.** ∵

∴ **Taste thicker than cherry.** ∵

Flicked
easily
aside.

My Love

Then, slowly—sunshine emerges.

— Yevgeny Zamyatin

Nothing close to what military firepower could have done to that building, let alone that room. One clip from their small
arms would have done worse. In the light of
day, this brightness that shredded direction would have perished. It was
night that answered her blast with
blindness.

Cas never even saw the
one who came too close.
Who had known to cut
them off there but had
not known about the
closet. The Approxi-
mate had given him
an edge, but as Cas has
learned time and time
again, precision paves
the way to survival.

The scariest part was
how quickly her fin-
gers had conducted the
Orb to detonate. Maybe
Deakin stood as an inspira-
tion. He too in the last hour
had managed to force a distraction
— to whatever unknown effect.

Bobby's brutish taste for accelerants and material velocity had saved them. Both Sorcerer and Deakin had argued in favor of self-destruct coding that would only corrupt the data. Anything more and someone might get hurt. But Bobby wanted to know how many would die if the erasure failed. For some reason the immediate violence packed inside the Orb appalled everyone, but Bobby's addition had prevailed. And for the first time Sorcerer followed Bobby's design to a T. In the end, Deakin confessed he had feared more for himself than for any harm he might carry out against another.

Cas had done harm.

It didn't matter how the Orb's awful glow, in that fractional moment before ignition, illuminated not only two awful eyes but also the glint of a weapon, what both Bobby and Marnie swore fired twice, even as they hauled Cas through the closet, through the back door, locking themselves in that blind space, with nothing but a long ladder descending between the walls of that strange brick building to the metal door opening out into an alley where Marnie's car waited.

Cas knows that much of what she saw is not what she would see if it were possible to Orb the scene.

Likely a small flash, a burp of cracking crystal, followed by the tinkling of metal, and then screams.

They'd all heard those as they struggled rung after rung, nine floors down with no way to see how the darkness would end.

Outside, fire trucks, ambulances, and police cars began to arrive. Too soon, Cas knew.

Marnie swore she had no clue how they had gotten there so fast. She did cop to parking near the emergency exit ever since Bobby had pointed out what resembled a tall electrical box.

Bobby seemed almost proud of her during those first few hours when they got the hell out of Dayton.

However, he soon recognized his naiveté when Marnie refused to let him drive, zipping them along side streets and back roads, stopping only to hand out bus fare and all their electronics to the homeless.

"Not advisable," Marnie replied when Bobby mentioned returning for Joel and the Airstream.

Other expressions like "unknown-size element" and

"our cut-out" eased from her lips as they continued to head south. By morning they were in Athens, Georgia. When Bobby objected to the idea of a motel, Marnie had nodded. "This isn't my first pie-eating contest," driving them past the bi-level stack of doors, across the parking lot, and onto a dirt road that seemed to dead-end in a grassy area crowded with dumpsters along with some rusted bicycles propped up against a tree stump.

Marnie didn't stop there, but maneuvered around the obstacles until they were soon rattling down a still narrower path and finally parking behind a barn of sorts. At least from the outside you'd call it a barn. Inside, though, was a warren of cubicles and tiny rooms, if with just one bathroom. Plenty of water and gas but no electricity.

Marnie could only confirm that Sorcerer had arranged for the safe house. Her assurances weren't enough. At least not on that first night. In the bath together, Bobby and Cas gave voice to their sudden mistrust of Marnie, whispering feverishly about escape, even as they had to admire the size of the tub and the endless flow of warm water.

Not that either one of them thought trying to flee in the darker hours had any chance of success. Neither slept a wink but when morning arrived without an "unknown-size element" emerging from the Georgia mists with high-powered rifles, they began to accept that Marnie might know a thing or two outside of massage therapy.

Not that the massages ceased. It took a couple of days but Marnie eventually admitted the first night had been hard on her too. "They would have gotten us then. I kept going over it in my head, trying to see if I'd

forgotten something, made a mistake. With any luck, they're in Cleveland now." Cas remembered how Marnie had scattered the shells of her bracelet on the fire escape below to mislead their pursuers. "I left stuff, like half burned, or in the trash, or on the back of a notepad." Cas had smiled, patted her hand, and didn't mention that their pursuers never followed the sea glass but headed straight up.

With one already ahead of them all. The one Cas keeps dreaming about. Not Recluse but his apparatus. In constant flux.

The mind is nothing like the math that makes scrying possible. Orbing produces unalterable scenes or clips. Unless the links deteriorate. Is that what happened to the little girl named Xanther who went from spinning rainbows to brewing storms? Cas needs her Orb. If just to puzzle out that corruption a little more. Its absence aches a hole in her. Hardly eased, no matter how many baths Cas takes, within the untranslatable creaks of century-old wood sunbaked and home for birdsong and the brightest disruption of all . . .

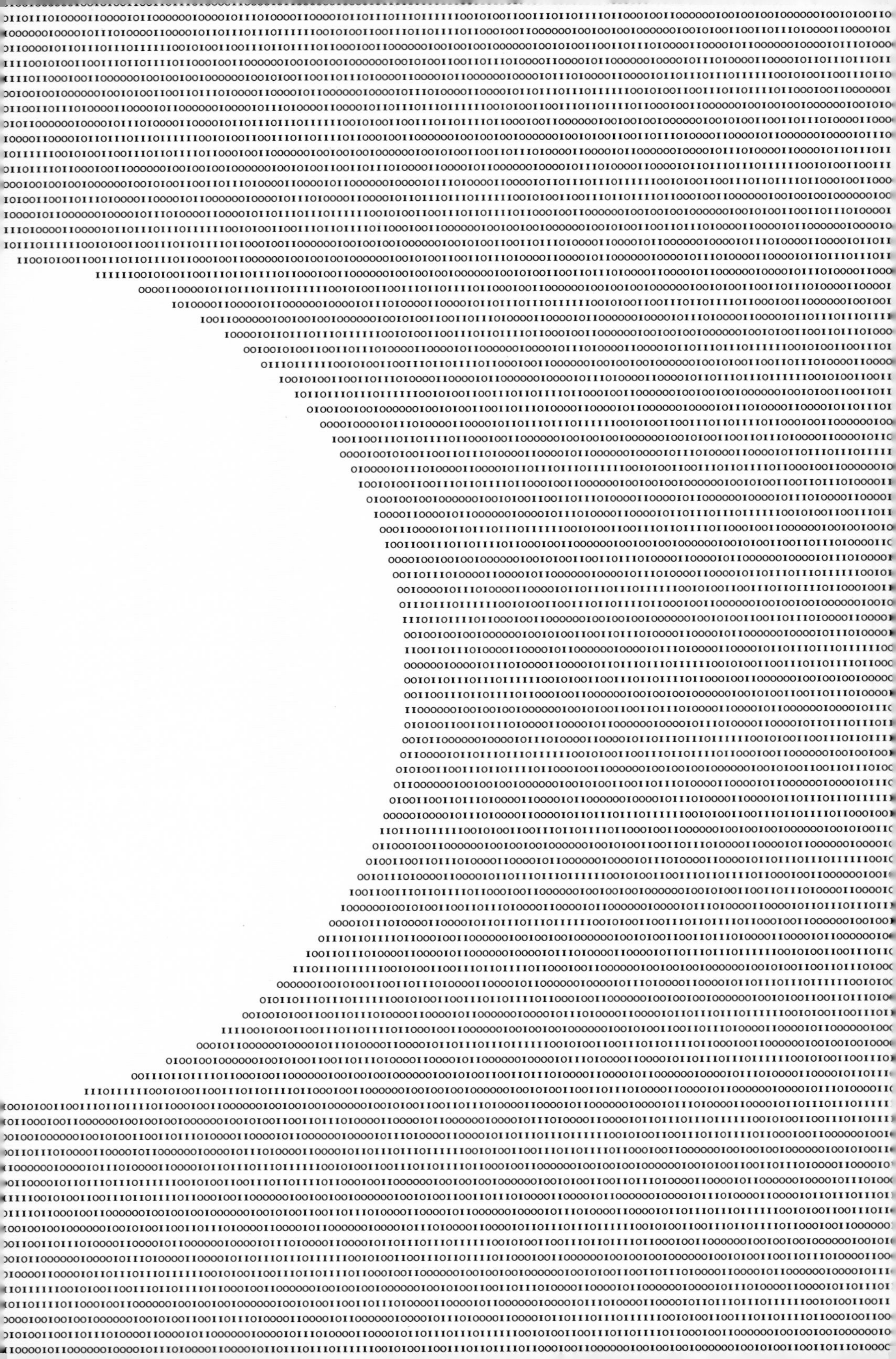

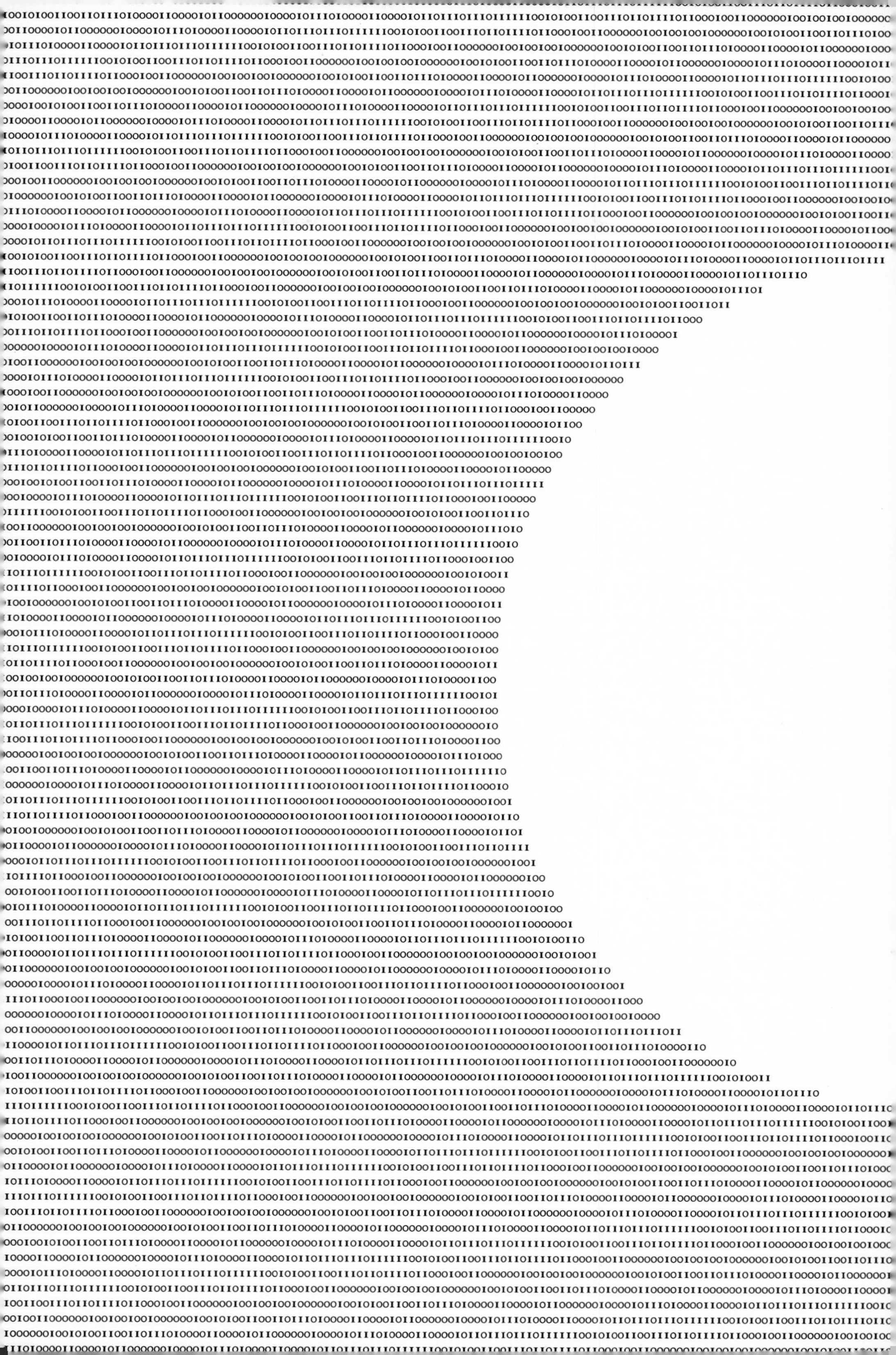

On Thursday, after breakfast, after lunch, after their afternoon naps, while Cas is under her hands, Marnie asks: "Can it see the future?"

"Have you ever looked?"

"Oh, he's let me try. But it's, you know, not like something I can Vine on my phone. It's . . ."

"Different?"

"Well, for one thing, you need both hands, right?"

"The more fingers the better."

"I crashed and burned."

"How do you mean?" Cas lifts her head a little.

"Just, you know, spiraled down into all that static."

"Maybe you just need a better teacher," Cas says softly. "If anyone has hands sensitive enough for Orbing, it's you, Marnie. It just takes practice. Like any skill. Or art."

"Are you offering?" Marnie laughs, her unseen smile already in her thumbs and index fingers, itsy-bitsy-spidering along Cas' spine. Cas hasn't thought of that childhood game in years. Strange.

"For a second I thought it was raining," Cas drifts. Barn wood cracking above. No birdsong.

"You miss it, don't you?" Marnie asks later.

"It?" Cas asks.

"The Orb?"

"You have no idea."

"An addiction," Bobby says from
the doorway. Flowers fill his
hands.

"For me?"

"Always for you," Bobby smiles,
knowing they're never talking about
flowers when they talk about flowers.

Bobby's doing his best, considering. No
beer's rough enough. But they've all had
to make do with ramen, tuna fish, Special K,
instant coffee, and condensed milk. Forget fruit.
Not even canned peaches. The closest they've come to
anything green is what was growing on the Wonder Bread.

Last night Bobby began ranting about cutting out, Marnie's urgings to wait nearly ignored, had Cas not sided with their young accomplice.

Cas trusted Marnie. Even if Cas feared it was only because the kid had grown familiar. Like the goofy way her shoulders rose when she admitted something, like that her last name was Shrap. "Close to crap, right?"

"Is it really an addiction?" Marnie asks now.

"I'm . . . inclined that way."

"AA?"

"Bunches of times. The OCD doesn't help."

"Though it does help, right?"

"That's Sorcerer talking."

Marnie's hands pause. "Maybe you don't even need an Orb."

"Orbless Revelation. One of our friend's favorite fantasies."

"And the future?" Marnie persists.

"Trust me, the present is impossible enough."

"Said that about the Year Window, didn't we?"

And just like that Sorcerer strolls in. Wide as a sail. Big as rain. Even wearing a t-shirt that — despite its stains — reads:

> Take the rain
> out of brain
> and just . . .

Talk about impossible to miss. A miracle he wasn't the first one grabbed. Flappy green camo shorts. Worn sandals. Afro like an ongoing A-Test threatening rafters above. Grin further tizzying the madness of a world that needed those A-Tests in the first place.

Cas bursts into tears.

"Hey," he says, going to her at once.

"So good to see you," Cas coughs but still can't stop, sobbing outright then, for Deakin, for all of their friends, dead, lost, or just squandered. Her big friend — now less like a weapon and more like some lopsided xebec sprung to life in a Miyazaki movie — puts down the groceries and wraps his big hairy arms around Cas.

Not that Bobby's to be outdone. "Sorcerer!" Practically a squeal, delight overwhelming any frown and all surprise.

"Necromancer!" Their big friend answers, already bracing for another embrace.

Cas hasn't seen Bobby this happy in a long while. The brown paper bags on the floor might have something to do with it, loaded with cheese, grapefruits, kale and asparagus, hummus, chips, cartons of eggs, olive oil, and pints of local ice cream. Bottles of Terrapins Hopsecutioner help too. Though it takes more than beer to redden that old man's cheeks.

"We thought . . . " Bobby trails off, eyes gleaming, an IPA already in hand, if still unopened.

"Hey now. Give this deviant fella his due."

"We were unprepared," Bobby darkens, palm trying to twist loose the cap.

"You too Wizard?" Sorcerer sighs.

"I didn't doubt but I feared," Cas answers.

"With good reason."

"Tell us the worst," Bobby demands now. "Don't spare us."

"Merlin's dead."

"Fuck!" Bobby growls.

"And we're only safe here for a few more hours."

Bobby almost throws his beer. "How were we tracked? By way of that Dayton place of yours?"

"Not mine," Sorcerer chuckles. "Though I did squat there a few months. For dolls and drones."

"Then will another innocent suffer for our intrusion?" Cas whispers.

Sorcerer shakes his head. "It was his place."

"Whose?" Cas and Bobby ask together.

Silence speaks the name.

"Why do you think the WiFi was so good?" Sorcerer grins. "One of Recluse's many properties."

"You made a safe house out of his—?" Cas can't finish.

"Remember your scriptures: The Eye always fails to look at Mordor. I needed time to figure out how he was finding us."

"Well, he did find us."

Sorcerer shakes his head. "He found the Orbs. And that's my fuck-up."

"His resources are too great," Bobby hisses. "He has everything."

"Not us."

"How long will that last?" Bobby scoffs.

"He wants to meet."

"You're kidding?" Cas this time.

"If we can agree to terms, he says he'll release those still alive and leave us be. Likely a trap but there's some semblance of choice."

"Morton's Fork," Cas sags. "It was just luck then that I detonated the Orb?"

Sorcerer nods. "Though I suspected enough to tell Marnie to destroy anything with a plug or battery before you left Dayton."

Cas turns to Marnie. "She was so brave. We wouldn't be here without her."

During this little reunion, Marnie has hung back, fidgeting behind her table, toying with the bottles of oil holstered in her belt, if her gaze never leaves the big man gently swaying between Cas and Bobby.

"Is that true, baby?" Sorcerer asks then, like he doesn't already know the answer, his smile widening the way sails fill after a dead calm.

For whatever reason, when Sorcerer's out of sight, without the locative illusion of corporeal fixity, he becomes an ever-expanding mystery, especially in light of the thoughts only his mystery can produce. Here though, mind well out of sight, scudding slowly toward Marnie, he's just their brilliant buddy: something Greek and fortunate in that belly, with a hint of Venezuelan ancestry, or is it Argentinian?, glinting like smelt gold in those warm brown eyes. Something else too. What should have been obvious from the start. The same as with all of them:

Fear.

Not that fear has any chance when Marnie at last bounces
his way, a skip first, then something faster, throwing all of
herself around the giant in their midst, waves of long blond
curls hiding her face, hiding his face, though not before the gold
in his eyes reveals far more than just relief, what no Orb or scrying
will ever match.

"My Love," Sorcerer murmurs.

"Mefisto," Marnie sings back.

FONTS

Xanther .... Minion
Astair .... Electra LH
Anwar .... Adobe Garamond
Luther .... **Imperial BT**
Özgür .... **Baskerville**
Shnorhk .... Promemoria
jingjing ....rotis semi sans
Isandòrno .... Visage
The Wizard .... Apolline

TF-Narcon 27 .... **Arial MT**
TF-Narcon 9 .... MetaPlus-
TF-Narcon 3 .... Manticore

MORE FONTS

TITLE .... DANTE MT

Preview #1 .... ᖴᑌᑌᖇᕮᕼᏆᏞᏞ & **MetaPlus-**
Preview #2 .... **Rockwell CE**
Preview #3 .... Nimrod MT

G.C. ....MetaPlus-

TIMESTAMPS .... **SYNCHRO LET**
Epigraphs .... *Transitional 511 BT*
Copyright .... Apollo
CREDITS & ATTRIBUTIONS .... GILGAMESH
Dedication .... *Legacy*

T.M.D. .... *Minion Italic*

THE FAMILIAR

VOLUME 2

Copyright © 2015 by Mark Z. Danielewski

All rights reserved. Published in the United States by Pantheon Books, a division of Penguin Random House LLC, New York, and in Canada by Random House of Canada Limited, Toronto, Penguin Random House companies.

Pantheon Books and colophon are registered trademarks of Penguin Random House LLC.

Permissions information for images and illustrations can be found on pages 834 & 835.

Library of Congress Cataloging-in-Publication Data
Danielewski, Mark Z.
The Familiar, Volume 2: "Into the Forest"/ Mark Z. Danielewski
p. cm.
ISBN 978-0-375-71496-2 (softcover: acid-free paper).
ISBN 978-0-375-71497-9 (ebook).
I. Title.
PS3554.A5596F36 2015   813'.54—dc23   2014028320

Jacket Design by Atelier Z.

Author Drawing by Carole Anne Pecchia.

Printed in China

First Edition
9 8 7 6 5 4 3 2 1

www.markzdanielewski.com
www.pantheonbooks.com

THANK YOUS

Edward Kastenmeier

Lloyd Tullues

Sandi Tan

Detective John Motto and
Lieutenant Wes Buhrmester

Rita Raley

Translations

Arabic ....Yousef Himnly
Armenian .... Niree Perian
Hebrew .... David Duvshani
Mandarin/Cantonese ....Jinghan Wu
Russian ....Anna Loginova
Spanish.................................... Juan Valencia
Spanish.......................... René López Villamar
Turkish .... Gökhan Sarı

More Thank Yous

Peter Andersen,
Nikolai Beope, Seth Blake,
Scott Milton Brazee, Lydia Buechler,
Michiko Clark,
Christopher J. Danielewski, Katherine Ewell,
Dan Frank, Emily Giglierano,
Andy Hughes, Altie Karper,
Chris Kokosenski, Shona McCarthy,
Anthony Miller, Christopher O'Riley,
and Peter Schoppert

ATELIER Z

{in alphabetical order}

NOAM ASSAYAG-BERNOT

REGINA GONZALES

CAROLE ANNE PECCHIA

MICHELE REVERTE

Exploring...

Gizmo, M. November 2016

Orangina Fall 2014

Will Coe
Little lion in a Sunny Maze
Fluffy

JASPER
Wife
Undentified

Greylock
"Locksie"
Fluffy pants
♡ 2/8/2010

May 12, 2015
Caspian,
Who thinks he is an Owl,
His purrs make the whole
house hum.
VJH.

Juno
Marissa Jager
April 30, 2015

Olyver Snow
By: Alexan Khatcheri

"An Existential
Meowment"
04/04/2015

Zoe
sept-99

through
a glass
darkly

Lula:

All black cats
are magic

Caramel
Ivan Saracz 5/5/15

"Poppy"
Owner: The Hedge company
Poppy was born in a barn to
a feral mama Cat.
He was king at the Camp

Alabama
Ana
23 August 2014
It was really hot
that day. I threw a blanket
over the couch. Thought she'd
sleep better.

"Summer"
Snoball, 2013

The Cat Who Stares at Dew.
(Potbelly Henry on a sunny day in April,
by Kitty F.)

TAY-TAY
a little girls best
friend and companion
from birth to age 16.
The most patient and
loving cat in the world.

Biscuit - 16 July 2012

Grobis gillar glass
-84

His name was Little Man
but we called him Chicken.
7-29-10
Jenn

D-Con always carried leaves from
the forest to the porch. I w
if he came back as a tree.

954283 11852 613 22112085

Life of the Party
02/12/2015

A CIRCLE
ROUND
A STONE

PRODUCTION

COMING SOON . . .

THE
FAMILIAR

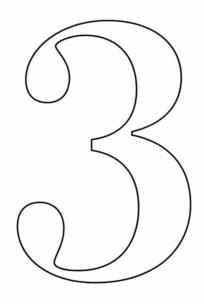

SUMMER 2016

And Marvin

      the Markhor

            wobbled.

And then he snorted.

    Marvin always snorts after he

        wobbles, and these days

                he snorts quite a bit.

Balance has become something of a problem.

              Not exactly a good thing for

 a life spent dancing

       the tot teeter tat
          of narrow ledges

             at vast heights.

Granted Marvin has led a long life.
           A good life even.

 What of one slip
      one happy spin or two in the air

            answered by quiet?

 There are worse ways to go than

            falling off a cliff.

Beats getting hauled off by a Snow Leopard.

Still, Marvin isn't ready yet
                                    to take that

happy spin

                    or two

                                                    into quiet.

            Though he isn't against quiet.

        Marvin just enjoys grass more. He enjoys grazing.

    He even enjoys the crickclick of climbing a tree now
                                                    and then
        to see what he might graze on up there.

    Though all this wobbling of late makes such adventures
                    a little more
                            challenging.

    Narrow steps of rock are one thing,
                                trees are tough.

        And then there are the billies.

On that front, things have not gone well.

Marvin is still a little dizzy.

high spires
highspire s
highspires turning high spires turning highsp
high s p i r e s
high s p i r

high s p i r e

Three had come around sniffing up his nannies.

Of course Marvin did what had to be done.

What he's done before, what he will do again.

Marvin knows what to expect.

Marvin knows how to do what to expect best.

Billie One charged too fast, so that

when he got near,

when he rose up on his hind legs,

Billie One nearly stopped,

hooves stutterskidding to catch a balance

already lost.

Marvin just had to do a little side hop, plant, and then
at an angle meet the charge with high spires and
a twist from his hips.

Billie One flopped over onto his side.

ng
urning

high spires
turninghighspiresturninghighs
spiresturninghighspiresturninghighspiresturning
highspiresturninghighspiresturninghighs
highspiresturning
spires turninghighspiresturninghighs
spires turn
highspires turning.

iresturninghighspiresturninghighspiresturninghighspires
highspiresturninghighspiresturninghighspiresturn

highspires

highspires
spiresturninghighspires
highspiresturninghighspiresturninghighspires

Billie Two was better.

Heavier too.

This time there was a lot more

knockclocking

and lockknocking,

sheercreer twisting too,

until Marvin felt strange and clumsy,

and ready to drag himself away, until

he saw Billie Two already

dragging himself away.

highspiresturning highspiresturning highspires
highspiresturning highspiresturning highspires
highspiresturninghighspiresturning
highspiresturninghighspires
highspire
spire
spire

highspires turningh
highspires turning
highspires turning
highspiresturnings
highspiresturninghighspiresturnings
highspiresturninghighspiresturning highspiresturn
highspiresturninghighspiresturninghighspiresturning highspiresturn

Billie Three never charged.

Billie Three just followed
                        Billie One and Billie Two away.

And Marvin's nose flared with relief.

Marvin had seen Billie Three around.

He was the thickest and heaviest,
                        but also quickest with wild
sheercreer spires to rival Marvin's.

Once Marvin had seen him
                        high in an oak tree nibbling
            leaves and the occasional acorn.

Even Marvin had to wonder how such a young billie
            could climb so high and stand so still,
                        as if born of the tree, a branch itself.

            Marvin had kicked up his back hooves then.

Then threw his head around.

Billie Three might have finished Marvin off.

Spirebattered him across the meadow.

Spireclattered him down the grass-pocked hills.

> *All the way to*

> *the first ledge.*

All the way to

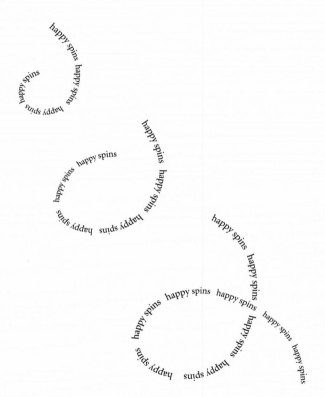

answered by quiet.

> *Once and for fall.*

Maybe Billie Three had been scared.

Maybe Billie Three was one of those big beautiful

strong kinds

ruined by fear.

Marvin is many things, but he is never afraid.

Unless getting fed up counts.

Marvin is fed up a lot these days.

Fed up with locking horns.
Fed up with the kids, their annoying bleating.

                                                    Even

fed up with his nannies.

Oh, the racket they made when he had returned
                from shocklocking
                                the billies.

In seasons past, Marvin would have loved that sound.
          Marvin would have raised his head.
          Marvin would have puffed out his chest.

Then he would have taken one nanny.
          He would have taken all the nannies.

Today, though, Marvin wants nothing to do with nannies.

  Let the billies take them for all he cares.
                        Take the kids too.

Not that Marvin really means this. Or he means it not as
something to accept but reject by another way he elects:

He prefers his solitude.

So Marvin wanders off again.

Well, wobbles off is more like it.

Wobbles away from the junipers and pines.

Up   and   up

beside the icy brooks.

Until from those waters,

after a too-long

totterteeter, Marvin hoptocks

stone *step* to

stone *step* to

rock ledge to

stone *step* to

rock ledge

along a **sheer** face to

rock ledge to

step

stone

along another **sheer** face to

rock ledge to

stone *step* to

stone *step* to

stone

stone to

step

stone

step

which by sharp turns finally

turning cornice and wall

up toward still higher

mountain beams,

which by tatateetertaps lead at last to Marvin's particular spot

for a view of things.

Another kind of quiet.

Though with all his wobbling,

               the canyon still echoes with snorts.

Marvin couldn't help it.

               Worse, several times on the way
   up he had to pause.

                      He still feels winded.

But here his snorting stops, his breathing slows.

Here on his table of rock.

   High above junipers, pines, and old oaks.

       From where Marvin can still keep an oblique eye

on his nannies.

         Where he can still find among patches of

  ice and snow

            grass to nibble on.

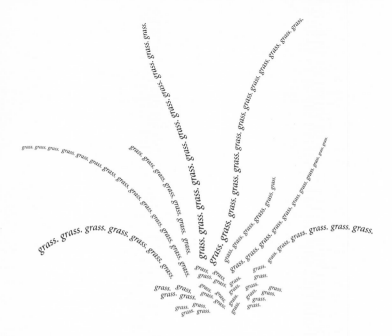

And a snake.

Marvin freezes.

No hoof moves.

Marvin doesn't even lift his head.

What an idiot.

Didn't even take a look around.

Just dragged himself up past the last step to his rocky table, and while still snorting, still panting, lunged straightaway for a mouthful of sweet grass.

Didn't even take in his view.

Which is when Marvin discovered

the intruder

But hadn't the green
tasty offering been so close?

How could Marvin resist?

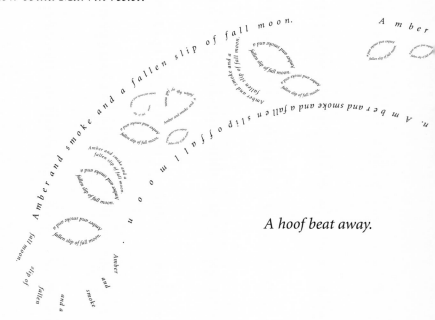

A hoof beat away.

Strange looking snake too.

Marvin might have even figured it for a strange stick

                               had it not twitched.

But when had Marvin ever seen a twitching snake?

Marvin had never seen a twitching snake.

Of the three he'd stomped, none had ever done this.

One lashed out,
                but Marvin was much too quick for that.

The other two had just slithered, spat, attempting

                         to *thruuuuuuush* their way free.

Amber and smoke and a fallen slip of fall moon.

All were much darker.

Perhaps this smokiness kept Marvin from stomping at once.

Perhaps this amberish kept Marvin from hopping back.

Perhaps this hint of a fall moon stilled Marvin.

Perhaps because a twitching snake

                                      of smoky amberish moon glow

*is so un*familiar.

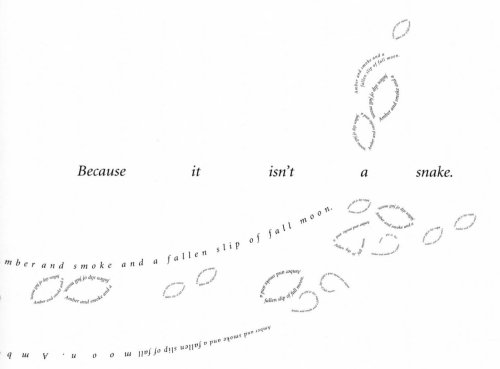

Because   it   isn't   a   snake.

It's a tail.

Which Marvin realizes when it whips from sight,

Marvin jerking his head up then

to follow the strangest lash,

spitless and hissless,

finding instead

the round

yellow eyes

high spires turning
high spires turning
high spires turning
high spires turning
high spires turning
high spires turning
high spires turning
highspiresturning
highspiresturninghighspiresturning
highspiresturning

high spires turn ing
high spires turn ing
high spires turn ing

highspireturninghighspireturninghighspire

high spire turning highspire
high spire turning high
high spire turning high
high spire turning high
high spire turning high
high spire turning high
highspiresturninghighspire
highspiresturninghighspiresturning
highspiresturninghighspiresturning

Marvin the Wobbleless
Marvin the Wobbleless
Marvin the Wobbleless
Marvin the Wobbleless
Marvin the Wobbleless
Marvin the Wobbleless
Marvin the Wobble less

Marvin the
Wobbleless
Marvin the
Wobbleless
Marvin the
Wobbleless
Marvin the
Wobbleless
Marvin the
Wobbleless
Marvin the
Wobbleless
Marvin the
Wobbleless

of a Snow
Leopard.

highspiresturning highspiresturning highspiresturning highspiresturning highspiresturning highspiresturning highspiresturning highspires

Marvin the Wobbleless

Well, if this doesn't just wreck an already crappy day.

Not that Marvin is afraid.

Marvin is never afraid.

So Marvin just stands and waits.

        Actually he wobbles

                        and so snorts

while he stands and waits.

The Snow Leopard doesn't wobble or snort.

The Snow Leopard keeps perfectly still.

Crouched. Ready for Marvin to run.

Marvin doesn't run.

Fat chance there.

This is his perch and his view.

At most, he stomps a leg because all these wobbles and snorts have started to annoy him and he wants them to stop.
Even if the stomping makes him wobble more and so snort more and so it goes.

If the Snow Leopard is going to spring, it will have to spring straight on,
and however old Marvin is, he knows a thing or two about straight on,
how to highspire twist and throw.

Even this Snow Leopard will have trouble.

But the Snow Leopard doesn't spring.

                                      In fact, she shows no
     interest in moving at all.
                      She even seems bored.

And when she eventually yawns, Marvin yawns too.

She isn't so big either.

Aren't Snow Leopards bigger than this?

Marvin has actually never seen one this close.

He's caught the scent plenty of times . . .

                        on the wind, or

                              by a claw
 of moon,
          spotted the blur of something much icier slipping
out upon the snow fields or
                  once heard the bleatelps of a nanny
dragged away across a scree,
                 the mountain walls finally
echoing only the sudden stifling.

                        But that was all.

Maybe this isn't even a Snow Leopard.

Maybe she is some kind of Lynx.

But she isn't a Lynx.

And her eyes stay fixed on Marvin.

Only now does Marvin realize he still hasn't caught a scent.

Only clear sheets of cold air fall from the cliffs above.

Maybe she isn't there.

Maybe she is part of Marvin's wobble.

Maybe recent lockknocking sheercreer shocklocking
has got Marvin seeing tails in sticks, Snow Leopards in stone.

Marvin catches the scent of pine trees, though.
There is even a hint of his nannies, and suddenly
he wants to look at something he knows.

Marvin wants to take in the day at its fullest even if it isn't
full anymore. Then watch the mountains and fields below
burn with the day's last light.

But as that need begins to turn Marvin toward

a familiar comfort, something awakens

                    in the Snow Leopard
                                   and coils up.

*Perhaps if Marvin hadn't wobbled then, snorted too, and
stomped to halt that foolish teeter,*

                  *he would have gone ahead with turning
and discovered what*

                         *a Snow Leopard feels like
     at his flanks, at his throat.*

*Marvin knows how easily those claws could slice into him,
how savagely her jaws could crush away any breath.*

*Marvin considers backing toward the steeps below. But
even if he could have managed such a feat when he was
young, all this dizziness rocking his head,*

                    knocking his knees,
makes such a retreat impossible.

So Marvin settles down instead.

*High spires high, forehooves firm if back haunches fold.
Belly too might as well rest on stone.*

Because when she moves, and she must move,

                    Marvin will
   have to scramble up fast enough

               to brace for her attack,

    because she must attack.

Except the Snow Leopard also seems to settle more.

Already her belly presses down against stone.

She even extends her front paws.

The paws surprise Marvin.

They are far bigger than he expected.

While tucked beneath her, they had appeared small as tufts of just-grazed brush.
               Now, though, they seem bigger than river stones useful when crossing dangerous

       waters tumbling down when spring thaws.

Maybe all of her is like this.

                      Bigger.

      Than expected.

Sometimes her whiskers tremble.

Sometimes her ears flick independently back and forth.

Sometimes her tail reappears,
                              wraps around her, twitches,
     only to disappear
                    behind her again.

But always the Snow Leopard holds Marvin in her unblinking gaze.

Marvin wants to look away.

Does the Snow Leopard want to look away too?

Ending light has crept in between them.

                    Below, Marvin's nannies will be heading into the woods.

                    Maybe with the three billies following, taking turns, having their fill.

                    Or maybe just lockknocking one another.

                    Or maybe Billie Three is up an oak tree again

           nibbling leaves

                  and the occasional acorn.

Not that Marvin lingers long on such strange stirs.

                    Not with ending light shimmering around them.

                    How it still sparks off rock and snow too.

                    Marvin even feels it in his nostrils, as if ending light could smell,

                    and fizz in his ears too,

                        as if

              it could sing, finally

                  achieving something that stills the wobble of a thought

                  and makes of stillness something strange and welcome.

And beautiful.

As beautiful as the round yellow eyes

of the Snow Leopard.

Something strange and welcome there too.

As if what Marvin thought was about light
                                        had never been
about light but always
                    the darkness of that stare.

                Her stare.

                        Without a care for the world.

Not for pines or junipers or old oaks,
                                not for billies or nannies,
not even for the shadow of night
                            starting to cloak valley
                and brook.

                        Caring only for Marvin.

Which is when Marvin knew he was going to die.

For Les Parents.